GALLOP FORTH TO ADVENTURE . . .

Harry Turtledove's "Precious Treasure"—The price of freedom was his sight, and as a Horse-clansman, he would risk any peril to regain it!

Sharon Green's "Damnation"—She had been taught that her role was to obey without question. But she would never cease to think for herself even if it meant aiding one her people named foe. . . .

John Steakley's "The Swordsman's Place"—He had never been at home on our own Earth, but could he carve a place for himself among those who lived—and died—by blade and bow?

Roland Green's and John Carr's "Dirt Brother"—The townsfolk called him witchboy and hated him for his mindspeaking skill. Would he find a new home or a quick end among the warriors of the Horseclans?

FRIENDS OF THE HORSECLANS II

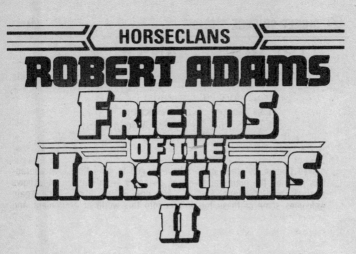

HORSECLANS

ROBERT ADAMS

FRIENDS
OF THE
HORSECLANS
II

Edited by Robert Adams
and Pamela Crippen Adams

A SIGNET BOOK

NEW AMERICAN LIBRARY

This book to the memories of
four departed friends:
Lin Carter, Ray Peekner,
Cliff Simak and Kirk Thompson.

NAL BOOKS ARE AVAILABLE AT QUANTITY DISCOUNTS WHEN
USED TO PROMOTE PRODUCTS OR SERVICES. FOR INFORMA-
TION PLEASE WRITE TO PREMIUM MARKETING DIVISION, NEW
AMERICAN LIBRARY, 1633 BROADWAY, NEW YORK, NEW YORK
10019.

SIGNET TRADEMARK REG. U.S. PAT. OFF. AND FOREIGN COUNTRIES
REGISTERED TRADEMARK—MARCA REGISTRADA
HECHO EN DRESDEN, TN, U.S.A.

SIGNET, SIGNET CLASSIC, MENTOR, ONYX, PLUME, MERIDIAN
and NAL BOOKS are published by NAL PENGUIN INC.,
1633 Broadway, New York, New York 10019

First Printing, March, 1989

1 2 3 4 5 6 7 8 9

PRINTED IN THE UNITED STATES OF AMERICA

Contents

Introduction

Well, ladies and gents, *The Friends of the Horseclans* ride again! Some of those who appeared in the first volume of these stories appear also in this one—Sharon Green, Steven Barnes, Paul Edwards, John Steakley, Roland Green, and John F. Carr—but they are joined on this go-round by Dr. Susan Shwartz, Mercedes Lackey, and Harry Turtledove. (And if you have not yet read Harry's Videssos cycle, then I order you to troop out and buy it, yesterday! Rousing good adventure tales, splendidly crafted, meticulously researched.)

There is no story by me in this one, however. I never have been able to do shorter fiction—anything of less than novel-length—easy or comfortably; every one of my attempted short stories or novelettes has eventually wound up becoming a novel. I suppose that this is just the way in which one's talent is put together.

To date, there are eighteen Horseclans books in the Horseclans series. (The first collection of Friends of the Horseclans and this one are not included in that numbering system.) I contemplate a total of about thirty novels. The next one, Horseclans 19, will take up from the ending of Horseclans 18, continuing the exciting tale of the twentieth-century genesis of the prairiecats and the twenty-second-century discovery of them by Milo Morai, their domestication of the smelly twolegs, etc. There will also be another volume of Friends of the Horseclans, probably in 1990.

For all you Middle Kingdoms buffs and Bili the Axe fans, yes, we will eventually get back around to your special interests. There are to be at least two more Bili the Axe novels and also a brace of Sir Geros novels in which *Thoheeks* Bili of Morguhn will be a peripheral character.

In addition, we also will get around to finishing the story left dangling at the end of Horseclans 17; there will be two more novels set in that cycle, then another loosely related to those chronicled events.

And for all you fans of role-playing games, there is now a Horseclans game available. It's a production of Steve Jackson Games, and the game book has a great Ken Kelly cover, of course. I put in many long hours of consultation with Steve on the preparation of this game book and, therefore, it can serve as an excellent glossary on the Horseclans books. It also includes several maps and quite a number of drawings and sketches of Horseclans characters, weapons, and equipment. And by the time this introduction sees print, there will be a supplementary adventure, Up Harzburk, out from Steve Jackson Games.

This book you are reading constitutes my eleventh published anthology; there will be more, both original stories written by some of the best authors working today and reprints carefully searched out and collected by me and my able collaborators. If you enjoy this collection, then you will enjoy all of my others, five of which you will find advertised elsewhere in this book.

> —Robert Adams
> Somewhere in the
> wilds of darkest
> Florida

Precious Treasure

by Harry Turtledove

HARRY TURTLEDOVE has a degree in Byzantine history. Possibly this is where he gets his puns. It has proven valuable in his Videssos Cycle series, which are establishing him as a writer to watch.

> *He that is stricken blind, cannot forget*
> *The precious treasure of his eyesight lost.*
> —*Romeo and Juliet*, I,i

The lowing of the cattle and the constant rumbling of their hooves were almost enough to lull Peet Staiklee to sleep. Almost, but not quite. Any rider of the Horseclans who lost alertness around the longhorns deserved whatever happened to him.

Peet stretched in the saddle. He was a strapping blond young man, tall for a Horseclansman, and in all respects but one a perfect physical specimen. He wiped sweat from his forehead with the heel of his hand. This far south, close to the domain of Don Jorge, *El Rey del Norte*, summer was a sauna of torment. The sweat re-formed as soon as Peet's hand was gone.

He lifted his glasses from his nose to rub away the moisture that had gathered under them. He sighed with pleasure as he took off his straw hat and fanned his face. The moving air felt particularly good against his damp eyelids.

"I wish," he said aloud, "I could leave the damn things off all the time." He was as practiced a telepath as any other Staiklee, but sometimes, riding alone on a flank of the herd, he liked to hear the sound of his own voice.

No, his flaw did not lie there. But while he was holding his glasses instead of wearing them, the world, or at least that part of it farther than about six inches from his face, became an indistinct blur. These were not easy times for a nearsighted man.

Sighing, he put the glasses back on. The world jumped into something close to focus. The frame was made of wood, and heavy; he'd carved it himself, a slow, careful job made even slower because he'd had to bend over until his nose all but bumped the work. The lenses were from the time before the Great Dying. No one, these days, could make their like.

"I suppose I oughta to count myself lucky," Peet said. Not many Horseclansmen had trouble with their eyes. Most of those who did were older men whose sight was growing long. The convex lenses that helped them were worse than useless to Peet.

Only wildest fortune had led to the Kindred Clans a few years ago a trader with a couple of concave lenses looted from some dead eastern city. "I don't even know why I picked these up," the fellow had said. "Not much call for them." He'd sold them cheap, glad to find anyone even a little interested.

For Peet, though, they'd made all the difference in the world. Without them, he'd been tied to the yurts, a man doing mostly women's work because he could not see well enough to hunt or herd or fight. But he had a man's strength and a man's desire to match his fellows—and a man's burning shame at being unable to do so. With his glasses, he could.

All the same, they were miserably hot to wear. He took them off, rubbed his eyes, and wondered how long it would be till Mikk rode out to relieve him. Mikk had been late two days running. If he was again today, he'd regret it. A little friendly wrestle, Peet thought—he didn't need to be able to see much to wrestle, and if Mikk's face got ground in the dirt a bit more than was quite needful, well, that was one of those things.

* * *

A sparrow hawk circled, high overhead. The little hawk approved of the Horseclans' herds. As they rambled on, they stirred up plenty of grasshoppers and mice. The sparrow hawk was plump and sleek; its plumage, gray-blue and ruddy, glowed with life.

Something caught its eye. It cocked its head to one side, peered down. It was as curious as its fierce nature would allow. It had never seen anything like the flashes of light that sparkled up from below. Ultimately, though, only one thing mattered: Was that food or wasn't it? Sleek or not, the sparrow hawk was always hungry.

There! The flash came again. It had to be something alive. The sparrow hawk folded its wings and plummeted.

Peet was holding his glasses again when they were suddenly, rudely, struck from his grasp. He had no idea the hawk was stooping on him till it hit his hand almost hard enough to break his wrist. One talon scored a thin, bloody line across the backs of three fingers.

He jerked reflexively. Taking its cue from that, and from the startled alarm shouting in Peet's mind, his horse reared, snorting. The beast bucked and plunged until, using knees, hands, and telepathic soothing, he calmed it again.

He gentled the horse quite without thinking, for his heart was like a cold stone in his chest. He had heard the crunch the first time its forefeet descended. . . .

Maybe, he told himself as he jumped from the saddle, the pounding hoof had just split the frame he'd carved. He could always make another frame. "Sun and Wind, let it be so," he murmured. Even then, he knew how slim the odds were.

Simply trying to find the glasses gave him a foretaste of the helplessness he dreaded. He had to put his head down to the ground like a tracking tooth-hound. If Mikk should come now and see him groping around with his butt in the air, he knew he would never live it down.

He was spared that humiliation, anyhow. Something glittering soon drew his eyes, as, unbeknownst to him, it had drawn the sparrow hawk's only moments before. Soon he was holding a few precious, irreparable fragments of the lenses that let him pass for a normal man.

He slowly got to his feet. His horse pressed its soft nose against his shoulder. "Not your fault, Snowdrop," he beamed, though now the white blaze that gave the beast its name was fuzzy-edged to his weak eyes. "Not your fault," he repeated. "Just—one of those things." He flung the bits of broken glass to the ground. "But why, curse it all, did it have to be one that came down on *me*?"

There was no answer to that. There was never any answer to that. Peet set his foot in the stirrup, swung onto Snowdrop. He needed no eyes for that. Like any Horseclansman, he could have got into the saddle stone blind. Men had, now and then, and got themselves into songs afterward.

He kept riding with the herd, his mere presence helping to keep the cattle on course. In his brief, haphazard boyhood schooling, he'd always had trouble understanding the notion of zero. "A placeholder," old Eyereen had called it, and boxed his ears when he failed to catch on. Now he understood. Mounted on Snowdrop, he was a placeholder until Mikk got here.

A zero, in other words.

"Don't do anything stupid," he beamed at the longhorns. He knew that was wasted effort. They were too stupid to catch the beaming, and certainly too stupid to obey it if they did.

He glanced at the sun. That, at least, he could still see. Mikk was late. He started to remind himself to do the other rider a bad turn, stopped with the thought half-made. Why bother? He would not be doing any more riding with the herds himself. His place would be with the yurts again.

He hated the idea of going back to them. Before he got his glasses, he had never known the full freedom of the plains, or what he was missing. Now he would be returning to a cage he thought he had escaped.

He swore out loud. Beaming the foul words did not

pack the same punch. He needed the feel of them in his mouth, their sound in his ears—

Laughter broke into his cursing. He wheeled in the saddle. The blur behind him was a man on horseback. Of that much he was sure, but it might have been any Horseclansman on any horse—or, for that matter, one of Don Jorge's *soldados*, even if none was supposed to be close by.

Most likely, though, he thought, it was Mikk Staiklee. "Took you long enough," he tightbeamed, operating on that assumption.

"Sorry, Peet." Yes, it was Mikk, not sounding any too sorry in spite of his beamed apology. He was still laughing, with his mind and with his mouth. "What happened to get you so riled? Hornet sting you, or—" He suddenly stopped, noticing for the first time what was different about—wrong with, Peet thought—his fellow clansman. "Your glasses."

"Yeah." Peet spoke now instead of beaming, the better to hide his hurt. He kept his voice flat, laconic. "Somethin'—hawk I guess it was—knocked 'em out of my hand, stupid damn bird. Snowdrop went and tromped on 'em."

"How's your eyes without 'em?" Mikk spoke too.

"Same as always—not worth a tooth-hound turd."

"Oh." Mikk thought that over. He took a while; he was a long way from being a quick thinker. Finally he asked, "Want me to ride back to the yurts with you?"

Peet's mouth dropped open. Just when he had worked up a pretty fair grudge against Mikk, the fellow had to go and offer a favor like that! Peet slowly shook his head. "The herds come first," he said, a creed more basic to a nomad even than Sun and Wind. "If I can't make so much as one short ride on my own, I don't deserve to belong to the clan."

"The herds come first—reckon you're right," Mikk said. His blurry image shifted. Peet guessed he was waving. "Luck to you."

"Thanks." But as he turned Snowdrop back toward the yurts, Peet thought Mikk's wish came too late to do him any good.

*   *   *

"Nope, nothin' like that," the trader said. Peet was hunched forward, leaning so close to the fellow that he could see his face clearly in the firelight. It did him no good—like any trader worth his salt, this one let his features reveal nothing. "Might have some next year, now I know you want 'em. Might not, too."

"Next year!" Six weeks of being chained within sight—his own short sight—of the yurts had driven Peet close to wild. The prospect of a whole year—and maybe longer than that—trapped this way was more than he could bear. He jumped up, started to stamp away from the trader's wagon.

The man's voice pursued him. "They'll cost you plenty, too." The trader knew desperation when he saw it.

"Shut up, curse you," Peet muttered under his breath. He headed back toward Clan Staiklee's camp, a hundred yards away. Halfway there, his foot went into a hole he—of course—had not seen. Only a wild scramble kept him from falling on his face. Even a man with good eyesight might stumble at night, he told himself. The thought did precious little to console him.

As he entered the circle of light the Staiklee fires cast, someone called aloud to him: "Peet, there's some boots here need fixing. Come sit by me and help?"

"Sure, Ann," he answered, walking toward the sound of her voice. He stumbled again three steps later, this time tripping over a child's wooden toy. As he slowly picked himself up, he tried not to hear people snickering. It wasn't easy. He'd fallen like that before, more than once. Swearing under his breath, he managed to find Ann without any more mortifications.

As he sat, she leaned over to kiss him. He responded, but with mixed feelings. Before he lost his glasses, he'd planned on marrying her one day. Probably one day soon; they'd been sharing a bedroll for more than a year now. His plans had shattered with the lenses. How could she stand having a helpless husband? How could he stand being one?

He could see the boots, but where was the sinew to repair them? He did not beam the question, but the moment it formed in his mind Ann handed him a threaded needle. "Thanks," he said; he would have spent five minutes patting the ground before he found it, and likely stuck himself in the process. Even so, needing the help was galling.

Nothing he could do about it, though. Grumbling, he got to work, holding the battered boots close to his face so he could tell what the devil he was doing. He finished repairing a rip, set the boot to one side, and reached for another.

Ann touched his hand. "You do such fine, tight stitches, Peet. Mine aren't anywhere near so nice and neat."

He knew she was trying to cheer him up, but her words had the opposite effect. Was this what he had to look forward to, years of pity-born praise for things that by rights were hardly worth mentioning? Better the way of some of the outlaw bands, who knocked defectives over the head and had done!

"Any luck with the trader?" Now Ann tightbeamed; she was sensitive enough to realize he might not want the whole clan to know if the answer was one he had not hoped for.

And it was. "No," he answered flatly.

"Oh, Peet." She looked away from him. Her hopes had ridden on the trader, too.

"Plague on it," he said, and got back to work. He kept stubbornly at it even after she was yawning. He worked like a machine from the old times, sewing up boot after boot after boot. One thing, he thought— after this night was done, Clan Staiklee's shoes would be in better shape than they'd been for years.

Finally Ann set down her needle. "I'm turning in," she said, with a smile that invited him to do the same—with her. It was wasted, and not just because he was so shortsighted—he was paying more attention to the boots than to her. Angrily clicking her tongue between her teeth, she got up and stalked away.

By then, hardly anyone was left around the campfires. Peet patched another boot or two, glanced in the direction Ann had gone. Odds were she'd still welcome him into her bedroll. She sympathized with his unending, agonizing frustration. He knew that. He was damned if he wanted her going to bed with him from sympathy.

That thought crystallized the decision that had been growing in him since he'd failed with the trader. He slammed a fist into the dirt, so hard he winced. Then he too rose and walked over to the little cart that held his meager wordly goods.

He ignored his bow and quiver. They were about as useful to him now as a hat on a frog. A mace, now—a mace was a proper weapon for somebody who couldn't see what he was doing. The pouches on Snowdrop's saddle held enough hard cheese and jerked beef to keep him from starving for a few days. He lifted the light rig off the cart, carried it toward the line of horses on the far side of the camp from the trader's wagon—no sense giving a natural-born thief any unnecessary temptation, Peet thought with a grim chuckle.

He made no special effort to go quietly, not that he could have anyway. The challenge that came out of the night was both spoken and beamed: "Who goes?"

"Me, Djo Bob," Peet beamed back. He could not see the sentry at all, which meant Djo Bob probably —he hoped—could not see him very well. "I'm just going out to see Snowdrop. You know how it is."

"Sure, Peet. Go right ahead. I understand," Djo Bob answered at once. He was a good fellow, Peet thought—a shame to deceive him this way. But he'd had a bellyful of sympathy. One more bite would choke him.

He sent out a mental call to his horse, was answered at once. He grinned—he had Sun and Wind with him for a change, at least in a small way. Snowdrop was at the far end of the line from Djo Bob. Peet hurried toward the beast.

Snowdrop whickered happily as Peet put the saddle over his back, then fell silent at his master's urgent mental command. Peet untethered him, mounted. Slowly and quietly, he rode away from the camp. No further challenge from Djo Bob. Peet hoped the sentry would not get into trouble when he was discovered to have disappeared.

But Djo Bob was not the last of Clan Staiklee's

protectors. Peet was a mile or so from the fires when a prairiecat's sharp question beamed into his mind: "Why are you riding off by yourself?"

"To make myself a man again, Crooktail," Peet answered respectfully. "My eyes are too weak now to let me serve the clan as a man should. I am going to hunt for the lenses that will let me see properly."

Crooktail considered that, then asked, "Why by yourself?"

Peet shrugged, though he doubted the cat could see him. "As I am, I'm worthless. If I am lost hunting, the clan will not suffer because of it. That would not be so if anyone came with me."

"You think like a prairiecat," Crooktail beamed— the highest praise his kind could give. "Hunt well, Peet Staiklee."

"I thank you, Crooktail." Peet's face was hot with pride. He felt the prairiecat withdraw from his mind. That too was a compliment; Crooktail must have decided he posed no danger to the clan.

Riding alone and near-blind in the dark, though, he was a danger to himself. Steering by the stars was no good for him—he could not see the stars. He could make out the moon, as a blob of light in the sky. It would do to guide him roughly south, toward the ruined ancient highway he remembered from last year's journey into south Texas. The highway would eventually lead him to a town.

Of course, people had been picking through towns ever since the Great Dying. But who, he asked himself, would have wanted to carry off lenses useless even for starting fires? Some should still be in the ruins, if he could find them.

If . . .

Lenses, unfortunately, were not likely to be the only things in the ruins. "Well," he said aloud, "that's why I brought the mace along."

Three days later, Peet came on the highway. He was on top of it before he knew it was there, in the most literal sense. What alerted him was the clop of Snowdrop's hooves on old asphalt, very different from the softer sound they made on dirt.

He reined in, peered down. He could see the faded black asphalt through the dust that had blown over it. Raising his head, he made out more patches running in a line east to west, straight as a stretched string.

Which way? He left it to Snowdrop. The horse chose east, walking by the side of the ruined road. Peet did not try to make the beast stay on the asphalt; too much time on that hard surface would be bad for its hooves.

As he found an hour or so later, staying off the road had another advantage. Again, ears rather than eyes were what told him Snowdrop had walked over something strange. He dismounted to clear the dirt from it and find out what it was.

He'd come across two thin, flat pieces of metal. They had been facedown; paint still clung to them, and even where it was gone, reflectors and inset dots that showed where others had been let him pick out letters and words.

US 90 EAST was all one of the pieces said: a highway sign, Peet supposed, though he had trouble conceiving of a nation big enough to need ninety highways.

The other sign was more informative. UVALDE 17 MILES, Peet read slowly. LODGING. FOOD. GAS. Truly the folk who lived before the Great Dying were a considerate people, Peet thought. He could not imagine any taverner these days being so kind as to warn customers that his food would give them gas.

Seventeen miles . . . not quite a day's ride, he thought. He would be in this Uvalde before noon tomorrow. Then he would search for—however long it took. Or until he starved, he added to himself. But if he starved, he'd be too dead to worry about glasses anyhow. Now, at least, he had a goal. He started to whistle. Snowdrop's ears twitched at the sound.

That afternoon, Peet came to a little creek not far from the roadway. He rode over to fill his water bottle and let Snowdrop drink. He squinted, trying to make out why the land on the other side of the little stream looked different from his bank. It was greener, somehow.

He had just realized he was looking at cultivated ground when someone called to him, "Go your way, rider." He jumped, turned his head toward the sound. Yes, that was a man there. He was holding something. It might have been a farm tool, it might have been a weapon. Peet could not tell.

He raised his empty right hand in the ancient gesture of peace. "By Sun and Wind, Dirtman, I have no quarrel with you and yours. If you harm me, though, Clan Staiklee will." That was purest bluff, and Peet knew it. The farmer, though, would not.

"Drink your fill and go your way," the man repeated, but he made no hostile move. Sensitive to tone, Peet could hear how cautious he was. That eased his own mind. If the Dirtman had a bow, he could pincushion Peet before the nearsighted nomad was sure he'd started shooting. But few farmers would casually take on a Horseclansman.

Peet said, "I'll ride on soon. Tell me, though, if you will, what you know of the old town of, uh, Uvalde east of here. Is it pretty well preserved, or have the looters picked it down to bare bones?"

"Uvalde? You're going to Uvalde?" The farmer dropped whatever it was he had in his right hand, made a violent crisscross gesture over his chest. Peet knew the motion had something to do with Dirtman religion.

With a sinking feeling, he asked, "Are there bandits holed up there, then?" If there were, they'd never tried raiding Clan Staiklee. That showed better sense than a lot of bandit bands had. The Horseclans made bad enemies, Clan Staiklee worse than most. Still, a single Horseclansman, especially one who could not use a bow, could not take on a robbers' roost alone.

But the farmer was saying, "No, not bandits. Worse than bandits. *Things.*" Bard Herbuht would have envied the horror the Dirtman packed into the word.

"Things?" Peet echoed. "What kind of things?" Of itself, his hand went to the mace at his belt. He willed it away, made the sign of peace again.

"That I do not know, but they come out sometimes, to hunt meat from our flocks—or from us. Three men

I know of have been killed since I came to manhood,
and more in my father's time, and in his father's, and
as far back as we recall. Always they die with terror
on their faces; always tracks lead back to Uvalde,
tracks like men's, but with claws.''

Peet was a Horseclansman. When something struck
him, his instinctive urge was to hit back. ''Why didn't
all you Dirtmen gather together, march in, and burn
the ruins down, then?'' he demanded.

The farmer's sigh was old as time, the sigh of the
oppressed and helpless. ''When my father was a boy,
we tried that. Thirty men went in. Three came out
again, one still with his wits, or some of them at least.
Since then, we have left Uvalde alone. If you wish to
live, rider, you will do the same.''

''The way I am now, it doesn't much matter to me
one way or the other,'' Peet said. ''I'm going to
Uvalde.''

The farmer made the crisscross motion again. ''I
have spoken with a dead man,'' he said.

''Not yet you haven't.'' Peet swung himself back
into the saddle. ''I thank you for the warning, though.
Sun and Wind with you.''

''God with you, rider,'' the farmer replied. ''If you
are going to Uvalde, you will need Him.''

A little nettled at the Dirtman's having had the last
word, Peet rode on. He saw the green of other cultivated fields and once or twice, squinting and peering,
made out men working in them. He did not hail the
farmers, and they let him ride past.

He worried over what the Dirtman by the creek had
told him as if it were a bit of gristle stuck between his
teeth. Things—things with tracks humanlike but for
claws. Mutant apes, maybe, whose ancestors, freed
from zoos, had passed through the fallout patterns of
the bombs that had fallen on Texas.

Mutant men, maybe, too. That would be worse.
Now when his hand closed on his mace handle, he let
it stay.

The fields dwindled and petered out as afternoon
passed into evening. As far as Peet could tell, the land
had not changed. No one, however, seemed to want to

live too close to Uvalde. After what he'd heard, Peet
decided he could not blame the Dirtmen.

The evening stayed hot and muggy. Peet decided
against a campfire. He suspected he would have done
the same in chilly weather. No telling who—or what—
might see it. He gnawed tough jerky and went to
sleep. Nothing ate him during the night, so presumably his precautions paid off.

The sun rose red in his face the next morning as he
mounted Snowdrop and trotted on toward Uvalde.

They watched the lone rider ford the little sun-
shrunken river and ride up toward the ruins. They
blinked in surprise; in their experience, meat did not
usually come forth to be slaughtered.

They were also suspicious. That raid so long ago
had hurt them as badly as it had the farmer folk
around Uvalde. And they were suspicious because
their nature was to be suspicious. They preyed on each
other too. There would have been many more of them,
were that not so.

But it was only the one rider, coming their way in
broad daylight. As well suspect a juicy steak! They
waited. The hoped-for meal kept coming.

Now that the ruins surrounded him, Peet wondered
in some despair how—or, more to the point, *where*—to
begin. Even before he'd set out, he'd known old cities,
even ones reckoned small, were vastly bigger than,
say, Clan Staiklee's encampment. But saying that only
made him imagine a larger nomad camp. The reality
of block after block of silent, tumbledown houses was
something else again.

He wondered how people could have chosen to live
their lives perpetually cramped together, then decided
that did not matter. Plainly, they had chosen so. His
job now was to deal with that reality.

He rode along the overgrown highway toward the
center of town. A ruin caught his eye; it was set off
from its neighbors by wide grounds and what once
must have been impressive fences, though now they

leaned drunkenly and had fallen down in a couple of places.

Curious, he rode through one of the gaps. The house, once two stories tall, had fallen in on itself. In front of it, a granite post fought its way clear of the rank weeds that filled the grounds. A bronze plaque was set into the front of the post. It had withstood the elements well. Peet leaned close to see what it said.

"Home of John Nance Garner, Vice-President of the United States, 1933–1941," he read. One of the chief's cronies, the nomad gathered. The plaque went on to list Garner's other accomplishments, none of which meant much to Peet.

Then, suddenly, he laughed out loud. One of Garner's rivals had characterized him as a "poker-playing, whiskey-drinking, evil old man." To Peet, that made him sound like an excellent crony indeed.

Peet decided not to explore the house. If this Garner had been an old man, he was probably long-sighted, in which case any glasses of his that might by some miracle be left in the ruin would do the Horseclansman no good.

He rode back to the highway, went deeper into Uvalde. Now the wreckage was no longer of houses, but of bigger structures. Sometimes a ruin would stretch uninterrupted from one cross street to the next. Curious to see how far back one of the bigger piles extended, Peet turned off onto a side street.

When he finally reached the back of the ruined colossus, he found a wide, open space, asphalt still visible here and there through brush. Enough tales had come down from the days before the Great Dying to let him recognize what the space had to be.

"A parking lot," he said aloud. Riding the open plains, he'd never understood why anyone needed a special place just to park anything. Here, though, almost everything was built up. The lot had a reason for being, after all.

And if that was a parking lot, then the huge ruin ought to be that other legendary creation, a shopping mall. And if, in a shopping mall, he found no lenses to suit him . . . "Then I'm screwed, that's all," he said.

He tethered Snowdrop to a bush close by an entranceway where a few pieces of jagged glass still stood like the last teeth in an old man's mouth. He took his mace in his right hand and a knife in his left as he walked into the ancient mall. Those fanglike shards of glass over which he stepped only heightened the impression of walking down the throat of some great beast.

The light inside the mall was not as bad as he had expected. There had been skylights in the roof. All the glass was gone from them (some crunched under his boots), but they let in the sun here and there. Weeds, some waist-high, grew in those patches, and less vigorously elsewhere.

Peet heard small animals scurrying about, smelled the telltale stinks of skunk and bobcat. Likely they denned in the ruins. They would not bother him if he left them alone. He paused, frowned. Something else was in the air too, something he could not quite name. Whatever it was, he did not care for it.

He walked along like a shopper from a bygone age, peering into stores to see what they had sold. Many had been looted; mannequins sprawled in old clothing stores like so many dismembered corpses. One shop was nothing but wreckage inside. The sign above it was in letters big enough for Peet to make them out and understand why: UVALDE GUNSMITHING. A few shops farther on was a cutlery store, similarly sacked. Looking behind a counter there, Peet found a skull grinning up at him.

"Was this yours, or are you just a thief who got what he deserved?" he asked, then chuckled. "Tad late to worry about it now." He left the plundered shop, started for the next one.

A grunting cough disturbed him. Startled, he looked up. Something—someone?—was standing under a broken skylight not far away, as if waiting for him to see it.

It had made the noise deliberately. The man was armed and alert; ambush would not have been certain. But men always froze in fear when they spied it. That made them easy meat.

Shrieking in hunger and fury, it leaped at the intruder.

The creature was on Peet before he had time to do much thinking. The Dirtman by the creek had been right—it did run on two legs, like a man. Past that, to Peet it was only a brownish blur.

He set himself, swung the mace at the top of the blur, felt it thud against flesh and bone. The thing's scream took on a sudden new note of shock and pain. He hit it again. Claws scored his arm. Then he rammed his knife home, twisted it, felt hot blood splash his left hand.

Now the once-fierce shriek was a bubbling wail. Peet swung his mace once more, screwing up his face at the stench that filled his nostrils. The creature toppled. He hit it several more times to make sure it was dead.

When it moved no more, he took a deep breath and bent close to see what he had killed. He rose still unsure. It had more hair than a man, less than an animal. His blows had pulped and bloodied its face past recognition.

"I doubt it was beautiful to begin with, though," he said aloud. He pulled up his tunic sleeve to see how badly his arm was hurt. The thick suede had absorbed some of the damage. His cuts bled freely, but none was deep.

Feeling a full man for the first time since his glasses had been broken, he stirred the thing's corpse with his boot. "You won't try that again," he told it.

He walked on to the next store. Most of the big black letters over it were still intact. He squinted up at them. "Sun and Wind," he whispered. The sign said H. P. LENSCRAFT.

He had no idea what the H and P stood for, and did not care. He rushed into the shop. Only overturned chairs and couches were in the outer room. He stumbled over a chair, almost fell.

The door inward screamed on its hinges as he forced it open. He paused at the threshold as his eyes adjusted to the gloom within. He saw another couple of overturned chairs—these two large and heavy—as well as some smashed gadgets he would not have understood even if they were whole. He did not see anything that had anything to do with lenses.

His feet scuffed old dust as he walked into the room. He waved his arms, knocked aside thick cobwebs. He was not the first to have come here; some drawers in the cabinets along the walls were open, others missing altogether. If those had once held lenses . . . Frustration threatened to consume him.

He fought for calm. If those drawers had once held lenses, he couldn't do anything about it now. He repeated that to himself several times. At last he began to accept it.

Another door stood at the far end of that second room. He kicked it and slammed it with his shoulder. It finally opened wide enough to let him through. Cautiously, he stuck his head in. If the last room had been gloomy, this one was black as tar inside.

He had to find out what was in there. He went back outside the shop, crushed dry leaves to make a little pile of tinder on the floor of the dead mall. Then he began the slow, patience-testing process of starting a fire with flint and steel.

The blaze caught at last. Peet crawled on hands and knees, his nose to the ground like a tooth-hound on a scent, until he found a stout piece of wood a couple of feet long. He stuck one end of it in the fire.

He went back into H. P. LENSCRAFT. He reminded himself to carry the torch carefully; if fire got loose, the whole ruin—and he with it—would go up in flames.

When he looked into the third room, he gasped and almost dropped the burning stick in spite of his best intentions. Tray on tray of lenses glittered dustily in the flickering firelight, hundreds more than he had seen in his whole life before. Other trays had been tipped onto the floor, the lenses in them smashed to smithereens.

Peet rushed in, snatched up a tray, carried it out of the store under one arm. He went back for two more before he noticed that one wall of the third room held a great rack of frames. Many had been stolen, but the

ones that were left were better than any he could hope
to make for himself. He piled several handfuls of them
onto another tray, carried out his loot. By then his
torch was nearly burning his fingers.

He sat down by the lenses, blew one more or less
clean, and held it close to his eye. The world grew
sharper, but not enough. He set the lens down, reached
for another.

Outside, Snowdrop screamed, aloud and in his mind.

Peet sprang to his feet, dashed for the entrance
through which he'd come. He fell once, scrambled to
his feet, and ran on. Two of the creatures that gave
ruined Uvalde such a dread name were attacking his
horse. One was on Snowdrop's back, the other kept
trying to dart in and tear at the horse's throat with
teeth and claws. Snowdrop bucked and plunged as
much as the tether would allow, and flailed hard hooves
at the monster in front of it.

That one was so intent on its prey that it did not
pay any attention to Peet until too late. It turned just
as his mace slammed into the side of its head. The
shock traveled up his arm. The creature swayed,
stunned and hurt. He hit it again. It went down.

The other monster shrieked. It leaped off Snowdrop. The horse lashed out with its hind feet. One
caught the creature a glancing blow. It reeled away.
Peet sprang after it.

It turned to glare at him, just as the one inside the
dead mall had. Its mouth gaped wider than a mouth
had any business doing; it was a great black hole in the
monster's blurry face. That made as good a target as
any for the next swing of his mace.

At the last possible instant, the thing ducked. All
the fight was gone from it, though. Instead of closing
with Peet, it turned and ran. He chased it for a few
steps, then gave up. It was faster than he, even if he
could have seen where he was going. It vanished into a
ruin on the far side of the parking lot.

Could have seen . . . Peet looked down at his left
hand, which was clenched into a fist around something
that should have been, but was not, the hilt of his
dagger. He opened his fingers and proceeded to call

himself eighteen different kinds of damn fool: he was still holding the lens he'd picked up just before the monsters jumped Snowdrop.

He walked back to the horse, gentled it with mind and hands. Then, when Snowdrop was approaching calm again, he put the lens up to his eye and took his first at least half-focused look at the creature he had slain.

He'd held that stupid lens all through the fight. He almost dropped it now. "Monster" was too kind a word for the hideous thing on the ground before him. And those grotesque features could only have been more terrifying when animated with life.

He put the lens down, shook his head. The sight of the horrid creature and reaction from the fight were both making him shaky. "Sun and Wind," he muttered under his breath. "If I'd seen what I was fighting, I'd've been too damn scared to fight it."

He looked toward the wrecked building where the other monster had fled, wondered how many more lurked in Uvalde. Alone, he did not care to find out.

He climbed onto Snowdrop. The horse shuddered but bore his weight. The monsters' claws had gashed it in several places, but none of the wounds was disabling. "Come on," Peet beamed soothingly, and rode the horse into the mall.

He used leather straps to convert the trays of lenses to makeshift panniers hanging from either side of Snowdrop's saddle, then stuffed every saddlebag full of frames. That done, he urged Snowdrop into a trot— out of the ancient mall, out of the parking lot, and out of Uvalde. Not until the ruined town was well behind him did he begin to breathe easily again.

The creature hiding in the wrecked building across from the dead mall thought about pursuing the rider as he headed north toward the edge of town. It hated to see so much meat escape, and in addition the horse-man had slain its comrades. Those killings cried for revenge.

But doubt and fear clouded the creature's mind. Always the barest sight of it and its kind had frozen a

man with fear, and frightened men made easy prey.
Going after one who not only defended himself but
ferociously attacked was a different—and daunting—
prospect.

The creature shivered. It would stay where it was.

Peet made camp with more than an hour of daylight
left in the sky. For one thing, he found a good spot—by
a little stream, in the middle of thick brush through
which nothing could come silently. For another, he
wanted time to find lenses which really suited him.

That took most of the time till sunset. A lot of the
lenses were like the first one he'd tried: better than
nothing, but not as good as the ones that had broken.
Peet clenched his fists. For all he knew, a dozen lenses
perfect for him still lay in that third room of the shop.
He laughed mirthlessly. Going into Uvalde once had
been quite bad enough. Going back . . .

A few minutes later, he picked up a concave lens
thicker than any he'd tried so far. He held it up to his
right eye, and yelled out loud when everything in the
world abruptly became so sharp-edged that each blade
of grass, each ripple on the stream might have been
individually carved out.

"So *that's* what I need," he breathed, and set about
finding another fat lens. Most, he discovered, were off
in a corner of one tray. A bit of experiment let him
pick one from among them.

He put the two lenses he had chosen in front of his
eyes, looked around. "Better than the ones I had," he
said, awed. Even the first stars of evening seemed
almost clear enough to reach out and touch.

He got the glasses frames out of Snowdrop's saddle-
bags. The first thing he saw was that not all of them
would fit the lenses he needed. Then he noticed that
all of them were steel or plastic; none was gold. He
remembered the gaps in the wall of frames. What the
looters had been after there was plain enough now.

He picked a steel pair; several of the plastic ones
were already cracked. Then he had to figure out how
to get the lenses into the frames. Most people, even
after realizing how the tiny screws worked, would

have had a tough time manipulating them. Peet found
it easy to slip the blade of his dagger into each screw's
narrow groove, even though he had to hold the frame
so close to his eyes that it kept hitting his nose.

For once, he thought, his shortsightedness actually
gave him an edge. "Yeah, for once," he answered
himself. Once in a lifetime wasn't worth it.

He tightened the last screw, cleaned the lenses with
a scrap of cloth, set the glasses on his nose. The right
earpiece was tight. He hardly noticed. He'd fix it later,
if he remembered to. It was still better and lighter
than the frame he'd made for himself. And he could
see again.

He sorted through the rest of the lenses he'd brought
out of Uvalde, searching for the ones most like those
he was wearing. He carefully wrapped the potential
spares in cloth. With luck, they would last him a
lifetime and keep him from depending on the vagaries
of traders—or on desperate adventures like the one
he'd just gone through.

Was going through, Peet corrected himself. If he
started thinking of himself as already safe and back at
his yurt, odds were he'd never get there.

"Now I can even tell what to be wary of," he said.
But not for much longer—it was almost full dark now.
Peet took off his glasses, rolled himself in his blanket,
and slept.

That tiny dot on the horizon had to be Clan Staiklee's
rearguard rider. Peet had been following the track of
the clan's herds and yurts a day and a half now: about
time he caught up. He clucked at Snowdrop. The
horse began to trot.

As Peet drew closer, the way the rider sat his horse
began to look familiar. Whoever he was, he wasn't
doing much in the way of rearguarding, just riding
along without a care in the world. That also seemed
familiar to Peet. "Yaah, Mikk!" he tightbeamed. "What
would you do if I was really trouble?"

He had the satisfaction of watching Mikk Staiklee
almost jump out of his skin. "Peet!" Mikk beamed
back as soon as he had enough composure to think

straight. "I was afraid you'd be buzzards' meat by
now, headin' out like that without bein' able to see
where you were goin'."

"Not me," Peet answered. He went on, "Sun and
Wind, that shirt you're wearing is an ugly shade of
yellow. You piss on it, or what?"

Mikk looked down at himself, then his head snapped
toward Peet. "You even got yourself new glasses. Sun
and Wind." He shook his head in wonder. Peet could
see him shake his head in wonder, and that was the
most wonderful thing of all.

Peet caught up with Mikk, rode past him. "I'm
heading on to the yurts," he told him. "My belly's
growling like a prairiecat in heat."

"Want me to beam ahead an let 'em know you're on
your way?"

"Thanks, no. Let's let it be a surprise."

"Fair enough. I'd say you've earned the right." Mikk
waved Peet on.

He was within fifty yards of the yurts before anyone
noticed him. But when the beamed and shouted cry
"Peet's back!" went up, the commotion that followed
was plenty hectic enough to keep from disappointing
him.

Drivers jerked on their reins to bring the yurts to a
halt. Men, women, and children came spilling out and
crowded around Peet, pounding him on the back and
pulling him off Snowdrop as if they were dragging
down prey. And so in a way they were, for his return
was news, something they all needed as much as fresh
game.

He started to tell his story several times, only to be
interrupted by greetings from people just fighting their
way through the crowd to him. One of those people
was Ann. That greeting was more thorough, that in-
terruption lasted longer than any that had gone before. The rest of the clan watched and leered and
whooped.

Peet finally, reluctantly, let Ann draw her lips away
from his. Her eyes shone—that he could see how her
eyes shone gave him a pleasure different from but
hardly less than her kisses. She studied his face, stud-

ied the look of the new glasses. "I like these better than the ones you used to have," she said. "They let me see more of you. Do they do as much to help you see?"

"More," he answered. "Now I can tell better than ever how beautiful you are." Watching her cheeks flush let him have that strange double pleasure again: knowing he had pleased her and *seeing* he had pleased her.

"I was afraid you would be—" Ann thought better of that beginning, tried another: "Going off like that by yourself was dangerous, Peet, with your eyes the way they are. I'd love you whether you could see past the end of your nose or not."

"I know you would," Peet said, but he remembered how pity had been mixed with that love. He went on, "But to everyone else in the clan, without glasses I would've just been a buffoon the rest of my days, always falling over my own feet or bumping into things. I didn't want that—those last few weeks were nothin' but torment to me. So I decided I had to go and fix things up if I could. Sun and Wind, Ann"—he paused to grin at her—"I just purely got tired of makin' a spectacle of myself."

Damnation

by Sharon Green

SHARON GREEN has a business card that says: "Novelist, Student of Chaos, Supporter of Barbarians and Chocolate Chip Cookies." *Believe it*. She is the author of the well-known Trevillian series.

How small is the difficulty in remembering back to the time I was no more than a babe, the time I first became truly aware of those around me. We who were very young were taken for the first time to hear the words of Mr. Skeel, the leader of our community, who spoke to us rather than to the adults about us. I myself found the occasion less than impressive or frightening despite the presence of so many large people around me, a reaction shared by none of my age group except for Pember.

Pember was the son of Mr. Skeel, and although I had never been quite so close to him before, I had seen him running about among the houses, making a great nuisance of himself wherever he went. He once took the carved stick Arris's father had made for him and simply walked away with it, and when Arris went crying to his father, he had been told the stick must be considered a gift to Pember. The boy was the son of Mr. Skeel, after all, and was not to be denied anything he wished. Arris had done no more than snuffle over the loss, but as Pember stood himself beside me that day, I knew I would have done a good deal more.

Mr. Skeel spoke to us for quite a long time, telling us that it was our duty to help the community please God, and then God would smile on us all. I quickly grew bored with the slow words that were repeated many times to be certain we understood them, almost as quickly as the boy who stood beside me. Pember had been in a sullen mood to begin with, resenting the need to stand before his father as the rest of us were required to do, but apparently knew better than to attempt to leave or disrupt the proceedings. His father was the one adult he dared not offend or disobey, and as the time passed he grew more and more outraged. I stood so near him I could almost feel the flames burning higher and higher inside him, and as soon as the address ended, his self-control did the same. As the adults left their places to either side of us and began speaking words of thanks to Mr. Skeel, Pember turned to me, bared his teeth in a grin of delight, and kicked me hard.

To say I was surprised would be to lie, for I'd known the boy would need to do something of the sort to ease his sense of outrage. That he chose a girl to do it to must have seemed even better to him, for he had already begun bullying the girls and making them cry. To him I was no more than just another of the girls, but I saw the matter differently. To me I was someone who refused to be a victim of his bullying, which I showed him rather quickly. His kick was hard and brought tears to my eyes, but I doubled my hand into a fist as I'd seen one of my older brothers do, then brought the fist around just as hard into Pember's eye. The boy screamed with shock as much as with pain, clapping one hand to his eye as he bent forward, and that was when I kicked him back, just as he had kicked me.

Quite a lot of shouting and yelling erupted then, intensified by Pember's screams that made it seem as if he'd been cut into tiny pieces, but no one seemed interested in quieting the uproar. Mr. Skeel added his own volume by shouting names as he pointed to me, and my father took me by the scruff and shook me harder than he ever had before. No one asked the reason for what I had done as I thought they might, but as they already knew the reason there was little sense in asking. They cared only that I had dared to touch Pember, and I was beaten hard for that, almost as hard as when I refused to apologize to the boy. I continued to refuse and continued to be beaten, until one day the matter was replaced with something else of concern and was never brought up again. Everyone forgot about it—except for Pember and me.

That was surely the beginning of it, but certainly not the end. Our community was one large farm, with everyone taking turns working the land and caring for the stock and occasionally hunting and doing everything that needed to be done. Our houses all stood close to one another inside the stockade walls, and at night the gates were closed and barred while everyone watched. Pember's father, Mr. Skeel, was the leader of our community, even though he didn't do any of the work. He was the one who got to say whether or not he liked the way things were being done, and if he didn't like them he told people it was God's will that they be done a different way. I remember following him around all of one day, not letting him see me, trying to find out how he found out what God's will was, but I hadn't been able to do it. The only things he'd done had been to sleep late, eat a better meal than most of us ever got, walk around with a frown on his face for just about everything he saw, and then go back home for another meal. If God spoke to him during that time, I wasn't the only one who didn't hear it; Mr. Skeel didn't stop to listen to anybody, not at any time, which made me wonder how he ever heard anything from God.

Growing up in the community was a time of learning for me, and not only of the things my sisters and brothers and I were told we had to learn. Under the heading of "had to" came the Laws that made us a community, the Laws that said we were born to work for the good of all and never complain, that what we wanted wasn't anywhere near as important as what our elders wanted, that to waste time laughing and playing was an affront to God and man alike. We were all given jobs to do as soon as we could walk and talk, and those jobs had to be done no matter what. If we had to be sick we could be, but not until after our chores were done. We also had to spend a lot of time sitting in one place all together, listening to Mr. Skeel tell us about all the things we did that weren't pleasing God, and then mumbling out promises that we would try to do better next time.

What I learned for myself had a lot to do with the "had to" list, but it came at problems from a different direction. I learned that if I was sent to collect eggs left in the straw by the hens and did it too fast, I wasn't told I had done a good job, I was given a different chore to see to in the extra time I had. I asked my mother why that was, and she answered without hesitation.

"God hates idle hands, Banni," she said, paying attention only to the shirt she was sewing for my father, none to me. "We must all do as much as we can in this almost-barren land, so God will love us and give us more of what we need."

"How do we know God hates idle hands?" I'd asked next, raising up on tiptoe to watch the needle flying over the old cloth. I wasn't far from being old enough to learn to sew, and I was trying to see if I would find it interesting.

"We have Mr. Skeel to tell us what God likes and doesn't like, child," she'd said, glancing up to see how my older sisters were doing with preparing breakfast. "We're very lucky to have Mr. Skeel, so we have to be sure to do everything he says."

"If God hates idle hands, why doesn't Mr. Skeel ever do anything to make his hands busy?" I'd asked next, peering over at the small, quick stitches that had been put in my father's shirt. "And if this land is so bad, why don't we go someplace else instead of just waiting for God to make it better? What if Mr. Skeel is wrong and he doesn't know what God likes and doesn't like? Then God won't ever make this land better, and we won't . . ."

That was the point I discovered my father had come in for breakfast, and had heard what I'd said. He grabbed me by the arms and shook me hard, yelling that no child of his would ever voice such sinful thoughts under his roof, and then he beat me with his belt.

After the beating I was locked in the dark place under
the stairs, and wasn't allowed out again until it was
dark outside as well and it was time to go to bed.

I remember that time better than almost anything
else of my childhood, how frightened and confused
and all alone I felt, how I hurt with no one to comfort
or help me. When I'd first been put under the stairs
I'd cried with the pain in my back, aching terribly and
waiting for my mother to come and make it better, but
time went by and then more and more time, and no
one came. My father and brothers had left a lot earlier
to tend the herds, but my mother still made no effort
to see if I were all right. I heard her and my sisters
moving around the house, all of them very carefully
making sure they didn't have idle hands, and after a
long while I'd realized she had no intention of coming
over to me. At the time I remember not understanding why that was, thinking that maybe my father had
forbidden her to come near me, but eventually I learned
better. My mother believed the exact same things my
father did, and she hadn't come over to me because I
had sinned and she refused to encourage me to do it
again by offering comfort. That was one of the major
things I learned as a child, that my mother thought
offering comfort would encourage sin.

"That and never again asking questions," I muttered to myself, chewing on the latest blade of grass
I'd plucked. There wasn't much else to do while watching our small herd of goats chewing up all the grass
they could reach, a chore I was given much too often
those days. I had grown to be a big girl rather than a
little one, but I had made the mistake of being too
good with the goats the first time I'd watched them
when my brothers had been busy with something else.
I hadn't thought anyone had noticed, but my father's
attention was never very far from the things I did.

"For some reason known only to God, they mind
you better than they do anybody else," my father had
said after that first time, frowning down at me the way
he usually did. "Since you don't get on with people, I
suppose you gotta get on with some creature of His.
But the next time you go out there, you take sewing or

some such with you. No sense in wasting time you can put to use doing more of your share."

I knew better than to point out my brothers never took anything extra to do when they minded the goat herd, not when my father had made it his duty to listen to every word I said and teach me when I said something wrong. My father taught me by beating my back into welts that didn't fade for days and days, but part of what I learned early for myself was not to care about that. I continued to do the things I considered important, to believe as I wanted to believe, two things all the beatings in the world couldn't change. Pember had gone on terrorizing everyone in the community after our fight, but he had never again tried it with me.

"And you also learned how much better it is to be by yourself," I muttered around the blade of grass, watching the herd and nudging them back when they began to drift too far. I had my sewing folded up in the sack beside me where I sat, and if the herd drifted too far away I'd have to move me and the sack after them.

"The one good thing about her is how little time she wastes talking to the other girls," my mother had once observed to my father, her tone more grudging than in any way approving. "She'll soon be having the boys coming by to look her over, and they'll like that. Girls who chatter end up marrying the last of all."

At the time I hadn't given any indication that I'd heard what my mother had said, but I'd taken a brief moment to wonder if she had really forgotten the reason I deliberately refused to be friendly with any of the girls my age. One of the beatings I'd had had been the result of thinking I had a friend, someone I could talk to without worrying about what I said.

"Honestly, Banni, I don't understand why they all act the way they do," Dinella had said that time we were washing clothes together in the stream, her words referring to the grown-ups usually around us. "Mr. Skeel told my papa I would be really pretty when I grew up, so my papa ought to start teaching me the right way now, before that happened. After he left

I heard my papa talking to my mama, and found out that I was going to be given all that extra praying my older sisters do all the time. I don't know why I have to say all those silly things, or why my papa and mama listened to Mr. Skeel. They all listen to Mr. Skeel, but I don't understand why.''

"They're too afraid not to listen," I'd said in answer, paying more attention to the washing than to the conversation. "It's like being lost in the community root cellar when you're very little, finding yourself alone in the dark and not knowing which way to go to get out. If you hear somebody's voice calling out to say they know the way out, you follow the voice without stopping to wonder if they really do know the way. You're so scared you don't want to believe the one calling out is just as lost as you are, because if he is you might never find your way out. You keep following the voice and following the voice, and as long as it doesn't start sounding as scared and lost as you feel, you never stop to ask if it's telling the truth. If you ever did that you'd notice you'd been following the voice without getting out for a very long time, and then all your hope would be gone."

"Oh, Banni, that's so silly!" Dinella had exclaimed, kneeling back away from the stream with a dripping shirt in her hand. "My papa doesn't get lost in the root cellar any more than any of the other grown-ups, and Mr. Skeel never goes down there except when he chooses what his portion is to be. That doesn't have anything to do with why I have to do all that extra praying, and doesn't tell me how I can get out of it. Don't you have any ideas?"

"Well, you can simply tell them your last prayers were answered by God, and He said you don't have to pray anymore," I'd answered with a small laugh, sighing only on the inside. Dinella had been fun to talk to, but she'd never understood anything I said and had always had a problem that needed solving by someone other than her. I'd helped her out when I could, which was more often than not, but that had only made her ask more and more in the way of help.

I hadn't noticed that she hadn't said anything more

after that about her latest problem, which had clearly been a mistake on my part. If I'd had less to do I might have wondered why she didn't keep on asking, but my mother had decided not long before that I should be responsible for more chores than I'd been doing. Because of that I had very little time to think my own thoughts, and therefore stole every moment I could. By the time I realized I should have paid more attention to my very good friend, it was far too late.

It was the night of the following day that I found out how badly I'd done, every detail told me by my father. I'd not only encouraged Dinella to lie, I'd encouraged her to lie about God, and on top of that I'd said some awful things about the grown-ups in the community. Mr. Skeel might be trying to guide us into the light, but that didn't mean we were all lost in the dark. Only damned souls were lost in the dark, and I had to be taught that there were no damned souls in the community—at least until I'd been born. I was taught that in my father's usual way, which at least gave me some undisturbed time to think once he was done.

The first thing that became very clear very quickly was the fact that Dinella had listened to my joking comment, hadn't been bright enough to realize I was joking, and had used the excuse to get out of the praying she'd been complaining about. Once caught in the lie she'd probably lost no time blaming the whole thing on me, and had added as much of the rest of what I'd said as she could remember in order to take everyone's attention away from her. Mr. Skeel always taught us to forgive those who wronged us, but after spending a night locked beneath the stairs I was more in the mood to act the way he did: He never forgot a wrong done him, and never forgave it until he saw it well punished.

After I was let out I was eager to see how punished Dinella had been, but it was a good thing I hadn't been counting on the sight to make things better for me. It turned out Dinella had hardly been punished at all, and as soon as she saw me she began complaining about her latest problem that needed solving. It took me a minute to understand that she had no intention

of apologizing for what she'd caused to be done to me,
and fully expected me to take up right where we'd left
off in my doing her thinking for her. For a very short
time I pretended I wasn't angry at all, and then just
before community prayer meeting made sure she "accidentally" fell into a mud puddle in her meeting clothes.
That time she didn't get out of being punished by
being able to find someone else to blame, and after
that I was simply too busy with my chores to have time
to talk to her. I was also too busy to find anyone else
to be a friend, which did make life a good deal easier.

I sighed aloud and shook my head, then got to my
feet to urge the goats back toward the stockade. Both
the goats and I would have been happier not going
back at all, but that would have left us with nowhere
to go once it got dark. I brushed at my skirts, thinking
about how much easier it would have been if I could
have done as everyone else in the community did, but
I knew far better than to even wish for such a thing.
There was something within me that refused to allow
the following of others to the detriment of my own
beliefs, and the passing years had done nothing to
change that outlook. If only there had been one other
who thought as I did, one person who—

I stopped very still with my head to one side, trying
to catch the sound I had almost heard, a sound very
much like a moan. It was difficult to imagine who
might be out there making such sounds, as it was
growing nearer the time the gates of the stockade
would be closed and barred. Earlier it might have
been one of my brothers teasing me, or one of the
other boys of the community doing nearly the same,
but at that late an hour . . .

The noise came again, and this time I was able to
tell it was more of a feeling than a sound, strangely
wordless but filled with a great deal of pain. It seemed
to be coming from the small stand of trees to the side
of the pasturage, away from the stockade I should
have already started for. I wavered very briefly, knowing without doubt what I would get if I was late
bringing the goats back inside the stockade, but that
very knowledge seemed to make up my mind for me.

If I was to be beaten again then I would be beaten, but not before I found out what was making that noise.

I didn't quite creep up on the stand of trees, but moving silently through thick grass isn't difficult for anyone. There were bushes as well as trees in the stand, and it wasn't until I looked behind the third bush that I saw him. Yellow hair, tanned features, slender and wiry rather than broad, dressed in trousers and shirt that showed more blood than dirt—a savage, one of those who made our stockade necessary. He moved feebly behind the bush he had chosen to hide him, unable to rise, and then he looked up to see me. Had it been possible for him to regain his feet he would have done it then, but it was patently impossible. The last of his strength had been used dragging himself into the bushes, and he simply had no more of it left.

Over the years I had been given very little reason to feel concern even for the people I knew, let alone for a stranger and an enemy. I might have simply walked away, possibly to tell someone about his presence and allow them to finish him properly—if not for the look in the blue eyes that came to me. Badly wounded, deeply in pain, helpless even against an unarmed girl, the look the savage sent told me he refused to surrender, would rather die than surrender. Caught he might be, but beaten he would never allow to happen to him; I was challenged to do as I wished, but could expect nothing in the way of victory over him.

I made a sound of great annoyance at myself, but it wasn't possible to turn my back on someone who faced life so closely to the way I did. The savage's people had undoubtedly left him behind to live or die on his own, too busy with their own lives to concern themselves with someone who was so badly wounded, and that, too, felt more than familiar. Rather than turning and walking from him, I moved closer and then knelt beside him in the grass.

For some unknowable reason I had brought my sack of sewing with me into the stand, which saved me the trouble of having to go after it. My habit was to take a number of finished articles along with one that needed working on, a ruse my father had never been able to see through. From time to time he met me on my arrival home and demanded to see evidence of hands which had not been idle, which I then gave him. The single unfinished article, usually partly done by the end of the day, had always been enough to show that I had sewed the entire time I also kept watch over the goat herd. Each time the partly finished article was a different one, and had always earned me a grunt indicating lack of disapproval. Approval was never given to anyone under any circumstances, but lack of disapproval had become more than enough.

My sack held a variety of sewing materials, which meant I was able to bare the savage's wound, discover it was made by an arrow which had already been broken off and pulled from his shoulder, and then stitch it both front and back. It was scarcely the first time I'd stitched a wound, but must surely have been the fastest I'd ever performed the task. The savage gritted his teeth at the first touch of the needle, attempting to hold fast against the greater pain, but although he made not a single sound the pain was quickly too much for him. He sighed as his senses left him, and then I was able to do as I had to as rapidly as I had to, ending with binding his wound with a length of my supposed sewing. It was all I was able to accomplish with the time and materials available to me, but there was one final thing I did before hurrying away. The apple and cut of bread I would have had to rid myself of before reentering the stockade I left beside him, to be accepted or not as the savage was inclined and able.

Had I been outside the stockade alone, it was quite possible the gates would have been shut without me behind them. As I hurried the goats inside I knew my lateness would not be overlooked, but it made very little difference. I was filled with a sense of triumph that I had no need to speak of, a sense of having accomplished something that no one would have approved of. It was childish to feel that way, not to mention dangerous, but I was far too delighted to care—until a figure stepped out to block my way up the street leading to the goat pen.

"Shame on you, Banni," Pember said in the bantering tone he had lately taken to using with me, clearly enjoying the thought that I was in for it. "You really must remember how dangerous it is to be outside the stockade when darkness falls, most especially these days. Didn't you hear about that great band of savages our hunters came on and fought with, and then drove off? If that band had come on you instead of grown men, they most likely would have carried you off to a lifetime of shame and degradation. Since I would find that most annoying, it will likely be necessary that I speak to your father about your tardiness."

"Our hunters fought with a band of savages?" I asked, not surprised that I had been told nothing about it. "When did it happen, Pember, and how many of them were there?"

"It happened late this morning, and Arris swears there were hundreds of them," Pember answered, his snort of disdain coming immediately after the words. "Of course we all know how Arris enjoys telling tales, which means there were probably no more than twenty or thirty of them. Arris also said he would be busy tonight asking your father if he might call on you, but that, you see, was just another of his tales. He won't be calling on you tonight because I will be, and I expect you to greet me in something other than the clothing of a goatherd."

I stared up at Pember in shocked speechlessness, all thoughts of savages gone out of my head, disappointment and dismay mingling inside me. I'd known Arris was intending to ask my father if he could call on me, but Arris was shy and had kept putting it off. He was still much of a boy even though he was now considered a man, and although I had no real interest in him I'd realized I might have caught the eye of someone much worse. Now Pember was saying I had caught the eye of someone much worse, and I simply couldn't understand why he was doing it.

"You're going to call on me?" I asked, barely able to see the smirking face looking down at me. "After all the years of our hating each other? That makes no sense at all, Pember, not even for you."

"You've never hesitated to be insulting to me, have you, Banni?" he said softly, strangely sounding very satisfied as he raised his hand to stroke two fingers down my cheek. "All the people in the community, knowing I'll be taking my father's place, give me the respect they give to him, but not you. You do as you please, and even refuse to give me that apology you've owed me for all these years. How long do you think you'll continue to refuse once you become my wife? You've grown into a deliciously delightful woman, Banni, and I intend enjoying having you as my wife. You go home, now, and we'll continue this discussion later."

I refused to let myself shiver until he had turned and was walking away, and then I began following the goats toward their pen, to close it before going home. Pember thought he had found the perfect revenge, choosing me as his wife so that he might spend the rest of his life tormenting me, but he wasn't going to get that any more than he had gotten his apology. If I refused to say the vows with him I would never be his wife, and refuse I would no matter what they did to me. I would sooner be dead than married to Pember, and once they all understood that they would persuade him to find someone else to torment.

I reached our house after the dinner prayer had already been said, which meant the meal had become one I would miss. No one was allowed at table after the prayer had been said, and no one not saying the prayer was allowed to eat. My mother pretended she couldn't see me, but my father took a moment to order me to my room before going back to what was being put in front of him. I didn't need to be told I would see and hear more of him once the meal was over; if nothing else, the silent smirks of my brothers and sisters would have told me that. All I could do was go upstairs and wait, which was precisely what I did.

The sound of my father's tread on the stair was a very familiar one to me, but that time I wasn't aware of his approach until he actually entered the tiny room I shared with two of my sisters. I looked up from the pallet where I sat, just in time to see the frown grow deeper on his face.

"Lateness in one thing breeds lateness in all things," he said, quoting one of Mr. Skeel's favorite sayings. "God alone knows why, girl, but you've been chosen for a great honor that you had better start preparing for as soon as I'm done with you. I was asked my permission for a man to come calling, and it won't be long before he gets here. You'll pretty up and put on the best dress you have, and you'll greet him with a proper smile on your face."

"Father, I won't marry Pember," I said, staring down at the bare wood floor of my room. "He stopped me just inside the stockade gates and said he would come calling, but it won't do him any good. I won't marry a man who means to spend his life torturing me."

"You'll marry who you're told to marry," my father returned flatly, disgust and scorn in his voice. "A girl who never done things right in her life don't get many chances, and never like the one you're about to get. One day Pember will be called Mr. Skeel, and then the father of his wife will be looked up to with respect. I don't much care what he means to do to you, girl— you'll learn to take it just the way he wants. Don't think you won't, girl, don't even think you won't."

By then he had his belt off, and the beating he gave me was certainly more thorough than the one he'd meant to give when he'd first come in. Once it was over he called my mother to be sure I dressed the way he wanted me to, and she hummed happily while she obeyed his orders. I tried once to keep from having that dress put on me, but my father came back and held me while my mother did her part. They wanted badly to be respected and honored, and I was the one who would get that for them.

I was sitting quietly at the edge of the settle when Pember came to knock, and after he was greeted warmly and happily by both of my parents I was sent outside to sit on the porch with him. I wore nothing of the smile I was supposed to be wearing, but Pember joined everyone else in ignoring that fact as he settled himself beside me on the old but sturdy bench.

"How lovely you look, Banni," he said in the sleekest of voices as he took my hand, pretending he was any man calling on any girl. "I've been counting the hours since we met at the gate, and now I'm finally here. I hope your father wasn't too hard on you for being late to table."

I sat silent in the dark, hearing the sounds of the night in a new, not particularly pleasant way, very aware of the feel of Pember's hand on mine. His skin was even smoother than a woman's, and I found that more repulsive than callus would have been. Then I gasped in pain as his arm went around my shoulders, and he chuckled without releasing me.

"How delightful to find a girl as shy as you are, Banni," he said, deliberately misunderstanding my reaction. "It's perfectly all right for me to put my arm around you, just as tomorrow night it will be acceptable for me to kiss you. I'm really much too impatient to go through a sevenday of this before asking for your hand, but tradition is tradition and must be observed even by me. Tonight we'll do no more than sit here and enjoy the night, but tomorrow night—ah, I can hardly wait."

He chuckled again then settled into silence, but his arm didn't leave me until he himself was ready to leave. I said not a single word despite the words of extreme satisfaction exchanged between my parents after he was gone, and simply went slowly up to my room and slept.

The next day I was sent out with the goats again after I had finished my household chores, and I barely remembered to steal what food I could and put it in my sewing sack. Despite having missed a meal the night before I hadn't eaten much that morning, something that had put a very small, very satisfied smile on my mother's face. I had no idea why she would be satisfied—unless it was the thought that I might still be in pain—but her reaction served the purpose of taking her attention from me in the kitchen and keeping it away. If I hadn't eaten what had been freely given, there was no reason to believe I would steal what I obviously had no appetite for.

I moved the goats into the same general area they had been in the day before, then walked around watching them as though I had nothing else on my mind. As soon as I'd gone through the gates I'd gotten the feeling that I was being watched, and because the feeling had more than once proved to be true, I knew I had to wait until it went away before I could see if the savage still lived.

I thought that if I found him dead I would envy him, and then I thought about how pleasant it would be if I were dead. Killing yourself was supposed to be a terrible sin, but I'd long since decided I knew why that was: If people killed themselves Mr. Skeel would no longer be able to make them do as he wanted, and if enough killed themselves Mr. Skeel would then have to work if he wanted to eat. Pember was very much like Mr. Skeel, so much so that he would deserve being called Mr. Skeel after his father was gone. Neither of them wanted to do any real work, so they frightened and bullied people into doing it for them.

I sank into my thoughts for a while, and when I became aware of the sunlit grazing area again the feeling of being watched was gone. I waited another moment or two to be certain, then made my way to the bushes where I'd found the savage the day before. If he'd been dead or gone I wouldn't have been surprised, but he was neither. I rounded the bush to see him up on one knee and waiting with a knife in his hand, ready to attack. I stopped short without making a sound, but when those blue eyes touched me he settled slowly back to the ground and smiled.

"Have no fear, I mean you no harm," he said, the words more strengthless than soft. "It was you who saved me, and I would not offer hurt in return."

"I see no cause for you to be different from everyone else," I answered, making no effort to respond to his smile. "Yes, I helped you, but for reasons of my own. You owe me nothing, and would be wise to be gone from here as soon as you can force yourself to it.

Our hunters defeated a force of your people once
already; if they come across you alone and wounded,
you won't stand any chance at all."

"The—'force'—your people defeated consisted of
me and two of my younger brothers," the savage said,
his face twisting into a grimace as he settled more
comfortably on the ground. "I held them off after
ordering my brothers to ride like blessed Wind, but
was clumsy in seeing to my own withdrawal. An arrow
took my shoulder and then took me from my horse,
but my horse-brother was able to draw the pursuit
after him while I hid. We knew nothing of there being
a Dirtman group in this area—but now we do."

"Which means in future you will wisely avoid us," I
said with a nod, understanding nothing of the hardness
that had entered his eyes. "Here, I've brought you
what to eat, although I probably won't be able to do it
again. There's very little even for us, and if I continue
to take things someone will certainly notice."

I knelt beside him and opened my sewing sack, then
brought out what I had stolen. A wedge of bread, two
small apples, a thin slice of salted pork, and a leather
jar of goat's milk. I had taken much more than I
should have, more than I would have gotten if I had
taken the noonday meal at home, and it would certainly have to be the last time. The savage sat up with
a small amount of effort to examine what I gave him,
and then those blue eyes were on me again.

"Will you share this with me?" he asked, that odd
smile on his face again. "My people believe that none
should go without unless all go without, and I would
dislike seeing you hunger because of your kindness.
While we eat we can talk, and . . ."

"No!" I said abruptly, straightening out of the crouch
I had taken. "I want none of it, and none of you as
well! Eat or not as you please, savage, and stay or not
as you will. I have chores to be about, and will not
come again."

I turned then and hurried out of the bushes, firmly
putting out of my mind the confusion I had seen in the
light eyes that had not left my face. I had not expected
a savage to be so strange, to sound more gentle than a

wobble-legged lamb, to speak to me as though I had
some importance, to smile as though I had gained his
approval. I wanted none of his approval, none of his
gentleness, and certainly had no intentions of speaking
to him. I spoke to no one, shared my thoughts with no
one, and was far better off for the lack of it all.

Once I returned to the goats I wandered around for
a while, nudging my charges back into place with only
half a mind. The day was lovely, the air cool despite
the sunshine, as was usual for that time of the year,
but it quickly became impossible for me to enjoy it.
There were so many things I had no wish to think
about that I barely knew which one not to think of
first, and the confusion was making my head spin.
What I most wanted was to give it all up, to let them
win over me as they had done over everyone else in
the community, but I couldn't give them that satisfaction. I couldn't give them that satisfaction, even if I
wasn't quite sure who the "them" was. Pember was
one of "them," that I knew, but the rest . . .

The balance of the day disappeared behind forced
thoughts of the goats and the sky and the grass and the
pleasure I would find in a death I would need to refuse
even if it were offered, and at last it was time to return
to the stockade. I closed the goats in their pen and
made my way home, got there in time to help carry
platters and bowls from the hearth to the table, then
joined my family for the meal. After the prayer I sat
with my brothers and sisters, waiting for what food
there was to be passed to us, and for the first time
noticed how much of what there was ended on my
father's plate. There were times some of it went un-
eaten, but my father was always the one to help himself first, to as much as he wished, and then my brothers
were served. After my brothers came my mother, and
then my sisters and me, to share what was left. Our
father and brothers worked hard and therefore needed
more, we had always been told, but we worked just as
they did, expending all the strength we had, ending
bone-weary and drained at the dimming of the day.
Why were they always given the most, sometimes taking all but the barest taste, which was then left for us?

Why didn't my people believe that one should not go hungry unless all went hungry?

I nearly shook my head to banish the whirling of my thoughts, but shaking was hardly the way to empty my head of the unwanted. I chose instead to study my plate, took only a little when the vegetable stew finally reached me, then began eating very slowly. After having eaten almost nothing the entire day, I still had no appetite worthy of the name. I chewed and swallowed with my full attention on those actions alone, and when my father spoke my name it took a moment before I was enough aware of it to look up at him.

"Time for you to be changing your dress, girl," he said when my eyes were on him, that all-consuming satisfaction showing again. "First, though, you got a lesson coming. I looked in your sewing sack, and didn't see nothing like what I should have. Upstairs, now, and I'll be there directly."

It came to me then that I had completely forgotten to change the things in my sewing sack, and my father had obviously looked in it last night as well as tonight. I stood up from the table and walked away without saying a word, but a small coldness was growing in the pit of my stomach. I felt as though a tightening, binding pattern was newly being imposed on my life, but I couldn't yet see a way out of it.

I was dressed and downstairs again by the time Pember got there, but I wasn't moving very easily. My father knew I hadn't changed my mind about marrying Pember, and showed me in the usual way his determination that I would. When my caller and I were again seated in the dark on the porch, the stiffness of my movements was, for the first time, deliberately noticed.

"How far do you expect to get by continuing to provoke your father, girl?" Pember demanded softly, staring down at me from my left. "At this rate there will be little left of you by the time we marry."

"There will never be so little left that I do marry you," I said in answer, staring straight ahead into the night. "I won't be bullied, Pember, and you of all people should know that."

"Children bully in one way, adults in another," he responded, not as angry as I'd expected him to be. "Adult methods are a good deal more effective, my dear Banni, and you'll find them more undefiable as well. When you become my wife you'll discover some of those methods are labeled duty, such as the bearing of my children. How large a family will we have, do you think, before you can bring yourself to beg for a respite before the next arrival? My mother begged after the sixth, but my father had no interest in her desires and continued on with the making of his family until the ninth babe took her life with its birth. You are a good deal smaller than my mother, less robust and more delicate. The time, I fear, will be much harsher for you."

I realized then that he was trying to frighten me, and strangely enough that made me feel better rather than worse. My own mother had borne fifteen babes, twelve of whom had lived, and she was no larger than I. She, however, was well matched to the man she had married, a strength I would certainly be lacking. If I was foolish enough to allow the thing in the first place.

"In order for a woman to be subject to wifely duties, Pember, she must first become a wife," I said, still staring straight ahead rather than turning to look at him. "I resisted your bullying once, and mean to continue doing so."

"How delightfully brave and persistent you are, Banni," he said with a small laugh, still showing nothing of the anger I'd been trying to provoke. "Your naiveté is certainly a large part of your charm, and I'm greatly tempted to give you the calling gift I meant to offer in another day or two. But no, why spoil the surprise? You'll have it soon enough, and tonight we have other things to occupy us, do we not?"

His arm came around me then, caring nothing about the pain he gave, and then his other hand came to my face to raise it to him. I tried to fight as I had that time he had kicked me when we were children, but his strength was no longer that of a child and I no longer his size. He took the kiss he had said he would, that one and more after it, and I could do nothing but endure the insult. Another daughter might have been able to call out for her father's help, but my father would have come to help him sooner than me. I accepted the insult in silence, then, and afterward went wordlessly to my bed.

The next day I was again sent out with the goats, and learned in an accidentally overheard comment that the time alone on the grazing tracts was for a purpose. I was meant to use the time thinking about the foolishness of the position I had taken, and eventually come around to seeing that cooperation was my only real choice. Because of that I made the effort to steal more food, and again had little difficulty in doing it. The reason was the same as it had been the day before, but this time my mother's satisfaction with my lack of appetite was less than it had been. I was told that she would see to the choosing of my dinner that night, and also expected to see it completely consumed. I left the house without commenting, reserving what argument there might be for the time it became pertinent.

Again I wandered around the outside of the herd once it had settled to grazing, waiting until the feeling of being watched was no longer with me. I wondered if it was Pember or my father who had taken to watching me, then realized that my father had work of his own to do and would have stayed with it longer if it had been him. Pember must have been the one, possibly checking to see if it was likely that I would try to run away. For a moment I raised my head, vowing silently that I would never give him the satisfaction of running, and then the moment was gone and I was left with the truth.

I would have loved to run, pelting at top speed into the woods and not stopping until the lack of breath threatened to break my body apart. I wanted escape so badly I would have sold the soul Mr. Skeel thought so tarnished in order to get it, but the only one interested in buying my soul was a devil I would never sell it to. True devils, I'd learned, tell you exactly what damnation you can expect from the exchange, and I'd begun to suspect that it was hurt and weariness and despair that caused people to give in, not evil and greed and sinfulness as Mr. Skeel insisted. I bowed my head and hugged myself around against the chill wind blowing beneath the clouds of the day, wondering how many other people had been lost in the name of the privileges of the righteous.

I spent quite a bit of time trying to fight off the despair of the damned, but only managed to get closer to losing the struggle. I knew I needed a distraction from my thoughts if I was to survive, and only then remembered I had stolen food waiting to be delivered. I took a deep breath, using the moment to be sure I was no longer being watched, then sought out the bush the savage was behind.

The bush the savage had been behind. I think I was more startled and shocked to find him gone than I'd been to find him ready to attack me, and I stared stupidly at the empty grass, which retained nothing of his previous presence, taking a long while to understand what I was seeing. When it was finally clear that he really was gone, I moved forward three slow steps and then sank down to the place that had been his, feeling worse than I had just a few minutes earlier. The savage had been nothing to me, really, no more than an injured animal I had taken the time to help, which meant there was no reason for the way I was reacting. There was a hole inside me I couldn't understand, as though a friend I had trusted had been taken from me, but I had no friends and certainly no one I could trust. There'd been nothing I'd wanted to say to him, but he'd spoken once about his people and might have again. I didn't have people like his, but maybe if I'd heard enough about them I could have pretended . . .

"You've returned after all!" a pleased voice said from behind, startling me into twisting around. He stood there, looking much stronger than he had the day before, two rabbits dangling from his belt. "I was hoping you would, and now you have. Will you pity me further by this time staying longer?"

"I don't pity you," I said as I watched him sit down beside me in the grass, not knowing what else to say. "I see you've soaked your bandage in an herb mixture of some kind, and the effort has obviously helped you. People who can take such good care of themselves have no need to be pitied."

"We all of us can do with gentle pity every now and again," he answered with a grin, reaching right-handed to his belt to unhook the rabbits. "My time comes when I try skinning rabbits one-handed, as I had to do yesterday. If my family and friends had been watching, they would have been too horrified at the results to give me anything but pity. My name is Jak Maklaruhn of Krooguh."

He put the rabbits down in the grass in front of him and just waited, his pretty blue eyes smiling gently. I knew what he was waiting for and almost got up and left, but something kept me right where I was. It had been years since I'd tried sharing anything with anyone, but such a little thing like a name couldn't hurt. . . .

"My name is Banni Akins," I offered with more difficulty than I'd thought I'd have. "Of—here, I guess you would have to say. Where is Krooguh?"

"Krooguh is a clan, not a place," he answered with another grin, but not a ridiculing one. "My mother was a Maklaruhn who married into clan Krooguh, which makes me Jak of sept Maklaruhn of clan Krooguh. Dirtmen don't know much about Horseclansmen, do they?"

"They know enough to put an arrow through the shoulder of one," I returned, just short of feeling insulted on behalf of people I didn't even like. "If you're so smart and capable, what are you doing still hanging around here?"

"Something has caught my interest," he said, his grin lessened but still very much there, those eyes looking directly at me. "I mean to leave as soon as I find it possible to satisfy the root of that interest, but for now must remain. You certainly have a fine herd of goats you bring out here each day."

"The herd isn't mine," I began to say, then grew immediately indignant when I thought I understood what he'd been talking about. "And even if they were, I would never let you take any of them! They're mine to guard, not give away as gifts, and if you try putting a single hand on any of them, I'll—I'll—"

I began getting to my feet, seriously thinking about looking for a good, heavy stick, but the savage laughed and shook his head.

"No, no, Banni Akins, I have no intentions of stealing the goats you guard," he said in amusement, putting his right hand to my shoulder to keep me from rising. "If I took the notion, I would make them mine when another stood guard, never when it was you who— What is it? What have I done?"

I couldn't have held back the gasp of pain even if I had been expecting the touch of a hand, and suddenly I was sitting again on the grass, fighting to keep from being overwhelmed. My back was one large mass of welts, and the previous night's rest had done no more than stiffen my body and make the welts even more painful than they'd been. I sat with my eyes closed and breathed deeply for a moment or two, demanding silently that the dizziness go and bedevil another, and finally it did.

"You did nothing," I husked when I could, waiting for the stolen strength to return to my arms and legs. "I—injured myself not long ago, and its time of pain has not yet passed. I think I had better go now."

"No, wait," he urged, his hand now on my arm with a grip of exquisite gentleness, upset clear in his voice. "You must rest a short while longer because of the—injury, and I would tell you more of us who are called Horseclansmen. Once you have rested you may leave."

He began talking then, giving me no chance to argue, giving me no chance to ask why he had sounded so strange when he had said the word "injury." He spoke of many clans roving the plains, all of them free and happy and knowing they were where they belonged, and I lost myself in the words and the pictures they evoked. After a while I opened my sack and gave him the food I had brought without interrupting him, and he took it and shared it with me without breaking into his narrative. He ate and talked and I ate and listened, and every now and then I nudged the goats back to where they were supposed to be. The first time I did it coincided with a pause and a look of surprise from the savage—from Jak—but after that he went on smoothly, doing nothing more than smiling more strongly.

The day ended long before I wanted it to, and I was nearly back to the stockade with the herd when I remembered I hadn't done anything to help Jak skin his rabbits. Such thoughtlessness would have bothered me under other circumstances, but just then I was too filled with confusion for other feelings to have a chance. I had never known it was possible to share that completely with another person, and yet not share anything of myself. Jak was the one who had done all the sharing, but it hadn't been a burden it had been a delight. I almost wished I could have added something of my own, but then I admitted the wish was useless. Jak would return to his people, his unbelievably wonderful people if he'd been telling the truth, and I would stay in the community. There was no sense in getting used to sharing, as there were no opportunities for sharing in my world. The only things my people shared were accusations and pain.

At dinner my mother made good on her promise to supervise my meal, but there was no argument as a result. I ate everything I was given and wished there were more, and then was actually sent to my room to change without my father promising a visit before that. Since I had deliberately left the same sewing in my sack and hadn't touched it at all I didn't understand that, but then it came to me that Pember might have spoken to my father. None of them wanted me to escape the fate they had decreed by letting me be beaten to death, and as I closed the same dress I'd worn for three nights in a row, I couldn't decide how to feel about that. The thought of death was more enticing than terrifying, but the thought of having the strength to survive in my stand was enormously more satisfying. If I had the strength I would survive, and fewer beatings meant greater strength.

And then Pember came, and took me out to the porch in the dark and began kissing me again. I hated the feel of his lips on mine, but presently there were other things to hate even more. For the first time he put his hands on my body, groping my breasts and trying to slide one under my skirts, and an insanity of sorts took hold of me. I screamed in outrage the way he had done as a child, and then I beat at him with both fists and all the strength that seemed to flow out of the night air and into my body. I beat at him over and over until I was free and he was shouting and holding his face and then my father was there and then—

And then the nightmare really began. If Pember had kept my father from beating me earlier, he didn't do it again. The pain was so great it even took my senses, and when I awoke I was in the place under the stairs, a place that was more cramped than it had been when I'd been younger. I greeted it silently as an old friend, a snug refuge in which to hide, and after a moment was able to smile. I still wore that vile dress, the one Pember had insisted on so, but would likely never be able to wear it again. I could feel the blood flowing from my back, and because of that and despite the pain, could also feel grim pleasure.

Whether I slept or my senses fled I have no idea, but quite a lot of time passed without my being aware of it. I knew the night was behind me when sounds of movement came into my refuge, but no one came to release me or lecture me or even to give me more pain. By then I thought I already had possession of all the pain there was, but the agonizingly slow passage of the day taught me I was wrong. I had the room to do no more than shift in place a very small amount, and could hardly have managed stronger movement even if there had been the room. The very act of breathing drew screams of agony from body to mind, and I thought I might well be fortunate enough to have them leave me there until I died.

I should have known better. Toward the end of the day I was helped from the place by my mother and one of my sisters, was cleaned and salved despite my absolute lack of cooperation, and then was put into an old dress of my mother's. Dinner was a grim affair, most especially when I refused to join in the prayer by closing my eyes and remaining silent, but my father said nothing about it. He and my mother both tried demanding that I eat the food put in front of me, but in that, too, they were unsuccessful. I had reached the point where I cared less about what was done to me than I had at any time in my terribly rebellious life, and I came to believe they finally understood that.

After dinner we had callers, more than the one I had been expecting. Pember came, but so did Mr. Skeel, and they both seemed to be filled with more satisfaction than the bruise on Pember's face should have called for. Our distinguished visitors took the settle and my father and I made do with chairs, and once we were all seated Mr. Skeel gave me one of his usual cold, small smiles.

"You must be quite excited, young lady," he said, sounding and acting as though I were eagerly there rather than not being allowed to leave. "I will admit the arrangements made between your father and my son are somewhat unusual, but they certainly are not against any of God's laws. Rather than first calling on you for the customary sevenday before asking for your hand, Pember has already asked and been granted approval. Your nuptials will be celebrated tomorrow night at this time, and I, of course, will preside."

"If it's your intention to make your son—and yourself—look foolish in the extreme, schedule any celebration you care to," I answered, at long last speaking to the man as I'd always wanted to. "I refuse to marry Pember, and will continue to refuse from now through forever."

"Ah, good, then you also agree," Mr. Skeel said with a wider smile, just as though I hadn't said what I had. "The ceremony will be private, of course, just your family and ours, and afterward the marriage will be confirmed to the rest of the community by me, just as the betrothal was announced. We all look forward to welcoming you to our bosom, daughter-to-be."

I looked around more carefully then, saw not only his smile but Pember's and my father's, and finally understood. No matter what I said, Mr. Skeel was going to hear only what he wanted to hear, only what

he and Pember and my father wanted to hear. With a
private ceremony everyone in the community would
believe I was married, especially when Mr. Skeel told
them I was. Pember would then be able to do anything
he liked to me, and no one would even think about
objecting.

"I'll still tell them you're lying," I tried, feeling
more trapped than I had in the dark place under the
stairs. "I'll scream it out even if they try not to listen,
over and over for as long as I live. And I won't ever
let Pember touch me, not ever!"

I discovered I was on my feet by then, my voice
more shrill than I'd wanted it, but all the outburst did
was widen the smile on Pember's face as he rose to
stand in front of me.

"No dutiful wife would try to refuse her husband,"
he said in a drawl, looking down at me with vicious-
ness in his dark eyes. "And no husband needs to
accept such an attempt even if it happens to be made.
Our wedding night will be quite active, Banni dear,
that I promise you."

His arms came around me then as he pulled me to
him, and I found I no longer had the strength to push
him away again. I panted as I struggled, appalled over
how easily he held me, how easily he kept me from
freeing myself, my father's chuckling the most evil
backdrop it was possible for me to imagine. At first
Mr. Skeel chuckled as well, and then suddenly, unex-
pectedly, the leader of our community was on his feet
with a frown.

"What is that noise?" he demanded, already beginning to stride to the front door. "Revels, from people
who should certainly know better, most especially at
this time of night? Have they lost their minds?"

His righteous indignation carried him forward quickly,
and by then we also could hear the whooping shouts
and raucous laughter he already had. It was impossible
to imagine what it could be, what situation could produce the sort of sounds that had never before been
heard from anyone in our community. I tried again,
vainly, to free myself from Pember as Mr. Skeel reached

for the door, and then everything happened so quickly I was barely able to follow it.

The door burst open right in Mr. Skeel's face, knocking him aside and down with the violence of the action, and then strange-looking men were streaming into the house. Dressed in trousers and shirts and carrying swords and knives and bows, they were smaller and slimmer than the men of our community, but seemed to possess a good deal more energy. It had just come to me that they were very much like Jak when Jak himself appeared, holding a sword and grinning broadly. My father had begun scrambling for a weapon at the first appearance of the men, but Pember stood as though struck in stone, and then he really was struck. Jak backhanded him away from me with the fist still holding a sword, and then turned his grin on me.

"We must leave now, Banni Akins," he said, a pool of calm in the midst of human chaos. The men who had entered first were taking weapons from my father and brothers, sacks of other things from the house, and in general keeping everyone from interfering with Jak. "The others will have taken what they wish from the herds, leaving only what I wish needing to be taken."

"But—the goats are in their pen, not here," I protested, still understanding nothing of what was happening. "Who are all of these people, and where have they come from?"

"They are Ohlsuhns and Hwilkees and Bakuhs, all of whom were visiting with my clan, led here for a raid by my brothers," he replied, sheathing his sword. "I would have come alone had it been necessary, even with no more than one good arm, but Sun and Wind sent a warrior force whose aid I was not so foolish as to refuse. And my desire is not for goats, Banni Akins. My desire is for you. I have come to claim you, and carry you back to my clan with me."

"But—that would be running away," I whispered, wishing with all my heart that I really could go with him. "If I run away, I won't have beaten them."

"Victory comes in many forms, girl," Jak said gently

as he put his hand to my face, not really having understood what I'd said but replying to it anyway. "Your victory will lie in finding a life with me, one far better than the one you currently live, and you cannot be said to be running away. I have come to carry you off, and no woman like yourself can resist such an effort from a savage."

His grin made me giggle in a way I never had before, as the absurdity of what he'd said struck fully home. He stood no more than three or four fingers higher than I, only a small bit broader, and still was unable to use his left arm. Had he been in full health he might have found it possible to "carry me off," but certainly not as he was.

"Girl, you must not let them take you!" Mr. Skeel shouted from where he lay on the floor, trembling back from the men who had knocked him down with their entrance. "You must kill yourself immediately rather than face such a shameful fate, else you will surely be punished with eternal damnation! Do you hear me? Eternal damnation!"

"Yes, I hear you," I answered with a full smile, then turned to Jak, took his hand, and eagerly followed him out. I was on my way to eternal damnation, and I could hardly wait.

The Swordsman's Place

by John Steakley

JOHN STEAKLEY is that kind of larger-than-life personality that can only come from Texas. The author of *Armor*, he is currently working on a book for New American Library.

Cri had called to me through my dreams nine nights in a row.

I knew what it meant.

I was going back. . . .

1

Some time back something happened to my best buddy, Lanny Weaver, and me. It was the worst thing that could happen to two young bucks with more muscles than sense—we had our wishes granted.

Don't talk to me about dimensions and different planes of reality and magic and all the rest of it, okay? I don't *know* how it worked but somehow he and I were transported to a different . . . Place. A Place described in great detail in the Horseclans novels, our all-time favorite adventure stories.

We were young, understand, like I said. Young and romantic and stupid and convinced that the world—this entire rich and varied Earth—was boring. (I know, I know. I *said* we were young.) And we used to fantasize about living the Horseclans life, about how much more fun it would be to be swaggering around with our swords, etc., etc., and then . . .

Then we were there and it was just as we had read it was only more so. More beautiful, brighter, more hypnotic. And more bloodstained and more brutal and more piteously savage than any modern war. And if you wonder how I can say that, think of this: A war, even a modern mechanized genocide, ends eventually. In that Place, violence was not due primarily to war, but to life-style. Wanton, slogging anarchy.

You know, freedom.

We told some people there about our world and they were amazed and we told them we liked it there better and they were more amazed and said we were crazy and they were right. Soon, once the fighting started, we agreed with them.

We were awfully glad to be back. Further, we had no desire to return. None. Zero. Only . . . maybe I'd better start with the nightmares. I had a lot of 'em about that Place. But not about what had already happened. Mine were about being back there, being dragged back to the mud and misery.

There was absolutely no reason for these fears. I didn't even understand how I'd gotten there in the first place, so why should I think I'd be forced to return? And Lanny didn't have those nightmares, I knew, because in a drunken moment I'd confessed them to him and he'd told me so. For a time I did manage to convince myself that only I was having the dreams because I had hated the place, had feared the place, so much more.

Wrong.

I did hate it and I did fear being drawn back there to the stumbling peasants and poleaxe justice and chaotic swordplay. It was awful so often and mindless so much more, a terrible place, and as much as I had hated it and had feared it I had also, God help me, loved it. Not all of it. Not even most of it. But enough of it to tell you a lot about me.

I'm big for six feet and 210 pounds and I'm fast and strong as a bull and I can use a sword like you can a tennis racket and I have no excuse for deciding to learn so senselessly hostile a skill. But I did.

So maybe that's why I feared going back. For loving

just enough of it—for being the *kind* of man who
could love it at all—that maybe, just maybe, I deserved no better.

So when Cri called out to me in my dreams, I knew
what was coming.

Cri (from a family name) Palema was the biggest
beauty I had ever seen. Long blond hair, glowing
eyes, lustrous features of near-perfect skin, all packed
into five feet five inches high and 250 pounds wide.

Fat, you say. Well, yes and no. I thought she was
overweight—I like 'em skinny. But she didn't. She
knew just what she was doing. She liked her weight,
liked the look and the feel of it, and she was by no
means alone. How that gal could attract men! Her
face and hair were wonderful, of course, but I think it
was the way she moved and swirled or maybe it was
just the way she had of caressing herself into an easy
chair and smiling like the Cheshire Cat. It made a man
think of those chubby naked cherubs from ancient wall
murals advertising the Eternal Orgy in Paradise. There
is something fundamentally carnal in the look of those
women. Carnal and, somehow, pure.

Cri had that look. And, therefore, her pick of men.

She had been the only person Lanny and I had told
about our experiences. About the Place. About Smada.

Trebor Smada was the main focus of our adventure.
He conned us, stole from us (both money and women),
outfought us, outthought us, and outdrank us and I
never hated anybody so much in my life. Or, I guess,
loved, too, and Cri seemed fascinated by our descrip-
tion of him, asking me over and over to try to recall
the smallest detail of his appearance. Actually there
weren't many small details—Smada was a bigger-than-
life type in most ways. But Cri seemed satisfied with
what little I had to offer. And she certainly made the
most of it. She was an artist in charcoals and one day I
jumped about three feet when I saw a dead-on portrait
of Smada in her studio.

At the time, of course, I just thought I'd described
him so well. Live and learn.

Cri called only my name in the dreams. But I knew
more was being said. You see, I owed her one.

Three years back, even before my trip to that Place. A hotel suite in Miami. We were down there for a science fiction convention. We had heard the guy who wrote the Horseclans was going to be there and maybe he was but we never got a chance to see him. Anyway, it was Thursday and the show didn't start until Friday and Cri had conned her current lover (some writer whose name I can't recall) into letting us use his suite for a little seven-card stud. By five in the morning, only six of us were left. Myself, Cri, two guys down for the convention to sell old collectors' comic books, and two Cubans who had just sort of wandered in at midnight and joined the game. We hadn't much minded. They had been losing steadily. But they were a scary pair, believe me.

They got scarier-looking in a hurry when I won the last and biggest pot of the night. They exchanged glances, visibly deciding whether or not to let it go or just start the rumble right then. Looking at them I had the strong feeling that armed robbery was more than just a hypothetical concept to them.

But then they relaxed, sighed, said adios, and split along with everyone else but Cri (who was staying there, of course) and me. I sat happily dragging the winnings against my chest and I noticed Cri was staring oddly at me. Or rather, at my cards. I smiled proudly. I had won with a small diamond flush: the nine, the six, the three, and the two fives.

Huh? *Two* fives? But there they were. I hadn't noticed it before, and neither, thank God, had anyone else.

But Cri had been hip to them all along.

"Why didn't you sing out?" I asked.

"Several reasons, my lad. I'm too tired to care, I know you're not a thief—and I didn't want that Cuban carving you up."

"He had a knife?"

"Matter of opinion. Something big enough to paddle all the way here from Havana can still be considered a knife, I suppose."

I gulped. "Where was it?"

"Inside your standard, everyday, foot-long shoulder holster."

I gulped again. "Thanks, luv. Want some of the pot?"

"I didn't win it."

"Neither did I, apparently."

"Hm. Good point. I'll take . . . that hundred." And she scooped it up off the pile and out of sight down the V of her blouse and scooted me out of there.

"Thanks again," I said as she closed the door. "I owe you one."

It was just one of those things you say. But by the morning it was true.

The Cubans came right through the door twenty minutes later carrying shotguns and had her down on the floor before she could scream. They were very disappointed to find only the hundred in her blouse and demanded to know my name and room number. She knew both but wouldn't tell so they beat her bloody and semiconscious. They hadn't spotted the extra five of diamonds. They weren't there to avenge an injustice. They just wanted their money back, and, being the kind of scum they were, they'd decided to steal it.

For the same reason, no doubt, they took turns raping her until seven a.m., when they heard the writer's wake-up call from the bedroom and ran off.

She was in the hospital three weeks. But when first aroused in intensive care, her only concern was for me. Seems she couldn't remember if she'd told them about me or not.

She hadn't. Quite a broad. I definitely owed her one.

Which only means she had a right to call for my help. It doesn't mean I didn't still hate her for doing it. I did hate her for it.

Because I could tell she was calling to me not from this world, but from that other one. Cri was in that Place.

2

The ninth dream in as many nights ended at three a.m. and I woke up. I stared at the shadowy ceiling a moment, then swung my feet over the bed and turned on the light. I lit a cigarette. My house felt even lonelier than usual. Even the surrounding woods were silent and thoughtful. I was used to the place being empty; I'd been losing what little family I had for three years. My mother was long gone since I was small, but my father and two of my stepsisters (I was adopted) had all died within fourteen months of one another. The third had moved to New England, of all places, with a new husband; he hated my guts and I his. The grandparents were gone even before my mom and that left only a black sheep Uncle Luke doing three to six for mail fraud.

So, alone. No real family and so no real holidays to mark my life and no real job, either. I'd inherited quite a bit I had quickly sold off. I still kept three bookstores in the city (science fiction, of course), but the college kids who ran them could catch those little comic-book shoplifters without my help.

So what did I do? I worked out with my swords in the woods every day until my lungs and muscles were raw, carving up on trees and sometimes myself. And I maintained my swords. Every day. Sometimes I watched television and sometimes I took a bath and changed clothes and sometimes I reread favorite books or went into town for more cigarettes and two or three times a week I drank myself blind and woke up somewhere on the property.

Everyone should have a routine.

Several times a year I would make plans to attend another science fiction convention or SCA (Society for Creative Anachronisms) event but at the last minute I'd get drunk instead. I still loved the things. But those plastic-thonged kids in costume swords are saddening after you've been to the blood and back.

I was semi-engaged for a while but she left me. She took the microwave oven, both dogs, and my pool man to Long Beach, California. I thought it was an interesting choice.

Lanny Weaver and I had drifted apart since the Place. My bizarre life-style, or lack of it, depressed him, I suppose. I didn't blame him. Neither did I consider telling him what I knew in my heart was about to happen. The last time Lanny had gone there, he had "died." No point in bringing him along again even if I had wanted to risk him, and I didn't.

This was my punishment. No one else's.

I wrote him a note, though, and addressed it to him and propped it on the broad hearth downstairs. I owed him that much to keep him from wondering.

By then it "felt" like time to go. I can't explain it any better than that. I could just feel the transition coming on to my soul, surrounding and enveloping my sense of myself as part of the space around me. Okay?

Well, it'll have to do.

I smoked another cigarette through and drank a scotch and water. Then I drank another one sitting in the tub. I sat and drank for several minutes. I was trying to come up with a new way to think.

Because this was going to happen. Now. That night. I was going to be there soon. In that Place. And I had to find a way to keep from . . . from what? Panic?

Yeah. Panic the moment my foot touched on those dusty roads. Complete utter panic. Damn. I could see myself throwing my weapons down and running in circles pleading to the heavens to send me back home to . . . to what? To passing out three times a week? To whom? Nobody?

To hell with it, I thought suddenly and with that thought the hairs on the back of my arms stood up. To hell with it. If I was going to die anyway, why not die fighting? Why not go out with a little touch of Style?

I could feel my wide grin forming and I knew it would have been a scary sight to anyone who had seen it. I didn't care. The scotch was helping this bravado a bit. But Style was pulling me the rest of the way.

I rose from the tub, carrying drink and cigarette and grin, and went into the other room to get ready to have at it.

Ten minutes later I was a lethal weapon. Boots, leggings, all my soft armor, the broadsword, the small knife, three daggers—most everything I had that hurt people. Everything "legal," that is. For I knew once I went over my zippers would change to buttons (as before) and anything else I carried which didn't "fit" wouldn't come across with me at all. I carried a leather pouch with goodies in it, metal coins and the like.

At the last moment I got Wishful-Thinking Disease and shoved a pack of cigarettes in.

Then it was time. I stood in front of a full-length mirror wearing my new short life and stared myself as hard as I knew I could be.

"C'mon," I growled sourly, "let's get this done."

There was a flash of sound-light and then subzero ice-cold darkness. I felt myself falling. . . .

3

I woke up, sure enough, on another dusty road. The trees on each side of the road spread a rich canopy above me, all but eclipsing the deep blue sky. There was a slow-moving river off to my right, broad and deep, a thick woods to my left, broader and deeper, and, right in front of me, a saber-toothed tiger eyeing me calmly.

At first I thought it was a dream. The sky too blue, the woods too green—that sort of thing. Then I saw it was no dream. Or rather, smelled it. Trust me, a cat that size has a whiff to it. By "that size" I mean . . . well, imagine the biggest fastest motorcycle you've ever seen with teeth the size of the handgrips running around loose looking for fuel.

"Are you the One?" it asked me without speaking, reminding me where I was, the Place, the Horseclans Place, and reminding me also that this was no saber-toothed tiger. It was smart. It was a telepath.

It was a prairiecat.

"Are you the One?" it beamed to me again.

"The way my luck's been running—probably," I replied out loud.

It turned its head this way and that like a housecat. It beamed confusion. But not, thankfully, anger or irritation. It seemed to be intrigued, though. He did, I should say. For it was clearly a male.

"Come with me," he beamed. "I am your Guide and your Shelter."

"My Shelter?"

"Your thoughts cannot be stolen within my closeness."

"I see. Who would wish to steal them?"

"Enemies."

"That's a lot of help."

"You are welcome," he replied.

I laughed shortly. Prairiecats weren't hip to sarcasm, it seemed.

"You are pleased?" he asked, noticing my laughter.

"That depends. Where are you taking me?"

"Lord Smada."

Now, *that* figured. Who else would be in on this but the old con man himself? I thought of objecting but what was the point?

I sighed, nodded, stood up. We started off down the road. We walked for a pleasant hour, the leafy ceiling rolling slowly above us, the great animal padding softly in front. This Place, whatever else it was, was indeed beautiful. And rich and full and wondrous. It was impossible, walking beneath such majesty, taking in that healthy soft air, not to feel more alive.

Even if you had been brought here to kill.

To hell with it! I thought again, even more strongly than before. Whatever happens, happens. There was a touch of righteous anger involved as well. For I hadn't done anything wrong! I had never really hurt anyone except when I had been in this Place, and it was damned unfair to bring me back to do it some more.

Just because I enjoyed doing it was no reason to make me do it.

We turned away from the river road after a while and started cross-country. It wasn't much harder going. The few really thick sections of undergrowth were easily avoided and the grass was luxurious and deep. It made you wonder why anyone would want to use the roads at all if he wasn't with a caravan or something.

Still, I wasn't used to this sort of sustained tramping and asked the cat if I could rest. "Of course, little two-legs," he beamed, and we sat.

Maybe he did have a sense of humor after all, I was thinking, until I felt the cat's disdain come over with his thoughts.

Sitting there I decided to take inventory. As expected, every single aspect of my possessions that did not fit this Place had been altered. Zippers to buttons, plastic shoelace eyes replaced by wooden ones, that sort of thing. There were odd runes and mysterious hieroglyphics instead of American presidents on my coins. My Premium California Red Table Wine had been changed to something like the stuff my aunt used to keep in an uncovered carafe in her formal living room for years at a time. My army-navy store magnesium match was now a couple of hunks of flint.

All my toilet paper was gone.

Incredibly enough, my cigarettes were not. They looked different and tasted awful but there they were, right down to the coarse parchment package with "L&M" on the front.

Weird. But then again, nice to know Someone had a sense of irony in this Place.

We began again a few minutes later. We walked several miles, stopping twice more. And everything was amazingly vibrant and alive and breathtaking and I remembered something Lanny had said when last we were here. He'd said he thought it wasn't really the Horseclans world. It was too perfect. Too much like a movie. It wasn't the world of those books or the world of our birth. It was something in between.

It was something raw and full of purpose.

It was getting almost too dark to see when we spotted the campfire. The cat stopped on a knoll and sat down, its huge tail curling behind it.

"Smada?" I whispered.

"No," he beamed back. "Your comrades-in-arms."

4

They didn't want me.

They sat or lay sullenly around the fire surrounded by the cracked and broken masonry of what used to be some sort of building and stared hard-eyed in my direction. No one stood up to greet me after the cat told them my name. No one spoke to me or to anyone else. A couple of them exchanged disgusted looks.

There were eight of them, ranging in age from late teens to one old salt who was sixty if he was a day with the thickest gray hair and beard I had ever seen. He would have looked like a hippie had it not been for all those jagged scars on his face and the huge broadsword lying beside him. Oddly enough, his face was the most pleasant of the lot. Well, not his face. But his eyes. Clearly, he was not automatically ready to hate me as the others seemed to be.

But neither had I sold him. He did not return my nod. The cat then made an interesting little statement. He backed away to the edges of the firelight and lay down with his muzzle propped up on his forepaws. Watching.

It looked like audition time.

And you know what? That pissed me off. I hadn't asked to be here. I hadn't asked to be the One. I hadn't asked to be stuck out here in the darkness of Never-Never Land with a bunch of raggedy-ass swordsmen too stupid to know what antiperspirant was, much less know how very badly they needed it. A little dentistry wouldn't have hurt either. Make that a lot of dentistry.

I snorted as loudly as I could, stepped over to the fire, and lit one of my prehistoric cigarettes off one of the embers. Then I plopped loudly down on a stone and blew a smoke ring in the most impudent and irreverent manner I could manage.

To hell with it! Remember?

I don't think they'd ever seen a cigarette before. But "Well, screw you, too, buddy!" translates everywhere.

Their reply came right away. Gruffle was the guy's

name. Long tangled black hair, a tall wiry build, a short wide sword, and a barroom-bully sneer. Did I mention dentistry?

He stood up with an exaggerated groan and raised himself to his full height, which was maybe two or three inches beyond my own. He put his hands on his hips and stared at me for a bit in a way calculated to have me see how unimpressed he was. Then he regarded his fellows.

"For one full day and part of night we have waited for such as this? We were told to await a leader—I see none. We were told to await a man of power—I see none. I see no power. And truly, I see no man."

And with that he took a couple of dramatic steps around the fire and stood staring down at me.

I had to admit it—there was a certain perfection to this crap. Not enough that I'm brought here against my will. Not enough that I'm obviously meant to do a little fighting with these dudes. But no, first I've got to run for office. Well, I've always hated politics.

I stood up slowly, stepped up to him, smiled, and kicked him in the balls. He folded up nicely.

"You say you saw not a leader, a man of wisdom or power . . . you saw not a man at all. Clearly, you are a man of truth." I leaned down and stared into his groaning red face. "For neither did you see my boot."

There was a pause, then a titter from the far side of the campfire. Then another and another and soon all of them, led by the old gray one, were laughing uproariously. They were still laughing when Gruffle finally managed to unwrap himself and climb to his knees. I pointed him toward the spot he was in before. He clambered over and sat down, rubbing himself. I remained standing.

"To be sure," I began, "his words are not without merit. I do not know how I have come to this Place. I do not know why. I do not know what is desired of me. I do know this, however." And with that I strode right into the center of them, just beside the flickering fire so they would be looking up at me. "I do know that I am the One. And if you have need of me, then you should tell me what you want. And I . . ." I looked directly at the old gray one. "I will tell you what I will do."

The old one met my eyes. I saw a grin begin to form on his mouth and something else, respect, appear in his gaze. He stood and held out his right hand. I gripped his forearm almost to the elbow and he mine.

"We are well met, I believe, Fee . . . ?"

"Felix," I finished for him. "And who might you be?"

He was their daddy. Well, daddy to several of them anyway. He was grampa to the two youngest. I'm not much good at names and I never got all of 'em right, I don't believe. But the old one's name was Orman. His sons were: Gruffle, the tall one. Grussle, the blond one. Temblar, the pretty one (and he really was, folks—pretty enough to be a girl—and, while I'm at it, strong enough to be a Volkswagen). And . . .

Dammit, I just don't remember. There was another black-haired one with a sharp nose, really pointed. And there was one who chanted quietly to himself a lot but almost never spoke. There were five boys altogether and two grandsons. I was bigger than all of them except for old Orman and taller than all of them except Gruffle.

Intros over, I sat down on a rock next to Orman to get the lowdown. The cat came over to "listen." I made it clear from the beginning just how in the dark I really was. Briefly, I related to them my only experience with Smada—which they all found hysterically funny as well as typical of the old smart-ass. Particularly the part about Lanny and me passing out in the hallway outside his room waiting vainly for him to send some of the tavern whores out.

The part about how we—Smada, Lanny, and I—had taken out the Greydon and his dark soldiers impressed the hell out of them. Seems that one was one of those oft-told legends thereabouts. I had the distinct impression from Gruffle's look that he never would have messed with me at all had he known I was *that* Felix.

It didn't seem a good time to tell them how utterly terrified I had been the whole time.

Finally we got down to it.

"Smada," began Orman, "has been taken by the Dead."

"You mean he's dead?" I asked, surprised at my own alarm.

"He may well be," offered Grussle (the blond one).

"I don't dig you."

"What?"

"I don't understand," I translated. "Is he dead or isn't he?"

Orman looked grim. "I know not," he said quietly. "I know only that he has been taken by the Dead."

I sighed. "Okay, let's try again: Who are the Dead?"

They were, it turned out, just that: dead. Corpses, stiffs, old news, etc., etc. Only they didn't know it. They kept walking around. Sometimes they did more than just walk. Sometimes they killed people. And sometimes they ate them afterward.

I was in a zombie movie.

Smada had been nabbed by these critters. He was being taken by them to a place called Keep of the Dead, where their leader, some scumbag named Gor, was going to have what he called his "final revenge." Seems he and Smada had had a little difference of opinion upon occasion.

It was nice to know the old fool had *some* standards.

But hang on, it gets worse.

The entire countryside was infested with these ghouls, stalking blankly around looking for—are you ready?—us. The Orman family, long indebted to Lord Smada, were known to be the only people brave enough or loyal enough to help him out. They were being led, rumor had it, by the One. Or rather, Smada's One. Felix. Me.

Ouch.

It was getting late and we had a long way to travel to try to cut off the procession dragging Smada to the Keep. We decided to turn in. I lay on my back puffing on one of my burlap L&Ms and stared at the most beautiful starry sky imaginable.

Well, except for not wanting to come here in the first place, and then being dragged here against my will and then having to fight damn near the first person I met and being expected to go save the life of a man who delighted in making a fool out of me *plus* being chased around by flesh-eating zombies . . .

Except for all of that, it was great to be back.

I rolled over and dreamed of shopping malls and Saturday-morning cartoons and the Democratic Party —all the things I had always hated and now missed with an almost sexual fervor.

Oh, well. Live and learn. And die.

5

The first zombie killed Grussle, the blond one, by ripping half his throat out with black teeth the moment we stepped through the tavern's side door. I had my sword in my hand without recalling having reached for it. Out and at the ready and . . . nothing. I just stood there and stared at the nightmarish sight. They had gray dead skin and black teeth and long black nails and shiny red eyes and they were everywhere, filling the tavern, rushing at us, and they *lusted*! How they *lusted* for us! Coming at us in a wild frenzied jumble, and I heard someone scream to my side, one of the Orman boys, and I saw poor Grussle trying to scream, oh, how he tried to scream, but he had nothing left to scream with, and then one was on me and I shoved my blade right through its throat with a two-handed perfect lunge and . . .

And it didn't care.

It just kept jamming itself forward at me, *along* my sword through its neck, black blood flying and splattering through the air, and I jerked my blade to the left and free, collapsing one side of its neck, but the other side still wanted me, and I spun all the way around, I spun and brought my blade around like a propeller and beheaded it, but there was another one right behind it leaping through the air at me, black teeth shining dully, red eyes flashing, and I ducked and it went over my shoulder and down, its awful hiss close and warm against my ear, and I turned and drove my blade through its forehead into the tavern's wooden floor, but only made it hiss and scramble more frantically, and I knew, suddenly, what to do. I popped my blade loose, leaned one step to the side, and brought the full force of my blade down across its clavicle and the head burst free and rolled out of sight into the rest of the battle.

I stood up, mouth open and blowing like a whale, to get my bearings, and felt something grab my leg. It was an arm. Just the arm. And the clutching hand.

I tore it loose and flung it away just as another ghoul came rushing at me from the side. I swung a long powerful backhanded slice for its neck but it ducked underneath or maybe my aim was just off but suddenly it was on me, face to face and hissing those glistening black teeth arched wide and back on its neck to come forward and do to me what had happened to Grussle and I couldn't get the broadsword into position so I just dropped it and grabbed the fiend by the hair to keep those black teeth from my throat and my dagger was in my other hand, my left, and I drove the blade up under its chin and we fell backward to the hard floor.

The smell! That awful deadman stench of decay! I gagged, whimpered, struggled, shoved the dagger in deeper. But it didn't care! It didn't care about the dagger or the wound or the fountain of black blood it was spilling across our faces. All it cared about was my throat, my blood, my flesh, and never had I known such complete, utter terror.

Then there were other hands, human hands, and they had the creature and were lifting him up and Orman held it off the floor by the hair on the top of its head while Gruffle chopped its head off with his short wide blade and it was all over and those of us still alive stood there huffing and puffing for the several seconds it took for the various sections to stop jerking and reaching.

I had thought there were thousands. There were only six.

And I had gotten three. Imagine that. Or two and a half.

While I was still trying to get it together, one of the Ormans released the proprietor and his staff from the locked cellar. Turned out the place was more than just a tavern and more than an inn. It was a Hall. And Markus, the owner, was famous for running the best Hall on the river. He was quite a guy. Small and lean, with a trim beard and elegant manner, he immediately dispatched his staff to clean up the carnage with no more apparent alarm than you'd expect over a dropped tray during the noontime rush.

A small covey of buxom lovelies appeared with warm water and soft cloths to clean off our gore. They also brought ice-cold mugs of ale to give us something to do while they worked on us.

The whole time Markus was watching me out of the corner of his eye. It was beginning to make me a little nervous. He apparently noticed this and came over to our table. I stood warily.

But his manner was completely friendly.

"You are the One," he said with a smile.

It felt right to nod and say: "I am."

Markus's smile was broader. "Lord Smada is my good and dear friend." He just stared at me for a moment, looking pleased and—I dunno—satisfied or something. Then he turned and snapped his fingers in the direction of a middle-aged woman supervising the clean-up. She hurried over bringing her own smile. "His rooms have been prepared for two days. This is Nasus. She is my wife." We nodded at each other. "She will show you the way."

It sounded pretty good. We had been marching cross-country since dawn, and sleep sounded better than sitting there and thinking about what had just happened. I turned to Orman, who looked pale and drained and sad, and I was thinking he was getting too old for this until I realized he had lost his son today. Tonight. Ten minutes ago.

"I am sorry about Grussle."

He nodded, looking vacantly past me. "He was my One."

Ouch. His son *and* his best fighter.

"I'm sorry," I said again.

He looked at me this time. His smile was thin. "It is the Price," he said.

I didn't have an answer to that. I just beheld his Style.

"Sleep," he said to me after a few moments. "Sleep and in the morning we will talk."

Smada must have been some good friend, all right. Or at least a big tipper. His rooms were on the third-story corner, the only rooms on that floor. They looked spacious and wide and elegant and perfectly suited to his orgy-rhythm life-style.

Markus's wife, Nasus, made me nervous. Too respectful, too much bowing. The food and drink, lavish and tasty, made me nervous, too. It felt a lot like I was being fattened up for something.

I drank some ale and smoked a cigarette. Then I drank some more ale. It wasn't much good, but it worked. But nothing would have worked as well as I wanted. I tried for a blank brain and held it awhile, pretending fascination with the way the cigarette smoke spun and whirled. Then I took great interest in noting how these rooms, this entire Markus Hall, was the cleanest place in this Place I had ever seen.

Then I gave up and admitted how well I had fought and how smug I was about it and even the rest of it: how full of shame I was and deserved to be.

The food looked great. Steaming fresh meat and a fresh salad-something. I took my nausea and ale out onto the balcony.

It was a great broad terrace with a wide carved stone railing just even with the treetops. It was an incredibly beautiful night. The moon was full and glowing, the stars shining. The river was there sending gently rippling reflections towards me and with it a lush warm breeze that smelled of affection and reward.

"It is very pure," beamed the cat.

I started, looked around. My Guide and Shelter was sprawled with lazy magnificence on a flat cornice where the railing met the wall.

"How'd you get in?" I blurted rudely.

" 'Get in'? I leapt," he beamed back.

I walked to the railing and looked over. Thirty-five feet if it was an inch and sheer except for a small shack perhaps six feet high. That still left it about a thirty-foot jump straight up.

I grunted. I doubt if I could *fall* that far.

I turned back to him. "I thought you didn't like being around so many people." At least that had been his reason for not entering the village with us.

"I do not like herds of two-legs, that is true," he replied with a truly gargantuan yawn. "But many nights have your Lord Smada and myself spent thus, he with his ale and I with my moon."

"He's not so much *my* Lord Smada."

I could have sworn he looked confused. "Are you not his One?"

I thought about it, sighed. "So I hear."

It was quiet for a while.

"It is very pure," he beamed again.

I nodded. "Lovely night."

He turned his great head and eyed me to the core the way only cats can. "No. I mean not the night. I mean the Struggle." He stood, stretched, replaced himself. "The Swordsmen and the Dead. It is very pure. It is very clean."

I knew exactly what he meant but decided to be an ass instead.

"It was pretty messy tonight," I growled and drained the last of the ale.

He didn't respond and I didn't look at him but I could feel him staring at me for what seemed like forever until at last I had had it. I rose, said: "I'm to bed," over my shoulder and headed back inside.

"Felix," he beamed gently to me.

I stopped, turned reluctantly to face him.

"Felix, you hide your fear well."

There were a lot of things I could have said. But . . .

"Thank you," I said at last and went on in and flopped down fully dressed and slept.

6

I dreamed of my starving-artist phase.

When I was twenty-three I took my years of doodling fighter planes in the back of the classroom to the edges of the ghetto to become a painter. I lived in an old warehouse with several other artists surrounded by lots of worn-out, usually abandoned buildings, a couple of rubbled lots, a few bars, a Vietnamese grocer, and some crime.

I was so determined, so hardworking, so pitifully eager that I got some work. Some covers on local magazines. Some caricatures. Some illustration work. That sort of thing. By busting my ass working all day long every day I made just enough money to pay my rent and buy enough food to bust my ass working all day long every day.

I was happy to do almost no thinking at all.

Amber and his wife, Simone (at least black parents *try* names more original than Bob and John and Pamela), lived in the loft above mine and were the center of our lives. She was always sweet and their place always clean and his work was so damned good it made your heart ache. Everyone loved them and everyone was there the night he unveiled his sketch for a two-story wall mural for the outside of our building. Amber was a tall and handsome young man the color of his name who rarely let his feelings show and when his voice choked up as he described his plan it jolted and inspired and made all of us get misty.

The sketch had already done that to me. It was of a young black couple, sweaty and hard at work. You couldn't tell what they were doing except that you knew it wasn't sex but the point was that in the midst of their work, they were looking up and sharing a private smile of satisfaction and accomplishment. It was all about hope and faith and hard work and pride and it was wonderful.

But Flash Phil thought it wasn't "black enough." Flash Phil was our local crime boss. Every shadow neighborhood, even one as deserted as ours, had a chief pig. Flash Phil was ours. He ran a little dope, a little stolen merchandise, a few junky hookers. He spent a lot of time driving around in a purple Caddy convertible, stopping occasionally to shove people around. He was a coward and a bully, but also six foot four.

He wore a huge black Abraham Lincoln stovepipe hat with a purple feather in it.

When the word came through that Flash Phil thought the preliminary sketches on the side of the building weren't "black enough," we all knew what he meant. There were lots of other murals in the area, all of them depicting the inevitable misery of blacks and other minorities under the heel of white racism and white money. Poor downtrodden classes with no chance of success no matter what, so if the game is rigged anyway, why not get it while the getting is good? Drop out of school and join Flash Phil and get high and . . .

You get the idea. A coward and a bully, yes. But not stupid. Flash Phil was a crafty and cunning politician.

The first week the penciled outlines were erased; Amber redrew them. A week later they were rubbed out again; Amber redrew them again. A week after that our pitiful scaffolding was trashed and we helped Amber with carpentry.

There were ways Flash Phil could have finished it sooner but he liked once-a-week attacks because they helped draw the whole business out longer. There was a lot of tension in the air and fewer people willing to publicly support the mural and in the middle of it all poor sweet naive Amber, who thought Flash Phil would stop if he could just get enough done between vandalisms to show how pretty it was going to be.

The fourth week Amber spent almost twenty-four hours a day on the scaffolding, painting like mad under Coleman lanterns and sparking jury-rigged spotlights, and managed to complete almost half of it.

It really was lovely—anyone could see that—and when another week went by without trouble it looked like Amber's strategy had worked.

It was getting dark the night I found Flash Phil and his punks laughing and talking on the curb in front of our building. We nodded to each other as I stepped inside and trotted up the steps. At my door I heard weeping above me and knew, right then, I knew. On the landing above I found a sobbing Simone cradling a very bloody Amber. Not seriously hurt but slapped around plenty.

It was all very strange. I had never been much of what I thought of as a tough guy. In point of fact, I was scared of Flash Phil. But the next thing I knew I was skittering full-speed down the steps. I rocketed out of the building's entrance across the sidewalk and, still holding the sack of groceries I had been carrying, slammed into Flash Phil like a locomotive. He was too smart to carry a gun and he never got near his knife. I broke his nose, blackened and closed his eyes, knocked out some of his teeth. I kicked and butted and bit and gouged and screamed and roared and seconds later I had won.

And when I stood back up with Flash Phil unconscious on the street and his great black hat gray and squashed beneath my boot, I sneered at his punks and twirled his purple feather in my hand, gone completely mad, and asked: "Anybody else?" and just then the streetlamps came on.

They ran.

I knew it wasn't over. So did everyone else, and they told me so. I remained quiet, keeping to myself. I slept with a tire tool, when I could sleep at all, and resolved not to wait for hurt.

When Flash Phil reemerged bandaged and angry three nights later it was in the abandoned lot next to our block's only apartment house. As reported, he was with two new—and larger—goons. I watched from the darkness a few feet away for several moments while they passed around joints and wine and muttered vengeance. Then I stepped forward and bashed the tire tool against the side of Goon #1's neck. Goon #2 got the pointy end through the cheek, and there was Flash Phil, wide-eyed and mouth agape, reaching for a pistol. I broke the reaching wrist and the collarbone above it and his jaw and a lot of the rest of him and then had some other short vague struggle with one of the goons and then . . .

Then it was over and they were groaning at my feet and above me, high above me, came the sounds of wild cheering and applause from the people in the apartment-building windows and seconds later they were surrounding me and smiling but looking at me kind of funny and some time after that a cop was standing in front of me gently taking the tire tool from my hand and pointing out, just as gently, how it would be better for me to sit down seeing as how there was a knife sticking out of my chest.

Ever the hero, I fainted dead away.

It wasn't that bad a wound, but any chest wound is serious. I was in the hospital three weeks. I had to answer some friendly questions, but there were no charges brought and some of the many people who came to visit were the cops from our beat. Almost everyone else came as well but I think only Simone guessed why I was so quiet.

The mural was finished but covered because they had decided the unveiling should be a joint celebration for Amber and me. There were tables set up with food and wine and claps on the back and then the mural was released into the glare of those shorting spotlights.

The mural was incredibly beautiful and wildly cheered and Amber and I were wildly cheered and people were sweet to me and warm and full of compliments and I stood there and took it. I took every bit of it. I even smiled.

When it was finally over and everyone had gone home and I was sure no one was around I grabbed up all my paints and charcoals and materials and all my sketches and went to the river bridge and threw them off and sat down and cried and cried and cried and still found no relief from the facts.

For the facts were too hard. What I was, was too clear within them. What I was and what I would always be. The mural, Amber's mural, was not simply good, it was better than anything I could ever have hoped to accomplish. Sure, I had made it possible. But Amber had made the mural. And I didn't want to make murals possible. I wanted to make the murals.

But what *I* could do, I had already done.

I moved out that night and wandered back to my white-semirich-kid life. I got into a little karate and into a little shooting. Then one day, at a Horseclans convention, I saw a sword I liked and I bought it.

7

The next night we cracked Smada free.

It was easy, once they told me the rules, and yes, there were rules to the Dead. The Ormans hadn't told me about them because they simply assumed that I, Felix, being Smada's One and therefore his best rough-and-tougher, would already know them. Wrong.

Most of the rules were pretty simple. They even made sense, in a Hollywood sort of way. For one thing, they could only be killed by decapitation, which I had already figured out the hard way, or by flame. They were really scared of fire. For another, they could only come out at night—or at least out of direct sunlight.

Like I say, it made a sort of macabre sense, particularly the part about their victims inevitably rising to become one of the Dead themselves unless cremated.

I really *was* in a zombie movie.

The procession carrying Smada was technically that of the Lady Gor, also on her way to the Keep of the Dead. Her carriage was really just a huge, intricately carved wooden box the size of a motor home drawn by a dozen oxen almost as large. She was in the rear, surrounded by half a dozen mounted swordsmen. At the front of the little parade was the wagon for the Dead. It was huge and flat black, enabling the Dead to be transported during daylight hours.

In between came Smada. In a cage. They had him naked, each wrist leather-thonged tight to either side of the cage, him sagging limply in between, his great belly crisscrossed with ugly red whip marks and uneven lines of dried blood.

I was hiding in the upper loft of the stable when

they came through into town, and when I saw him I
. . . Well, two things. First, I was angry. Furious.
Enraged. The sight of what they had done to him and
what they were and what they'd probably done to
others . . . I was boiling and dangerous and more than
a little crazy.

The second thing was the sight of Smada's face.
Even like he was, beaten, strapped up and swaying,
clearly exhausted, he . . . shone. He shone, radiated
some something that normal men just don't have and
no one can explain, and I realized that, dammit, I
really had missed the old fart and, double dammit, I
really was glad to see him again.

But I shoved those thoughts away, and seconds later,
we got into it. And when I got into it this time—even
though I didn't even see it then—I was in it, all of it,
to stay.

It was almost dawn when we hit them, and the Dead
were closed up and not a factor. We found out later
their theory was that we'd be less likely to attack them
inside a village so they had planned to spend the
several hours without the Dead in relative safety.

Wrong.

But even without the Dead we were outnumbered.
Two riders in front, the two men on the Dead wagon,
the two drivers of the flatbed wagon hauling Smada's
cage, plus their two riding guards, plus the six riding
alongside the Lady Gor's carriage added up to fourteen.

We had seven Ormans, me, and a prairiecat. It
wasn't close.

It had to look like an attack on the Lady Gor to give
me time to spring Smada. But it wasn't quite dark yet,
and the Dead had to be kept inside their box to keep
from cluttering things up. Orman had done a little
thinking along those lines. He had this weird bulky
locking mechanism designed to clamp the wooden bolt
on the black box shut and keep it that way. He took
his youngest grandson along to help him. At the other
end of the train, Gruffle led the other boys in a mounted
assault on the Lady's carriage. A beat later, the cat
and I were to go for Smada.

It was a good plan and worked well enough, I guess.

Would have worked better if the enemy had cooperated, but isn't that always the way?

Gruffle led them in screaming and hollering, and shouts of alarm went up almost at once. I could just see Orman up ahead move up with his grandson to the lock on the box of the Dead. I turned to my Guide and Shelter to see if he was ready and I could swear he looked at me and nodded but by that time we were already moving. I was sprinting full-speed by the time I reached my particular targets, the driver and, closest to me, the pike-bearing guard sitting beside him. My first step took me up onto the seat beside him just as he was turning toward me. I slammed my hilt into his forehead as hard as I could and he slammed sideways into the driver, who cried out and tried to keep from falling off. From the corner of my eye I saw the cat leap into the air and damn near *through* the two guards sitting atop the cage. Hell, it was only about six hundred pounds traveling at forty miles an hour and when I saw them both flying off in pieces and myself in good position for the already cowering driver, I thought: This is going to be easy.

About then is when the oxen pulling us smelled prairiecat and decided to leave.

I banged my head against the bars of the cage when they vaulted forward. It took me a couple of beats to clear my head, and by that time we were really moving. If they're scared enough, even oxen can rock and roll.

They careened right through the center of the village square, scattering the couple of dozen locals who had come out to gawk and missing the town well by at least three inches, then rolled to the side and headed down a side street large enough for all six of them but not for the wagon, and there was a helluva crash.

And then I was flying through the air into the midst of stomping, rearing, groaning, panicked oxen whose tether had miraculously withstood the impact and half a second later the limp body of the guard crashed in on top of me and knocked me off one of those broad backs and the hooves were cracking sparks on the street tiles around my head and by the time I managed

to right myself there was the driver holding the guard's
pike and jabbing it at me. He missed, missed again. I
flung out my sword and didn't and he sank like a sack
of fireplace ashes. The bellowing of oxen freak-out
reverberating between the narrow stone walls and tiled
street was lifting the top of my head right off. I clambered back atop what was left of the driver's seat,
planted my feet, and brought my sword down on the
tether to the rigging. It snapped free, and the oxen
bolted forward out of sight into the shadows.

When I turned back to the cage, Smada was looking
at me. And for perhaps five seconds I looked back and
neither of us moved a muscle and I thought: Who *is*
this man?

Then the cat was there with us and I turned my gaze
deliberately away from Smada and set to work on the
cage's lock. It was primitive as hell, of course, but also
quite strong. There was no sign of a key in the seating
compartment, and, hearing increased sounds of fighting from the others' struggles, I was in no humor to go
looking for it.

I reached over and grabbed the prairiecat's paw.

He resisted a moment, tensed, and for just a
second I was a dead man. Clearly I was taking great
liberties, but for some reason or other the great beast
let it slide. He relaxed and let me guide a paw the size
of my thigh into a position of leverage behind the
cage's door.

"Hold still a second," I ordered breathlessly as I
leaped off the wagon seat to the ground, and he tensed
again but let me live through that little impertinence,
too. I fetched up the pike, hopped back aboard, and
propped it against the door alongside that great paw
and said: "Pull."

I never even got a chance to get my weight into it. If
not for that shrieking rasp of crumpling metal, you
would never have known the damn cage was locked.

Whew! Nice kitty.

I stepped inside and, still not looking at Smada,
used my dagger on his thongs. Then I handed him the
robe I had strapped to my back alongside the extra
broadsword. I stood there holding the sword for him

while he tied the robe on tight. Then he took the **sword,** pulled the blade halfway out to check it, and **froze.**

Me, too. We were both looking down at his bared blade. But, as one, we raised our eyes and peered at one another and a rush of emotion went through us both and I could not tell you to this day if we would have kissed or killed each other if someone hadn't called out at just that moment.

"Lord Smada!" shouted a hoarse Orman.

As I tore my gaze away toward the sound, however, I did notice the prairiecat's fur standing straight up on his back.

Killed each other, I think.

"Lord Smada!" called Orman again, sounding a little frantic, and *that* tone coming from *that* man had us out of the cage, swords drawn, and beside him in a heartbeat.

His face was smeared with blood not his own. He turned and gestured with his head back toward the village square. "The others!" he gasped. "It's a trap!"

We could already hear the galloping horses approaching through the dusk, but Smada ignored it and instead put an arm on the old man's shoulder.

"Thank you, old friend," said Smada with infinite tenderness. Then with equal affection, he walked the old man over to a stoop in front of some doorway and sat him down. Orman obeyed like a little child.

Neither of us mentioned the body he carried in his arms, a body obviously devoid of life to anyone but a grieving grandfather.

The riders were, of course, the force which trailed ten minutes behind the procession for just such an eventuality. I never got it straight just how many there were because at least some of them were taken out by Orman's other sons, led by Gruffle, who, I understood later, was some ball of fire that night.

Whatever. We faced six, gunning their mounts on either side of the village well just as the light of dawn broke about us.

Smada and I exchanged a quick look—a much different one than before—and backed up to a wall about a sword's length or so apart and stood there, braced and ready and mean.

They dismounted first, which was a mistake, and then they just sent the first pair at first, which was a bigger mistake. But I think they were trying to prove their bravery or something. And I suppose they did, for they were courageous and . . .

And that's not what I want to tell you. I don't want to tell you about them. I mean, they were fine. They died well. Fought well, too. But that's not what I want to tell you about.

I want to tell you about me. Or rather, about us.

We were goddam fabulous.

I don't think I can explain it to anyone who wasn't there at that time and not one of us, but: Think of absolute clarity and certainty of resolve and a sense of fullness and . . . I dunno, *rightness*. I'm not advocating killing or even fighting, but neither am I going to spend my life feeling sorry for punks who enslave entire peoples and then feed them to the ravenous ghouls they make of the few men around with guts enough to die resisting them.

It was right what we did. Right, and, much more, we did it well. We fought as if we had rehearsed it. We fought as if it was the only fight that had ever been or should have had to be and pity it was not. We fought well and hard and we fought together. And when Smada turned his death's-head grin briefly to ask for a dagger I found that I had *already* noticed he needed one and had it out and was tossing it to him. And later, during my third enemy, when I felt myself getting tired, it was not a source of fear, but rather the distant noticing of just one important fact among many, like glancing down on a trip and realizing it's time to start looking for a Mobil station.

It was incredible. It was so *full*. Full and rich, and something else: It was the only time in my life I had not rolled in shame under my love for this.

That's not just my opinion. When it was over and they were dead and we looked up we saw Gruffle there standing with one of his brothers, the one who chanted, I think, and just staring. Not shocked. Not frightened. Not too selfish to help. But awed. Awed by what he was seeing.

Then we were shaking off our fugue and exchanging little smiles of satisfaction—it was impossible not to, no matter what we thought of each other. Smada stepped over to Orman and helped him up with the help of Markus, of all people, who had appeared out of nowhere carrying a sword as big as he was.

I noticed a small procession being led by the Orman boys. Three men with their hands tied behind them and an obviously feminine hooded form walking before them, and distantly I realized we'd captured the Lady Gor.

But I didn't care. The results were irrelevant. I headed for the Hall and found the door open and the broad hearth roaring and a mug of ale with my name on it. I drank that one and then another and tried to concentrate on what the others were telling me and finally some of it did sink in.

We had lost every Orman but the old man himself, Gruffle, Temblar (the pretty one), and the one who chanted. We had killed every guard and driver save for those three riding inside with the Lady Gor.

And the next day we were supposed to travel to the Keep of the Dead and kill Gor himself.

That woke me up. I stood up, my head clearing in a flash, and saw Smada leaning against the hearth with a mug in his hand watching me. And back came all my anger and resentment and whatever the hell else it was I felt for him and I said: "First you drag me back when I didn't want to come and then I save your fat ass and now you want me to die killing your enemies? What in *hell* makes you think I'd do all that for you?"

"But you won't be doing it for him, Felix," said a familiar voice, and I turned around to see the Lady Gor pulling back her hood. "You'll be doing it for me."

It was Cri, of course.

I sat back down again. I think my mouth was probably open.

Cri smiled sweetly a smile unique to her. "We'll talk later," she said.

Then she walked over to the stairs and stood meekly at their foot and waited. Smada drained the last of his ale, nodded in a strangely friendly way, and walked over to her. For a second he stood looking down at her and she up at him. Then they embraced the way people do who have had practice with each other.

"Smada?" I blurted dumbly.

She smiled, knowing I wasn't calling to him but asking her.

She smiled, said, "Of course," and together they climbed the stairs.

Another, smaller, room was found for me.

8

"I don't understand anything, and I mean *anything*, about *any* of this," I said to her when she came to my room that night to talk.

"I know," she said with understanding. She sat down in the chair across from my bed. "I hear you have cigarettes."

I stared, said, "Uh, yeah," and fetched one for us both.

After they were lit we sat and smoked awhile in silence.

"This is not really the Horseclans world, is it?" I blurted suddenly.

She smiled. "No. It is . . ."

"A Place," I finished for her.

She looked surprised, then smiled again. "Yes. A Place."

"Is it real?"

"Of course. As real as the books."

"But you said this wasn't the Horseclans world."

Her tone was patient. "It isn't. But it is close and somehow . . . connected to the mind of the man who wrote those stories. It is—I'm sure you've seen—a wonderful place, Felix. But it is clogged these days with the grip of horror and darkness. Evil is very real here. Evil and magic and they both work and if you had been here these past few years you would feel it and . . ."

"And what?"

"And it would have felt you, too." She was quiet a moment, looking genuinely scared. "It would have worked its way on you and into you as it has all of us. Let me tell you right now: as brave as the Ormans are, they wouldn't have dared this fight without you. They can tell you haven't been touched by it yet, Felix. We all can. Anyone who sees you can see it."

"Smada has it, too?"

"Everyone has it," she answered without hesitation, and that thought chilled me and raised the hair on the back of my arms.

"So that's why I was brought over?"

"Among other things," she replied and smiled knowingly at me and . . .

And . . . for . . . just . . . one . . . instant . . . I understood something about it all, I knew, I *saw*.

And then it was lost, fluttering away in my mind like a single mote in a shaft of sunlight.

I couldn't even remember what I'd seen. And suddenly I didn't want to remember.

"How come you're Lady Gor?" I asked too loudly.

She studied me, chose to answer. "It was the only way to get Smada free *and* have someone inside the Keep."

Knowing I was being unfair, knowing that, I still said: "So you're whoring for Smada, too, is that it?"

She bristled, held her breath, answered calmly, "We all use what tools we have. Do you like killing people?"

Ouch!

"Touché," I said with a sort of smile.

"And let me tell you something else, little man," she said, rising. "I'd rather kill them than have to sleep with them."

And with that she was gone out the door.

Touché again.

What was that Orman had said? About the Price?

Yeah. Quite a broad.

9

They bought Cri's story about the attack.

But I'll be damned if I know why. She was about as believable as Richard Nixon saying "I am not a crook." Her voice faltered and her eyes rolled and sweat appeared on her upper lip and none of it mattered one single bit. While I was sitting there on the front of the carriage by the "driver," Gruffle, looking around for a place to run, the guard at the gates to the Keep was just nodding and waving us on through.

Cri's story had been so unconvincing I thought the guy was joking. But he wasn't. The gates opened, Gruffle gave the oxen the giddyup and we were in.

It was weird. The guard at the gate looked and sounded just as frightened as Cri did. And so did the little dude that supervised the parking of the carriage and so did the toadies who rushed out to carry the Lady Gor's things. And so did everyone else.

And I mean *everyone* else. And that included Smada.

It had started about five miles from the Keep, I guess. There were just the four of us: Cri, Smada, Gruffle, and me, all riding on the front seat of the carriage (which was huge) for the air. The plan was pretty simple. When we got to the gate, Smada was to literally hide under the bed inside the carriage, Gruffle was supposed to play driver—which was easy, his uniform almost covered his face—Cri was supposed to spin her little tale of how she had been attacked, and I was to be the mysterious traveler who had come to her aid at the last moment when she was fleeing Smada's loyalists.

Smada was supposed to have been killed during the fight.

It was a garbage story—nobody should have bought it. But the other three were utterly convinced it would play, and they were right. That was pretty weird, too, but all part of the same dim weight we'd been carrying since, like I say, about five miles from the Keep.

It started—no fooling—with a buzzing in the ears.

Look, I know, I *know* how that sounds, but it's a fact. It felt to me like there were gnats or something.

At one point I actually slapped the side of my head trying to swat one.

Cri had given me a thin smile and said, "It is the Cloak of Dead," and the other two had just nodded.

Which didn't explain a thing to me and I said so, and they tried to explain some more and they did, eventually. But it wasn't any better. Seems it had to do with—are you ready?—a magic spell.

The Cloak of Dead was the deal Gor had made to give him power over the land, power over the Zombies, power over the fears of everyone around him. I mean everyone, which explained why so few people were willing to help Smada and why none of them were willing unless an outsider, me, who hadn't had a chance to be influenced, was coming along.

By "influenced" I mean scared. Really scared. Deeply scared. *Always* scared. It infused their thinking and their movements. It filled their dreams with gut-wrenching, tortured nightmares every night. The people were off balance and cowed and always, always, exhausted by this never-ending fear and the buzzing I heard meant we were approaching the source.

I, personally, just found it irritating. But so had everyone else when it had first started. It took a while, apparently, for it to creep down into your marrow and suck you small.

It had been long enough for my companions. They were uniformly pale and their breathing was too quick and they had a tendency to jump about a foot at every sudden sound, their eyes darting this way and that all the time like trapped fawns.

It was sickening at first. Particularly Smada. I still didn't know how I felt about him but I knew damn well I didn't like seeing him sitting there *trembling*! That's right, trembling. Actually shaking, quivering, from terror and I wanted to reach over and slap the sumbitch for shaming himself so.

Which was not only insensitive, I realized later, but outright stupid. Later I thought about how I would have acted feeling such fear. How any normal mortal would have acted.

I decided I'd have probably run away. But would I

have hatched some crazy plan through chattering teeth
and then, so bloody scared I could barely control my
bowels, tried sneaking into the most dangerous and
awful place in this Place to fight the most horrible
monster alive?

Like I said, I'd have run away. But they didn't; they
fought. Petrified, pale, and, yes, trembling, they had
fought back. Not your average folk.

But I wasn't thinking that at the time. I was being
an ass again. I was letting my disgust with them show,
snorting and deliberately ignoring them.

Nice guy, huh?

The Keep was huge and perched atop a rock crag
high over the river and it was dead flat black from its
outer walls to its tallest turret, where Gor lived. Absolutely black. And dusty, as if made out of coal. The
inner courtyard was filled with the dust as some flunky
passed us through into the interior of the main Keep.
There was another flunky waiting there for us who led
us up a couple of stories to still another flunky who
wanted to hear Cri's story again.

He was a slimy little rat, and the idea of squashing
him was so sweet a thought I almost forgot about the
plan, about Gruffle and Smada waiting down at the
carriage to sneak up later, about Cri at my side—about
anything else but hearing him squeal.

But I cooled it. He bought Cri's story, too, and we
were sent climbing once again. The third-level scum
bought the bit, too, but he was a little tougher. He
actually sneered when Cri started explaining about
how I had appeared, a mercenary, and offered to help
and her voice really skittered out of her mouth when
she was talking to him. I thought sure she was going to
blow it, so I interrupted his sneering inquisition, stood
right up and over his face, held out my palm and
pointed to it.

"Do I get my coins or do I not, little toad?"

For just a second he and I met eyes and I really and
truly wanted him to make some smart-ass remark—
fear affects everyone differently—so I could shove it
slowly back in with my gloved thumb.

But he got smart and shut up, except to nod.

We went through three more levels of stooges before we got to the audience room. Apparently word had spread ahead about the foul-tempered mercenary. The squid were actually bowing to me by the time we reached the chamber.

This was shiny black. Looked like marble and maybe it was. There was a huge black throne with a carved black inverted pyramid behind it and on either side there were tall thin oil lamps sending flickering yellow flames twelve feet into the air.

Lined up around the throne but a level down were half a dozen priest types and a couple of scythe-wielding guards and one old fat bald man with a pregnant paunch and a hook nose who beat three times on a black drum. He was naked and sweating and he smiled the most repulsive gap-toothed smile imaginable in my direction. I sneered at him. He just laughed and spittle flew and he pounded the drum three more times.

Gor entered. He was tall with jet-black hair and long flowing robes trimmed with red satin curlicues, and never in my life had I ever seen anyone whose every motion so totally exhibited control. This was his little universe and he damn sure knew it.

So did everyone else. They visibly shivered at his appearance. And these were his friends!

He had red eyes. And they glowed when they were pointed at you.

Cri managed a little extra something from somewhere and started off on her spiel once more. But it was clearly too much for her. Gor would smile patronizingly and interrupt her and she would panic and start all over again and I expected the guards to start hacking away with their scythes any moment.

When my turn came I ignored the red eyes and went into my mercenary improvisation. I was pretty good. Snarling, stomping, scratching, demanding my payment about every third paragraph, I gave a decent show. The tension in the room dropped steadily as I got into my little fable, embellishing this part and that and all the time being sure to remain aggressive about demanding my bread up front.

I was damn good and I knew it and so did Cri and

when it was over I sat down, unasked, knowing I had pulled it off.

Gor smiled, unconcerned with my breach of protocol. Instead he sat down on his throne and propped his chin on long thin fingers with long thin shiny-black nails and said:

"So, you are Smada's One."

10

So I killed him.

I was up out of my seat with my sword drawn and he raised his right arm up to stop me and I blocked it with my left and grabbed his black shiny hair with those same fingers and I drove my blade through his chest and bright red gas came from his throat with his laugh and he fell dead at my feet but . . .

But it didn't help much.

There was a flash and great booming thunderclap, the sound rocketing around the stone room. One of the guards screamed and dropped his scythe and clutched his hands around his throat and his features—his neck, his arms, his wrists, his *forehead*—began to swell outward, ugly, misshapen, grotesque, and he tried to scream again but his ballooning throat clogged the sound and his eyes, bugging and panicked and beseeching to all of us, started squeezing themselves out of his sockets and . . .

And there was another flash and some smoke and I heard the laughter once more and the smoke cleared and there stood Gor where the guard had been, black robe and shining red eyes, spinning that great huge scythe in his hands like a cheerleader's baton.

I was too scared to do anything but run—either forward or back. I chose forward and as I closed the distance between us all I could think of, oddly, was that Smada and I hadn't exhanged a word during the entire dusty ride up in that carriage, just sat there with Cri between us, swaying and bouncing and not talking and . . .

And Gor was laughing again and rushing right at me and as he laughed more red light flashed from his eyes and more red gas from his mouth and I jumped to my right to avoid the scythe and brought my sword across in front of me to block it and there was a loud clang as the two weapons met and a burst of sparks and then I was down and rolling and then back up to my feet just as the scythe's handle slammed me full in the left temple. I saw stars and felt the back of my head thud against the floor.

There was more laughter, but it was distant now along with the rest of the room. It was hard to focus on the black robes, hard to get my legs up under me and balanced. I was hurt bad and I knew it—a concussion at the very least. I was swaying as I rose and so totally out of whack that I tried to block not an actual lunge, but merely a feint from the scythe, and that took me off-balance so far I fell to my knees.

The laughter increased as the shadowy form approached and stood over me. I could only see him in spurts before my eyes would cloud over, so I was constantly blinking, and this made Gor laugh all the more.

"Die, little one!" he said and grabbed the hair on the top of my head with his left hand and swung the great scythe back with his right, swung it back high over his head, and he smiled bright red light at me and started his head-chopping motion and I stuck blindly out and clamped my left hand onto his Adam's apple and jerked him toward me and my sword, which pierced cleanly through his lower abdomen before cracking through the spine three inches out his back.

He screamed as he fell the rest of the way forward across me and there was more red gas and a bone-numbing rush of cold air. I held on frantically, jerking the sword deeper and deeper into him and farther and farther out his other side, and he thrashed and warped above me like a burning insect for what seemed like a very long time.

Then all was still and quiet for a few seconds. I lumbered about and managed to shove his body off just as the second thunderclap shook the room.

It was the bald sweating gap-toothed drooling pig at the drum who now approached me with shining red eyes. The laughter was of a different tone coming from this creature, this repulsive naked ogre with his foul smell and round wet belly and crimped genitals swaying. His bare feet slapped wetly as he danced around me, darting in and out. I was still zonked and confused and tired and I could not understand why he didn't just rush me and be done with it and then, when he darted in closer than before, I met that deformed gaze and saw his fear.

And I understood it all, suddenly. I understood his power. It was not power at all, but the spell of fear. It was why all shook in his presence but would not come forward to help him. He didn't control them. He simply ruled their paralysis.

And I knew something else, instinctively. This gross body was his last. This gross body was his own.

I was still thinking this when he leaped forward and clamped his gnarled hands about my throat. We rolled over and over on that shining black floor and my own hands went up to meet his but his grip was too strong and his smell too foul—I couldn't breathe, I couldn't think, I couldn't seem to bring the last of my strength into my hands. He was too awful and too close and too strong, and I was losing, I knew it, sinking down as my face went red from the pressure and my throat began to collapse under those gnarled hands, and we stopped rolling with him on top and his eyes lasered red and his breath red gas and spittle and his laughter began once more.

I was going under for good when Gor screamed and let go. It took a couple of seconds before I could make out anything at all, before I could discern the beast writhing in front of me to pull the dagger from his back or the frozen figure of Cri still posed in the position from which she had delivered the stabbing. It was incredible. She was *still* so frightened she couldn't move, and how she had managed to force herself forward to deliver that dagger I will never, ever, know.

Quite a woman, indeed.

The beast had finally grasped the hilt and had actually managed to drag it halfway out before I could clamber over and slam my own dagger into its chest.

Its eyes went wide and it stared at me and shrieked

an ungodly sound and exploded into a nightmare burst of flesh and red gas and arctic cold and this time came not only a thunderclap, but the lightning as well, sizzling up from Gor's forehead to ricochet insanely about the black walls of the chamber before turning bright, dazzling crimson, and then . . .

Then it was gone. I got up and grabbed hold of Cri and hugged her and she hugged me back, gasping and smiling. We stood like that for several seconds, and around us stood Gor's people, blank-eyed and staring, awake from a coma or nightmare, and I thought: It's over! We've made it! just as the great black doors to the chamber burst inward and the Dead came jamming through to feed.

I managed to get my sword loose and up but was too weak to hold it steady. Cri, beside me, was no better. Even free from the spell she was spent—that saving thrust had been all she had.

What saved us at first was the people in the chamber between us and the ghouls. If we had been closer to the door, we would've been eaten in the first ten seconds. But there were others there to feed upon, and the Dead did just that and the chamber was filled with a mind-melting cacophony of screams and blood and ripping black teeth. People were running wildly about, falling and shrieking and dying, and the Dead just lurched at them, outnumbering them, out-eviling them. Eating them alive.

We had managed to stumble over to the throne toward where I figured Gor's own exit had been when the first half-dozen zombies reached us. I raised up my sword to fend one off, but my legs were wobbly and my wrists shook with fatigue, and I yelled: "Run, Cri!" and shoved her away just as a strong hand grabbed my collar from behind and threw me backward out of range of the clutching black talons.

Smada, of course, saving my butt once more. Gruffle was there with him, his sword already red and flashing in the air. It was Gruffle who gathered Cri and me together and got us to the exit, stopping twice to behead ghouls grasping at us. It was Gruffle who got us through the exit and who led the two of us, now

numbed and wasted and following like children, down
the long dark passage and out of the Keep.

But it was Smada who saved our lives. I was worthless, standing there swaying and staring. But even
though I could do nothing to help, I knew what I was
seeing. Never in my life had I imagined, much less
seen, such a spectacular display of power swordsman-
ship. I lost count of the number of ghouls he carved
up, and after the first three or four I watched only
him, his movement, his sureness, his balance. It was the
first dozen or so to reach us that would have gotten us.
Gruffle got two of those. But Smada, standing astride
that shiny black platform in front of the throne like a
colossus, saved the day. Even in my dazed state, I
knew what I was seeing.

And then I'd been dragged out of sight through the
exit and down the passage. The night air was cool and
made me shiver. From the Keep came more screams
from the upper floors and especially from the inner
courtyard wall. The feeding frenzy was just beginning.

We were in a wagon and about to move before
Smada appeared beside us. Old Orman, whom I hadn't
even noticed, helped him aboard. We rode perhaps
three miles before stopping to camp and tend our
wounds. When the river breeze was just right, we
could still hear faint echoes of massacre.

I hadn't realized I was asleep until someone bandag-
ing my temple woke me up. It was Cri, smiling down
at me. I smiled back and rolled out of her lap into a
sitting position.

"I wouldn't try to stand just yet, lad," said a voice.

I looked over. It was Smada, sitting across the campfire from me looking concerned. I stared at him a
moment, then nodded.

Around me Orman and his boys were lounging about or,
in Gruffle's case, worrying over wounds. Temblar was
cooking something sweet-smelling and looking worried.

It seemed he was worried about the Dead in the
Keep coming out again tomorrow night. But that was
foolish, and I told him so. The Dead would, come
morning without Gor, be really dead at last.

Temblar wanted to know how I knew that, and I started to answer before I realized I didn't *know* how I knew. I looked at Cri, who tried smiling at me again. But it didn't help. I felt a stab of fear and vertigo.

I stood up, knowing what was coming. I backed away from the campfire, the people there seeming menacing all of a sudden. Then I just stood, staring, feeling panic starting to swell from within.

"Do not fear, my two-leg friend," beamed the prairiecat I hadn't noticed from his spot on the ground at Smada's feet.

Curiously, his thoughts calmed me down a bit. But when Cri approached me a few seconds later, it was good she did so slowly.

When she was but a foot away, it burst from my mouth at last:

"I know this about the Dead . . . I feel this, because . . . because I am from this Place. I was born here. Wasn't I?"

Cri nodded sympathetically. "There was much danger when you were born. You were sent Over to spare your life."

I knew she was telling the truth. I could feel it. I could feel much more as well.

"I was brought back because I had to return," I said aloud. "Isn't that so?"

Cri nodded again.

"Who sent me?" I asked, and during the moment she hesitated, the answer came to me. "Smada!" I cried out angrily.

"Yes." She nodded gently to me. "He—"

"Why?" I demanded, still mysteriously furious somehow. "Why did he do this to me? *Why?*"

"Because," said a gentle deep voice from behind me, "I could not bear to lose my wife *and* my only child."

I spun around and stared at him, and I knew but still I blurted my confusion. "What . . . what do you . . . ?"

And then his great hands were on my shoulders and he said:

"One means Firstborn."

Goodbye, Earth.

Goodbye, forever.

I am home.

Traitors

by Susan Shwartz

SUSAN SHWARTZ was a 1987 Nebula finalist for her story "Temple to a Minor Goddess." She lives in New York, where, when her cat Merlin allows her to, she is working on an anthology, *Arabesques*.

Look what the cat dragged in, Milo Morai thought, then lifted his cup in ironic, reminiscent tribute to the ancient observation. Besides, he never knew just what a prairiecat would decide to drag in.

This time, it had been a woman.

The Ahrmehnee girl with her arm splinted, the one whom Steeltooth had brought in from his last scouting trip, might keep a wary distance from the prairiecat's steel battle spurs and long fangs, but that was the only fear she displayed. Once or twice, she even leaned against the big cat's flank, steadying herself against his back with her uninjured hand. Milo did not know which was stranger: that the girl dared to lean on Steeltooth or that the big cat permitted it.

Did she, perhaps, have mindspeech? He sent out a tentative probe, but it turned up only exhaustion, guilt, confusion, and—strangest of all—pride. Even as he intensified his mental investigation, she shook her head as if a mosquito buzzed in her ear.

The girl had need of her pride in the next moment as Vahrtahn Panosyuhn, *nakharar* of the battered tribe of refugees that had joined up not two weeks earlier with Milo's army, entered the tent.

"Where is my Rohzah?" he demanded before even greeting Milo himself. Milo allowed himself a bleak

nod of understanding. Panosyuhn had turned heaven
and earth upside down trying to find his daughter,
Rohzah, and his niece, Shahron, who had disappeared—
captured and feared dead. Judging from the girl's
headshake, this must be the niece.

"Dead, uncle," Shahron said without raising her
head. Her voice was soft and would have been gentle
if she had not been so hoarse from the autumn rains.

The old *nakharar* drew himself up. The white hair
stippling his brows and beard seemed to quiver as if he
were a cat scenting something foul. "Yes," the girl put
in before the old warrior could launch into a display of
the fabulously volatile and fierce Ahrmehnee temper,
"I do wish that I had died in her stead. I should have,
I know that." She watched hopelessly as the old man's
eyes grew bleak and distant and his mouth curled in
disdain. Ahrmehnee had strong family ties; old Panosyuhn
had been her uncle as well as her lord. And now,
clearly, she expected him to cast her off.

"There is worse to come," she added. Reaching into
her sling, she pulled out what looked like a well-kept—
and certainly well-used—revolver, and offered it butt-
first to Milo. Two guards pushed at her. Not bothering
to spare her broken arm, they forced her down onto
the rugs that lay on the ground about Milo's chair (not
that the revolver could harm him, even if the girl
could aim and fire it). She cried out sharply, but only
once as her arm was jostled, then fell silent, her eyes
steadily regarding Milo.

*Cool-headed despite her breeding and whatever it is
that she's been through,* Milo thought, and Steeltooth
purred approval. He examined the revolver, of a type
that he himself had taken from the bodies of the
so-called Witchmen. Had they started to recruit
Ahrmehnee, too? Then another, more insidious question gnawed into his consciousness. Perhaps this girl,
who looked as if she had lost so much—perhaps she
was a spy.

To the surprise of most of the men in the tent, the
girl attacked, not with a concealed weapon, which
would have won her only a quick death, but with
words.

"You think that I am a Witchman, is that it?" She laughed unhappily. "You do not know by how little I escaped . . . but it is no matter. I always knew that it would probably come to this, but I did not want to die—or worse than die—among Witchmen."

Milo grimaced. This girl was a matter for King Solomon, not for Milo Morai or even God Milo, as some of the plainsmen still called him. She was perfect, either as a spy or a victim. *Damn, I wish I had Aldora or Bili here,* he wished. *If only we were in Kehnooryos Atheenahs.* The experts could interrogate her more skillfully than he, with his limited mindspeak.

Already, the old *nakharar* had spat at her feet in repudiation and was striding from the tent. Shahron watched him go, her eyes hot with shame and anger and unshed tears. When he was gone, she suppressed a shudder. Clearly, she had expected to be killed.

Perfect, Milo thought.

"God Milo?" Just as the rangy, shock-haired man of Clan Sanderz spoke up, advancing on the girl, Steeltooth yawned. Milo snapped his fingers. "Thanks for reminding me, cat-brother. The Test of the Cat!" Milo muttered. He set his chin and walked toward Steeltooth. After all, why fear her? Any knife that she bore could cost him but a few instants' pain.

"Girl," he asked, "do you know aught about the Test of the Cat?"

She glanced at Steeltooth and jerked up her own chin in the Ahrmehnee negative.

"You know that the great cats can talk to those people with mindspeak. They can also probe and learn when people, even those who lack mindspeak, are lying to them. This is the test: Steeltooth opens his jaws. You place your head within them, and let him listen to your story, which he will relay to us. If you are lying—" Milo brought his hands together in the gesture of jaws snapping shut.

"Will you submit to this test?" He asked. *And what if she does not, Milo?* he asked himself. *Will you kill her right now, right here?* One innocent, injured girl. She could be an enemy; years ago, such girls had proved to be his enemy. But old prejudices and old chivalries died hard.

She smeared her free hand across her face, rearranging grime and tears. "It is good to know," she said, "that one creature here does not already despise me. But—what is that? The cat says that if I am lying, he will send me gently and mercifully to Wind?

"God Milo, I shall take your test," she declared and knelt quickly before the great cat. "Here and now. What reason can I have for delay?"

She knelt, and after Steeltooth had opened massive jaws, she placed her head between them with almost no sign of fear.

"No, down this way!" Shahron heard. Her skirts, the cumbering, heavy layers that Ahrmehnee girls wore, threatened to trip her with each step that she ran, and as for climbing—! But she and Rohzah had taken out the herds, refugee herds of a refugee clan, when they themselves had been taken. Having little choice, they had accepted food and fire from their captors, and those only long enough to escape. Shahron's only regret was that she had left the tiny knife from her felt boot behind. She did *not*, however, regret where she had left it scabbarded. Fear clawed at the two girls, fugitives now from a Witchman's hearth, and made them run faster.

To fall unarmed into the hands of the Witchmen! That was worse than war, worse than feud. Witchmen did not fight fair. They had those long tubes that spit fire and dealt death to the tribe's flocks, and probably, for all they knew, to the tribe itself.

The girls ran gasping through the forest and finally brought up short against a sheer rock face. "The ropes," gasped Shahron. Each pulled from beneath her skirt the ropes that they had braided from petticoats and blankets in haste and in secret. They tied their rough ropes together, then knotted them around a projecting stump.

"Test it!" Rohzah insisted.

"But they're coming! I can hear them!" Shahron

cried. Nevertheless, she jerked twice on the rope. "It
looks strong enough. Let me go first."

"I'm eldest," Rohzah protested, as she had protested since they were tiny girls. Older she might be,
and the daughter of the *nakharar*, but Shahron was
stronger and fiercer. She had always protected her
cousin, and she would do so now.

"Yes," she agreed, "you are the elder, but you are
the *nakharar*'s daughter, while I am but his niece. So I
go first." Wrapping the rope about her, she swung
down, hoping that she could walk down the rock face
the way that she had seen young men, jealous of their
reputations for bravery, do long ago, when they still
had a village and time for the luxury of such games.

She froze as an ominous tearing came from above
her. The rope vibrated. Then, abruptly, the rending
noise stopped.

"I've got it!" Rohzah cried.

Shahron went totally still. If the rope tore apart, she
would fall. *Bright lady, don't let me fall, with my
brains splattered all over the rocks, I beg you!* she
prayed. She kicked out with her feet, seeking toe-
holds, then reached with one hand. There! Panting in
triumph, she clung to the naked rock. Below her lay a
ledge toward which—she heard the sound of ripping
once more as her rope gave way—she must aim. As
the rope gave way, she coiled herself, hoping to land
on the ledge . . . and none too soon.

"Cousin!" shrieked Rohzah, as the rope frayed and
snapped, and she fell. Her last thought before the rock
ledge rose up to strike her down was a kind of furious
irritation at the noise that her cousin made. Did she
really want to bring their pursuers down upon them?
Silver Lady, what an idiot!

Which idiot? she thought, a moment—or an hour—
later. Her head ached, but not as savagely as her left
arm. She lay in a tumble of fabric, and found herself
staring at the pattern of red on white of the shreds of
cloth that had once been an undergarment. Overhead,
with an annoying regularity, came Rohzah's shrieks.

"Don't! They'll hear you!" she tried to beg her
cousin, but all that she could force from her mouth

was a croak. Red specks of flame danced in front of her eyes and threatened to engulf her vision. Then darkness beckoned, a spinning black tunnel of it that drew her into its depths.

As she entered, it occurred to her that being recaptured by Witchmen might be the best fate that she could hope for now. *I would rather die!* she thought. But she was blacking out, and she was very much afraid. . . .

"This should bring the little bitch around!" A slap jolted Shahron back to consciousness, and that was very bad. Worse yet, the slap sent jagged streaks of pain, like steel slivers from a shattered sword in a wound, up and down her left arm. Just in time, she bit her lip against a shameful cry of pain. Behind her, her cousin Rohzah showed no such self-regard; she wept, as a *nakharar*'s daughter should not do in the presence of enemies even if her cousin, almost her sister in fosterage and in love, did lie injured before her. And if her enemies were Witchmen, she must definitely not show fear or grief.

"For God's sake, Ehrikah," came a man's voice, "do you want the girl to scream and spew all over your boots?" Shahron set her jaw and vowed, even as a stab of pain made her dizzy with nausea, neither to cry nor (if she could at all prevent it) to vomit. The man who warned the woman called Ehrikah was of no account: a warrior, perhaps, of some minor house, warning a great lady. But, Shahron thought, if she broke her vow, she would try to break it by spewing all over that Ehrikah.

"Let her be, both of you!" ordered another member of the party that had hunted them down. Shahron remembered that voice, rumbling against her ear. Its owner had swung down on a rope and borne her off the ledge that had bid fair to be her bier. The man speaking was a tall, heavily muscled warrior whose dark hair and clean-shaven chin belied the impression that Shahron had had of him since she and her (praise the Silver Lady!) now quiet cousin had been dragged in, the last survivors that she knew of from their village on a mountain slope . . . a slope no longer.

Now their home was a pile of smoking rubble, and its folk, who had dwelt there for generations, near the Vale of the Moon Maidens, were become beggarly wanderers.

Tending the paltry remnants of their flocks, she and Rohzah had strayed too far and been swept up by what she knew in her heart and bones had to be the Witchfolk, so strangely did they speak and dress, and so boldly did that woman Ehrikah stride out among the men, daring even to rebuke the man who now prevented her from striking Shahron again.

Nakharar and leader this man seemed, yet he deferred to Ehrikah like a youth to a priestess. He looked young, but he spoke like a man seasoned by many battles, even though many of his words were strange to her, and his accent wrapped them even more strangely.

"Let the chit be, Ehrikah," he repeated, more quietly. "Clearly she wasn't taken in by our 'welcome,' so she tried to escape. An honorable attempt, at that," he added, glancing down at the ledge from which he had rescued Shahron.

If she had fallen . . . ! She swallowed hard against a sudden stab of dizziness and nausea.

"Two girls untrained in technical climbing, wearing skirts and those idiot boots, on a rock face that I'd want ropes and spikes for, assuming I was fool enough to try it in the first place? That girl has guts. Stand back, and let me set her arm."

"Before you go all misty-eyed over the chit, as you call her," Ehrikah snapped, "let me remind you, Jay, that that *chit* half-blinded a guard, whom we had to send back to the Institute to transfer, just when we need every able-bodied man and all of our equipment."

"She was within her rights to try to escape," said the man Jay, "and is entitled to medical care. Now, can you control yourself, *Doctor,* long enough to provide it, or will you leave it to a mere soldier?"

Ehrikah snorted something in the Witchman's tongue that sounded like "geneva-convention sob stories," and tossed her head, an arrogant one, too, with a dark mane of silver-streaked hair that any Ahrmehnee woman would have taken pride in and adorned properly and bravely with scarves and the silver coins of her dowry.

"You can coo over little Miss Purple Heart later," she told Jay. "Damn! I could have used her strength. But now, well, I guess that I have business with the cousin."

Shahron could hear Rohzah gulp, suppressing a sob but not a quiver of fear. "I'm sick, I'll make myself ugly," threatened her cousin.

"Nonsense!" Ehrikah snapped. "I'm not after your paltry maidenhead, and I'm not going to hurt you. Now, come along, or shall I send for the men?"

Rohzah went quietly, more afraid of the threat of men, of male lust and male violence, than of the present danger posed by Ehrikah, who—as Shahron suspected—threatened something else, though what it was she did not know. But then, Shahron had never based her love for her cousin on brains. A twinge shot up her arm, and before she could stop herself, she finally cried out. Her eyes filled with tears of pain and embarrassment.

"Brave girl," the man whom Ehrikah called Jay and whom she had heard younger men call "sir" murmured. "I've seen strong men faint and foul themselves after a spiral fracture such as you've got." He raised his voice. "You, Cabell, have we got a flask hereabouts?"

"As the general wishes!" cried one of the lesser warriors in a voice that seemed to shake the top of Shahron's head off. "Sir!"

"As you were, Cabell. Give me the flask, and take yourself off. Can't you see the child needs quiet? No . . ." He held up a hand. "Quietly. At ease, man." He flicked fingers at his forehead in response to the younger man's stiff gesture, then opened a very old, dented silver bottle.

"I don't know how morphine"—whatever that was—"will affect you, so I think you'd better have a gulp or two of this. Watch out; it'll burn," he warned as Shahron swallowed. The fire from the drink made her eyes water again and took her mind off the fire in her arm, worse now because of the way it had been handled. Once again, this *nakharar* among Witchmen prodded at her arm, muttered to himself, then wound cloth about a straight stick and bound her arm deftly to it.

"Another?" he asked, offering the flask, and smiled as she grasped for it with her right hand. "No, no more now, or you *will* be sick. Don't worry if the world goes a little out of focus," he told her. "Let it blur. God knows, child, you're entitled."

Tears trickled down Shahron's cheeks. She was disgraced, doubly disgraced, to weep before even a noble enemy. Unless, of course, he wanted her as a wife. She could not imagine why he might want a girl with a broken arm, niece to a *nakharar* though she was: he must have wives at home. Perhaps as a wife for a younger son? Brides had been stolen before, had wept, but then become the mothers of strong sons.

"What's wrong—*God*, Corbett, that's a foolish question to ask!" Jay Corbett spat. "No, I'm not shouting at you, girl."

"I have . . . something terrible, something *evil* is happening," wept Shahron.

"That's not blue-devils from the brandy. No fool, are you?" Corbett's mouth tightened, and his eyes went hard, the way her uncle's had when he looked over the smoking ruins of their village and knew that his younger brother, Shahron's father, lay buried with half the tribe, under the scree and the rubble. "Here, I think that you had better have another shot after all."

He held the flask up to her lips and let her drink her fill. The fire's bite had subsided to a hearthfire now, and she smiled up at him treacherously. When she finished, he stoppered the little bottle, but not without shaking it to gauge its contents and a thirsty glance at it.

"Sorry, General," he muttered. "Sun's not over the yardarm for you yet; you're on duty. Go to sleep, Shahron. You need that more than anything else."

She was surprised that he had even bothered to learn her name. "Oh yes, I know your name. I know that you're a refugee, that you lost most of your family

when the mountain . . . blew up." He grimaced and
shook his head. "If it were up to me, I'd have you
back in Broomtown so fast—I could name three fine
fellows who would fight over a girl like you . . ."

"No . . ." Her lips were thick. "No . . . *dowry*!"
She produced the correct word with a kind of groggy
triumph, but he shrugged.

" 'The lady is a dowry in herself,' " he muttered in
the Witchman's tongue, then switched back into accented Ahrmehnee. "No, never mind what I just said,
child. You wouldn't understand. Try to sleep. Unfortunately, when you wake, things will probably be
worse."

Her captor enjoined her to courage? Surely, she
must have lived her life properly or she would not face
such a noble enemy. How proud her uncle would be to
have such a one, and how glad . . . if she had both her
arms hale and the use of a knife, if she won free, how
he would praise her if she could return bearing her
enemy's head. Or the head of that Ehrikah! Now, that
was truly a pleasant idea. She yawned, and felt the
warmth of blankets tucked about her. Already, she
knew enough of this Jay Corbett, this Witchman general, to know that even his kindnesses were well planned.

"Poor thing's got a smile like a grubby-faced angel,"
she heard him say as her eyes fluttered shut. The ache
in her arm now seemed blessedly far away. And so,
after a moment or two longer, did the rest of the world.

Shahron woke to a feeling of contentment. The ache
in her broken arm still seemed very remote. She was
warm and dry, as she had not been since the village
was destroyed—or was that as much a dream as her
present existence seemed to be? She had been out
tending sheep with Rohzah, and she had fallen. . . .

Terrible fear about Rohzah lashed through her.

"Good morning, sister!" Sweet Lady! That was
Rohzah's voice. Shahron threw off her blankets and
leaped up.

Then it *was* a dream, all a dream. Once again, tears
flooded Shahron's vision, and she held out her good
arm to her cousin, who took it . . .

Or was this woman who looked so like Rohzah truly her cousin? she wondered suddenly, horribly, as the girl pressed her hand, smoothed her hair as gently as a sister would, and offered to bring her food—but all in Ahrmehnee so thickly accented that Shahron could scarcely make sense of it. Rohzah did not speak that way.

But Ehrikah did.

The happy tears dried in Shahron's eyes. Other things about this "Rohzah" came into her mind. This girl strode; the cousin whom Shahron had spent her life with sidled. This girl spoke out; her cousin's voice was very soft. Now, "Rohzah" grinned; and that was not at all like her own cousin's smile.

Madness threatened, dancing at the borders of her consciousness. Shahron was captive to Witchmen and Witchwomen. They could do anything. And, apparently, hideously, Ehrikah had. This was not Rohzah, who stood before her, but a terrible masquerade in Rohzah's flesh.

"Jay was right," murmured the Witchwoman in her cousin's body. "You're brighter than you look. Why'd you have to break the damned arm?"

"Where is Rohzah?" Shahron faltered out before the force of Ehrikah's gaze silenced her.

She gestured at the familiar face, the familiar dark hair, dark eyes, and aquiline profile, even the torn, stained clothes that Shahron knew as well (and had come to dislike as much) as her own garments.

"No." Shahron shook her head stubbornly. "Where is what makes Rohzah herself and not you? Where did *that* go?"

Ehrikah shrugged. The very indifference of that gesture made Shahron tremble.

"Gone?" She *was* going to go mad, but before her wits left her, she would refuse to scream or plead. Beneath her panic ran a tiny, treacherous thought: *This is why she hit me. This is what she wanted me for until I broke my arm.* She felt a passionate, shameful gratitude for the pain in her arm, the pain that had damned and destroyed her poor cousin.

That came close to breaking her.

"Does it matter where your cousin's . . . surely, let's not call it a soul . . . went? She's gone, but I am here," Ehrikah said. "Here, and ready and willing to be your loving cousin, to return with you to your family. They go, I believe, to seek the God Milo?" Her lip curled scornfully around the venerable name; and that too was unlike Rohzah. The familiar, strongly marked features seemed suddenly strange and hateful. Once again, Shahron longed for a knife and two good hands. *On which of you would you use it?* she asked herself, and was honest enough to admit that that was another thing she did not know. But she was stronger than Rohzah, and she knew it. Perhaps even one-handed . . .

"I wouldn't," said Ehrikah. "I have a Black Belt" —whatever that meant, Shahron thought—"and even in this body, I can probably break your other arm before you even pull my hair.

"Sit down."

Shahron sat. Outside the tiny room in which she had been pent, so unlike her own room of thick, white-washed walls and colorful blankets, she could smell hot food cooking. Abruptly, sickeningly, she was hungry, and she hated herself for that too. Rohzah was dead, or worse than dead, her mind was stolen—and all that Shahron could think of was food.

Well, maybe not quite all.

"I won't take you back!" she told Ehrikah, too angry and too afraid to spit or to shout. "I won't betray my family." *At least, not more than I already have.* Then, more cleverly, she continued, "Besides, just listen to yourself. You can scarcely speak Ahrmeh-nee. You know nothing about Rohzah, about us, our family. How do you expect to be Rohzah in front of the people who have known her all her life?"

"*You* have known her all her life. You can teach me."

"No!" This time, Shahron did shout.

"Anything wrong in there, ma'am, miss?" came a drawling voice that Shahron recognized. It belonged to Jay Corbett's young soldier.

"No!" snapped Ehrikah.

"Then, with the doctor's approval, I'll be bringing in breakfast—"

"Get *out* of here!" Ehrikah ordered, nearly hissing in anger. "Look. I haven't time to sweet-talk you into this. You're not a total moron, so I'll give you all the facts straight, and I'll only do it once. Either you coach me and bring me in, or you will wind up like your cousin Rohzah. Or worse. For example, there's a man I know who told me that he'd like to try walking about in a female body. He likes to play rough, too. Do you know what I'm talking about?"

Just as well that Shahron hadn't eaten after all, she thought, even though the idea of fouling Ehrikah's boots still appealed to her. She tried, in any case. Bile spattered out. Dimly, through spasms of gagging and dry heaves, she heard Ehrikah swear and footsteps retreating fast. Then gentle hands held her head, and the words "Let it all out," rumbled in her ears. Finally, those same hands wiped her mouth and eased her back down to sleep.

Why was a man as important as the Witchman's general standing guard over her?

When Shahron woke again, she was truly hungry this time. Hot breads and smoked meats steamed gently on a plate that the trooper Cabell was setting out. "Afternoon, miss," he said easily.

"Why do you call me this 'miss'?"

Inexplicably, Cabell looked disappointed. "The doctor . . . she says she has to be called that or this 'Miz' thing. The general says that 'miss' is a title for a young lady and a guest, so I call you miss."

"I am a prisoner, not a guest."

Cabell shrugged. "Well, I reckon that's something you'll have to take up with the general, miss. He said that you were to eat this, all of it. I could help you with soup and cut up your meat for you, if you're feeling too poorly to do for yourself, though." Shahron remembered what Jay Corbett had told her about the three young fellows who'd fight to accept her, even without a proper dowry. Could this young man be one of them?

In his presence, Ehrikah's threats seemed very far away—and the food was close at hand. This Cabell couldn't be more eager to see her eat than she was to try. The meal tasted good, and she found herself careful not to spill on the clean white napkin that Cabell tied kerchief-fashion about her neck. Finally, she pushed back from the emptied tray.

"Now for a face-wash," Cabell said, and, much to her surprise, did so. "Lord, you clean up pretty. How's the arm?"

"Better." Shahron didn't need to see Cabell snap upright, his face suddenly a mask of duty and attention, to know that there was another man in the room.

"Excellent. And you, Cabell, anytime that you want to be a nursemaid, just say so."

The trooper looked straight ahead.

"And you, Shahron, do you think that you're all over your sickness?"

"How did you—"

"How did I know that you were awake?" asked General Corbett. "Let me tell you, child, that there is nothing about my camp that I do not keep aware of. Nothing at all."

Including what your Ehrikah plans for me? Do you know about that, and do you approve? Do you know that I would rather die?

"You could let me go," she attacked doggedly.

"Where would you go?"

"I don't know. But at least I would be free. And safe from . . ." she grimaced.

"I cannot. I have oaths I cannot betray." He paused, and the silence was long and heavy. "I am sorry, child."

He might be a general, but as he left her room, his face twisted with distaste.

All that day, Shahron was left alone to sleep, to dream, to wake, sweating, and to fear all over again. Sunset came in a blaze of red, and she began to await . . . someone. She was afraid that Ehrikah would come, but instead Cabell entered.

"General says that you are to eat all of this too," he told her, grinning.

There must have been enough food on that tray for
three meals, not to mention extra dried fruit and bread.
Cabell turned and, with his back to her, stood facing
the door. The holster that held his strange weapon,
the one that dealt death at a distance, lay ready to her
hand, ready to steal. She dared not shoot it, and
would not shoot him, but a quick blow over the ear . . .

Stealthily, she groped for the gun, snatched it, and
just as Cabell turned—surely, he turned too slowly!
—she struck him on the temple.

He fell without a sound, and Shahron searched him,
awkwardly, one-handed, for a more familiar weapon.
Ahhh, there was a clasp knife. She wished that she
had the strength to bind him, but one-handed . . . She
made do with a gag. Then, wadding up her food in her
napkin, and tossing a blanket over her shoulders, she
grabbed up Cabell's keys and ran. Miraculously, no
one stood guard outside, and no one loitered about.
Except that, as she left, she thought that she saw a
shadow, a shadow as of a man leaning against a wall,
looking up at the sunset, then down at his wrist, and
she remembered Corbett's words.

*Nothing happens in my camp of which I am not
aware.*

She was glad that she had not hit Cabell any harder.

Then real fear set her running, and she fled.

The pressure of the huge prairiecat's jaws on her
skull had not abated. But, thank the Silver Lady, it
had not increased either, Shahron thought.

"I wandered for a couple of days," she whispered.
"I ate all my food, all the food that the general knew
that I would need. I knew that I dared not seek out
my uncle. I had betrayed his daughter. There could be
no welcome for one who had done that. And besides,
after seeing Ehrikah, I had another fear. How could
they know that I was not myself an Ehrikah? I dared
not expose anyone to that risk either. Thus, even
when I saw families on the road, I dared not approach
them. And now . . ." Her voice thickened and broke.
"I cannot forgive myself, and I cannot forget."

She sank to the ground, aware for the first time that

Steeltooth's jaws had relaxed, releasing her, and that she was still alive.

The big amber cat rubbed against her, purring and licking her face clean with . . . as much care as Cabell. Poor Cabell, whom his general, no doubt, had ordered to stand still while she hit him. She hoped that the headache wasn't too bad, or that he hadn't gotten into any trouble. Somehow, she suspected that Jay Corbett could protect his soldier.

"You, an Ehrikah?" repeated the man, who, astonishingly, she had been told was God Milo himself. "That's not what Steeltooth says."

"So I passed?"

"You passed both tests," said God Milo. "The first test was simple survival. You kept your wits, you kept your nerve, and you made your way to us. The second test . . . let's just say that if you had lied to Steeltooth, you and I would not be talking. Somebody get the child a chair!" Milo ordered.

To her continued amazement, he held out a goblet to her and splashed an inch or so of rich brown fluid into it. "I gather that you have a taste for brandy. And you look as if you could use it."

Numbly, she took the cup and sipped. *This much,* she told herself, *at least I have accomplished this much. My honor is unstained. Yet Rohzah is dead and my uncle has disowned me. I have nowhere to go . . . and Ehrikah is still alive.*

"You know," said God Milo, "if you ask, I will order your uncle to reinstate you in the clan."

"A loveless hearth is cold," Shahron said.

"Where will you go, then?"

Abruptly, Corbett's words came back to her. In that Broomtown of his, there might have been a place for her, a husband for her, of his choosing. Even if she did not have a dowry.

The brandy warmed her, all the way from her mouth to her belly. And the bargaining instinct that nothing could ever drive out of an Ahrmehnee's mind suddenly woke. "I have no place to go," she said, as if making a preliminary offer on a pot. "And no dowry."

"That can be taken care of."

Shahron suppressed a smile and heard a stifled sound. When she dared to glance upward, she saw that God Milo had one hand over his mouth. "If I needed more proof, there it is!" he commented. "Ahrmehnee to the core! The girl offers me a bargain in my own tent."

Around him, the Horseclansmen laughed, but watched Shahron with some wariness.

She smoothed her hands down her hips as if she were at market, chaffering for vegetables or for the pot that she had thought of earlier. What sort of bargain could she drive?

"The question is," God Milo said, "where do you go next?"

A shrewd stroke. But she had known from the moment that she saw him that he was no common trader. He had knowledge that could provide her with a future; she had knowledge that could ease his plans. It only remained upon what terms they would trade it.

She took a deep breath and started to bargain. "I could stay here," she volunteered. "Perhaps there are other Ahrmehnee in God Milo's camp, clans who would accept me? I can work, tend flocks, cook, spin, and—" Her strongest bargaining points flashed into her mind. "I have been a prisoner of Witchmen. I can tell you about them."

"Child, I *know* about Witchmen." Shahron sipped her brandy. Was she going to allow him to drive down her price with that statement?

"God Milo, I am certain that you know more about Witchmen than I will ever learn," she said, countering his assurance with mock humility, emboldened by the humor in his eyes. "But do you know about *these* Witchmen, their names and their natures?"

"Well played!" God Milo approved. "Have some more brandy. Lord, I wish my wife Neeka were here. The Witchmen had her too, you know."

Shahron hadn't known, but that was interesting. She started to suggest that she would be glad to speak with this Lady Neeka, then clamped her lips shut. In every bargain came the time when you had to stop speaking and let your adversary persuade himself that he had made a good deal. That time had now come, she could tell.

"I wonder what the two of you could come up with. . . . Hmmmm, that's a good idea. And then, once the campaign is over, I am certain that some of Bili's Ahrmehnee clan-kin, like Tahm . . ."

God Milo trailed off into thoughtful mutters. Shahron knew that type of muttering from older, happier days. Men did it when you had given them an idea that they liked and that they had to turn around in order to claim it for their very own. Usually, once the muttering started, it meant that you got what you needed.

As she would too, she suspected. She sipped her brandy, aware that the world was receding at a rate too fast for good sense. She set the cup down and met God Milo's eyes. Of course he was wiser and kinder than her uncle. After all, her uncle was only a *nakharar*, but Milo was a living god.

But she couldn't shake off the notion that he reminded her of someone else who knew everything that was going on in his camp. And who had let her have what she needed to go on living.

But he had been muttering approval. Generally, once that happened, it was prudent to withdraw so that you could be sent for and given whatever you had inspired the man to think he had had in mind all along. She rose, bowed, and . . .

"What's that, Shahron? No, don't go yet. There will be dinner in a moment. And I want you to tell me about this General Corbett. One day, I think that he and I are going to have to sit down and do a little bargaining."

Dirt Brother

by Roland J. Green and John F. Carr

ROLAND J. GREEN lives in Chicago with his wife and daughter. He is currently working on a series to follow his novel, *Peace Company*. This is the second story about Djoh, and they say that there's more left to tell.

JOHN F. CARR lives in Southern California with his wife and two children. A war-games enthusiast, he is well known among students of medieval and Renaissance history. His most recent projects are coediting *War World*, a shared-world anthology, and writing *Gunpowder God*, a novel set in the world of H. Beam Piper, with Roland Green.

Prologue

Djoh cupped his hands over the butt of the rake handle and rested his chin on them. The raking had fired up all the old familiar pains. Now they were radiating out from his bad knee, up and down his right leg.

The pile of manure was taller than a horse and as wide as four of the stalls. At the moment the dung heap seemed to be the most he'd accomplished in years. Djoh grimaced. *What have I done with my life?*

The job of chief handyman on his rich father-in-law's farm didn't strike him as anything to be proud of. Certainly his wife, Marthuh, would have agreed. Granted, his game leg made him nearly useless for most farm work. Granted, his skill as an archer, a rider, a storyteller didn't count for much in Oskah's Book of Life. (But then, Oskah had never had much affection for his son-in-law from the first.)

Djoh hadn't even been a very good carpenter, except on finish work. By the Sacred Caterpillar, how much call was there for fine joining and shaping in a town like Blue Springs?

So after his parents died in the fire that destroyed their house, he'd had to hire assistants for the heavy work, more than the shop could support. By the time he gave up the shop to dower his sister Nee, he was far in debt. He'd practically had to indenture himself to his father-in-law, just to get the man to take him, Marthuh, and his baby sister Lilla in!

It didn't help, either, that many of the townsmen didn't care about the warning his mindspeak had given about the river pirates, twelve years ago. To them, that mindspeak still meant he was the Witchboy who could read their innermost thoughts and sins. . . .

Some of them even thought he could use his mindspeak to force them to do things he wanted. Ha! If that were true, what was he doing raking horse manure in his father-in-law's barn? The mindspeak was a gift, and with it came certain responsibilities. One of these was to keep his mind out of other people's business. His mother, Behtee, had passed on that message from his mysterious real father, Bard Willee. The prairiecat Iron Claw had reinforced it.

But try to explain that to a bunch of farmers and townies!

The squeak of hinges brought Djoh out of his reverie. For a moment he thought the massive woman coming through the door was his mother-in-law.

No such luck. It was Marthuh, bloated and misshapen by the useless years and her sour life with him. There wasn't much left of the graceful, winsome girl he'd married twelve years ago.

"Wastin' Pa's time again? It's bad enough we have to take his charity and board. If you were any kind of a *man*, we'd have our own house. Why couldn't I see past your pretty face? Look what it's gotten me!"

Djoh had heard much worse than this from Marthuh. He made a polite grunt. "Whatcha want?"

"Some of your drinkin' pals from the militia are out here to talk to you. Old Scratch only knows why. You ain't much of a hero anymore, just a half-breed cripple!"

Djoh no longer took offense at Marthuh's words. They were just there, like the manure he had to rake. Certainly they'd had bad luck in the matter of children—one daughter, stillborn, and she'd been barren afterward. A curse of his Witchblood, according to Oskah. They hadn't been man and wife much after that, and not at all for several years. It might have been even harder here for Marthuh than for him, under Oskah's reproachful eye. *He'd* never been the beautiful daughter who could have had any man she wanted!

"Where are they at?"

"Pa told 'em to park their carcasses on the front porch and wait for the no-count there."

Djoh slowly and deliberately placed the rake back on the rack. He squelched the urge to use the handle on his wife's ample buttocks.

"Last time you went off to a militia muster, you came back stinkin' dog drunk," she went on. "You do that again and I'll break one of Ma's rollin' pins over your head!"

"Marthuh, enough is enough! I don't ask you where you spend your nights when you go to town to 'visit your sister Aldora.' So don't ask me things I don't ask of you."

Djoh was surprised to see his wife blush, a sight he hadn't seen in years. Her weekend visits to town had started about a fortnight ago. He knew from her high color and good spirits when she came back that something was going on.

He also didn't give a damn anymore. Anything or anybody that got her out of the house and off his back was a blessing. Just as long as she didn't rub it in his face. Their marriage was as dead as their daughter, and if there was any other way but death to end it she'd have put him out like an unwanted kitten years ago. *Can't blame a mare for itching a mite.*

"What do you know about that?" she snapped. "Did Aldora say something?"

"No," he said, trying to control his temper. "But I'm no kind of fool. A man can see when his mare's in heat."

"You son of a bitch! If you weren't crippled in

more'n your leg, you might do something about it!"

Before he realized what he was doing, Djoh's hand snaked out. It stopped a hair short of Marthuh's face.

"Why don't you hit me, lizard guts? 'Fraid my pa might finally throw your ass off this farm? Then where'd you go, Witchboy? You stole my heart and then you killed my baby—"

"Shut the fuck up and get out of my sight, woman! Or I'll skin you like a rabbit!"

Something must have shown in his eyes that hadn't been there before. He'd never seen her move so fast. In an eyeblink, she was out of the barn and halfway across the farmyard, bawling for her mother.

Djoh shook his head, dusted off his pants, then made his way toward the porch. It was hard to believe now that once he'd loved Marthuh more than himself. Now, some days it was all he could do to keep from squeezing that fat neck until her mouth closed for good.

The worst of it was that he was beginning to share her low opinion of himself. The boy who'd saved Iron Claw from starvation and then the town from river pirates was a distant memory. There'd been too many years of shoveling manure for Oskah since then.

Maybe being a hero was the easy part. It was how you lived day by day that really separated the men from the boys. If that was true, then he was *some* kind of failure.

Waiting by the porch were Kahrl, the captain of the militia and one of the few townies Djoh dared call friend. With him were Djeffree, the town bully, and Rik, who'd actually spent a year as a mercenary serving one of the Ehleenohee lords up north near the Great Seas.

"I'd offer you something to drink, but—"

Kahrl raised his eyebrows, to show he understood the situation here. Djeffree snickered.

Not for the first time, Djoh wished that Djeffree could have married Marthuh. Then Oskah would have got the son-in-law he deserved!

Actually, Djeffree had never married, not because he was holding on to any big passion for Marthuh but because he roughed up those girls who encouraged him at all. Someday maybe he'd be able to persuade some fool woman that he wasn't really such a pig's ass after all. . . .

Djoh's mother-in-law mercifully interrupted his thoughts with a big pitcher of cider and glasses for everyone. She was taking a chance, with glass as scarce as it was, but Djoh appreciated the gesture. Let the Sacred Caterpillar save her from Oskah's temper if one of them broke a glass! Myrah was the only one in the family who'd ever showed him any kindness; it was mostly her doing that he hadn't gone completely crazy years ago.

After they all had washed the dust out of their throats, Kahrl began. "Djoh, we wanted to talk to you about some trouble down south."

"What kind of trouble?"

"Big band of nomads from the Great Plains. Horseclans people, I think they're called."

Djoh nodded. "I've heard tell of them. What brought them across the river?"

"Outlaw band, maybe. They're mostly men and a few women. The women fight too!"

Djoh smiled at the thought of Marthuh stuffed into a boiled-leather cuirass.

"How many?"

"Different reports. One peddler claims he saw five hundred. Sami Two Shirts says he only saw about a hundred or so. We do know they're a war party. They've burned two villages and ask for food, weapons, and jewelry from every place they visit. When they don't get what they want, they butcher the townsfolk, take what they want, then torch everything."

"What's the Town Council want us to do?"

Djeffree snorted. "Half of them old geezers think this'll blow away like a thunderstorm. Other half, they're already buryin' their silverware and sendin' their womenfolk to kin upriver."

"Cork that hole!" Kahrl snapped.

"Yessee, Captain sir."

Rik looked ready to do a more permanent job of closing Djeffree's mouth, but Kahrl's look stopped him.

"The Council's still talking, not doing," Kahrl resumed. "After all, it's too close to spring planting to have half the young men in the area running around not knowing where to go. Considering what we might be up against, that makes some sense.

"What we need is reliable information. I'm suggesting that we send a small party down south to scout around. Your name came up during the discussion."

"Yeah," Djeffree said, "your Pa-in-law said he wouldn't miss a worthless gimp like—"

Djoh's hands were around Djeffree's neck before he realized that he'd moved. He felt the windpipe beginning to give under the pressure. It took both Kahrl and Rik to pull him off the bigger man.

Djeffree lay on the porch for a minute, his face the color of a fresh bruise, massaging his neck. When he had his breath back, Kahrl reached down and helped him to his feet.

"Apologize to the man," the captain ordered.

"Fuck you—"

A backhand from Rik knocked Djeffree down. He stayed seated, dripping blood from his mouth. As he spat out a tooth, Kahrl stood over him.

"Djeffree, you're as dumb as the day is long. Right now, you stupid sodsucker, you're about this far"—he held thumb and forefinger a crack apart—"from a court-martial. Now, you give Djoh that apology or I'll have your ass slung in jail so long your pecker'll dry up before you can use it again. Understand?"

Djeffree nodded. The look in the bully's eyes told Djoh that the townies who hated his guts had just gained a new recruit.

"I—I'm sorry."

"Good. Now, Djoh, I suggest you rein in your temper a bit too. I suspect a nice long trip might cool things down around here a bit for you."

"Can't do any harm. When do we leave?"

"Not for a while. I have another meeting with the Town Council. Two, three days likely. Not longer. The Council's got the sense to know that Blue Springs is the biggest town for fifty miles. We're going to get a visit from these Horseclans, whether we like it or not."

I

The dirt-scratchers' village was called Two Tanks. Or so Karee Marshul had heard, from those who had questioned the captured farmer last night. The man was too badly hurt to make up any lies, so it was probably true.

It did not really matter anyway; what the Dirtmen called a village that would not live to see dawn. Its doom had been sealed by another of Warchief Djimmi Marshul's ruses. Some of the older warriors had dressed in captured Dirtmen clothing, cursing and grumbling every time a seam gave.

Karee studied Two Tanks while Djimmi inspected his sham Dirtmen. The village was little more than twoscore huts and buildings inside a wooden palisade with a gate and two towers. The wooden log walls were taller than her horse's ears, and recently watered so that they would be hard to burn. She held her hand over her horse's mouth when Chief Djimmi lifted his axe.

Moments later half a dozen of the decoys ran out of the woods that had grown too close to the gates of Two Tanks for safety. They were crying out in word-less fear.

The Two Tankers foolishly took pity on their fleeing fellows. They opened the gates. The instant the gates swung wide, a score of Clan Marshul's fastest riders thundered from the woods.

Some carried ropes with hooks on the ends. These were the best climbers. Along with a half-dozen prairiecats, they mounted the walls and cleared them of archers. Others carried long poles. These they thrust into the gates as the Two Tankers struggled to close them.

Already the air was rent with the cries of horses and the screams of dying Dirtmen. Karee had to tighten her grip on the reins just to keep Yellow Tooth from bolting. "Wait your turn, my lovely," she mindspoke. "Your time to send Dirtmen to Wind will come soon." She did not understand how men could willingly en-slave themselves to the land as these Dirtmen did. Was she perhaps freeing them from some terrible curse by killing them?

At last the chief of the Two Tankers did the only thing left to him. He opened the gates wide and led his folk out, matching his militia who'd fought only drunks and robbers against the picked warriors of Clan Marshul. There were more than Karee had expected, but doubtless the farmers and trappers nearby had rallied to the village.

The clansfolk gave ground just enough to draw the Two Tankers out from their walls. Then Chief Djimmi led a charge that cut in behind them, barring their last retreat. Karee joined in the ensuing melee, dispatching one Dirtman with her lance, then taking another's head with her saber. For Dirtmen, the Two Tankers died well—Karee had a cut on one knee from a desperate knife slash. They still died.

Now their village was dying too. Karee heard flames crackling, almost as loud as the screams of the newly made widows. Karee stalked through the reeking back alleys of the village, in search of her own share of that particular pleasure of a sacking.

A barrel rattled. She whirled, drawing her second sword. It was a short weapon, better suited than a saber for work inside a village's walls. On horseback it was of little use, but on horseback Karee used bow and lance as well as saber.

The barrel rattled again, then rolled. A man sat behind it, a bandage on one arm showing why he'd not died beyond the walls. He could barely be older than Karee's own twenty summers, and seemed handsome for one who had never ridden the Plains under Sacred Sun.

Footsteps sounded behind Karee. She whirled, nearly spitting Lewee Half-Thumb just above the manhood he'd so often offered to demonstrate to her.

"Peace, Karee," Lewee said. "You wandered off, so I followed to be sure no one lay in wait for you."

"No one did, save this dirt-scratcher here. And I know how to deal with him."

"So do I. If that arm isn't crippled, he'll bring a fair price—"

"Lewee! It is told that among the Ehleenohee men love men. Have you taken to that strange way?"

Lewee choked, and even in the shadows she could see his face darkening. He had never been able to best her, at any contest of weapons or even in bandying words. Perhaps that was why he sought to bridle and saddle her for his bed. In no other way could he hope to defeat her.

"Lewee, is there anyone left in this Sun-forsaken hole you or I need fear at our backs? Truly?"

"Well—"

"I thought not. Find your own pleasures and leave me to mine!" She emphasized her words with a gentle prod of her sword. Lewee knew that the next prod would not be gentle. He left. Karee wished him luck and turned back to her own prey.

He hadn't tried to flee, and another time Karee would not have cared for that. The seed of a coward or witling in her could bring no good fortune. As it was, she now not only heard the screams and flames, but smelled smoke thick enough to cut with her steel. She had little time for the pleasures of chasing down game.

Karee began with a quick slash of her sword that opened the man's breeches without touching his flesh. He stared with eyes that seemed too large to be human as Karee peeled off her own breeches.

Women were at something of a disadvantage when it came to forcing an unwilling partner. However, Karee had learned arts that made up for what nature had not provided. The man was young and his flesh responded as she wished. Indeed, before it was over she had stripped herself bare of all save weapons so his good hand could play upon her breasts.

The waves of pleasure that swept through her didn't blind her to the flames now leaping above the rooftop, or deafen her to the subchiefs' shouted orders. She had heard them all before—rally in the village square, bind slaves, dispatch those who couldn't walk, and so on, as their experience and their fear of Djimmi Marshul's wrath bid them. Hearing them still meant that it was time to add this man to the slave chain.

"On your feet," she said, with a jab of her sword at the part of the man's body that had served her so well.

"I'm probably not your first woman, but I'll surely be your last if you wink without asking a clansman!"

Fumbling and shaking, the man pulled on his clothes. "What—what do you horsefolk mean to do with us?"

"If you've the strength, sell you to the river pirates. What they do with you is their affair."

Likely enough a boy this fair would fetch a good price from some northern blackhair. Knowing this, the pirates would probably sell him to an Ehleenohee agent. A pity, but not her problem. There was no room in her life for a concubine, no matter how comely or skilled.

Clan Marshul's riders were moving too fast to be burdened with slaves on foot. When they sacked a town to provide an example to its neighbors, able-bodied survivors ended in the hands of the nearest band of river pirates. The pirates were friends to no one but themselves, and twice they had tried to ambush the clansmen. That made two pirate bands the fewer. The rest grew wiser, from that lesson and also from the silver to be gained selling able-bodied slaves farther south or ransoming them to any kin they might have in larger towns such as Blue Springs.

The man trembled again, then found courage somewhere. "As the gods wish," he said. Karee stepped back, to pick up her clothes.

In the next breath, she learned she had not stepped back far enough. The man's good arm leaped out like a striking snake. His hand closed on the blade of her sword. The sharp edge cut his fingers to the bone, but the oozing blood didn't weaken his grip. It was sure and firm as he plunged the sword into his own throat.

The last sound he made was something that might have been a laugh, if the blood hadn't choked it. Then he fell, and the sword clattered to the hard-packed earth beside him.

For a moment, Karee was too shaken by the Dirtman's unexpected courage and her own narrow escape to pick up the sword. It might have been her own throat gaping, as well as his.

I was his last woman. And may Wind take him with honor, for he had more of it than most.

Now louder than anything else, the voice of Djimmi Marshul rose, rallying the laggards. Karee jerked her clothes on with hands not altogether steady, then wiped her sword on the ground and sheathed it. When Djimmi rode in and began giving order in person, it was best to be there to obey.

"Farewell, Djoh," Oskah said. "Don't try too hard to be a hero."

"I'll do what must be done," Djoh replied, fighting to keep his tongue civil. His crippled leg gave a sharper-than-usual twinge as he swung himself into the saddle. Once mounted he was as good as any man, better than most because he could use his mindspeak to control his horse.

The horse pawed and whickered restlessly, at least sparing him the need to make any further reply as he brought it under control. Then he rode off toward the gate, not looking back. Marthuh had been in town since their last fight and hadn't even returned to wish him off. Only his mother-in-law seemed to really want to see him again.

To anyone listening, such as the militia waiting at the gate, Oskah's farewell might have sounded like a fond wish for the safe return of his daughter's son. To Djoh, it had another meaning.

Don't come back a hero everyone will honor. I don't want to have to give you anything more. The last time you were a hero, I had to give you my daughter, and look what's come of that!

Not that Oskah would really have forgiven Djoh for taking his daughter, even if he'd become the wealthiest man in the Ohyoh country and the father of six stout sons. But he would not have had the power to force Djoh to marry off his baby sister Lilla at fifteen, to a laborer who would take her without a dowry because she was cheaper and comelier than the waterfront whores!

Nor would Djoh have to endure people like Hwul. Oskah's farrier was standing by the gate as Djoh rode up. He drew himself up and brought his hand to his forehead, in a mockery of the ancient gesture of respect from one warrior to another.

"See the hero ride forth!" shouted Hwul, as if the gesture hadn't been enough. Djoh had a moment's dream of making his horse rear and trample Hwul. But the elderly hack Oskah had given him could barely manage a decent trot. Few horses in Blue Springs were really fit for war, and Djoh's mount was not one of them.

"Wait until you see him riding back before you crow like a cock on a dunghill!" Captain Kahrl snapped. Kahrl was the nephew of the old Sacred Caterpillar who'd freed Djoh at the time of the pirates' raid and kept an eye on Oskah until his own death five years later. Kahrl had had hardly more use for Oskah than his uncle.

Djoh reined in his horse close enough to Kahrl that they could talk privately. The captain was frowning.

"If you didn't have that power of hearing thoughts, I'd not be taking you. To Scratch with the Council! Not that I doubt your courage, but these Plains riders are a very different matter from the river pirates. Besides, I suspect you want to be a dead hero more than you want to return a live one."

"I'm not eager to go to Wind. Besides, the faster the Horseclans move, the more warning we need."

"You understand war, Djoh."

Yes, and what good has it done me? I don't understand my wife or her father or my elder sister Nee. The only house in Blue Springs open to me save from charity is my sister Lilla's, and hers only when her husband's sober. Too often he drinks, to forget the "witchblood" in his wife.

Aloud, he said, "I hope I understand war against the Horseclans. It won't be like anything any of us have ever seen. What's brought them across the river, anyway?"

Kahrl signaled to his men to close up and dug in his spurs. "Some say they have a prophecy, of a great leader who will take them back to a sacred city. Others say that even the Plains are growing crowded, and some clans would rather fight us than their equals."

"They may find the pickings less easy than they think, in time," Djoh said. It sounded like whistling in the dark even to himself, and it drew a sour look from Kahrl.

"Tell that to the riders near Two Tanks," Kahrl growled. "Ever since the town burned, they've had all the other villages and farms offering them food, forage, leather, beer, women—just for snapping their fingers."

"Maybe that's why they burned Two Tanks," Djoh said.

"I told you, you understand war," Kahrl said. "And the gods grant it does us some good."

They reached the Y in the road that took half the riders back to town, the other half into the unknown.

Kahrl reached over to shake Djoh's hand. "Good luck. I'd go with you if I could. But the Council's decided we need most of the able-bodied men here to protect the town. They wouldn't even let me send Rik!

"Well, I got you the best that bunch of old women would give me. Gil's the blacksmith's second son. He's strong, if maybe a little thick between the ears. Djak's a yahoo, but good with a sword. Steev grew up on a horse. He's the best."

To the others he spoke up. "The plan is to bring back *knowledge*, not scalps. If anyone here forgets that, he'll answer to me!"

"All right!"

"Bye, Cap."

"Remember, Djoh is in charge. You obey him."

This time there were no "all rights." Djoh knew this was going to be a long trip.

Karee Marshul knelt by the stream and scooped up another handful of mud. To the west the sky was the color of hot coals, all that remained of Two Tanks when Clan Marshul left it behind. Soon it would be dark enough that her clothes of dark leather and her mud-smeared face and hands would make her all but invisible.

Along the bank the other riders of the scouting party were doing the same. Only Djilz needed nothing to darken his skin. When he stripped off the fine white leathers he wore, he was darker than any mud could make him. So he was horse handler while his comrades turned themselves into creatures of the night.

"This mud stinks," someone muttered.

Without raising her head, Karee snapped, "You'll stink even worse after Chief Djimmi hears you disobeyed his orders. We are to slip south like prairiecats on the prowl, not make a din like challenging stallions."

"Or like mares in heat," came the reply.

Before Karee could shape her tongue to a reply both prudent and adequate, she felt the unmistakable ghostly touch of human mindspeak. It was as intangible as the urge to sneeze—and when it came where she expected none, it was far more frightening.

"Red Striker," she mindcalled the prairiecat keeping watch. "Do you hear a two-legs' thoughts?"

"I do. But—he is not of the clans! How can this be?"

"Sun and Wind only know." *Nor will they tell us, in time to save us the burden of facing this mystery unaided by anything save our own wits.*

Now, let us see if those wits are as good as I have always said they are.

"Red Striker, come here at once! Mask your thoughts as you come, as though your deadliest foe sought your life."

"I have no such foes," came the reply. "I have slain or driven off every one."

Karee's thought crackled with anger. "No doubt you have bred such vanity into all your cubs. Have you bred disobedience into them as well?"

This time the reply was silence, both physical and mental. The silence ended in the rustle of grass as the big orange cat slipped from his hiding place to stand beside Karee. Karee laid a hand on his head. That way he could read her thoughts and she his, with less chance of the mysterious mindspeaker overhearing them.

"Circle behind them, silently. Count them and tell me how many. Then use only eyes and ears and nose to guide yourself on their trail."

"As you wish."

Red Striker had vanished before Karee could even

turn to her comrades and begin giving her orders. Djilz's eyes grew white and round in his dark face as he listened.

"How have the gods allowed one of the dirtfolk to have mindspeak? The true gift is rare enough among the Kindred!"

"When I learn, I'll tell you. Meanwhile, take it that they have done so, and mask your thoughts as you would against warriors of the clans."

"I'll do my best."

She slapped him on the shoulder. "That's always been good enough in the past."

Djilz's teeth flashed white in a grin. He had a number of virtues, one of which was abundant manhood. Another was a willingness to obey orders.

In the time it would have taken Karee to examine the hooves of a horse, Red Striker reported that only four two-legs rode toward the stream. He added that he was staying downwind of them and smelled fear in both the men and the horses. He would doubtless have gone on if Karee hadn't sent him a peremptory order to stop talking and start stalking.

With whispers and hand signals, Karee ordered her comrades into place. None of them had enough mindspeak for her to reach them mind to mind, even had it been safe to do so. She could reach prairiecats and horses with ease, but seldom a human without powerful mindspeak of his own. Nor could any save the most powerful mindspeakers reach her.

What this said about the man riding toward her was something she did not much like.

In the time it would have taken Karee to groom her mare, Yellow Tooth, the dirtfolk riders had approached close enough to hear. They were riding at a walk, seemingly loose-reined as they argued. Clearly the one with the mindspeak sensed danger but had been unable to persuade his comrades.

"What the horses smell is water!" came one voice. "All that talk about the big cats is so much owl dung!"

"Djak's right. How would the clansmen train a cat, anyway?" came a second voice.

"Maybe the clansmen can speak to them, mind to

mind," was the reply of a third voice. Karee swallowed. Something in the words matched what she'd sensed in the mindspeak touch. That third voice had to be the mindspeaker!

Laughter came, harsh and hostile, from three throats. "A whole folk of witches? Djoh, you're dreaming! It's hard enough to believe you can do what they say!"

"I didn't—"

"Djoh, I don't care what Kahrl said. One lucky guess about when the river pirates were coming doesn't mean you know much about fighting. There's no way you could have one of those big cats around horses without spooking them."

Karee bit her lip to keep from laughing. She went on biting it until the sound of hooves slowed, then stopped. A thought came from Red Striker.

"Shall I prove to that fool that I am no tale?"

"When we have them busy, yes. Take their horses, so they cannot escape."

Beside her, a leaf rustled as Djilz drew his sword. "They all die?" he whispered.

"Save the one with mindspeak, if we can tell who he is in time."

Djilz rolled his eyes but nodded. Karee drew her own sword and flattened herself on the earth as she would have done on a lover.

The voice who had dismissed the mindspeaker's warning came again.

"I'd wager there isn't anything more dangerous than a wolverine in half a day's ride."

Karee leaped to her feet, bow in hand. An arrow seemed to spring from its quiver to her string, then from her string to the throat of the speaker.

He lived long enough to hear Karee say, "You lose that wager, I think."

Djilz sprang up beside Karee. From the opposite side of the clearing, another arrow flew. This one glanced from a rusty but stout breastplate. The breastplate's wearer lifted a crossbow already cocked and loaded and shot Djilz in the chest.

"Red Striker!" Karee screamed.

In one breath the prairiecat was in the open. In the

next he was on the rump of the archer's mount. The man's breastplate gave no protection to his throat, as Red Striker's teeth closed on it.

Two of the other three horses were now rearing and shrieking in terror. The fourth horse was the mount of a middle-aged man, with no very warlike look to him save for the hunting bow he was unslinging. As she ran toward him, Karee noticed that he wore an elaborate boot on his nearside foot.

Her sword wasn't long enough to reach him, but its razor edge did well enough in cutting his bowstring. He raised the bow to bring down on her head like a club. In her mind she heard a fierce, wordless command to stand and be struck down.

Exaltation filled her, at identifying the mindspeaker. It didn't slow her as she danced aside from the descending bow. A quick slash made the mindspeaker's horse dance wildly, in spite of his desperate efforts with both mind and body to command it. He couldn't recover his balance before Karee gripped his arm and threw herself backward with all her weight.

He tumbled from the saddle and landed hard enough to knock himself senseless. Karee lurched to her feet, knowing that she'd risked the same fate herself by trying to take him alive. If any of the dirtfolk had remained ready to take advantage of this chance—

None did. Her surviving comrades all had red swords; one had a cut across the knuckles of his left hand. He sucked it as he knelt beside Djilz.

The dark man was as pale as Karee had ever seen him. Blood trickled from his mouth, and he coughed more when he tried to speak.

"My own fault—standing like—a Sun-forsaken—tent. I—can you—?"

"Ride in peace, friend Djilz." Karee's sword thrust swiftly, and Djilz went to Wind. She knelt beside him for a moment, until all sense of life had left the hand she was holding. Then she turned to look at the senseless mindspeaker.

Capturing you cost us a good warrior and me a fine lover, dirt-scratcher. You had better be worth such a price.

* * *

The thoughts around Djoh awakened him before the sounds. They also told him as much about where he was—in a camp of the Horseclans. He hardly needed to discover that his hands and feet were bound to know that he was a prisoner in that camp.

He listened to both the thoughts and the sounds for a while, for lack of anything better to do. He'd taught himself the art of counting men and animals from their thoughts in the first years after he saved Blue Springs and no longer needed to hide his "witch power." He didn't know what the riders called his ability, but doubted he had much to lose by using it. What these people did with captives, the ashes of Two Tanks said clearly.

"You didn't knock out your brains after all!" came a voice in both ears and mind. The lips and mind belonged to a young blond woman sitting by the entrance to the tent. Djoh didn't know anything about the mind beyond that one thought, but the lips were definitely full and comely.

Blue eyes flared wide as Djoh completed that thought. The young woman rose in a single lithe motion and stood beside the straw-stuffed pallet where Djoh lay.

"Or did you?" she asked. "In your position, I wouldn't be stripping my guard, even in my mind."

"I think any guard in charge of you would gladly strip himself, with no prompting," Djoh said. Marthuh had liked such pretty speeches, back in the early years of their marriage when everything had been good and seemed likely to stay that way.

"What troubles you?" the woman asked. "You seem sad. Or is your arm paining you? We put it back in the socket, and your head was hardly hurt at all."

"I am well enough, I suppose." He tried to sit up, realized that was a mistake, then decided that he was somewhat hungry and incredibly thirsty.

That request produced a cup of water and a plate of fresh berries with a piece of smoked meat in the middle. "Not too much of the meat—and what is your name, Dirtman?"

"Is that what you call us? Well, I think I will not say *or* think what we call you after Two Tanks."

"That was war!"

"Not as we understand it, here among the farms and towns."

"We shall not agree, I think," the woman said. She hesitated, then said, "My name is Karee, of Clan Marshul."

"I am Djoh the Carpenter, son of Peetuh, of Blue Springs."

Djoh discovered that he was so hungry it was hard to eat slowly, with small bites. He wanted two or three platefuls the size of the one Karee held.

Gradually he realized that this was one of the best meals he'd eaten in years. Was it really the food, or was it that for the first time he was being fed as if someone wanted to see him eat? Marthuh had never been the best cook even when she was trying to please him. Now she slapped food down before him with an "Eat this or starve, I don't care which" air.

"You are sad again," Karee said. "What is it that troubles you?"

"I don't owe you people my life story!" Djoh snapped. "If you can read my mind, do it. Otherwise leave me in peace."

Karee jumped as if he'd slapped her. "You will tell us anything we want to know, whether you owe it or not! When the questioning begins, you will *beg* to tell us."

"And when will that be?" Djoh asked. "I should like to know if I can expect to die under torture, or be whipped to death by your tongue before then?"

The reply was a slap that made Djoh shake his head afterward, to be sure it was still attached to his shoulders. Since he had nothing to lose—

"Karee, I prefer to see you as I did in the battle, a warrior. I think you want to be remembered that way too, not as one who beats helpless prisoners."

For a moment he thought he was going to get another slap. Then she swallowed. "You—curse you, did you read that in my mind?"

"I need no—mindspeak—to tell one who loves honor

from one who does not." *All I need was to remember Oskah or Marthuh—gods forgive her!—and watch you.*

Karee looked away for a moment, but was almost smiling when she turned back to him. "Then if I show honor by not slapping you again, will you show honor by telling me what makes you sad?"

"It is remembering someone I once knew and loved. She looked somewhat like you."

"Is she dead?"

"She is—it is as if she was dead."

Again Karee turned away. This time she did not turn back, but rose and strode out.

Now *what did I say? I'll gladly take a few more slaps, if she'll just come back and help me go to the jakes!*

The hot iron slid between Djoh's left great toe and its neighbor. The hiss and reek of searing flesh reached Djimmi Marshul even where he stood, at a dignified distance from the pit where Djoh was being questioned.

No sound from Djoh reached Djimmi. Nor did any smell, save that of the sweat pouring down his naked body. Djimmi was surprised that the Blue Springs carpenter had not even fouled himself since the questioning began.

"What is the strength of Blue Springs, in men and weapons?" the man with the iron asked. It was the tenth time at least he'd asked. Djoh's body showed the signs of his refusal to answer the previous nine times.

The Dirtman's lips were bitten bloody, but he managed to shape them into a wry smile. "Surely you are asking me what you already know? I have more respect for your scouts than you do. They have ridden far and fast, and I have seen other prisoners brought in."

Once more Djimmi reached for Djoh's thoughts and found only pain, a trifle of fear, and no trace of the knowledge the clan needed. Djoh was a member of the Blue Springs militia; it was hard to believe that he knew so little. The Dirtmen might call mindspeak "witch power," but they had trusted this mindspeaker with a post among their scouts.

Rather, one of their chiefs had trusted him. Those who rode with Djoh had not trusted so much, and paid the final price for folly in battle.

So Djoh not only had the mindspeak but, perhaps without knowing it, the power to hide his thoughts from other mindspeakers. *That* was a power that few even among the Kindred had. Djimmi had it, but only a half-score of others among Clan Marshul.

For considerably more than the tenth time, Djimmi wondered how a Dirtman came to have such mindspeak. His musings ended as Karee Marshul walked up to stand beside him.

"What has he said?"

"Nothing that he did not tell you that first day. Unless he told you other things, during the ten days you nursed him?"

Unmistakably, Karee was flushing. "He told me only that he had once fought river pirates with the help of a prairiecat. He was a hero for a time, but they distrusted his mindspeak in Blue Springs. Even his wife turned away from him, in time."

"Then he must not have had a woman for quite a while. Did you think of that?"

Karee's flush this time was anger. "Suppose he'd had the strength? What could that have done?"

"Perhaps loosened his tongue better than the irons and what else awaits him," Djimmi snapped. "You have not hesitated to use the power of your loins over other men for smaller purposes. Why not this Djoh?"

Karee's hand was on her saber hilt, not resting lightly but gripping so tightly the knuckles were turning white. Djimmi realized that he had gone beyond wisdom, even for a chief. Sacred Sun did not shine warmly on chiefs who insulted proven warriors. Karee would have been that had she had three arms, two heads, and purple scales like some of the creatures unleashed on the land after the Wasting.

"I think Djoh would have said as much or as little as he chose, no matter what I did with him," Karee replied after a moment. "I think he will do the same today."

"Listen to her, Chief Djimmi Marshul," Djoh said

hoarsely. "She speaks the truth. You spend your time in the hope of learning what I either will not tell or do not know. You take my strength and in the end my life. From yourselves, you take honor."

"What is a Dirtman, to know of honor?" snapped the man with the iron. "Perhaps you want this up your arse?"

"I know more of honor than anyone who would do that to a captive!" Djoh practically shouted. "The more so, when you could take from my mind anything you want to know!"

Karee and Djimmi exchanged looks. It was no surprise that Djoh did not know all the aspects of his mindspeak. Among those who called it "witch power," he would have had small chance to learn. Yet such abilities as his were rare even when carefully trained.

It made Djoh an even greater mystery than before. *And you did not become Warchief of Clan Marshul by thinking you knew everything. Mysteries like Djoh are to be kept alive and answered, not killed to no purpose.*

"This Dirtman has the honor of a warrior," Djimmi said. "End the questioning, return him to his tent, and let him be healed."

"Honor in a Dirtman!" The man with the irons squalled like a mating prairiecat.

"Yes, honor!" shouted Karee. "The chief is right. Some among them know as much of it as you do!"

"Oh, there was one who refused you?" snapped the questioner. "Was that honor, or was he a eunuch—"

In the next moment only Djimmi's grip on Karee's shoulder kept Clan Marshul from losing a warrior and gaining a blood feud. Then he pushed Karee roughly away from the pit and leaped down into it. Buhrl, the man with the iron, was young enough to be his son, but Djimmi Marshul had fought and beaten three such with his bare hands not two years ago. The man dropped the iron on his own foot, yelped, and stepped back, hands raised to placate his wrathful chief.

"I think it is your tongue that will meet the iron, the next time it wags to so little purpose," Djimmi said. "Now—go to your tent and let your face not be seen beyond it this day. Otherwise I shall let Karee have you and see if your kin think your blood is worth a feud."

Djimmi did not take his eyes off the man until he was out of sight. By then Karee was kneeling beside Djoh, speaking soothingly as she would have to a fretful baby while she smeared lard on his burns.

Djoh saw and heard neither Karee ministering to him nor Chief Djimmi contemplating him with a frowning face. He had at last fainted.

II

Djoh set both feet firmly on the tent floor. They hurt, but not so much that the thought of standing made him cringe.

Karee knelt beside him, so that he could put an arm around her waist. It was a fine and supple waist to embrace, even though he was careful to touch her as lightly as he could. It had been years since he had touched such a woman at all; Marthuh's waist had long since vanished.

Karee slipped an arm around Djoh's shoulders. "Are you ready?"

"If I'm not, we'll find out soon enough."

Standing proved easier than Djoh expected, though not less painful. His game leg was particularly sensitive. It would be some time before his feet could bear much weight without protesting ferociously.

Keeping his balance was another matter. Without Karee's support, he would surely have fallen. She seemed to sense this and turned to stare anxiously. The motion brought her face almost close enough to kiss—a thought Djoh fought out of existence, though not before he saw Karee blushing. He seemed to have some power to mask his thoughts, but only when he and another were not touching.

Karee's face was returning to its normal tanned hue when Djimmi Marshul loomed at the entrance to the tent. There was no other word for his appearance. His legs were bowed from a lifetime in the saddle, but he still rose a head taller than Djoh. As for strength and prowess, Djoh suspected that for all his years, the chief could distribute Djoh's body in pieces to the four corners of the camp without raising a weapon or working up a good sweat.

Best to give him no excuse to do so, such as fondling one of his clanswomen.

Djoh pulled away from Karee. Too hastily; he lost his balance and sprawled on the sleeping pallet. Karee nearly fell with him. Djimmi laughed.

"You are the first man I have ever seen trying to escape our Karee."

"It would hardly be honorable for me to—"

"Djoh of Blue Springs, perhaps you should think that the chief of Clan Marshul may know something of honor. Indeed, that is why I have come here." He made a gesture of dismissal at Karee, who withdrew with evident reluctance.

"Djoh, you have twice shown a warrior's courage. It is my thought that you have earned the rights of a warrior. You may move freely within the camp. You may ask for what healing you need. You may have a message sent to your kin, that you live and heal."

"I appreciate that, Chief Djimmi. But I am not sure your messenger would be safe."

The chief smiled. "I feared as much. Few of the Dirtmen know honor. Well, we shall do what we can without throwing away a warrior."

Djoh nodded. "I don't want to doubt your word, Chief Djimmi. But—what do you want from me?"

"Your word of honor not to try escaping or doing any injury to Clan Marshul by word or deed, as long as you abide with us."

That's better than I got from Blue Springs, and I hadn't lifted a finger against any living creature there. Without the chief of the Sacred Caterpillars being both honest and shrewd, I wouldn't have lived long enough to lose my family, wife, home, and craft.

Come on, Djoh. Stop feeling sorry for yourself and answer the man.

"By my word of honor, I shall remain in the camp until given the right to leave it. I shall say and do nothing to harm Clan Marshul, its folk, beasts, and goods." He remembered the oaths he had used with the prairiecat Iron Claw; they seemed to be common usage among the clan riders.

"This I also swear, by Sacred Sun and by my hope of going to Wind."

Djimmi grinned. He had few teeth left, but those remaining were strong and white. Then the grin faded.

"Djoh, I will ask one more thing of you. Consider, if you will answer some questions about yourself. Not about your town or your people or their war strength. Only questions about yourself, that may not be my affair but can certainly do no harm to Blue Springs."

"What kind of questions?"

"Your parents' names. Your age. Where in Blue Springs you were born. When you learned that you had the power of the mindspeak. Trifles like that."

The chief's mind was so well shielded that Djoh could not have entered it without being not merely noticed but repelled. The shielding did not hide from Djoh a strong sense that these questions were anything but trifles, to the leader of Clan Marshul.

"I shall consider your request. Is that enough for today?" Djoh's feet were beginning to feel as though they had been returned to the pit of fire.

"More than enough. Now I shall cease to weary you, and leave you with Karee. If she wearies you, it will doubtless be in a more agreeable manner than mine."

From the flush on Karee's face when she returned, she had clearly heard Djimmi's parting remarks. Nor was her mind shielded; she might have been shouting aloud that she rejoiced in his company.

Djoh thought it best only to smile and press her hand to his cheek. Whatever might come of waiting, it would be better than what might come of haste. Moreover, despite the mutual attraction between him and Karee, he was undeniably married to Marthuh—and it did not matter to the law that the marriage had become a sham.

The odds were long against his ever leaving this camp alive, but if he did he would *not* go back to his former life. That was no life for a man. Indeed, since divorce was as despised as infanticide in Blue Springs, it might be best for all if he never returned. Let them think him dead.

Who would care, in truth? Little Lilla would miss him, but he had been able to do little to protect her from her husband. Sooner or later her husband would drink himself into an early grave, and she would be a widow young enough to catch the eye of some better man. As for his older sister, Nee, she would rejoice at this cleansing of a stain on the family honor.

No, Blue Springs was no longer home, and besides, he'd given his word to Chief Djimmi not to run back and warn them. If by some chance the Horseclans freed him, he could doubtless contrive some way to disappear.

It was sheer chance that brought the boy with a splinter in his thigh to Djoh's tent. A raiding party had just returned from Zhampayunsburk and all the other healers were busy. Even those whose task it was to aid the healers seemed to be in need of extra hands.

"It seems the Zhampayunsburk militia was well mounted and not easy to land into ambush," Karee said. "We lost few dead, fewer still so badly hurt that they could not ride. Many have returned needing healing and some days' rest before they draw bow or mount horse again."

A pardon for Blue Springs, then? No, only a reprieve, unless the Sacred Caterpillars and the elders agree to pay tribute. Oskah's tight purse alone would be enough to prevent that.

In the half-moon since he had given his word and become as much a guest as prisoner of the Horseclans, Djoh had learned much about Chief Djimmi's plans. Had they not been the plans of one who might still burn Blue Springs and all in it, he would have honored the man's wisdom in war.

The warriors who had crossed the river were the picked fighting men and women of Clan Marshul, scouting for the rest of the clan. Whether that clan was crossing the Great River to escape enemies, seek new lands, or itself scout for all the other clans was still a mystery. Djoh knew without being told that it was also a secret, one his new position still did not allow him to know.

In any case, Chief Djimmi did not wish to turn the

land about him into a waste. Towns, villages, and individual farms were summoned to pay tribute, of food, iron, horses, or anything else the clan might need. Those who paid were mostly left in peace. (Chief Djimmi kept good order among his warriors.)

Those who refused felt the wrath of Clan Marshul as Two Tanks had done. That wrath was heavy. (When Chief Djimmi turned his warriors loose on a town, they left only ashes, rubble, corpses, and slaves.) From time to time, a village or town was also sacked and burned without warning, to remind all those in sight of the smoke to pay tribute *quickly* when their turn came.

Chief Djimmi had a reputation for seeing far ahead. He also had a reputation for an exceedingly short temper with folly or treachery.

Zhampayunsburk had shown neither. It lay well beyond the Eeleehnoyah River, and Djoh suspected it had been attacked simply to confuse the clans' enemies. Where would they strike next? people would be asking.

What Djoh was asking was what he was supposed to do for this boy who'd suddenly appeared in his tent. He was one of the score or so of chosen boys who'd ridden with the war party as part of their initiation into manhood. Right now, the boy looked to Djoh like any other scared twelve-year-old away from his mother and in pain.

Why ask myself, when there's surely at least one person who knows and will tell me? He turned to the men who'd brought the boy in.

"Will one of you go to Karee Marshul and ask her to come here if she is free?"

"Oh, Karee never charges!" said one with a ribald laugh. "Indeed, it's as much as your manhood is worth to even hint that she does. She doesn't have much humor. Of course, she has everything else—"

"Including a tongue, which is more than you'll have if you keep flapping it," said the other bearer.

"Why should we obey a Dirtman's orders?"

"Because this Dirtman has been pardoned by Chief Djimmi. Also, because I will knock out all the teeth Karee doesn't if you go on insulting two better warriors than yourself."

"A Dirtman a warrior?" growled the first man, but he followed his comrade out of the tent. His receding thoughts held the message *Clan Marshul is falling on evil days, when warriors are sent to do the bidding of captive Dirtmen.*

Djoh sighed. The "once a Dirtman, always a Dirtman" faction was strong in the camp. Not so strong that he was in danger, but strong enough so that if he lost the protection of the "anyone with mindspeak and a warrior's courage deserves honorable treatment" faction, his fate was certain.

His life would probably hang in the balance as long as Clan Marshul remained on this side of the river. What happened after that depended on whether they chose to return to the Plains or remain and carve out a territory. They would hardly return, leaving one who knew all their secrets behind them.

If they chose to stay, however . . . Djoh had to wonder. Those who thought he deserved honorable treatment had treated him better than most of the Blue Springers ever had, except in the few years after the battle with the pirates!

Was his destined home among these wild riders from the Plains?

Djoh found his hands shaking so badly at this thought that he sat on them to hide them from the boy. Except for the splinter, the boy seemed to have no worse than bruises. That splinter was going to be enough trouble, though. The boy didn't need to see his would-be healer's hands shaking into the bargain!

By the time his hands stopped shaking, Djoh heard a familiar footstep approaching the tent. He forced his mind and voice to be as steady as his hands.

"Karee, this splinter must come out soon, and the wound be cleansed. Do you have a sharp knife, or one that can be sharpened?"

"Is that sharp enough?" Karee said wearily, handing the knife to Djoh.

Djoh pressed the knife against the ball of his thumb. The skin parted at the lightest touch. He sucked the blood and nodded.

"Sun be praised!" Karee said. "If I'd had to take the whetstone to it again, I think I would have tested it on you somewhere else."

Djoh seemed not to hear her. "Can the mindspeak put someone to sleep, so he feels no pain?"

"There are tales of those who can use it thus," Karee said. "The Undying Milo is one."

Djoh dropped the knife, then cursed as he picked it up. Karee noticed that his face had gone very white. Well, perhaps he'd realized how much he'd taken on himself, seeking to heal this boy.

"Did the knife lose its edge?" she asked.

"No—no. It's sharp enough. All right, lad. You'd better bite on something—"

"Here." Karee handed the leather sheath of her wrist dagger to the boy. He popped it into his mouth and managed to smile around it.

"What did they cure this with, Karee? Northhorse dung?"

His smile froze and sweat popped out on his forehead as Djoh slit the wound open. Blood poured out onto the pallet. Karee moved to hold the bandages ready as Djoh carefully lifted the splinter out, with hands he'd carefully washed in water as hot as they'd used for the bandages. He held the wound open with one hand while he gently sought stray bits of wood with the knife in the other.

Sometime during this seeking, the boy fainted. At last Djoh sat back on his haunches. Karee knelt beside him with the bandages ready, but he put an arm in front of her. Clearly without intent, his hand brushed her breasts. The gentle brushing could not have felt stronger had it fallen on her bare flesh.

"No, we leave the wound to bleed freely for a moment longer. Then all the evil that may come from horse dung will be washed out."

"Horse dung?"

"Yes. The chief among the Sacred Caterpillars always said that it was an evil element in horse dung that caused the Death of the Frozen Jaws. Not everyone believed him, but my father and I did. Carpenters often have splinter wounds."

"Curious. They say the Undying Milo taught the same. Did your priest ever speak of—Djoh, *what is wrong*?"

"The Sacred Caterpillar never spoke of anyone called Milo. But—a man my mother knew when she was young spoke of him."

"Who was the man?"

Djoh blinked at the tone in her voice. *Karee, you are as shaken as Djoh and hiding it no better!*

"He called himself Bard Willee. My mother did not think that was his real name, but it did not matter. He went away the year before she married my father."

Bard Willee! Was that not one of the names Chief Djimmi used, when he was in this land thirty years ago? And how well did Djoh's mother know him, when she was young?

Karee looked at Djoh so intently that he flushed and nearly dropped the bandages she handed him. *He does not look much like Chief Djimmi, but he might favor his mother.*

Djoh's fingers had seemed to linger on Karee's wrists as he took the bandages from her. His hands remained steady as he bound up the wound, making sure that the bandages did not touch the floor of the tent, the pallet, or anything else unclean. At last the blood stopped flowing. Djoh laid his ear first on the boy's mouth, then on his chest.

"He can be moved now. Does he have anyone who can tend him for a few days?"

Karee said nothing. She didn't trust her voice. It was all she could do to keep her hands steady as they tugged at the lacings of her vest.

Djoh stared at her. "Karee, the boy might wake—" he stammered. She replied by laying her vest over the boy's face—gently, so that he could breathe—and beginning on her shirt.

"Oh, Peeoryah," Djoh said. It was half a word, half a gasp, and most of both were muffled by Karee's breasts as he began kissing them. She ran one hand up his thigh as she started undoing her trousers.

"Djoh, I think you need some healing too, the kind only a woman can give."

His arms went around her, and after that she re-

membered very little for quite a while. He began like
any man who hadn't had a woman for some time, but
quickly found a pace that matched hers. When they
were done, she woke from a mist of fulfilled desire to
find him asleep on her breast, tears trickling down his
cheeks and making little pools on her belly.

She wanted to stretch but was afraid of waking him.
*And when was the last time I was afraid of waking a
lover? Karee Marshul, Sacred Sun has given you a gift
it may not be in you to understand.*

Well, then I will take it for as long as it is given.

Karee was cinching the saddle on Yellow Tooth
when she felt a hand on her shoulder. Thinking Djoh
had come to see her off with the scouts, she turned
with a smile on her face.

Instead of finding Djoh's arms reaching for her, she
found herself facing Lewee Half-Thumb's gap-toothed
smile.

"How 'bout a kiss, honey-lips?"

Karee reached for her sword, but Lewee's hand
pinned her wrist before she could draw.

"What do you want, midden-breath?"

Lewee's face reddened. "No Dirtwoman speaks to
me that way!"

"Dirtwoman!"

"Isn't it true you're sleepin' with that dirt-scratcher
from Blue Springs?"

"Yes, it's true. It's also true that even with his game
leg he's twice the man you've ever been."

"You tell 'im, Karee," someone cried out. Half the
scouts now encircled them. Some of the warriors were
already laying bets on the outcome of any fight, the
odds heavily in Karee's favor.

Lewee Half-Thumb was turning redder by the moment, not only from rage but from the strain of keeping Karee's sword hand pinned.

"Lewee, I swear by Sacred Sun, take your hands
off me, or you'll be missing half of something besides
your thumb."

"Go ahead, Karee," someone shouted. "Ain't like

he gets much use out of it anymore!" A chorus of laughs followed.

"All right, bitch," Lewee said, pulling his hands away and stepping back. "I demand a fight to the death with knives, under Clan Law."

"Fine by me, horse fart," Karee replied, drawing her dagger. She held it low, with the stance of a practiced knife fighter, waiting for Lewee to make the first move. The onlookers were calling out wagers as fast as heartbeats and the odds on Lewee were tumbling faster than his harsh breathing.

Karee let the man take the initiative, then jumped back and to the side in a single movement. Her dagger flickered and a long shallow wound opened in Lewee's forearm.

"I'll kill you for that! Bitch! Dirt lover!"

Karee smiled, crouched, and prepared to move in for the kill.

She'd just launched herself forward when two massive arms wrapped themselves around her. Two other warriors pinned Lewee's arms.

"What's going on here?" Chief Djimmi's voice bellowed. "This is a war party, not a drunken brawl. Who started this?"

One of the Clan Elders, Chuhk, spoke up. "Lewee Half-Thumb tried to force himself on Karee while she was saddling her horse."

"Is this true?"

A chorus of yeahs supported Chuhk.

"What do you have to say for yourself, Lewee?"

His hands still pinned behind him, Lewee looked like a man beginning to realize just what kind of trouble he'd made for himself. His voice shook as he replied.

"Ain't my fault. I've always had the hots for Karee and now she's taken up with that Dirtman prisoner. I figured she's givin' it out to everything that walks."

Karee hissed. "Let me go, Djimmi. I'm going to geld that bastard a finger at a time. Death's too good for him!"

Chief Djimmi's whisper was harsh in her ear. "Quiet. One idiot's bad enough!

"Lewee," he addressed the clansman. "By Clan Law clanswomen have the right to choose their own lovers and mates. We're not Ehleenohee who force ourselves on young boys and unwilling slaves. I want this settled right here, right now. We have a raid to carry out and some Zhampayunsburkers to put in fear!"

"By Clan Law, I *demand* the right to fight Karee Marshul to the death."

Djimmi let go of Karee and took a deep breath. "By Clan Law, Lewee Half-Wit, *I* have the right to your head for fighting with another clansman during a time of war. Now do you want to tell me any more about *your* rights?"

Looking at the ground, Lewee shook his head.

"Good. But if I hear of your bothering this woman again, I'll claim the right to fight you to the death myself. Is that understood?"

Lewee swallowed several times; his words still came out as from a dry throat.

"Y-yes, Chief Djimmi."

"Good. Now everyone mount up. It's past time for being on the road."

The sound of Kindred warriors mounting up swelled. Above the sound, Lewee Half-Thumb's voice rose furiously.

"I'll get you yet, dirt lover!"

The sense of danger was one Djoh couldn't have put into words. So he held his peace. Not that any of the youths and girls splashing with the horses in the shallow stream would have listened, if he had spoken.

Not all of them believed "Once a Dirtman, always a Dirtman." Even those who kept their weapons handy when Djoh was around obeyed Chief Djimmi. When the chief said that Djoh was to be allowed to go with parties watering the horses, they let him go. Those who grumbled did not do so where Chief Djimmi might overhear.

Even those who did not grumble, however, refused to believe that Djoh had true mindspeak. Sometimes Djoh wondered why the chief, who knew better, did not offer proof. One did not, however, ask Djimmi questions about matters on which he had chosen to hold his tongue.

So Djoh had gone from his own people, who believed that mindspeak made him a witch, to the Horseclans, who didn't believe that he had it at all. It could hardly be said that his life was standing still, but he often had the sense that it was going around in circles.

The idea of danger close at hand presented itself to Djoh, more strongly than before. He stopped combing the mane of the big gray stallion. Mountain Wind seemed to tolerate him more than any of the other Horseclan mounts. Combing him was a way to at least seem useful in the eyes of the young clansmen.

"What makes you uneasy, two-legs?" came the stallion's thoughts.

"Could bad two-legs be coming without being seen?"

"The chiefs send out riders, to watch for such."

"The chiefs have ridden off on the raid, most of them. Those who stayed behind might not be obeyed."

The stallion's unease at the thought of unknown danger to his mares and children came plainly. So did other thoughts, from another source yet also close at hand. Djoh forced himself to concentrate, as if he had to smooth an entire plank with a single stroke of the plane.

"Bad two-legs," he thought finally. "Some on the other side of the river. Some crossing—no, now on this side."

And do I call them enemies or rescuers?

Djoh looked up at the sky, but the sun, whether sacred or not, gave only light, not answers. He looked at the "Kindred" splashing in the water. He looked rather longer at the maidens than at the men, for none wore anything. Not that he was going short of women these days—or rather, of a woman, since Karee was enough woman for three men.

These people might not be *his* Kindred. It was still more than he could contemplate, seeing them butchered when it was in his power to save them. Some of the Maiden Archers were no older than his sister Lilla.

Besides, Mountain Wind would probably stamp him

flat if he threw away the lives of mares and colts.

A man had to be able to sleep at night, whether or not he slept in anything he could call a home. Otherwise Djoh might as well take the knife he'd been using to pare Mountain Wind's hooves and cut his throat.

"Four-legged friend, will you let me mount you and seek the bad two-legs?"

"You will not run to them for help?"

Not for the first time, it struck Djoh that the Horseclans' prairiecats and horses were sometimes smarter than the clansmen.

"They are not my friends. I will not help them bring death to your mares."

"Then mount."

As Djoh gripped Mountain Wind's mane, one of the youths who'd remained on the bank, armed and clothed, saw him.

"Ha! Do you think oaths are like the dirt you live in, that you can ride off anytime you please?" He hurried toward Djoh, drawing his saber as he came.

"I take oaths as seriously as any of the Kindred," Djoh said. "I heard mindspeech downstream that made me suspect danger. I wished to ride and see. By Sacred Sun and Wind and by mother's honor I shall return."

"Nothing has come to me," the boy said. "Nor do I lack the mindspeak. If nothing has come to me, then how has it come to you?"

"If you do not trust me, ride with me," Djoh said. "I admit that I do not know my mindspeak as well as those of the Kindred who have used it since they were children. Perhaps I see danger where there is none. If that is so, then we do no harm, and I will have no chance to escape.

"If there is danger, we are more likely to give warning if there are two of us. Two are harder to kill than one."

The boy frowned. "To hear you talk, anyone would think you had been a warchief instead of a Dirtman's carpenter." The frown deepened. Then he shook his head.

"No. I will not ride off on a fool's errand, leaving the horses."

"Then will you at least help me put the weapons of those in the water closer to the bank, so that they may reach them the faster?"

The boy looked along the bank and flushed. He could not be finding much pleasure in a Dirtman's seeing what some of his comrades had done—left their weapons where an enemy on the bank could come between them and the weapons.

"Ho, brothers and sisters! A Dirtman is wiser in war than some of you. Look to your weapons!"

Those were the last words the boy spoke. An arrow from across the stream took him in the throat. At the same time half a dozen men in wet green-and-brown clothing sprinted out of cover downstream. They carried short stabbing swords and long daggers, and only a witling could have mistaken their intent.

If they could seize the bank so that unarmed and naked Kindred had to climb up to face them, they could hold those Kindred under the arrow hail from across the stream. The half-dozen might die, but so would far too many of the Kindred.

In the time it took the boy to fall to the ground, Djoh was on Mountain Wind's back. He sprawled ungracefully across the stallion's barrel at first; even a grip on the mane hadn't made up for a game leg. Mountain Wind's thoughts held rage and bloodlust, but he kept still until Djoh was mounted as securely as he could hope to be. Djoh had seldom ridden horseback, never bareback on a horse this big, and never into battle at all.

Mountain Wind's legs seemed to uncoil, and he plunged forward. As he went, he screamed a warning to the rest of the herd. Djoh heard the lesser stallions and the mares replying, and the thunder of the whole herd starting into movement. He could only hope they would run to the camp and give warning, or at least not into the arms of new enemies.

He tried to search for any other traces of hostile mindspeak, but gave up in a moment. As long as he heard Mountain Wind, he could hear nothing else.

If the men who'd swum the river had carried bows, Djoh and Mountain Wind might have died before they had closed half the distance. As it was, the archers on the far bank were too few to make effective practice against both Djoh and the Kindred in the water. Djoh was a moving target, sometimes behind trees, and the Kindred could duck out of sight until they were ready for a sprint up the bank.

By the time Djoh was out of the trees, he was so close to the half-dozen that an archer shooting at him hit a friend instead. This drew curses, which turned into screams as Mountain Wind charged among the men. Instead of holding the bank against the Kindred, the men found themselves being driven down the bank into the water where the Kindred waited. The alternative was being trampled under Mountain Wind's hooves or savaged by his teeth. The men seemed to prefer death at human hands.

The fighting in the water was still going on when Kindred who'd reached their bows began shooting back. The arrow fire from the far bank slackened, enough to allow other Kindred to swim the river and press home the fight to close quarters. From the warcries and deathcries on the far bank, it seemed that the Kindred were prevailing, though not without losses.

Not what they would have been if you hadn't charged the raiders on the bank. In fact, if you hadn't, you might have wound up being "rescued" whether you wanted to be or not.

Unless they decided you were of the Horseclans and cut your throat along with theirs.

Any throat-cutting that actually took place happened on the far bank, out of Djoh's sight though not out of his hearing. When the Kindred who'd crossed the river returned, it was on an improvised raft of fallen logs. It bore two dead and another too badly hurt to swim, plus another soundly trussed prisoner.

The maiden who seemed to be the new leader came up to Djoh. By now he'd dismounted, but found that he needed a firm grip on Mountain Wind's mane in order to stand.

She looked him up and down with a look mingling respect and exasperation. Then she saw his empty hands and belt, and the exasperation vanished. Her mouth opened into a silent circle and stayed that way for some time.

Finally she found her voice.

"Dirt—Dirt Brother. Did you bear any weapon at all, when you charged?"

Djoh shook his head—carefully, because his neck muscles felt so weak that a hard shake might send his head rolling in the dirt. "I—well, Mountain Wind is enough of a weapon, isn't he?"

"I thank you for that praise, Brother Djoh," came the stallion's thoughts.

The maiden nodded slowly. "If it were possible for such a thing to be, I would say you have in you the blood of a Kindred chief. If that is not so, then—then Sacred Sun has allowed you to make yourself into one of the Kindred. That is not what I was taught, but it is what is before my eyes."

Djoh felt like kissing the girl, but since she was quite naked he felt that both she and Karee might misunderstand the gesture. At least he could now step away from Mountain Wind and stand without falling on his face. Meanwhile, the Kindred were laying out their dead, tending their wounded, bringing the bodies of the slain enemies across on the raft, and generally putting matters in order.

Djoh watched them with a mixture of admiration and unease. *A good part of these clansmen are young enough to be my sons and daughters. They were young enough to be careless with their weapons. Without my aid they would have paid a heavy price for that carelessness. Yet when they rallied, they did it so well that they prevailed against a fair-sized band of seasoned warriors. Zhampayunsburk scouts, I should judge, who are among the best in the whole Ohyoh country.*

If these people cross the Great River in strength, seeking their sacred city of Elay, I think we should let them pass in peace.

A scream broke into Djoh's thoughts. He looked behind him, then walked quickly away. The questioning of the captured scouts had begun.

III

Karee had dreaded this meeting during most waking moments of the past two days. Not that she feared Djoh would do anything dishonorable or foolish. That was the problem. Djoh might be doomed not because he deserved it, but only because he was not of the Kindred.

Would not be of the Kindred, Karee corrected herself. If Djoh swore the proper oaths, he need not die. But would he swear them, when he knew that the next town to burn might be his own Blue Springs?

That was the decision made in the warriors' council two days ago. Seldom did Chief Djimmi bring the council together, still more seldom did he need it. He had led for long enough that all knew he would not throw lives away through vanity or folly. Warriors died when he led, but they died from the chances of battle that came to all.

Now, though, Clan Marshul would be trying its strength deep in the Ohyohlands, against a strong town, well led, and with allies. It was learned from the Zhampayunsburk prisoners that Kahrl, war leader of Blue Springs, had sent the scouts to seek and wound Clan Marshul. But for Djoh's quick thinking and Mountain Wind's quick hooves, they might have succeeded in slaying more than their own numbers.

"A man who can make those not of his clan perform such deeds is a dangerous foe," Djimmi said. "It is best that we prove quickly that he is not invincible. What better way than by defeating his warriors, burning and looting his town, and throwing his head at the feet of his allies?"

"That's true enough," said Chuhk. He was nearly as old as Djimmi, but every bit as tough too. "But why not go at him another way? What can he do without allies? If we strike at Zhampayunsburk itself, they will know that the price of following Kahrl's orders is death. If we teach that lesson, Kahrl will be helpless as a child."

"There is wisdom in that," Chief Djimmi had said. "Yet not as much as in attacking Blue Springs. For one, the Zhampayunsburk folk are now alert and waiting for us. They will not be easy prey. For a second, we cannot march with all our strength against Zhampayunsburk without leaving Blue Springs in our rear. Blue Springs, and Kahrl."

"Since when have the Kindred feared foes in their rear?" shouted someone. Karee had looked, then recognized Lewee Half-Thumb. Djimmi's threats had improved his manners toward her, but done little for his wits.

"Who speaks of fear?" snapped Chuhk and Djimmi, almost in one voice. "It is not fear but wisdom to find new ways of war in a new country," Djimmi added. "If we were on our own Plains, we could ride freely around any foe who sought to block our path. We are in a different land, where even Dirtmen if they are numerous and cunning can find places to fight horsemen."

It was those who had ridden against Zhampayunsburk who turned the balance. They wanted to avenge their dead comrades, to be sure. They also felt that if Blue Springs and Kahrl fell, Zhampayunsburk would be ripe for the plucking. It would not be so the other way around.

So now Djoh had to hear that his hometown was doomed, and that if he did not swear to ride with the Kindred against it so was he.

Karee had prayed for the words to break this news. That particular prayer had not been answered, but another she had not thought to utter had been. Chuhk was coming with her. He would not allow Lewee Half-Thumb, who had insisted on joining the party, to shed Djoh's blood unlawfully.

Lawful or unlawful, does it matter if it is still death? Perhaps dying on Chuhk's dagger would be better than what other deaths might await Djoh, at the hands of Lewee or Burhl, another unwelcome addition to the party.

Do not bury Djoh before he is dead, Karee Marshul. There is much life in that man, as well you know. And at the memory of how much life there was in Djoh of Blue Springs, Karee had hugged herself.

Now the four news-bearers stood before the entrance to Djoh's tent. "Djoh, it's Karee. May I come in?"

Djoh rose but said nothing when Chuhk, Buhrl, and Lewee followed Karee in. "Greetings. To what do I owe this honor?"

Both Chuhk and Buhrl looked at Karee. She had to lick her lips three times before she could speak without fearing their cracking. They had never been this dry before a battle.

"Djoh, you have fought as one of the Kindred. Will you take the oaths by Sacred Sun and all else lawful, to be one of us? You cannot remain neither free nor prisoner, after what you have done."

Karee knew that her voice was not as steady as she had hoped. Even if her voice had been steady, Lewee Half-Thumb's expression would have given the game away. He was openly gloating at the possibility of Djoh's refusing the oath and dooming himself.

Would that we could have refused to allow Lewee to come. But then those who say no Dirtman is worth more than the dirt he turns would wag their tongues, and some might be ready to do more. Chief Djimmi has placed a burden on Djoh and me, but it was a matter in which he had no choice, as chief of Clan Marshul.

"We are grateful, and so are the kin of those you saved," Chuhk added. "But we cannot put the clan in danger to show our gratitude."

Djoh's smile was curiously lopsided. Or perhaps there was nothing curious about it. Only a witling could be unaware of the choice he faced.

"Your gratitude won't go as far as letting me go home, will it?"

Karee swallowed. "No."

"When we march against Blue Springs? Do you think we are fools?" Lewee cried.

Djoh's smile froze. Karee's heart nearly did the same, because in that freezing of his smile, like a stream in the depths of winter, she saw his answer.

"Most of the Kindred are not fools," Djoh said quietly. "It has been an honor, if not always a pleasure, to be among you. Yet there is one fool here. Lewee, did you think to tell me the secret so that you would have an excuse for killing me?"

The look on Lewee's face nearly made Karee draw her sword on the spot. From the look on Chuhk's face, it was a plausible theory that hadn't occurred to him. He felt ashamed that a Dirtman had been wiser than he, in the presence of three of the Kindred.

He also had his hand somewhat closer to the hilt of his sword than he had a moment ago.

"Karee," Djoh said, and for the first time his smile vanished entirely. "Karee," he repeated, and she had never heard her name pronounced so. It was almost a caress, of a kind not to be received in the presence of others.

"Karee, forgive me. I have had honorable treatment among the Kindred, and I hope I have repaid it in battle. I cannot swear to repay it further by lifting a hand against my own kin."

"They called you witch and nearly killed you!" Karee shouted. Her voice cracked.

"Some of them knew enough justice so that I lived. A few more have been decent, all through the years. Even those who have scorned me—I am not one of the old gods from before the Wasting, who hurled down wrath on whole cities because some of their people had been evil."

He looked at Chuhk. "Is it in your power to take my oath never to return to Blue Springs? It is true enough that I hardly have much to return to there."

Chuhk shook his head. "I would trust such an oath from you, but many would not. Also, what if you fell into the hands of other enemies of the Kindred? Any hint that you knew the slightest of our secrets and you would be praying for death in half a day."

Djoh shrugged. "So be it. I thought as much, and I will not shame Karee or my kin by begging further." He stepped forward, raising his arms. "Karee, try to find it in your heart not to hate me—"

"Djoh, any woman who hated you would be the greatest fool ever born under Sun—" she began.

Lewee Half-Thumb's face twisted. "He's trying to

get her knife!" he shouted. His sword leaped clear and he sprang forward, snatching Karee's belt dagger as he came. Karee was too surprised to stop him.

Djoh tried to leap clear, but his lame leg betrayed him. He stumbled over the pallet and fell, outstretched legs in Lewee's path.

Lewee Half-Thumb crashed to the ground, tried to rise, and made a faint bubbling noise. His wide eyes held amazement more than pain. Then he rolled over, and Karee saw that he had fallen so that her dagger had vanished up to the hilt between his ribs.

Chuhk and Karee looked at each other, unable to look at either the doomed honorable Dirtman or the dying Kindred fool. Djoh drew their attention back to them by sitting up and rubbing his knee.

"Not that Lewee's much of a loss, but—Karee, will you suffer for this?"

"Not if Lewee's kin have your blood as the price for his," Chuhk said.

"They will ask for a harsh death," Burhl added, an unwholesome smile on his lips.

Djoh shrugged. "I've had twelve years of life since the Sacred Caterpillars were going to burn me alive. Maybe they haven't been the best years, except for meeting Karee—" He reached for her again, and this time no one prevented the embrace.

When he had breath to speak again, he added, "I've lived better among the Kindred than I have most of the time in Blue Springs. Perhaps it's a kind of justice that my death come among you."

"Djoh—" Karee could not force more than his name out of her tight throat. It felt as if her dagger had been thrust into it, instead of into Lewee's chest.

"Karee, I'm going to give you an order, for the first and last time . . . since you can't do anything to me for giving it. I want my last memory of your warrior's face. Don't weep for me."

It was an order that she could not obey. When the guards Chuhk summoned appeared, Karee was so nearly blind with her own tears that he had to lead her from the tent.

She was ashamed of her lack of self-command, but

there was one consolation. She did not have to see the guards binding Djoh.

The mosquito whined savagely in Djoh's ear. He had given up wincing at such assaults. They merely made the leather thongs binding his hands to the post cut deeper. The thongs were so tight that blood had already joined the sweat on his hands, to attract the insects.

At least the snakes and day insects had vanished with the sun. Djoh had listened with his ears to the clansmen—he could not quite bring himself to call them the Kindred anymore—chanting their farewells to Sacred Sun.

He had tried to listen with his mind to anyone with mindspeak, in the hope of learning what death would be his. He had to listen with not only little skill but much caution, lest he convince someone besides Karee and Djimmi that he had true mindspeak.

It was just conceivable that evidence of his mindspeak powers would alter his fate. More likely it would put the clansmen even more on their guard than they were already, or even hasten his death. Lewee's kin would point out that if Dirtman Djoh didn't need to flee to warn Blue Springs, the sooner his mind and body alike were forever still, the better.

In their place, Djoh realized he would have thought the same. Even if his mindspeak did not hasten his death, the extra guard placed on him would make his one chance of escape impossible.

From his listening, he had learned two things. One, that the clansmen were far more concerned about any lingering Zhampayunsburk scouts than they were about him. The second, that he was staked out here not because that had some ritual meaning, but because the clansmen couldn't agree on what else to do with him.

No doubt they would eventually think of something sufficiently unpleasant, given time. With help from the one friend Djoh might still have in the camp and a great deal of luck, they would not have that time.

Djoh was still cautious as his mind searched among the horses. Some of them had mindspeak as powerful as Mountain Wind's. Few would dare disobey the stallion, but their thoughts might tell their riders more than Djoh wished them to know.

"Dirt Brother? I sense danger and pain. Is it yours, or another's?"

The stallion's mental voice was unmistakable. Djoh briefly retold the day's events and described his situation.

"Though they are my brothers, I say the two-legs have used you shamefully. They owe you much, yet seem unwilling to pay."

"Will you spare them that shame?"

"How?"

"Free me and carry me beyond the reach of the scouts."

"How am I to free you, Dirt Brother? We are battle comrades, and this much I owe you. But I have four legs and no hands to hold an iron stick."

"You have teeth." In fact, given a choice between Mountain Wind's bite and that of a prairiecat, Djoh would not have known which to chose. The stallion could certainly kill with his teeth as well as with his hooves, if not as swiftly as a cat like Iron Claw.

"Those teeth may well cut more than your bindings."

"I will take that chance."

A long silence, broken only by the whine of the mosquitoes. Djoh felt sweat trickling into his eyes.

Then:

'I take a chance too, Dirt Brother. Do you mean to return to your own folk?"

Lying in mindspeak was not absolutely impossible if one was very gifted and trained for many years. Djoh was neither. Besides, Mountain Wind was right about what battle comrades owed each other. One of those things was the truth.

"I do. But no word or deed of mine will put your two-legged brothers, your mares, your children, or anything else that is yours in danger. When I tell of the strength of the Kindred, I think those in Blue Springs who mean to fight will think again. If they do not offer peace to Clan Marshul, I will urge it upon them."

That was the truth. Djoh didn't expect to get much of a hearing, except possibly from Kahrl and a few people who valued their own skins above everything else. Odd allies, they would be—the crippled witchboy, the war leader, and the cowards. But if it kept the fire and the steel away from Blue Springs, it would serve its purpose. Then his last duty to the town would be finished and he could go wherever he wanted—if there was any place for him to go.

"Are you chief over Blue Springs, that you can be sure they will listen to you?"

Djoh mentally damned the horse's sharp wits, and heard the reply:

"Would you not ask such a question, if your mare Karee might be in danger from me?"

When Djoh had stopped laughing at the idea of Karee as a mare, he once more had to admit that the stallion was right.

"If I cannot persuade my kin not to fight Clan Marshul, I shall lead those willing to follow me out of the town." That would probably mean only Lilla and Kahrl's children, if Kahrl didn't feel he had to keep them around to reassure his followers. He had to try to save *something* from his town, if it would not save itself.

The silence this time was even longer. It was finally broken, not by mindspeak, but by the soft thud of plate-sized hooves. Mountain Wind trying to walk quietly would have been an amusing notion if the stallion hadn't been doing it. Djoh's hopes rose as the great horse loomed above him.

"Did anyone challenge you?" Djoh asked. He hadn't been guarded at nightfall, but they might have placed sentries after he could no longer see them.

"Neither man nor horse nor cat. Now prepare yourself for pain, Dirt Brother and battle comrade. This will not be pleasant, if it is to be swift."

That was a considerable understatement. Djoh's lips were bleeding almost as badly as his wrists by the time Mountain Wind was finished, from biting them in order not to cry out. He had to bind them with strips of his shirt before he could even try to stand.

"I trust you have some ideas about what to do next," came Mountain Wind's thoughts. The idea of a horse being sarcastic was not one that would have occurred to Djoh before he fell among the Kindred, but no other word would do.

"There is a stream that leads out of the camp, where sentries cannot see who passes. Before we reach the end, where there are sentries, we shall climb the bank. I know a place for that."

In mindspeak, he could not hide how he knew of that place. He and Karee had spent a whole afternoon there, making love as he had never dreamed it could be.

Mountain Wind's reply held amusement. "It is a pity that you will not take us as your kin. You and the mare Karee would produce fine colts. It would be an honor to have your get riding mine against the enemies of the Kindred."

"It is an honor that cannot be, my friend."

"It seems not. And when we have climbed the bank? My scent will mask yours from men, but not from the prairiecats."

"There is a pond of foul-smelling slime and mud just above the bank. I will smear myself with that. Prairiecats on the far Plains may detect the smell, but they will not recognize the smell of a man."

"And I, of course, must endure the stench until we part company?"

"You don't think you owe that to a battle comrade?"

"One who perhaps saved some of my mares and colts? Of course. But one does not have to enjoy it!" The stallion lowered himself to give Djoh an easier mounting. "Enough talk, Dirt Brother. Let us ride, and may Sun take you safe where you wish to go."

Even better, may Sun tell me where that is, was Djoh's thought as he gripped Mountain Wind's mane.

A full assault by the army of Zhampayunsburk and Blue Springs together could hardly have made much more uproar in the camp than the discovery of Djoh's escape. Lewee's kin were hurling accusations in all directions from the moment of the discovery. Only

Chief Djimmi's direct orders kept them from mounting up and riding out on Djoh's trail as one warrior.

"If he is fleeing to friends, he may be planning to lead you into an ambush, by night, in country those friends know and you do not. If he is fleeing into the wilderness, the bears and the snakes can have him."

The reply to that order stopped just short of outright defiance. It stopped there, because even Lewee's angriest kin knew Djimmi's wisdom in war. They also knew that to split the clan by disobeying their chief in a hostile land would not avenge Lewee. It would be far more likely to give the Dirtmen the chance to avenge Two Tanks.

At dawn, riders did leave the camp, on a trail grown faint but not cold past hope of finding. What might have come of the pursuit had it gone on, Sun only knew. The riders were only half a morning from the camp when they met men of Zhampayunsburk and another town in the north, called New Chikaga. These men fought as if they were the advance guard of a larger force, only retreating when most of Clan Marshul came up and forced them back.

By then, Djoh's trail was lost past finding by any mortal creature. None of the prisoners taken that day spoke of his presence among the enemy, so it began to seem that he had indeed fled into the wilderness.

Lewee's kin still had one arrow in their quiver, though. They demanded that Chief Djimmi mindspeak Karee at the deepest level, to learn if she had done anything to contrive Djoh's escape.

If they could not have Djoh, they would ask for her.

Chief Djimmi knew that he might have to give her to them, if indeed she had helped Djoh. That was a fear he could not conceal, as he sat beside her in his tent while she lay down and tried to open her mind.

He hoped he could better hide another fear. He could not mindspeak someone at the deepest level and keep all of his own shields up. There were things he now knew about Djoh that it would be best no one else knew. They might make some people doubt the chief's honor, and many doubt his wisdom.

The latter, Djimmi was now ready to doubt himself.

"I am ready," Karee said. "Or as ready as I'll ever be. Be warned, though. I won't be a tame sacrifice to those leeches of Lewee's kin. I'll stand against their best warrior in a fair fight and let blood tell, but I won't be butchered."

"No one will ask that. By Sun and Wind and Steel, I swear it."

"Then let us be done with the matter."

Djimmi knew the moment when he was certain Karee had done nothing to aid Djoh's escape. He could not keep a smile off his face.

He also knew the moment when Karee learned his secrets. Her smile might have been a twin of his, at least for a moment. Then the smile faded, her face twisted, and silent tears streamed down her face.

"You knew that he was your son, yet you permitted all that he endured? You would have seen him die without lifting a finger to stop it?"

"I am the chief of Clan Marshul, Karee. The clan's good is what *I* must serve, before my own heart. Or yours. Once Djoh had refused to swear the Kindred oaths and made enemies of Lewee's kin, what was there left for me to do?"

"You should have told him the moment you knew! You were a fool not to! To your face, and nowhere else, I say it. You were a fool!"

"Karee—Sun forgive me, but there is truth in that. I wanted to be certain, so I waited. It seems that I waited too long." He had never spoken with Djoh about Blue Springs, as he'd wished. Why? Probably because he suspected the truth even then, but didn't want to face the responsibility. A new son—and now lost!

For a moment Karee covered her face with her hands. When they fell to her sides again, the warrior had returned.

"It seems you did wait too long. Have we anything else to say to each other today—or any other day?"

"Karee, if you disobey—"

"I care as much about Clan Marshul as anyone not its chief can. I will obey. But I will not forget!"

She stalked out, leaving Chief Djimmi to contemplate his own folly. Perhaps he should see that the whole matter was laid before the Undying Milo, when Clan Marshul returned to the Plains. Certainly Milo laid much importance on finding those with strong mindspeak. He would not be pleased to learn that this escape had prevented a marriage between Djoh and Karee, whose own mindspeak was stronger than most.

Perhaps Milo would suggest that Clan Marshul find a new chief—peacefully, so that its war strength remained intact, but soon. If so, Djimmi knew that he would not quarrel with such a verdict.

Yet one glimmer of hope remained. Would Djoh have any more luck finding a home among the Dirtmen now than he had before? As long as Clan Marshul remained on this side of the Great River, Djoh would know that he had a second home. With a little luck, the wandering Dirt Brother might find his way back to the Kindred.

And perhaps Chief Djimmi Marshul might give luck a little assistance. He certainly owed it to his own honor, to Karee, to the memory of Behtee—and to the son he had let slip through his fingers.

"My son. The next time we speak, you will learn who you are and what you might be. And I will ask your forgiveness, for not telling you this time."

Sacred Sun, grant that there is a next time, and I will go content to Wind.

Aloud and in his mind, Djimmi repeated those words three times. Then he rose and summoned messengers, to bring the warriors together for planning the next battle against the Zhampayunsburkers.

Seek a Clan Sword

by Paul Edwards

PAUL EDWARDS started his writing career off with a bang, by winning a first place award in the Writers of the Future Contest with his fourth short story. He has decided that he wants to be a barbarian when he grows up.

The polished cabochons gleamed in their gold settings, drawing attention to the fat fingers which twirled the stem of the goblet, raising tides of dark wine against the faceted glass. Lord Omphalos, the greatest of the Ehleen merchant princes of the burgeoning city of Santalu, sniffed the small fragrant cloud with a slightly flared right nostril before moistening his tongue with the sharp and musty fluid.

"Yes, yes, the little green statuettes are quite nice. Truly the work of the Ice Dwellers of the far north, you say? Humph."

"Yes, yer lordship. I seen plenty of fakes in my day, but these're the straight goods. From a Horseclans singer they are; the most widely traveled men in the world." Bilijo MacCray, a plains trader, browned and wiry, stood on the patterned marble tiles before his parcels, his simulation of respect flawless. He found it hard to pretend that the fat Ehleen, reclining in his carved walnut chair before the red velvet hangings, had one tittle of importance more than any other bag of money he might slit to empty into his own coffers.

"Hmm, yes, yes, I suppose. But the brocades. If I were to purchase all four bolts, then I suppose we could consider a drop in the price? Say from ten ounces apiece to eight."

Bilijo smiled, looked down. "So you can jack up the price? Well, that's your bizness. I might consider nine, *if* you was to be takin' the barbarian embroidery." He stooped to pick up a saddle blanket, covered with intricate geometric designs favored by the Horseclans. "It's rare to find such a big one. The work is p'tic'ly fine. Lookit these spirals here." He took a step forward. Omphalos' bodyguards frowned, and the clerks around the great man muttered to themselves. Scribes hastily scribbled the changing terms of the negotiations.

Nikomedes, Omphalos' first son, stepped down from the dais to look at the object in Bilijo's hands. He extended his slender, pink fingers to the surface and gently stroked it. "No bloodstains on it, I see."

"What's that supposed to mean?"

"Senhor MacCray," Nikomedes said, "everyone knows that you trade the edge of your sword for at least half of your acquisitions. No one, you may be sure, would wish to sleep beneath the effluvia of a dead person, no matter how pretty the coverlet." A few other Ehleen youngsters tittered.

Bilijo MacCray looked at the fat little dandy. No one would ever deny Omphalos' paternity. Resisting the urge to backhand the nasty youth, and mindful of the sale he had almost concluded, Bilijo smiled, revealing a few broken but clean teeth, and said, "When you've faced the arrows of the barbarians and the claws of the meat-eaters that hunt the plains, then you can talk to me. But until then, sonny, you watch yer manners or I'll give you a public lesson that even yer old man there would approve of. Now git."

"You can't talk that way to me, you ignorant oaf! I'm just as brave as you are!" He turned to look at his father, who merely blinked, hiding his amusement. "Who are you to come into this house and teach *me* manners?"

"I ain't teachin' you nothin'. But if you come to my house, I promise you some teachin' yer not likely to ferget." Bilijo dismissed the boy with a glare and turned back to Omphalos. "Now, back to bizness, yer lordship—"

Nikomedes reddened with embarrassment and rage,

all the more since his younger brother, Ugarios, was grinning from the old man's side. Just because he'd actually raced a horse in the arena, he strutted in the favor of his father. Nikomedes shouted, "How dare you pretend your bravery, bartering for bits of cloth and stealing children in their sleep? I can do at least as well as that!"

Bilijo began to tire of sporting with the rich loudmouth. "Then why don't you go out on the plains and bring back one of their swords, if yer so hot?"

"Well then, I will! I'll bring back one of their sabers and throw it in your face! I swear I will! On my father's name I swear it!"

Instant silence. The legend that the barbarians never parted with their weapons under any circumstances had never been disproved. Omphalos knitted his brows but declined to intervene. Nikomedes was so impulsive! He was hardly fit to take the reins of a business that three generations of work had so laboriously built.

Ugarios glanced at his father, pleased to read the disapproval there. He leaned forward from the dais to goad his older brother. "Yes, Niko! MacCray only lives on the plains, while your Santalu sophistication has certainly made you the better man!"

Nikomedes wheeled around to shout at his brother: "You stay out of this! I don't need to prove myself to you, but I will, by every god in heaven, I swear to you I will!"

"You're rather free with swearing this and swearing that," Ugarios called. "Big words don't mean a thing, brother, without a little action to back them—"

"I don't need you to teach me the value of my word." Nikomedes reached into his vestment and withdrew a small locket. "Before you all, I swear on the grave of my mother that I will go the plains and return with a Horseclans sword, just as I've said."

At these words, Omphalos leaned forward, jowls aquiver, and every voice hushed to hear the old man speak. "You know, if you persist in this, and fail, I could deny you your birthright and cast you out. And I might, if you invoke Amadora's shade for your arrogant boasting!"

"I don't care! I won't suffer the insolence of this ignorant—I won't be insulted in my own home!"

"You bring back a Horseclans saber, sonny, an' you can have this blanket to go with it." Bilijo chuckled, relishing this condescension. "Too bad they never sell 'em. And I wouldn't go tryin' to steal one, neither, not if you value your right hand."

"We'll see about that!" Nikomedes cried, and stormed out of the hall.

"The plains will teach him all the lessons he needs to learn, Father," Ugarios said.

"Hmm. We shall see." Omphalos sipped another small draft of wine. Nikomedes could only fail his oath, to become an object of scorn and ridicule forever. So impulsive. This whole unpleasant affair might not be too inconvenient, after all. "In the meantime, son, pay attention. Now then, MacCray. You mentioned some herbs?"

Within minutes, Nikomedes' purposeful stride had degenerated into fretful stumbling. Should he see to his horse first, or have his provisions packed? What about maps, guides, money, trade goods? Indecision finally paralyzed him. Perhaps it was better to lose face than lose life. Hot with shame, he turned toward Omphalos' reception hall, colliding with Marisue Mac-Cray, the trader's daughter.

"Excuse me," he muttered and started to push past her.

"Niko, you look terrible! What is it?" The young woman touched his arm and brought Nikomedes' impulsive rush to a halt.

He remembered all the funny tales he had regaled the girl with, throwing his money around at the inns and taverns of Santalu, and felt like even more of a fool than before. It was hard to meet the friendship and concern in her eyes.

"Your father goaded me into daring a trip to the plains to bring back a Horseclans saber. I swore an oath on it. No, that's not true. I brought it on myself. I—I don't know if . . ."

"You're very brave, Niko. I always knew it. You'll give my father the comeuppance he needs."

"You'd favor me over your own father?"

Marisue looked away. "He's never been short with food or clothes, or getting me sums and letters, but sometimes, when he's drunk, he . . . I don't want to talk about it." She looked up to meet her friend's curious gaze. "I've been on the plains, too, you know."

Niko's heart started pounding. What kind of a coward am I, he thought, if this little girl, years younger than I, can so blithely speak of her familiarity with the plains? How could I ever face even her if I back out now?

His hands began to shake as he realized that he was truly going to go through with it. He took her arm and steered her away from the reception hall, back through the corridors of the great villa toward the storerooms and offices. Perhaps she noticed the clamminess of his palms; it didn't matter.

"I don't even know where to begin," he said.

She laughed, a comfortingly friendly sound instead of another piercing humiliation. Marisue seemed to have no doubts that Niko, city-bred and soft, could fulfill his impulsive oath. The young man allowed some of her confidence into his heart, and laughed with her. "Let's see," she said. "To begin with, you have to go upriver about three leagues, to a huge rock outcropping on the western side. One of their major trails terminates there. You'll probably meet them in less than a week's ride from the river, if you take the northern fork and head into the hills. . . ."

There was no fanfare at Niko's departure four days later. Only Marisue accompanied him to the stables, where he clumsily hoisted his saddle onto one mare and the pack onto another. He pulled himself up, and taking the halter of the packhorse, entered the streets of Santalu with the young woman at his side. He had never thought that the noise and bustle, the smells of animal excreta and cleaned fish from the river, the smoke of innumerable small fires, and a thousand other vivid sensations of his city's life would ever arouse longing or even affection. He breathed it all in, fearing that it might never comfortably envelop him ever again, but also strangely exhilarated by the real risk of his adventure. Soon they were at the docks, where experienced hands took charge of his beasts and his chattels.

Marisue embraced him. "Remember what I said: the barbarians respect only courage. If they think you're afraid, they'll despise you. And don't be too forward; when it's formal, don't talk to anyone who hasn't talked to you first. You'll win that sword, Niko. I know you will."

He smiled, trying to look as brave as she wanted him to be. "And if they don't want to make the trade?"

"Just don't plan too far in advance. We traders never do." She leaned forward to whisper in his ear. "Be safe, Niko. Come back to me."

He looked at Marisue, saw that her cheeks were a shade flushed, thinking it was only the wind off the river on this cool day. Marisue had always been the little girl he'd dazzled, yet for the past four days, she had been a serious little tutor, teaching him what she could of the plains and the strange brooding ways of the ferocious barbarians, the folk of the Horseclans. Suddenly what had seemed only precocity was revealed as the beginning of her adulthood. Niko saw that Marisue was no longer the wide-eyed girl whose entertainment had been his pleasant duty while their fathers conducted business. He leaned forward to brush her lips with his.

The mate called all hands, and Niko tore himself away to run up the gangplank. With a snap, the sail rippled into its lovely bulging form, and the ferry moved away from the dock, into the slow currents of the river. Niko stayed at the rail, watching Santalu recede into the south, until at last he was no longer able to see the figure of Marisue standing at the water's edge, watching him head into the unknown.

The circle of Clan Coopuh's yurts and tents had been erected to the east of a tall steep hill so that the afternoons would be cool and refreshing. Life had been so calm and uneventful that the elders were joking about the young men's lack of opportunities for experience and plunder, which wasn't funny for young heroes hot for a chance to earn a reputation. Babies were healthy, game was plentiful, the women were all getting along with one another. All the clan's wounds from a few disastrous raids of several years ago had completely healed.

Two hours before dusk, Stripes, a newly mature prairiecat of three years old, returned from the east to the Coopuh encampment. He padded in, past the children throwing spears at targets, past the women busily scraping stretched hides, answering with a self-important low growl all the friendly greetings. He went straight to the Coopuh's tent, and asked permission to enter. Coopuh's welcoming thoughts returned.

Inside, Coopuh was honing his axe as Morguhn, his second wife, gave their infant son the breast. The sight gave the huge feline a moment of longing for his own days as a kitten, the warmth of his littermates, the affectionate coarseness of his mother's tongue, before his importance as a scout of Clan Coopuh reasserted itself.

"We're getting some visitors before nightfall," he said with his mind. "One man and two horses. The two-legs has a strange mind; I couldn't make it out at all."

Coopuh loved Stripes. He knew he had to make this seem as important as possible to keep the youngster's pride from deflating. "Well, then. You've done well to report it. Did you get a look at the two-legs?"

"Yes, sir, and I'm sure he didn't see me. He seems very fearful. I think I would have terrified him, if I'd made my presence known. The four-legs were afraid, too, but I think they were picking up on him, not me."

"Considering how fearsome you are, that's probably true." Stripes purred with contentment at the praise; Morguhn worked at not laughing. "So what did he look like?"

"Black hair, smooth cheeks, fairly pinkish skin. Fat. Not at all like any of the traders we know."

True, thought Coopuh in the private spaces of his mind. Is this the first hint of some kind of territorial challenge to the traders we've learned to deal with?

"Good work. I think it will be safe to receive him here in camp. You're certain there's only one?"

"I doubled back three miles. No men, no fires, no other tracks."

"You are an outstanding cat. Go and eat; and be ready when the two-legs arrives. If he lies about anything you know for certain, we will deal with him appropriately."

"Thank you, Coopuh." Stripes turned to go, giving the baby a brief lick with his rough tongue before departing.

Morguhn chuckled aloud. "That's the most pompous animal I've ever known. You really shouldn't encourage him."

"He's all right," answered Coopuh. "He'll laugh at himself when he gets older. Little Hron certainly seems to enjoy the attentions of his cat brother."

Morguhn shifted the child from one nipple to the other. "Not surprising. He's learning to purr, too."

The sun was no more than a thumb's width above the horizon. Niko's horses, terrified of the cats at first, accepted the soothing cascade of human and animal thoughts and contentedly munched the prairie grass in the company of the free horses of the Clan. Except for an occasional whinny and the gentle crackle of the fire, the only sounds in the camp of Clan Coopuh were the voices of Coopuh, the clan leader, and the visitor, Nikomedes of Santalu. The clanfolk stood in a long silent semicircle around the stranger. Firelight glinted from their jewelry, from their golden hair, and most of all, from their well-worn, polished weapons.

Marisue's admonition burned in Niko's mind: Don't show fear! He answered their question perhaps a bit too loudly.

"Yes. I am Ehleenee."

A few wiry hands moved, came to rest on hilts and hafts.

"As I said, I'm from the Great City, Santalu. I was born there. Until I left to come here, less than a fortnight ago, I had never traveled farther than the immediate environs of the city."

Don't say too much! Niko watched Coopuh in the long pause, not glancing around nervously. Finally the clan leader spoke in the alien accents of his people.

"Did you have relatives in Kehnooryos Ehlas?" Coopuh asked, as twoscore clansmen had shouted in his mind to do.

"The siege of Kehnooryos Ehlas was four generations ago. If I had relatives there, I was never told so. The depravity of the Ehleenee of that city was burned out by the valor of the Horseclans. I am not a soldier, but that does not mean that I am degenerate! I am Ehleenee. I do not apologize for that."

Don't push! Niko desperately wanted to see all of them. Unable to contain himself, he dared a slow look from one end of the line of stern faces to the other. The distrust was universal, but no pair of eyes spoke silent murder in the night. He wondered if they could see the pulse pounding in his neck.

The thoughts of the clan flowed at Coopuh.

"That Ehleeneekos gibberish—I can't understand a word of it!"

"He's afraid and strong at the same time."

"He wants something here, but I can't figure what it is."

"Something about our weapons—well, he's not a soldier, that's for sure. Look at his hands."

None of the faces moved, not even to blink. Niko felt the sweat run on his face. He knew the history of Ehleen pillage, and like all the folk of his generation or his father's, he was ashamed of it. There were no more brothels where chained, kidnapped slaves awaited their repeated degradations in despair.

Coopuh spoke. "What have you brought to offer us?" he asked, and instantly the sharp tension in the air was gone. Clansfolk shifted their feet, a baby began to cry. Niko drew a deep breath. At least he would survive to see the dawn!

"I have knives, and fine steel for your smiths. I also have silver ingots. There is also some cloth, called 'linen,' which is particularly pleasant to wear during the hot months. I have seen your carvings; for the artists who make them, I have some rare woods which grow only a thousand or more leagues to the south."

"No Ehleenee has ever come to barter here before. Perhaps they consider it unclean to deal with us directly."

"I can't speak for anyone but myself. I am here."

A young man about Niko's age left the circle and came forward with a small object in his hand.

Coopuh shouted, "No, Wessli! It is not yet time!"

Wessli turned to face the leader. "He has spoken the truth, clan leader. I see no harm in him. He will be mine for tonight." Before Coopuh could interrupt, the boy raised a small bowl to the Ehleenee's lips. "Drink this!" he said.

Marisue had prepared him for the gesture, but not the flavor. It might have been milk once, but it was sour, sharp, and alcoholic all at once. Niko shuddered and swallowed, handing the small bowl back to the young clansman, who sipped in his turn.

The boy faced his clan. "Nikomedes and I have shared drink. Let him be your guest as well as mine this night." He waited until they began to turn away to their evening tasks, the hostility gone. He turned back to the startled Ehleenee. "I am Wessli of Coopuh," he said, extending his hand to clasp the newcomer's in the customary manner of the city folk.

"Among my friends, I am called Niko," the young trader replied. He responded with a clumsy attempt at the Horseclans greeting gesture, and both of them smiled.

The tent was smoky, and to Niko's discomfort, somewhat crowded. One fellow worked a piece of metal with a burin, two girls silently embroidered a shirt with fine stitches in red and green thread, while a younger couple pursued vigorous erotic games on a huge fur coverlet, most likely a bear pelt.

"So you really can read minds?" Niko asked. "Were you reading mine during the clan meeting?"

Wessli grinned. "We were trying. But you think in your own language. We couldn't figure you out. It's not that way with the traders, though. They've learned better than to pretend anything. They may not like us any more than we like them, but they would never dare cheat us." He pointed to the two girls. "Look at them. They've been talking without a pause since we came in. The one on the left thinks you might—"

The girl looked up with a dangerous frown. There was a pause, and then Wessli said, "If she wants you to know what she thinks, she'll tell you."

"Can't you ever be private?"

"Sure! But it takes effort to keep minds out. Why should we?"

Niko shook his head. The truth of these people was far stranger than the rumors or legends.

"You can't be used to riding this far," Wessli said. "The traders bring whatever we wish to sell across the Great River. So what is it that you want? Why are you here?"

Niko looked at the ground, made spirals in the dirt with his fingers. "I gave an oath that I would prove my courage," he said. "I swore to do it here, among the Horseclans. I could never face my people back in Santalu if I don't do what I said I would."

"Are we as fearsome as that? Well, anyway, you're here, and we can talk, and I'm not cutting your bowels out, am I?" He laughed again. It was a merry sound.

Niko looked up and caught Wessli's eye. "Isn't it true? Don't you torture people that way?"

"I've only seen it once. The man was a traitor. He deserved it." A smile played at the corners of his lips. "We don't disembowel people every day."

"To answer your question, yes, you *are* fearsome. I had a thought I might be killed, standing where I was."

Wessli shook his head. "That was Coopuh testing you. You were never in danger. If anyone had really threatened you, I would have stopped it."

"But why?"

"Because I trust you." Wessli yawned. "There's no rush. Your goods will be safe here. We do not steal from guests. I'm going hunting tomorrow—like to come along?"

Niko grinned. "Yes! I'll have to borrow a bow, though. I didn't bring any weapons."

"I know." He yawned again and reclined on his pile of furs, asleep in a moment.

Niko was looking around, wondering where he was going to sleep, when the girl who had challenged Wessli reached out to him.

"Sleep here," she said with a smile. Her accent was hard to understand. Niko was exhausted. He nodded in gratitude and lay back on an edge of the furs.

That wasn't good enough for the girl. She pulled him to the center of the warm pile, and then tugged off his shirt and pants. "Legs hurt from the long ride? I'll rub them."

It felt immeasurably fine. Niko wondered how Wessli had learned to speak the common parlance of the city so well, while this girl seemed to know only the strange argot of the Horseclans. I'll ask him tomorrow, he thought.

Strong hands rolled him over. "Ahh!" she exclaimed. "Your hair is really black, not paint! Maybe I'll get a black-haired boy, eh?"

Niko swallowed. Marisue hadn't prepared him for this.

The sky was still black when Niko felt a strong hand shake him awake. He opened his eyes upon a strange place where the smells were all strange, and the silence was absolute. For a moment he spun in the disquieting vertigo of not knowing where he was or who these people were until it came to him in a flash—he was days and days away from his home in Santalu, in a tent with half a dozen Horseclans folk! He looked down to see a naked girl curled up next to him. Vaguely he remembered his clothes being removed, but now, for some reason, he was already dressed. He stumbled up.

"Those shoes will never last," Wessli whispered. "Wear these." He handed Niko a pair. The boots were soft and snug, and fit him perfectly. Niko made a note to be sure they were included in the trade.

Outside, Wessli handed Niko a bow. The Ehleenee

pulled it. It was much heavier than it looked, but with extra effort, he brought the string to his cheek. He let it down slowly and nodded. With a full quiver and his eating knife, his armament was complete. Niko noted that Wessli's bow was a bit larger. He also strapped a scabbarded sword to his back. A small axe hung on a loop at his belt, and each boot carried a slender throwing dagger.

They left on foot. "We'd spook every deer for miles if we rode," Wessli said. "By the way, did you have a nice night?"

"Oh, it was great, slept well," Niko answered. "Sorry I had to disappoint the girl, though. I made a vow, uh, six weeks of purity. Perhaps if I return, maybe—"

They were far enough from the camp that Wessli's belly laugh couldn't awaken anyone. "We're not *that* fearsome, are we? What did you think she was going to do? Cut it off?"

Niko stopped to wait for the humor to wear itself out. Finally Wessli's chortling calmed, and Niko said, "I can't figure you people out. I come here to find that Kehnooryos Ehlas is still a freshly bitter memory, and yet you offer me real friendship, and the girl . . . she didn't even tell me her name! I just don't understand."

"There's nothing to understand. No one who treats us fairly need fear us. I know you are honest. Yet you are afraid."

"The traders are afraid of you."

"Certainly. There isn't one of them that wouldn't cheat us if he had the chance. We choose to live here, in freedom, on the plains, instead of cooped up in the choking stink of your cities. Does that mean that we should be easy to cheat? Hardly. They have no chance to rob us. But they earnestly desire it. We can read that too easily in their festering minds. But not in yours." He pointed to the hills. "Let's go. We have an hour of darkness to get to that ridge, if we're going to eat deer tonight!"

They set off at a brisk walk. A four-footed shadow veered away from them and padded back toward the camp.

*   *   *

"Wessli isn't pretending anymore," Stripes said. He and the black-hair are genuinely becoming friends."

Coopuh sipped the strong green tea his first wife had brewed. "The Ehleen is young; he doesn't prejudge us like most of his small-minded people. Perhaps that is what has attracted Wessli's trust." He pondered the peculiar situation in a wordless rapture, waiting for intuition to guide him. The traditions of a thousand encounters between the Horseclans and the Ehleenee collided with an infinity of possibilities which a friendship between Wessli and Niko generated. The history of the past grated against the experience of the present. "I can't force their feelings one way or another," Coopuh finally said. "Stripes, stay in the camp. Give them a chance to succeed in their hunt. They must have a chance to find a common ground of friendship. If the Ehleen learns to respect our ways from his heart, and if he really has the notion to trade, perhaps we may choose to keep MacCray and his ilk out of our dealings altogether."

Stripes growled quietly, vaguely unsure about the clan leader's decision. But Wessli could take care of himself. The soft little Ehleenee with no calluses on his body could not possibly be a threat to even a Horseclans child, let alone a scion of Coopuh grown adult-tall.

With a curse, Bilijo MacCray snapped the Dirtman seeing glass shut. The smartmouth Ehleen brat had actually lived through the night! Now the little bastard was going out with one of 'em—to hunt! Damn! Now there was no way to claim all that steel and silver for his own. The little moron had no idea what it was worth; he'd give all that treasure away to those thieving killers. Damn!

There weren't no way to sneak aboard the ferry, even if I'd known, he thought. The little bitch thinks he likes her, the stupid slut. Maybe my reddening all four o' her cheeks'll give her something to think about. A gold and two silvers to get across! I ain't taken the full fare out o' her hide yet, that's fer sure. And how'd he ride so fast on that fat arse of his? It couldn't've been luck to find 'em without wanderin' around out here for a few months. That bigmouth bitch must've told him! Told him our secrets! Damn! I'll show that little whore what that big mouth is for, soon's I get back to Santalu!

He led the horse two miles away, to the far side of the next ridge, and hobbled it there, grinning that all the noise had probably driven whatever game there was right into their laps. They'd be so busy with their kills that they'd never notice him coming. His mouth was quite calm; he was sure those killer lions the clans had trained were nowhere around. Too bad he couldn't use a bow, since he was a great shot, but an unguarded Horseclans boy was too much of a prize. He'd kept the manacles at his belt oiled for years, waiting for an opportunity like this. His bitch daughter and the Ehleen pig might rob him blind, but why pass up the opportunities to recoup that destiny provides?

The sun came up. Bilijo MacCray, hidden in a dense thicket, shielded the long tube in which the seeing glass was mounted from an accidental telltale glare and searched the hills a half mile away. He was a patient man when he had to be. In an hour he located their faces, and in a moment he had memorized the spot with his bare eyes. The sun moved its slow way across the sky, and the shadows twisted under him.

The game trail was apparently well traveled, but Niko had had the only good shot all day, and missed. The sun had gone down before they decided to stop their vigilance.

"There's more deer out here than this," Wessli said. "This is the first day I've seen less than ten right here at this spot."

"We've got enough food for at least one more day."

"I was thinking the same thing."

"Sure," said Niko, "but how was I to know that?" They laughed together.

It wasn't long before they had a little fire and some warm tea. Niko told his new friend of life in the great city of Santalu, which might have been exciting once, but here in the wilderness, the hectic busyness of it all

seemed like so much unpleasant raucous noise. Far
more interesting were the tales of Horseclans history
which Wessli shared, the wars with the Dirtmen over
the theft of the prairie, the ancient rivalry with the
Ehleenee, the great heroes of the clans: Blind Hari,
whose songs had united them, and Milo of Morai, the
God Who Walks Among Them, even to this day.
Their tales meandered from the great legends to each
one's everyday events, which profoundly fascinated
the other. Most of all, Niko and Wessli enjoyed the
strange and joyous experience of rapport with a creature from another world. The stories totally absorbed
both teller and listener, so that neither of them heard
the faint, almost silent approach of the two-leg preda-
tor. Finally sleep crept up, and Niko dozed off, pon-
dering the incredibly good fortune to have met this
"barbarian" who had not only offered friendship but
had taught him how little absolute value his "civilized"
way of life really had.

Only a few embers still glowed as darkness approached. The two young men could be easily distinguished by the color of their hair. A powerful fist
gripped the short iron bludgeon more tightly.

It was a sharp, unnatural sound, something heavy
falling at his feet. Wessli instantly sat up and groped
for his knife. Then his vision was filled with a bright
light as intense pain exploded in the right side of his
head.

Niko awoke to see a big man standing over the limp
body of his friend. He scrambled to his feet, hearing
the ominous metallic clatter of chain and locks. No
weapons! He backed away, but the big man threw his
prize to the ground and sprang at him, clutching his
shirt in a strong fist. Something sharp touched his
throat.

"Havin' a nice time with yer new little friend? Didn'
expect to see me out here, didja?"

Niko stammered, finally found words. "Bilijo Mac-
Cray," he said. "You didn't believe I'd actually come
out here like I promised."

"I don't give a shit whether you fulfill yer oath er
not! But you ain't comin' out here, tradin' with these

horsefuckers, cuttin' me out! And you ain't pryin' any more o' my trade secrets outa my girl, hear?"

"You know I'd never come out here more than once!"

"Shuddup." In a single movement he released the shirt, drew back his fist, punched Niko squarely in the face. He looked at the ground, where the Ehleen boy clutched at his bleeding nose.

"I ought to kill you, but you ain't worth the trouble. This here barbarian kid is *mine*, hear? I figure a big one like this'll go for eighty, mebbe even a hundred golds in them Eh-leen pig-cities back east. Then I ain't never comin' back. So I ain't got no problem 'bout leavin' you fer cat food if you don't do what yer told. So get up!" He kicked Niko in the ribs. "Get that blanket there an' pile all the barbarian's stuff in it. Now! And when yer done with that, kid, you can go on back to that barbarian camp and tell 'em what's happened, an' they'll have you dancing on a sharp stick up yer hole so fast yer head'll spin!"

Niko shook helplessly before the vicious power of the man, unable to conceive of stopping him. Terrified, he watched for a moment as Bilijo bent over the limp body and began wrapping a stout rope around his legs. Then he slowly began to pile the small weapons and clan fetishes which Wessli had brought on the small cloak.

Something made him look up, and in the dim red glow of the embers he saw Wessli's eyes. Bilijo was busy with his victim's ankles, and didn't see the clan boy signal desperately. The sword! Niko saw in the staring eyes. Take the sword!

I'm no fighter! Niko's mind screamed. I've never even held a sword in my hands! But there was no time if he was to help his friend. His hands reached into the dark, finding the hilt of Wessli's weapon without seeing or searching. The blade slid from the scabbard without a sound.

"Whatcha doin', ya Ehleen punk? Get to work!" the big man hollered over his shoulder.

He'll see me in a second! I can't!

In a single movement, Niko gripped the hilt in two hands, lifted it over his head, and brought it down where Bilijo's neck should have been. The keen edge grated against the skull, and Bilijo leaped up with a scream.

It was the moment Wessli needed to pull himself to his feet, as Bilijo, with a roar of rage, whirled on Niko.

The boy stumbled back, tripped over a root, and landed on his back. The trader snatched a dagger from his belt and with a gigantic, hungry grin went forward.

Something massive punched his back, and, losing his balance, he pitched forward. Niko jerked the sword up, but despite all his strength, Bilijo's weight slammed the pommel hard against his chest. The big man's fall seemed to take four or five seconds as he emitted a long groan. The knife fell against Niko's shoulder, pushed into the flesh by Bilijo's flaccid bulk. Niko cried out as his attacker twitched and gulped; a torrent of steaming blood poured out of Bilijo's mouth to splash in his victim's face and run into the grass and stones of the forest floor, where its shine faded into huge clots.

Absolute silence returned. Niko felt the weight of Bilijo MacCray on top of him, crushing the hilt of Wessli's sword into his breastbone. There was sharp pain in his shoulder, warm gore all over his face and chest. Silence.

"Niko, Niko! Are you all right?"

"I think so. I can't move."

"You've got to! I'm tied up!"

It took a few moments, but at last Niko was able to get his arms beneath Bilijo and push him off. He pulled himself to his feet, ignoring his wound where the knife had fallen free, and looked at the man who had tried to kill him.

Two feet of reddened steel protruded from the center of Bilijo MacCray's back.

A slash of a knife and Wessli's bonds were gone. A search of the body turned up the keys to the manacles.

Wessli stretched himself, rubbed the purple swelling on the side of his head. "You saved my life," he said.

Niko shook his head. It was a little hard to breathe. "*You* saved *my* life. I could never have beaten him if you hadn't told me to take up your sword, if you hadn't hit him when he was coming at me."

"But you did it. If it wasn't for you, he would have sold me at Santalu. Your arm!"

The blood had trickled to the elbow. In a flash Wessli had pressed it and bound it. In a moment he had the fire built up, and they lay beside it until the sun came. Niko seemed much weaker, so Wessli wrapped their belongings and helped his friend back down the path until the messages from his mind were heard by the horses, who raced along the trails to find them and carry them home.

"I should have followed them. I deserve to be expelled from the clan."

Coopuh looked at the flattened ears of the huge feline. He hadn't eaten in four days; the Clan leader could almost see the ribs furrowing his pelt. "Stripes, for the last time, *I* told you to stay! There's no fault, no blame. I tell you now, you must eat. If not, I'll have Yellow Fang try to convince you."

"You know I would never lift claw against the cat chief."

"Of course." He waited for the huge animal to slink away before turning back to the tent where the Ehleen boy was at last regaining his strength.

The wound had reddened and drained, and now the fever that had left him weak and confused for two days had abated. His appetite had increased; it was clear that he would survive. Coopuh looked down at the pale young man, his black hair matted. Lana, the girl who had teased him a week ago, cleaned the stale sweat from his face with a cool cloth.

"You look awake."

Niko lifted his eyelids, an effort. "I can think clearly, today—I think." He tried to prop himself up on one elbow. "They've told me I was raving for a few days."

"The fever disturbed you, but all that is over." Coopuh sat on the ground. "We all owe you a debt of gratitude. Wessli made it clear that your actions prevented him from a life in slavery."

The events had lasted for only a minute or two, so long ago. Niko tried to remember the blurred details. "He is too modest. Bound hand and foot, he attacked the slaver, threw him upon the sword. Did he tell you that?"

"Yes." He waited, but Niko couldn't think of anything to say. "You have already become well known. The leaders of two other clans have sent small gifts, and the promise of friendship here in our lands. That alone is worth more than any gold. And someday you will hear the song which the bards have already made in your honor."

"I am not a trader," Niko said slowly. "Or at least, this is my first attempt at it. All I ask of you is a fair bargain when we each bring out our wares."

"If you knew us better, you would be able to take that for granted. But you don't—therefore there is no offense given or taken. It shall be as you request." The clan leader rose and left the tent.

"Is he always so formal?" Niko asked.

Lana dipped the cloth in a bowl of water and twisted it dry. "Oh, no," she said, laying it against his head. "Only with people he respects."

Two days later, Clan Coopuh gathered at the center of the camp as Nikomedes of Santalu unstrapped the parcels which he had brought and spread the contents out. The men and women came forward to lift the knives in their hands and feel the balance, run their fingers over the finely woven stuff, lift the silver trinkets to the sun and see them shine. After a while they began to bring their own artistry to show: intricate embroideries of a thousand complex interlocking spirals, similar designs worked in thin, supple leathers, odd totemic amulets of feathers and semiprecious stones.

They brought no metalwork of their own. Niko looked at some of the pieces and began to haggle, seeing the nature of the game and enjoying it completely. But the one thing he craved was not there.

Coopuh of Clan Coopuh walked through the gathering, watching Niko conduct himself with far more respect for the clansfolk than any other trader. But it was clear that some dissatisfaction disturbed him. He had made a few trades for small carvings, but always his eyes roamed over the edges of the small crowd, looking for new faces bearing . . . what? Coopuh came up to the young Ehleen, proud of the fine work which his clan had brought to trade.

"Nikomedes, do not our artists produce things of great beauty?"

"Indeed, Clan Leader. I think perhaps you have asked your folk to bring their finest because of the incident Wessli and I shared. The traders my father deals with never bring pieces of such a quality."

Coopuh laughed. "Perhaps they sold what they had bought elsewhere, or kept the choicest pieces for themselves. But you are displeased in some way. What is it?"

"Are you reading my mind?"

"No, Nikomedes. Among us, it is a crass lack of manners to invade anyone that way without permission. No, I need no mindspeaking to read your face."

Niko looked at the man his stern features opaque to his empathy. They trust me without reservation, Niko thought, but who knows how rapidly their affections change? But I could never steal one. I'll have to ask for it.

"There is an object of Horseclans make that no one has brought to trade. I seek a Horseclans saber. I'll be generous for it. I have extra silver just for that one trade."

The gist of the conversation, impossible not to overhear, spread through the clanfolk. Talk ceased. The weapons of the Horseclans were beyond price. None had ever been sold beyond the Confederation of Clans; none had ever been seen in the hands of the city folk.

"You ask too much!" Coopuh said, his voice rising in a controlled shout. "We have cleaved Ehleenee blades before, but never has the steel of the clans shattered in battle. No, my new Ehleen friend. You shall take no Horseclans weapons with you to Santalu!"

Instantly, the warmth of the past week was frozen in

the wave of hostility that seemed no less than when he had first arrived. But there was no backing down now.

"Clan Leader, surely you cannot believe that I, who rescued your son, could ever lift a sword against Clan Coopuh, or any of the clans! My blood is Ehleen, but my honor is my own! And the lessons of my experiences here, as well!"

"Just so. We have learned that we cannot rely upon the honor of the Ehleen. And who knows what twisted lessons your people may have learned from Kehnooryos Ehlas, or a score of other battles where Ehleenee fell to fertilize the riches of the prairie? You may complete your trading, Nikomedes. Then you must depart, before thoughts of theft enter your head, if they have not already."

Niko looked around him at the universal disapproval. The pleasant spirit which had infused the gathering was gone, and with it, any chance to fulfill his oath.

A prairiecat growled behind them. Coopuh and Niko turned to see Wessli come forward, with Stripes at his side.

"Father," Wessli said, "Nikomedes proved himself to me in a duel to the death. Did we not discuss his brotherhood with the clan the night of our return?"

"That means nothing. You know full well that we decided not to—"

"My friend gave a sworn oath to his father and clan at Santalu. Here is an honorable way for him to fulfill it, with a worthy exchange. The steel he brings is well wrought. His silver is pure."

Coopuh became more obstinate the more he was pushed. "No, by Sun and Wind, I have made my decision! The swords of the Horseclans will never be sold!"

"I won't be dishonored by my war brother's failure!" Wessli shouted. He tugged at his belt, and the sword he had brought on the hunting trip fell into his hands. "Here, Niko! This is a gift! A free gift of Wessli of Coopuh!"

Niko caught it, a scabbard of intricately tooled leather, bound with brass. The saber had a complex cup to protect the hand, bands of twisted wire ham-

mered into a curved teardrop of steel. A beautiful,
and undoubtedly old, weapon.

"Return that at once," Coopuh said, and stepped
forward.

With a growl, the prairiecat was there. "No, Coopuh,"
the feline thought came. "Wessli named him war brother,
gifted him with weapons. The two-legs did what this
cat should have done, but didn't. Am I not Wessli's
war brother? Then I cannot let you retrieve what is
not yours, though you expel me from Clan Coopuh."

The great beast sat, twitching his tail, staring into
Coopuh's eyes. Niko knew that the man and the beast
must be exchanging thoughts, but in the silence, strain-
ing to perceive this mystery, unable to take his eyes
off the animal, he could not discern a single interior
clue to the debate which was taking place between the
two strong wills.

At long last the clan leader, Coopuh of Clan Coopuh,
turned to Niko and said, "So be it." Then he left the
gathering.

Wessli came to Niko with a big smile. "He'll get
over it," Wessli said. "Sometimes it's necessary to
make new traditions."

"This is a costly thing," Niko said. "You must let me
give you—"

"No, nothing!" There was a flash of anger. "Niko,
that sword is a gift. You saved my life. How can I
measure my life against a piece of metal, and deny it
to you?"

'But you must have a sword to defend the clans!"
Niko cried. "You told me that yourself!"

His war brother grinned. "I have an axe, too. Don't
worry about me, Niko. I can always earn another
sword. But, just between you and me, how many
chances will you have to do that?"

Niko stepped back, and bowed. "Thank you, Wessli.
I promise you that I will never be parted from this
sword, and that when I die, it shall be returned to the
Horseclans." He strapped it around his waist. The
length of it was just right and to wear it put a special
spring in his step. He grinned back at Wessli, and then
a clanswoman called his name to inquire about a heavy

silver buckle. With a confident air, Nikomedes the Trader took the bone carving she offered into his hands, and began to haggle.

There was no danger on the return to the river. A huge dark-striped prairiecat padding along at his side, Niko rode, leading his pack animal, upon which were heaped his treasures and his prize. There was no need to hunt, for the feline carried kills back every night. Niko talked out loud to it, but there was no telling whether the animal understood him or not. Days passed uneventfully until at last the Great River appeared. The adventure in the plains was done. Niko dismounted and reached out to scratch the huge cat's ears, which always provoked a loud rumbling purr.

"Stripes, I've been thinking about our friend. He's my war brother, as much as I'm his. I can't let a war brother face the life you choose to lead without a weapon. So here, take this." He reached to his waist and untied a pouch of coins. "Take this back to the clan, and when you next meet a swordsmith who can do work as good as this," he said, patting the saber at his hip, "buy it for him, and give it as a gift. Do you understand?" He bent down and held the fur of the great cat's cheeks in his hands. "Can you understand?"

Stripes leaned back and gave a roar which almost knocked Niko off his feet. Then he stood up, scraped his tongue over the boy's face, picked up the pouch in his teeth, and turned to trot off to the west. His heavy footsteps and the clink of gold disappeared into the brush.

Less than a mile to the south loomed the rock outcropping to which the ferries sailed. Niko waited only two days until the next arrived. Three other men showed up. They all eyed the exotic blade hanging from the boy's belt, and left him alone.

A singer stopped with half a chord unstrummed as Nikomedes walked into the reception hall. Although he had only been gone for a fortnight, he was completely transformed. Where once he had been occasionally interesting, now he was fascinating; conversations stopped as the fashionable courtiers discovered his presence, from which they could not pull away their gaze. The cheery insolence was gone, replaced by a quiet, careful attention to everything that swirled around him. His skin, freshly burnished by the sun and wind, glowed with a quality of health he had never before known. A servant carried an enormous bundle behind him, set it down in the center of the floor, and departed. All eyes were fixed upon him, but the most suspicious of those were Ugarios'.

"I found the Horseclans. I have fulfilled my oath."

"Why, then," said Ugarios genially, "you must be dead. No one has ever taken one of their weapons and lived." A few people tittered. "Too bad Senhor MacCray isn't here for his comeuppance."

Niko waited until the laughers had become too uncomfortable with their ill humor and silence had returned. "I brought trading stock and did rather well. For example, this." He reached into the sack to retrieve a hunting horn. The rim was a filigree of silver, and the horn itself was covered with geometric carving. Omphalos, on his dais, sat forward for the first time since Niko had entered to examine the object. He knew at first glance that he had never seen its match.

"Extraordinary, yes. This is your best piece?"

"I have others." He reached far into the bag and brought strings of lapis beads, enormous quartz crystals, an embroidered cloth so large that no fewer than three men were required to hold it up for display.

Omphalos looked on his son with a new respect. His agents had told him how much the boy had spent on his adventure. He had better than tripled his investment! Without a middleman! Ugarios saw the light in the old man's eyes and leaped up.

"So enormous luck has befallen you! You still haven't shown us the sword! Let's see how you've fulfilled your oath!"

Niko smiled. "You shouldn't taunt me, brother." He reached into the sack and retrieved the scabbard. There was a gasp from everyone. Not only was the work magnificent, but it was old, antique even. The brass fittings shone like golden mirrors, and the leather, originally brown, now had a greenish patina from many decades, if not more than a century, of hard use. A swirl of patterned steel enveloped a grip which had been carved to fit the fingers of the wielder. Niko buckled it around his waist, where everyone noticed how well it fit, as if it had been made for him. With his eyes on Ugarios, Niko's right hand instinctively found the hilt and drew the blade. It glowed from loving polishing. No razor was more sharp.

"I didn't buy it, Ugarios. You are right; these are not for sale. I saved a young man's life, and he gave this to me."

"You? Save someone's life? How?"

"It isn't a complicated story. We were hunting. A murdering slaver stalked us in the night, and tried to take us. I killed him."

The casualness of the remark frightened some of the girls, who sucked in their breath and clung to their swains. Ugarios swallowed.

"Of course, I couldn't expect you to believe me. So I brought back a bit of evidence to convince you." He reached into the sack until he found his prize. It weighed around ten pounds and stank of blood and salt, but no one would challenge the grinning head which Niko lifted by the hair, and, holding at arm's length, displayed to all the stunned people in Omphalos' reception hall.

"If you have any doubts, ask Bilijo MacCray."

With a heave of his shoulders, he tossed it at Ugarios. Instinctively the young man put out his hands to catch it. His spine chilled as one hand touched the matted hair, and the other sank into the red mush in the center of Bilijo MacCray's neck. With a squeak of alarm, he dropped the trophy. The skull clacked on the marble, bounced once at Ugarios' feet, and turned on a reddish smear to look up with dull, half-lidded eyes and a tight, empty grimace.

Desperately wishing that the nasty putrescence would simply evaporate from his hands, Ugarios stared frantically around the hall for support, but every face sneered back with only amusement and mockery. The

churning in his stomach strangled any possibility of
wit. With a look of rage at Niko, Ugarios rushed from
the room. The sounds of retching came from the hallway, where Ugarios could not have missed the derisive
laughter which followed him out.

"My boy," Lord Omphalos said, "I believe I've
misjudged you. You've done a grand job. Hmm, yes,
grand."

"Thank you, Father." He bowed. "But if you will
excuse me, I have a visit I have to make."

"Ahh, yes, I imagine that you do. She should hear
of it from you first, yes. Well, off you go. But be here
in the morning," Omphalos called after his son. "I'm
meeting with the Civil Affairs Committee, and it's
about time you began participating! Niko! Niko?"

They sat on a hillock overlooking the docks. Occasional faint shouts of men pulling massive ropes or
lifting heavy cargo came to them, but mostly it was the
sound of the birds and the smell of the Great River
itself, moist and inviting.

Marisue looked up at him, a faint greenish echo of a
bruise on her left cheek. There were tears in her eyes.
"I don't know what to think, Niko. I hated him! And
yet I sort of miss him, too. But I could never hate
you!" She leaned against him, for the comfort of his
embrace. "He hurt me so much! Hold me, Niko!"

He wrapped his arms around her. "I wouldn't have
lived if it weren't for my war brother," Niko said.
"And I never would have thought I'd be able to kill a
man and feel at peace about it. Especially your father."

"My feelings . . . It's almost as though I feel them
because I'm supposed to. I hate him! The way he
touched me . . ." She clung to him, shuddered. "Thank
you!" she whispered over and over. "I'm free, free!
Oh, Niko!"

Niko held her as she cried out all the secret horrors
of her life. Finally he lifted her chin and kissed her
gently. "All that is over," he said. "Soon you'll have
to begin to think about the future. The plains . . . the
city. Dear Marisue. You're so young to have to face
such decisions."

"And what about you?" Marisue asked. "Can you go back to eating delicate little foods and plotting little intrigues against your brother all day? A whole life of wandering up and down the familiar streets of Santalu?"

"I thought about it every mile of the journey from Clan Coopuh to the river," Niko said. "I love Santalu. I never thought I'd miss this city until I boarded the ferry. But the prairie, the beauty of it, the freedom . . . Wessli gave me this sword, but I don't know the first thing about using it. There aren't any fighters like the Horseclans folk, but I guess you know that better than I do. You've lived on the plains, and I haven't. Maybe it's time for me to turn my life around. I don't really want to turn into Omphalos. I think I'd fall on this sword before I turned into a fat, officious bore."

She sat up suddenly with a big sunny smile. "You mean you're going back? Back to the clans?"

"Why not? They've as much as invited me, and they made it clear how much they want to learn about Ehleen life. And Sun and Wind know how much I need to learn about . . . well, about everything."

Marisue laughed, and kissed him on his lips. "They're not the only ones who can teach you about the prairie, you know!"

It took a few seconds for him to realize what she was suggesting. Then, in a single moment, all his plans became complete, and he realized the perfection of his life.

The Fear-Beast

by Sharon Green

They made camp early that day, finding the meadow beside the small woods and stream too pleasant to bypass. They were many days beyond the city of *Komees* Sahm of Cambehl, and not since they had left had they had so attractive a campsite.

Lisah, once of the Cambehls and now of the Dunkahns, would have been willing to camp in a tree as long as Bryahn, her new husband, was there beside her, but even she was forced to admit the meadow was a good deal more attractive than a tree would have been. Not that the tree would have failed to be more entertaining, especially with Bryahn there—at least until they fell out of it. So far Lisah had found nothing Bryahn considered not worth the attempting, most especially where she was concerned, and her newly married life had been filled with more laughter than undying declarations of fragile feelings, more lovemaking than sighs and vows of unending devotion. She had been told by one of her serving women before the wedding that an active woman must resign herself to the boredom of marriage, but so far there had *been* no boredom. If Bryahn continued on the way he had been going, there never would be.

"My new two-legs brother is extremely strange, sister," White Feet bespoke her as she dismounted, the warhorse's confusion with Lisah's satisfaction clear in the thought. "Once he asked me if I and the rest of our city were a dream of his, meant to dissolve and disappear when he awoke. Or perhaps you and he were not truly wed, that you were another's and would never be his. Does he know nothing of what is and is not?"

"I think perhaps he feels as I do," Lisah answered the roan mare with a laugh and a pat before she began unsaddling her. "To marry because of duty and then find the marriage a greater delight than freedom ever was is not something we two-legs expect. I, too, sometimes wonder if I shall awaken to find him no more than a dream of my own devising, a dream never to be recaptured once the mists of sleep are gone. He seems far too good to be of flesh and blood, far better than what I deserve."

"Should *I* be asked, I would say my sister is far better than what *he* deserves," White Feet returned with a snort, waiting for the bridle to be removed from her before she tossed her head. "I find him adequate as far as two-legs go and his mindspeak is a good deal clearer than that of most others, but my sister remains the best two-legs of my acquaintance."

The girl smiled even as she let the roan mare feel her love and gratitude, and then she stood watching as the warhorse began moving away to graze. They had been sisters ever since the mare had been a gangly filly, and she valued the bond between them almost as much as what she'd found with Bryahn. She'd never imagined it would be possible to be closer to a human than to her beloved war destrier, but one human had shown her how wrong she had been.

"At least I think he's human," she murmured to herself with a grin hidden from those who moved around building the camp. Bryahn had spent so much time with cat brothers and sisters that at times his thoughts were more like those of a prairiecat than a man, a circumstance that made him *more* attractive for Lisah rather than less. She brushed at the road dust which had settled on her leathers, wondering what her life would have been like if she had managed to ride away from the marriage her father had arranged for her with Bryahn, who was now heir to his father, *Thokeeks* Hwill of Dunkahn. She was happier with Bryahn than she would have been without him, but what sort of happiness would she have found if she *had* managed to join her company?

Lisah sighed as she looked around at those who

were busily putting together the night camp, attempting to smooth over the one ripple in the stream of delight she had been bathing in. She had funded the raising of a new company, the Crimson Cat Company, so that she herself might join it and finally put to use the war skills she had spent so many years acquiring. All those men of their escort, Bryahn himself and his father as well, *all* of them knew the pleasure and glory of battle, a knowledge which seemed destined to evade her forever. The brief skirmish she had taken part in when Bryahn, his father, Bili of Morguhn, and their escort had been attacked leaving her father's city had only whetted her appetite for battle, not satisfied it. It was a small unhappiness which was most often buried beneath the weight of pleasure and satisfaction, and yet buried was not the same as satisfied or seen to—

"Women are truly marvelous," a voice said from behind her, a now familiar voice filled with the also familiar lightness of teasing. "A man seeing those engaged in the setting up of camp would feel constrained to join in the efforts himself. Only a woman can stand about inspecting the doings of others and feel nothing of a need to make herself useful."

"Proving women are considerably more talented than men," Lisah said with smug satisfaction as she turned to face Bryahn, her grin a full match to his. "We suffer seeing others laboring away without our help, but have the strength to bear the suffering without complaint. And how much has my noble husband contributed to the general effort he finds so irresistible?"

"No disrespect from you, wife," he growled as he put his arms around her, his mock anger making her laugh. "Because of my direction our tent is nearly up, and once it is you may have the honor of helping me out of this plate. My father has agreed that first use of the stream should be yours, which means I get to go with you. Having a wife is turning out to be handier than I thought it would be."

By then his grin had returned, and Lisah laughed again at the way he held her. Encased in heavy steel plate, Bryahn was free to do no more than run his hands over her, but once that plate was off—

"The honor certainly *will* be mine," she said, reaching a finger up to run it around his ear. "I wonder, though, how long it will take me to complete the task. A woman who has so much of the talent allowing her to merely stand and watch others must surely be on the slow side. . . ."

"She had better not be," Bryahn said with the growl returned when her voice trailed insinuatingly off, his gray eyes looking down at her in a very stern and direct way. "It's become my habit to look forward to camping for the night, merely to be out of my armor, you understand, and a delay would be entirely unacceptable. If you wore your chain instead of having it rolled up on one of the pack mules, you would surely understand the point a bit more thoroughly."

"Why, I believe you're right," the girl said with very thick surprised understanding, her widened blue eyes looking up at him in a suspicious way. "Wearing my mail would surely bring the point home, so the answer to the difficulty is clear. From now on my chain will be worn."

"Lisah, you are a devious, plotting woman, and I refuse to allow that in my wife," Bryahn said to her hearty satisfaction, regretting the need to disappoint her, but nevertheless speaking firmly and surely. "My father was right in his suggestion that you accustom yourself to your new place in life as quickly as possible, and for that reason your chain is packed rather than worn. By rights your sword should be with the chain, and perhaps from now on it would be best if it were. A wife and mother has no need of the trappings of war."

"I may be a wife, but I'm not yet a mother," the girl answered, the happiness gone from her face as she stepped back out of his loosened embrace. "This sword is *mine*, and anyone who wishes to take it is free to make the attempt. Perhaps then I'll no longer be a wife either."

Bryahn saw the hardness in the blue eyes looking up at him, and he sighed, realizing they were in the midst of their first serious argument. His Lisah was no more joking about her refusal to give up her sword than he would have been, but the attitude was totally unreasonable! He was a man and an experienced fighter, while she was a girl who might already be with child. He could see she had failed to consider that, most likely had not even thought about it, the innocence of a girl raised among men keeping her from the consideration. Best he soothe her quickly, and later make her see the wisdom in his decision.

"Ah, but for now you remain a wife," he said with an attempt at a grin and a sly wink, reaching for her again. "First we'll see to this plate, and then we'll see how private the area around the stream might be. I haven't yet caught you in a stream . . ."

"I don't care to be caught just now," she returned stiffly, stepping back away from his reaching arms. "As for your plate, let your father help you with it. A man with so large an amount of good advice must surely have other talents as well, many more than a lowly female. No need to settle for inexperienced help when such expertise is available."

With that she turned her back and marched away, leaving behind a man filled full with exasperation. Bryahn watched her go with a silent growl in his throat, shook his head, then turned toward the tent that had been erected for him. He would find other help to doff his armor, and then he would follow her and make another attempt to talk sense into that empty female head.

Lisah kept going until she was well away from the camp, the woods around the stream doing well in screening her from view. When there were no longer eyes on her she began making her way around the stream to the far side, and from there into the thickest brush she could find. Once in the middle of the bushes she paused to look around, then she settled herself on thin grass and twigs without noticing what it was she sat on. There were other, more important things needing her attention, and the first and foremost of them was Bryahn.

"I think it's safe to say the dream has ended," she muttered as she picked up a twig to toy with, her head down as she spoke to the twig. "If he thinks I'll obey him, *he's* the one still dreaming, but he has a rude awakening ahead. When he and his father give up their swords, then I'll give up mine."

She could almost see *Thoheeks* Hwill, Bryahn's sire, being told he must give up his sword so that she might be made to give up hers. The roaring and fury would be so great that the entire woods would be felled, and the picture evoked brought an evil grin to her. She could see she'd been wrong in allowing her chain to be taken, an error which would be corrected the very next day. The armor was *hers*, made and fitted to and for her, and come the next appearance of Sacred Sun she would reclaim it no matter who objected.

No matter who. The girl leaned down to her left elbow, all amusement gone. The one certain to object most strongly would be Bryahn, for although the original suggestion had been his sire's, the decision to see it done had been his. He had kissed away her attempted arguments, tickled her into laughter and lovemaking, and after that the point had no longer seemed important. It was then the terrible thought came to her, one that brought her pain and disillusionment, one she had no wish to consider despite her anger. It couldn't be, it simply couldn't be . . . !

"Why are you distressed, sister?" The question came through mindspeak, the thought-set one Lisah wasn't fully familiar with. "My brother is disturbed as well, which he has not been for quite some time. Wind Whisper would offer her aid."

Lisah looked up to see the prairiecat, staring at her through the bushes not five feet away. They two had exchanged thoughts before a time or two, but the girl had been so wrapped up in the man who was her husband that she'd had little time for anything else. Under other circumstances she would have gone out of her way to become acquainted with the prairiecat, but because of Bryahn . . .

"Your brother is what distresses me," the girl answered by mindspeak, finding it impossible to return the stare of those large yellow eyes. "It has come to me that the happiness I found with him was deliberate

on his part, not truly felt by him but used to make me
obey his wishes. If I find such a terrible thing to be
true, I will never speak to him again."

"The happiness you mention is not easily understood by this cat," Wind Whisper replied, settling
down in the bushes to increase her comfort. "My
brother has been filled with great satisfaction since
taking you for his mate, the satisfaction one would
find after a successful hunt followed by the drinking of
warm blood. Is it this sort of satisfaction which dis-
turbs you?"

"I have never known that sort of satisfaction," Lisah
replied, feeling even more miserable than she had.
"Your brother has no wish for me to know it, just as
he most likely feels no true love for me. I was a fool to
believe I would find happiness where others find only
duty, perfection where others find no more than flawed
hopes. I have given up all to gain nothing, and now
find myself in possession of that nothing. Perhaps Sacred Sun will take pity on me, and I will quickly go to
Wind."

The big, brownish-gray prairiecat watched in puzzle-
ment as the girl buried her face in her arms, feeling
the tears roll from mind to eyes. It was beyond Wind
Whisper why the two-legs would behave so, as though
she had displeased her mate and would soon receive a
sound cuffing. Wind Whisper's brother was far from
displeased, and would likely not cuff the two-legs female in any event. When he fought his thoughts were
much like those of a cat, yet when he played his
doings were far gentler. Best would be to leave the
odd two-legs female undisturbed till her brother came,
and then allow him to see to the matter. Till then
Wind Whisper would guard his mate, for she had
picked up strange scents in those woods and her brother's mate seemed not of a mind to guard herself.

Bryahn rebuckled his swordbelt about his hips and
then stretched hard, deliberately readjusting his balance to compensate for the lack of armor. Most of his
battles had been fought in full plate, but when he and
Iron Claws, Wind Whisper's sire, had ridden together

for a time, armor would have been more of an encumberance than an aid.

Just as the plate was an encumberance where Lisah was concerned, for most of the time at any rate. He sighed as he considered the words that had passed between them, harsh words he should never have allowed to be spoken. His bride was young and delicate, sensitive despite the boiled-leather exterior she most preferred showing, in need of the protection he was so delighted to give. He would take her in his arms and let her know again how much he loved her, and after a while there would be no protest when her sword was put away with her chain. It was the way he should have done it to begin with, the way he would see it done now.

Bryahn looked around as he moved through the camp, nodding to himself in approval at the easy manner in which their escort did everything that needed doing. Two tents had been erected, his and his sire's, billeting areas had been assigned, the horses had been mostly hobbled and turned out to graze, cookfires were crackling, and sentry posts were already being walked. A force as large as theirs had little to worry about even in lands as open and empty as the ones they rode through, but precaution was never a wasted effort. He wondered where he would find Lisah, decided she was probably with her mare, then stopped short when he saw White Feet grazing quietly with the girl nowhere in sight. If she wasn't with the warhorse, then where . . . ?

Firmly holding down anxiety, Bryahn began searching a bit more purposefully. With almost a hundred men in camp, one brown-haired girl should have stood out rather clearly, but no such luck. He began questioning people then, asking if they'd seen his woman, but most had been too occupied with tasks to notice a girl who rarely brought herself to obvious attention. He finally found one who thought he'd seen her heading toward the woods and the stream, and Bryahn cursed under his breath as he hurried in the same direction. She was supposed to have waited until he was able to go with her, but injured pride had undoubtedly made her ignore that fact. If anything happened to her because of that, he would—

He swallowed that thought as he moved quickly into the woods, his left hand loosening the sword hung at his side. Nothing harmful would come to his Lisah, for he would not allow anything harmful to come to her, and likely nothing was about to harm her in any event. He opened his mind wide to see if he could pick her up, heard nothing, then thought of tracks. It was hardly so late in the day that tracking her was impossible, even there under the trees. He slowed as he studied the ground, casting back and forth until—there! Boot tracks of a size that could only be hers. She had come that way, all right, and seemed to have been headed toward the far side of the stream. He should be able to follow her with no trouble at all, and once he found her they would talk.

Bryahn followed the high ground over the stream and then began angling left, the hurrying bootprints showing him the way. The poor little thing must have been really upset for her to have moved that quickly, and flickerings of guilt began intruding in the man's thoughts. He'd been too stern with her too soon, he knew, exercising his authority over her at a time when it wasn't necessary. She was probably crying her eyes out over having to give up a weapon she loved, and all because he hadn't handled the matter with the delicacy it called for. He would be very gentle with her when he found her, and might even allow her to keep the sword for another day or two. He was certain that would bring the smile back to her face, and then he would—

Bryahn's thoughts ended abruptly when the heavy branch struck the back of his head, sending him down to the ground with no more than a muffled grunt. The trail he had been following had occupied his attention and captured his thoughts to too great an extent, keeping him from knowing of those who lurked in the wood until it was far too late.

"I wonder what he would do if I left him," Lisah muttered, her thoughts dark as she studied what she could see of the prairiecat who still kept her company.

"I was duty-bound to marry him, but am I duty-bound to *stay* with him? He certainly means to take a second wife at some time, and would probably scarcely notice I was gone."

The girl's thoughts darkened even further at that, the tears she had shed quite a distance behind her. The thought of needing to remain with a man who had no true feeling for her was more angering than upsetting, a circumstance she was becoming determined to alter. She had thought at first that the only honorable course was to remain true to the vows she had taken, and then she had remembered that honor was viewed rather oddly when men applied it to women. Bryahn had made it all seem so clear that night they had spoken, but since then things had changed so terribly. . . .

"I refuse to give up my sword," she growled low, glaring at a prairiecat who looked at her with curiosity. "If he wants my sword he can try to take it, which means I may then end up with *his* sword. He'll be sorry then he began this whole thing, most especially if because of that Duke Hwill decides to name me heir in Bryahn's place. I think I would be helpless to keep from laughing aloud."

She grinned wide at Wind Whisper, and the prairiecat grinned back at the distinctly catlike flavor of the girl's thoughts. Her brother's new mate was a good deal like him, and— Suddenly Wind Whisper was on her feet with fangs bared and a growl in her throat, and Lisah knew immediately that something was wrong.

"What is it?" the girl asked, straightening where she sat so that she might reach her sword more easily. "Did you catch the scent of something?"

"I heard—my brother," the cat's mindspeak came, distracted as she searched with all senses. "I felt his thoughts as he neared, and then they were suddenly gone. I distrust the taste of so abrupt a change. I will go now to search him out."

"I'm going with you," Lisah said as she rose to her feet, a flat finality in the thought. Bryahn might have been only pretending to have deep feelings for her, but he was still her husband. If something had happened to him, it was her place to find it out.

Wind Whisper moved silently and swiftly through the woods, the girl following almost as quickly and quietly. The dimness under the trees hadn't yet changed to the darkness of night, but even if it had the prairiecat would have had little trouble. Her brother's scent was strong where he'd fallen to the ground, as strong as the scent of strangers despite there having been a greater number of the strangers. Her lips peeled back from her teeth in a silent snarl; the mixture of scents told her the strangers had taken her brother with them, but the lack of blood scent was what kept her from racing after and slaying them all. With no blood having been spilled her brother might still live, and if so, freeing him of capture was of primary importance. She moved carefully off through the woods, following the mixed scent of those who were not far ahead.

Lisah moved along behind the prairiecat, her sword in her fist, her eyes roving as far through the wood as it was possible to see. When Wind Whisper had stopped the girl had seen the scuffed ground, the prints from a number of sandal-shod feet, the broken branches on nearby bushes that suggested something large had been carried past them. There was no indication of who had taken Bryahn and certainly nothing to say why, but the tracks the girl and cat more or less followed showed in how much of a hurry the kidnappers had been. That had to mean they knew about the camp and how many men were in it, men who could be called on to follow after and take Bryahn back from them. Lisah had considered calling for those men, but had quickly decided against it. To bespeak Duke Hwill, Bryahn's sire, would have been easily done, but how long would Bryahn have remained alive if his captors found themselves in imminent danger of losing him to rescuers? No, she and Wind Whisper would follow and free him, and then a call could be sent to summon the others.

The chase led the prairiecat and the girl beyond the stream and to the right of the landbridge, deeper into the woods away from their camp. Those carrying the captive continued to hurry, those following kept pace a bit behind, and then Wind Whisper slowed. The ground a short distance ahead rose up to form low caves, and both girl and cat could see five men appear from the trees and rush ahead to enter one of the cave entrances. Four of the men had been carrying the burden of an unmoving body, the fifth scurrying a few steps ahead while looking back, and Lisah had never seen men dressed so strangely. Dirty white dresses were what they appeared to be wearing, and then the five were inside the cave mouth and no longer in sight.

"We must approach that cave very carefully, sister," Lisah bespoke the prairiecat, who was gliding forward ahead of her. "Are you able to sense the presence of a sentry?"

"There is no sentry," Wind Whisper replied, disdain clear in the thought. "All of the two-legs have gone within, therefore shall we do the same."

"But we may not show ourselves till Bryahn is no longer in the midst of them," Lisah cautioned, having no difficulty feeling the bloodlust coloring the big cat's thoughts. "Then we are free to take their lives for what was done."

A sense of reluctant but definite agreement came to the girl from the cat, and then the two rescuers gave full attention to approaching the cave mouth. Men who take captives but post no sentries, Lisah thought, shaking her head. What sort of people were these?

Entering the cave mouth gave no immediate answer to the question. Not only was there no sentry posted, the entire knot of people in the large cave were clustered around the five who had just returned. More than thirty, Lisah estimated as she and Wind Whisper eased themselves into the shadows to the right of the entrance, mostly men and women and a few children. The cavern itself, although large, was almost barren, with occasional torches on the walls and pallets of rags scattered about on the floor well to the left. To the right was where Bryahn had been taken, not far from a dark tunnel mouth, his body set down on the pebbly floor and bound with leather. Lisah could see him clearly when those who had been in the process of binding him stepped back, and then another man stepped forward, one who hadn't been with those who had gone out.

"Brothers and sisters, we must bow our heads and give thanks to God Almighty for providing us with a new brother," he said in a satisfied voice as he raised his arms. "This man, stranger though he be to us, will henceforth be considered one of our own, and we will bless him for his sacrifice all the days of our lives. Soon will come his finest hour, and he will be purified and made holy just as those who have gone before him. Let us pray."

All of those standing around lowered their heads above clasped hands, just as though they understood what the man had been talking about. Lisah had no idea what was going on, but was able to see that all of the people there, men and women alike, were wearing long, thin dresses of dirty white with no decorations on them. The man who had spoken also had a band of stained and faded red wrapped around his waist, but there wasn't a true weapon in sight anywhere. All of the men had long, unkempt beards, and some of them had lengths of tree branches hung from thin belts of white as dirty as their dresses, but not a single sword or dagger or dart or anything beyond the branches. And those weren't dresses they wore, Lisah suddenly realized, they had to be what were called robes. She had never seen anyone dressed in them before, but that had to be what they were.

"Brothers and sisters, the time approaches for the arrival of God's Instrument," the man who had spoken before said, causing the people around him to raise their heads. "Ever is sin punished, even sinning thoughts, and we stand humble as we are judged and accept that judgment for the good of our souls. Let us retire from this area, and leave our newest brother to the purification he would otherwise never find."

A murmur of pleased agreement accompanied the withdrawal of the people toward the left side of the cavern, their movement covering the sound of Wind Whisper's very low growl. Lisah had also seen that Bryahn was coming around, his head moving from side to side as his arms strained against the leather which bound him. Strangely enough his weapons had been left him, but tied hand and foot he had little chance of reaching them.

"You may now release your mate while this cat stands guard between you and those two-legs, sister," Wind Whisper bespoke Lisah, the prairiecat's tail moving in short, jerky arcs. "The scents in this place are exceedingly strange, and I feel it would be best if we were gone as quickly as possible."

Lisah wondered how the cat was able to scent anything beyond the stench of unwashed bodies, moldering food, and general refuse in that cavern, but rather than waste time asking she moved forward toward Bryahn while still remaining as much as possible in shadow. She hadn't thought freeing him would be that easy, not simply a matter of reaching him and cutting him loose, and the girl was just the least bit disappointed. Cutting down well-armed guards who stood over him would have been much more satisfying, but apparently one could not have everything in life.

Wind Whisper moved off to the left as Lisah neared Bryahn, the man now lying still and staring straight at the girl. Lisah had sent him a terse command to save his strength and wait until she reached him with the dagger now in her fist, and although he'd been startled and confused he hadn't tried arguing. The people in the cavern still had no idea they were there, which meant there was no need to hurry. Better to have Bryahn cut free before they knew what was happening, Lisah thought, and apparently Wind Whisper agreed. The prairiecat was also hugging the shadows, her urge to spill blood held rigidly in check. Lisah slid out of the shadows in a crouch, no more than three steps from Bryahn, no more than moments from freeing him, and then—

And then a growling roar sounded from the right, pulling Lisah's head around to the dark tunnel Bryahn had been put down near. From out of the darkness lumbered a—*thing*, somewhat like a bear but appearing like no bear the girl had ever seen. Standing larger and broader than the biggest man ever born, the thing had a scraggly brown coat of patchy fur, long, sharp red claws on both hind and front paws, a mouth full of red, jagged teeth—and no eyes. Smooth patches with slight depressions showed where eyes should have been, but even so the thing turned unerringly toward the man and the girl.

"Lisah, hurry!" Bryahn hissed, struggling where he lay against the leather which held him. "Cut me loose and then get back!"

"In the name of glorious God, I command you to leave that man where he is, girl!" an authoritative voice came from the other side of the cavern, the voice of the man who had spoken to the rest of the people. "To release him would be to rob him of his only chance at purification, a sacrilege in the eyes of man and God alike!"

Lisah glanced up to see that all of the people in the cavern now knew she was there, but that made very little difference. It wasn't Wind Whisper's sudden presence before them that kept them at a distance, it had to be the appearance of the thing that was now moving toward Bryahn and herself. After Bryahn's order she was tempted to leave him where he was and engage the beast herself, but she wasn't so foolish as to fail to realize what would happen to him if she fell. Wind Whisper backed from the crowd and came to stand growling beside her two-legs brother and sister even as Lisah reached Bryahn and cut him free, and then all three of them were able to stand and face the oncoming thing, drawn swords in the hands of two.

"Blood . . . flesh . . . hungry," Lisah heard suddenly, and a glance showed her Bryahn was just as startled as she. The thoughts had come from the beast they faced, the mindspeak sending more blurred than easily made out, but there was no doubt it came from the thing before them.

"We are not proper prey for you, brother," Bryahn bespoke the beast, sending warmth as well as words, slowly and with strength. "We are armed and will defend ourselves, but we have no wish to harm you. Return to wherever you came from, and none of us need be harmed."

"Will . . . feed . . . *now*," came the answer, heavy with annoyance, a sense of absolute rejection aimed

toward the offer of warmth and friendship. "Two-legs
. . . too frightened . . . not to . . . give . . ."

With a great roar the beast lurched forward then in
attack, its heavy paw swiping hard at Bryahn and
Lisah. The two jumped back and apart, swords coming up before them, and Wind Whisper darted in
under the swipe to slash and retreat. The beast howled
as its blood was freed by the prairiecat to run down
its leg, but it made no attempt to withdraw. Instead it
attacked again, and in seconds a full battle raged in
the cavern. Bryahn fought to the left, Lisah to the
right, and Wind Whisper circled to come in from behind. Lisah's sword bit deep and then Bryahn's after
hers, both trying to find a clear path through swinging
claws and slashing fangs to a vital spot that would end
the melee. Wind Whisper bit and clawed, trying to
draw the attack in her direction, but the eyeless beast
merely howled in pain from the wounds she gave,
preferring to keep its attention with the two who dared
to challenge it.

Lisah, hacking away at the thing without accompli-
shing any more than Bryahn or Wind Whisper, wiped
the sweat from her brow with a forearm and wondered
how long the fight would continue. It hadn't been
going on all *that* long, but the beast's thoughts had led
her to believe it was old. If that was so it should
already be tiring, but the way it fought showed nothing of the sort. It was intent on destroying all three of
them, an outraged determination seeping from its mind
telling her that, which meant the battle could continue
until one or more of them was badly hurt. The girl had
no real fear for herself, but Bryahn was, after all, her
husband, and even though he felt nothing of true love
for her it was obviously her duty to keep him from
harm. An idea had come to her, a somewhat dangerous idea, but to wait any longer before trying it could
be more dangerous still. If it worked the fight would
be over, and duty and honor would both be satisfied.

Bryahn's attention was so completely on the beast
he fought that he failed to see Lisah back away
a step or two, and also missed the way she dropped her point. Mindspeak would not allow her to

lie, so her sword really had to be down before she
began her projection.

"Here I am," she sent, keeping the thoughts clear
and direct. "As I no longer wish to defend myself, you
may try to take me. My weapon is down and can offer
you no further harm."

The beast heard and immediately turned toward her
with savage satisfaction, clearly believing it had won
what it wanted. It raised a paw to send claws hooking
fast and hard into her face and neck, but although
shocked and surprised, Bryahn and Wind Whisper
moved almost as one to take advantage of the opening
they had been given. The prairiecat leaped to sink
fangs into the side of the neck of the beast just as
Bryahn buried his sword in its lower back, and with a
scream of outraged denial the beast spasmed under
the dual attack. Wind Whisper was batted clear to skid
along the cave floor before rolling back to her feet,
but her jaws held a wide chunk of the throat her teeth
had fastened on, and the beast was stumbling about
with great gouts of blood gushing from it. An instant
later it was crashing to the floor, nothing of mindthought
left to it, and the three combatants were able to draw
the deep breaths of the end of battle.

"So much for that," Bryahn said, eyeing the unmoving carcass, and then hard gray eyes came up to fasten
themselves to Lisah. "As for you, my girl, as soon as
we leave this place and return to our camp, there will
be a number of words exchanged between us. There
was no need for you to expose yourself like that, and
once I have you past our kind hosts it will be time to
describe my displeasure to you in detail."

Lisah flushed at the tight anger Bryahn had spoken
with, but nevertheless turned with him to face the
knot of people who stood staring in shock, their eyes
on the hacked and bloodied body of the beast. Some
of the women wailed softly and some of the men wept,
but the man with the dirty red sash simply shook his
head as he looked at the two intruders.

"Killing and killing and killing," he intoned, sounding as though he were trying to condemn. "You savages are all alike, knowing nothing but killing and

destroying what comes past you. You spurned purification through God's Instrument, damning yourselves for all of eternity, but the terrible sin of what was done will not be ours. We and our intentions are pure in a way you can never know, and heaven will be ours as it can never be yours."

"What makes you all so pure?" Bryahn demanded, his anger now reaching out to those who were nearly responsible for his going to Wind before his time. "The fact that you *fed* that thing, extending its life beyond the time it was able to hunt for itself? What did you feed it when there were no strangers around to victimize? Carefully selected members of your own people?"

"Those who gave their lives for our community were purified of all residual sin and forever blessed!" the man returned stiffly, his bearded head coming up. "We have devoted ourselves to a life without violence, a life without the killing and destruction your sort revels in. We can none of us be completely free of sin, but we stand so far above you and yours that we are closer to godhood than you could ever dream of being. To slay a dumb beast of the forests can be accomplished by any barbarian; to accept the embrace of death instead, and through it to find eternal life, is an action only the truly chosen are able to rise to."

"You consider dying an accomplishment?" Lisah asked with a snort of disdain, her own anger pushing words out ahead of Bryahn's. "Dying is simply done and requires no skill of any sort, which is what undoubtedly attracts you to it. To remain alive and succeed in that life is what you find beyond you, you and those poor specimens of humanity hiding behind your fine words. You refrain from violence out of fear rather than piety, and think to hide that fear by calling it a virtue."

"There is little virtue in refraining from doing what you cannot do," Bryahn added with savage pleasure, disallowing the man with the red waistband an immediate retort. "You all feared that beast, but rather than facing up to it despite the fear you chose to make feeding it a sacred privilege. How much easier it is to die rather than fight, how much safer for a leader to send his people one by one to death rather than advise a battle which could take more lives than his people are willing to give up at once. Such a leader knows *he* will be safe from needing to feed the beast, and what power he exhibits when his followers go one after the other to waiting, slavering jaws! Deep, exhilarating power that makes him feel like a god himself."

"How typical for one of your sort to denigrate the efforts of a man you have no hope of understanding," the bearded man with red waistband said, shaking his head haughtily as though he heard nothing of the faint muttering of the people around and behind him. "I am a man of God, chosen to lead these people up the path to heaven, a far harder and more arduous journey than the slide down to hell. Of course, you sneer at the thought of peace and nonviolence—agents of the darkness could do no other thing. We are above you, and will continue to be so no matter what words you attempt speaking to the contrary."

"If you people are so wonderfully holy, how do you explain and excuse kidnapping a stranger to feed your fear-beast?" Lisah asked, still unimpressed with the filthy man who thought so much of himself. "You used violence to take him, and cowardly violence at that. If you hadn't come up on him from behind, you never would have been able to capture him."

"Our God, in His infinite mercy, at times allows us to give up a stranger in place of one of our own," the man replied, his tone pure condescension as he looked down on the girl, who was physically taller than he. "Such a stranger is forever blessed, and for so excellent an end we are allowed what means are necessary. We accept the small sin of violence on such occasions, in order to provide a share in our own good fortune for one who would otherwise never reap such sweet fruit. It is for their sakes rather than our own, and such generosity is a blessing in itself."

"In other words, you dishonor your own beliefs in order to occasionally get out from under," Lisah said flatly, finding nothing admirable in the man's doubletalk. "If something is wrong once it has to be wrong all the time, otherwise you have nothing but pure nonsense being spouted. And why should the road home be harder than the road away from it? Isn't going home always faster and easier than leaving it? I think you tell these people how hard it is so that you can control them and make them do what *you* want them to do. Sacred Sun demands no more than the best we can offer, whatever that is. Is it your own god who demands more—or a man who joys in running the lives of others?"

"And how admirable is it for a man—or woman—incapable of violence to refrain from violence?" Bryahn asked, pursuing the man, who had finally noticed the muttering going on about him. "If I were the sort of barbarian you named me, I would now be in the midst of committing violence against people who first offered violence to me. As I am a civilized man instead, a true, full, *capable* man, I offer you my disgust rather than my blade, my disdain rather than my arms skill, knowing as I do that you will none of you survive despite the death of your fear-beast. Those like you fear life itself, and will find another fear-beast to offer yourselves to in place of the first. If you fail to find one for yourselves, your—*leader*—will surely find one for you."

"After all, he needs your sacrifice in order to feel his power," Lisah pointed out with a small smile, enjoying the way the man she goaded now pretended to hear nothing from his followers. "If he fails to make you do what you would never do without him, his wonderful feeling of godhood will be no more. He could, of course, have forced you to face up to the life you fear, but if he did that then you might have sought to follow another, one who would cater to your fears. Or, worse, you might have listened to him and grown beyond your fears and therefore your need for him. Far better that he speak lies you all choose to believe, and then neither you nor he will miss what you so obviously prefer—lives spent enslaved to the lies of a fool spoken *for* fools."

"Get out," the man in the red sash said in a choked voice, his hand curled into a fist. "You are the ones

who speak lies here, and we will have no more of it.
Take your filthy animal and get out!"

"Our cat sister would rather remain in the company
of that beast than in yours," Bryahn offered back with
a grin, knowing the man wanted them gone so that he
could try taking over the minds of his people again.
"We feel the same, so we *will* go, with this one last
parting thought: if you willingly believe what another
tells you, what befalls you because of it is *your* fault,
not that other's. No matter how hard you try, you can
never escape the responsibility for your own life. If
peace is what you truly seek, seek it from a stance of
strength and skill, not one of weakness. Peace can be
stolen from the weak with the flick of a sword, not
quite so easily from those who are strong. There is no
virtue in weakness and nonviolence; virtue can only be
found where violence is possible, but tranquillity is
chosen instead. And is peace worth any price? I think
not. Consider those who went to feed the beast, feel
yourselves in their place, and then decide the question
again."

The man with the sash of red would have shouted
Bryahn quiet, but instead was too involved with answering the questions of those who stood around him—
distraught, almost hysterical questions. Bryahn's hand
on Lisah's arm guided her toward the cave mouth,
Wind Whisper leaving off cleaning herself to accom-
pany them, and a moment later they were out in the
clean, fresh air of the woods again. It was nearer
sundown than it had been, the dimness of overhead
greenery turning to shadowy dark, and once they had
put sufficient distance between themselves and the
cave, Bryahn wiped his sword on his pants leg and
finally resheathed the weapon. Lisah, reminded by
that that she still held her own weapon, did the same,
then glanced uncomfortably about. A difficult situation had been faced and overcome, but there was still
a far more unpleasant one ahead.

"I find it difficult to remember when I last met a
bunch like that," Bryahn said, still faintly put out. "It
would be pleasant to believe that what we said will
make a difference, but unfortunately I know better.

That chief fool will begin spouting his nonsense again, and as quickly as he does the bunch of them will be his once more."

He waited for an agreement from the girl who walked beside him, at the very least a comment or a grumble, but nothing of the sort was offered. Perhaps she had been more shaken by the encounter than he'd realized.

"Your silence seems rather heavy, Lisah," Bryahn observed after a moment, Wind Whisper having just confirmed the fact that they were not being followed. "Is something disturbing you?"

"I have no need of a pretense of concern from you, Bryahn," the girl responded, the words as stiff as her back. "I may have little experience with men, but as you can see I have finally found my way through to the truth. Do me the courtesy of no longer considering me a mere child who needs to be told tales of love and devotion. Duty and honor will see me through what needs to be done, and then you and I may part company."

"These woods have grown darker than I thought," Bryahn muttered, totally at a loss as to what her meaning might be. "I had thought I was in the midst of finding my way easily, but instead I discover myself suddenly lost. What pretense of concern are you talking about, and what is it that needs to be done?"

"You know very well what I mean," Lisah replied, the stiffness still fully with her. "You used a pretense of love to cozen me out of my chain, but miscalculated when you thought to simply demand my sword. I will not only not surrender my sword, I also demand the return of my chain. My entire panoply will be needed when I am finally able to leave you."

"I see," Bryahn said, taken aback by how far the misunderstanding between them had gone. "And the time you are able to leave me will be when?"

"When I have given you the heirs I agreed to bear," she said, her chin high with a definite air of martyrdom about her. "Duty and honor demand that I I fulfill the agreement made, but happily say nothing about the need to remain, once my duty is done, with

a man who hates me. With your second wife beside
you, you will scarcely notice I am gone."

"My second wife?" Bryahn echoed in confusion,
wondering if the encounter with the beast had unbal-
anced her. "I barely have a first wife, one it so happens I do love. How can you believe I hate you?"

"How could I believe anything else?" she countered,
giving him no more than a quick glance. "A man who
loves a woman accepts her as she is. Only when he
hates what she is does he continually try to change
her. Your own actions have shown me the truth,
Bryahn."

Bryahn stared wordlessly down at the girl, stunned
at the manner in which she had taken the perfectly
ordinary arrangements that any man would have made
concerning his new wife. It was his *duty* to be certain
she was safe, and how might she be safe if he allowed
her to continue wearing armor and weapons?

The man made a sound in his throat as he listened,
for the first time, to the tenor of his thoughts. If *she*
would be safer without armor and weapons, then so
would everyone else, he and his fighters included. He
had been lying to himself, and just like those people
back in the cavern, hadn't wanted to give up so com-
forting a posture.

"It seems those poor fools behind us are not the
only ones with fear-beasts," he said at last with a sigh,
putting his arm around the girl to stop her determined
forward progress. Their camp was not far ahead, the
cookfires showing more brightly across the landbridge
over the stream, and he wanted to say what he had to
say before they got back. "Lisah, you will come to
know that I *do* love you, but you may not have the
return of your chain, nor will you retain your sword
once we have reached Dunkahn lands and your new
home. The fear-beast I sacrifice to has as much sub-
stance as the one we slew—and just as little—and
therefore does it refuse to be denied."

"Your concept of love is to deny me utterly then,"
the girl said, her shadowy face looking up at him with
less expression than her voice. "Clearly, then, I must
learn to practice the same sort of love with you."

"You reply to an attack that has not truly been launched," he told her, tightening his arm and adding the second to keep her from pulling away. "There is no denial in my love, only full acceptance, and now you may riddle me this: if you should come upon a battle you find of interest and your armor and weapons are upon you, will you join the battle, or smile faintly as you pass it by?"

"Why—I would join it, of course," she answered, the words hesitant with uncertainty. "Would you expect me to do anything else?"

"No, I certainly would not," he responded, feeling himself smile at the woman who was his. "And that, my girl, is the reason you will not have your armor and weapons. My fear-beast is the thought of losing you before we have truly had one another to learn and love, and I am helpless to deny it. It must be *your* fear-beast which is denied, for our sake as well as the sake of others."

"What is it you think *I* fear?" she asked, uncertain whether or not to be angry. "And for what reason need I concern myself with others? They may do as they please just as I do the same."

"What you fear is that you will never have the opportunity to prove the skill you have acquired," he said, speaking gently as he stroked her light brown hair. "The fear is reasonable and is shared by every man and woman who has ever had battle skills to be proud of, but you may no longer allow it to rule you. The others I made mention of—they may *not* do as they please, for they are the children we hope to have, our beloved offspring who will never see the light of day if you are slain in battle. Do you still consider them ones you need not concern yourself with?"

"I—had not thought to look at it in such a way," the girl said in answer, staring up at his face with disturbance now filling her. "I would not deny life to my own children, but—what of *my* life and needs? Must I concern myself only with the needs of others?"

"There is nothing of 'must' about it," he answered, continuing to stroke her hair. "I have discovered another fear-beast of mine which I have already buried my sword in, and never again will I pay it homage. All decisions about armor and weapons and joining or not in passing battles—those decisions are now *yours* to make rather than mine. I have enough trust in the wisdom of your judgment to know the decisions will be the right ones, right for you, for me, for everyone. Wrong is sometimes right and right is sometimes wrong, and we all must learn to take life as it rolls past us. I shall no longer see you as a woman to be changed, only one to be accepted as she is. Are you able to accept *me* as *I* am?"

"Pigheadedly stubborn and with a tongue as well oiled as a sword properly wrapped for storage?" she demanded, but Bryahn was delighted to hear a laugh along with the words. Then she raised a hand to his face, and he knew he had chosen correctly. "Wrong is right when the fear-beast to be bowed to is yours, but right is wrong when my interests disagree with yours," she said, not having missed those very obvious points. "I will first need to think about all this, and then you may have my very proper, very correct decisions. And I may yet leave you when I have given you the heirs I promised."

"Should you eventually decide to do so, you may go with my blessing," Bryahn agreed smoothly, then pulled her tight against his body. "Where you would find a company who would take a woman who has borne two hundred children, however, is something I cannot imagine. That *is* the number of heirs you agreed to bear for me, is it not?"

"Bryahn!" she exclaimed, trying not to laugh at what he had said, feeling the heat rise in her as he touched soft, warm lips to her throat. She squirmed in his embrace, noticing at last that his plate was no longer a barrier between them, then gave in to the delight of feeling wanted again. "No more than fifty," she murmured, circling him with her arms so that she might press up against him. "Not a child more than fifty—"

His lips against hers ended their conversation, at least the words spoken aloud. Their minds had grown used to merging long before their bodies did, and now they each spoke unceasingly of the pleasure they meant to share.

Wind Whisper looked about the woods with a sigh, despairing of her brother and sister ever learning proper behavior while still in such close proximity to enemies. But she would stand guard willingly. The brief battle they three had shared had been rather pleasant, and the prairiecat knew it was her duty to guard the unseeing backs of the others so that they three might share battle again.

As she knew they would share battle again.

Killsister

by Steven Barnes

STEVEN BARNES is one of those writers who can write either by themselves or in collaboration. Being the author of two novels, and coauthor of three more, the most recent being *The Legacy of Heorot*, with Larry Niven and Jerry Pournelle, isn't enough for him; he also has written several television screenplays.

"We'll make them pay," Steel Tooth muttered for the thousandth time. His battered face, swathed in make-shift bandages, was slack with fatigue. Weariness had drained his eyes of their customary fire. His body, the strongest and most supple among the Crow, was numb with the day's dreadful labors. "The night is cold, Boone."

"For those of us who can feel it," his companion replied. Boone was a slender, wiry man, his face all angles and lines. He poked the fire beneath the cookpot. "We lost too many this time." He sniffed at a rising tendril of steam, pungent with the aroma of spices, vegetables and moor boar.

"We'll make them pay. We'll make them pay." Steel Tooth chanted it as a litany, as if mere words could keep the grief at bay, or change the day's events.

Steel Tooth flinched, the dagger wound in his side suddenly alive with pain. It was only an inch below the lung. If he'd been a moment slower to the guard . . .

Even considering the pain, he was luckier than many. The Crow camp was filled with wounded men, and his only satisfaction was that as many, or more, lay wounded in the enemy camp. The Horseclans had tasted Crow steel today! Even their leader, the gigantic Hezros, had been toppled from his terrible black horse.

Steel Tooth's wan smile dimmed as he remembered the inhuman fury with which the other clansmen had cut their way to their leader's side, before the Crow could press their advantage.

Damn!

Distantly, a wavering animal scream broke from the southern woods.

With an oath, Boone sprang to his feet, slapping one hand to the dagger at his belt. "What was that?"

They stood, looking south, downriver. Toward Killsister, the river flowing past the mountain which gave her her name. At the base of Killsister Mountain, the river created a vast network of marshes. Farther south it floated to the plains roamed by their sworn enemies, the Horseclans.

They listened, but heard nothing more.

Boone reluctantly sheathed his weapon. "Just a jackal, I suppose."

"Plenty of meat for them today," Steel Tooth said morosely. He shook his head in disgust. "I don't know why I said that."

"I do." Boone stared into the flame, blinking slowly. "Erin."

Steel Tooth grunted. He seemed to be feeling his way, clumsily finding words to map out unfamiliar emotional territory. "It's just that . . . it hurts to think Little Brother is gone now. First Tal, now Erin." He wagged his massive head. "I've lost half my family to the damned Horseclans. . . ." He smashed his fist into the ground and lifted his face to the sky. "Damn you, Erin! It should have been me!" He sank his head between his knees and locked his eyes tight. "He wanted this battle. He wanted to blood himself. Erin the Warrior!" His voice was heavy with remorse. "It should have been me."

Boone lifted the ladle from the pot, let the aroma waft temptingly beneath Steel Tooth's nose. "You have to stay strong. There are a world of clansmen to kill."

Steel Tooth grunted approval. "It's true. Well, be

damned. The next Horseclans throat is yours, Little Brother! Yours." He sighed heavily, turning back to the fire. "Let's have a bowl for Erin."

The world seethed with pain and dull color, jelling sluggishly as Erin came to his senses. The first thing he sensed was massive pressure from above, pressure that crushed him down into the ground, stifled breathing. Stones and broken sticks cut into his cheek. Everything ached.

Memories began to flow, like water from a crumbling dam. He remembered the moment of his death: Hezros, chief of the clansmen, astride his terrifying black steed, had fallen atop him. He remembered the heat of its breath, the sudden shock of the impact. What a glorious moment that had been! Standing full in the open, pulling and firing, pulling and firing again and again, as that nightmarish centaur bore down on him, man and horse armored in leather, indistinguishable one from the other in the dusk.

And Erin stood, firing, and brought them down! The animal plowed into the ground, screaming, a Crow arrow feathering its eye, Hezros sorely wounded but lashed into the saddle, battleaxe gleaming in his hand as the horse churned in its death agonies.

Not five yards from Erin the horse's front legs finally collapsed. Beast and master struck the marshy ground, tumbling, churning and furrowing the moist, rich earth until both collided with Erin, hammering him into the ground.

He ached all over, but especially in his leg. His feet were cold. Is that what he would feel in hell? Is that the way it began?

If this was the road to hell, at least he'd sent a hundred souls howling before him. He smiled. If the furnaces of hell needed stoking, it wouldn't be Erin's raw, blistered hands that carried the coals from one flaming heap to another. He had acquitted himself with honor. This day he had become Erin the Warrior, a slayer, a reaper of souls. He would have slaves aplenty in the next world.

The next thought that came to him was awareness of

the wind ruffling his hair. Wind, cool wind in the pits of hell? Who would have thought . . .

Of course, it was probably just more torment. Probably just the icy breath of a hideous demon hovering over him now, waiting for him to regain consciousness so that it could begin to devour his genitals and excretory organs.

Over and over again, throughout all of eternity.

If that was his fate, he would meet it as a warrior of the Crow. He opened his eyes, and was surprised that the sky of hell was identical to that of earth. The same stars, the same clouds drifting endlessly . . . but something was blocking the sky. He fought to focus his vision and couldn't. There was something lying atop him, pinning him to the ground. Ah . . . the torments of hell had begun! A demon had rolled a giant stone atop his chest. . . .

Wait. He found the strength to twist his head to the right. At first he could see nothing, then focused his eyes on his bloody jerkin. So. You wore clothes in hell—presumably only the clothes you died in.

There were interesting possibilities here, he mused. Teela, the tanner's daughter, had drowned last month while bathing. If he could find her amid the flaming pits he might satisfy a curiosity which had grown increasingly hungry these last three years. . . .

A distant sound, like night birds rustling in the bushes, came to him.

Erin managed to shake his head, focusing on that remarkable sky overhead. The dull eye of a full moon stared down at him without comment.

A moon in hell? Wait, now. For a few moments, he muzzily fought with the possibility that he wasn't dead. Impossible. He *had* to be dead.

There was death all about him. He could smell it. Wait. He could feel, and hear, and see . . .

I'm alive!

He gathered his strength, and pushed against the thing on his chest. It was *flesh*, dead flesh, and as his senses continued to return, he realized that it was *horse* flesh. In fact it was the very horse he had brought down, now dead and stinking, and lying partially atop him.

With returning awareness came a pulsating, engulfing tide of pain. He was alive, but injured, perhaps badly. Fear rose up to clutch at him, and at the peak of its grasp he felt younger than his sixteen summers. Then he remembered that he was Erin! Erin the Warrior! Brother of Steel Tooth, the champion of his tribe! He had to survive.

He stared into the filmed eye of that dead horse, the one good eye glaring at him accusingly as he struggled from beneath its awful weight. He wrestled with that dead thing for an eternity. Time and again he thought that he had reached the end of his strength. Then with a wrench and a lunge, he wriggled out a few more inches, and lay there panting, gazing up into that cold, uncaring sky.

"Damn you! I thought I was dead! Didn't have to—*uh*! Go through this . . . *uhh*! Any damned more! Wretched Horseclans can't even . . . *damn!* . . . kill a boy!"

Finally—wonder of wonders! He kicked himself free and rolled panting onto his side, weak and sick and spent.

He flailed one arm out to the left, and it struck a corpse. He snatched it back, hissing, then took a closer look.

It was a Crow warrior—what was his name? Sky! That was it. Sky of the ready laughter and pretty wit. That wit was silenced forever now. He lay cold beneath the stars, his slashed throat slit into a ghastly pair of rubbery wet red lips that grinned as if whispering a final, dreadful jest.

Erin pried a spear away from Sky's stiff dead fingers and used it as a makeshift crutch, levering himself to a sitting position.

His legs ached horribly, the stabbing pain of returning circulation almost more than he could bear. Erin clamped his mind down on the pain and began rubbing his calves, gritting his teeth as new blood brought pain from the abused muscles. The knee was wrenched, damaged, and Erin cursed fluidly.

Erin the Warrior would endure! Survive! And return in triumph! He couldn't let the pain or fatigue or anything else stop him.

The world swam. He was very weak, but feeling finally returned to his legs. He rolled over, each bump of his leg against the ground a source of new pain. The haft of the spear was wet in his hands, clammy with his own sweat. It slipped in his hands as he levered himself erect. He blinked hard, praying for his wavering vision to clear.

He stood in the middle of the marshes, the recent battlefield, the middle of the disputed land between the Crow and the Horseclans. Killsister, the river that brought life to this desolate land, ran sluggishly here. It soaked into the ground to create the marsh, the richest hunting ground for a hundred miles. On the marsh lived wild ponies, a hundred species of fowl and the terrible moor boars—night scavengers, fighters, and Crow delicacy.

It was a place of life and death, flesh and fantasy. "Don't wander onto the marsh at night," his mother had warned, long, long ago. "There's things such as a madman never dreams, shadow things, evil things that come down from the mountain at night, looking for them that walk alone. . . ."

Killsister Mountain, mist-shrouded and impenetrable, loomed over the battlefield like a dark god, laughing at his pain and fatigue. Miles north lay the camp of his people, the Crow.

Somehow, he had to reach them.

His face was cut and torn, his left knee flamed, his ribs were bruised and cracked, but he was alive. The wonder was that Hezros' steed had not damaged him more! It was easy to believe that his kinsmen had thought him one of the dead.

His mind was clearing, and the memories fell more clearly into place, arranging themselves like fragments of a child's puzzle.

Yes . . .

They had been two days fighting, without sleep, without rest, and it had finally come to the final charge. Erin stood, prepared for that moment, anticipating a glorious death. To be slain on the battlefield, sur-

rounded by the bodies of your comrades! To die dealing death to the enemy chieftain! He would live forever
in the sacred songs of his people.

And that day, death had come to countless hundreds. Crow warriors, whipped into a frenzy, threw
themselves at their foes with berzerker frenzy. Horseclansmen pierced by Crow pikes had been driven
screaming to their knees, blood flowing freely from
their mouths.

And the greatest of them had been the one they
called Hezros, the giant warrior from the south. What
a demon! It was Crow custom to acknowledge the
greatness of an enemy, even one as treacherous as the
Horseclansman Hezros, who had called for parley and
then slaughtered all who advanced under the white
flag.

It seemed strange, alien, that foes who fought so
well, died so bravely on the battlefield could act so
cravenly in the dead of night. But so it was, and so it
had been since before Erin had been whelped. The
feud had burned, and would continue to burn until
one clan or the other was no more. There would never
be peace between Crow and clansmen as long as
Killsister connected their lands, as long as the Horseclans
ambushed Crows in the Killsister marsh.

Erin investigated a couple of the nearest bodies,
trying to determine whether either of them retained
life. One, a Horseclansman, stared back at him, face
already puffy and blackening with death.

There were insects in the eyes, picking, eating. And
beneath the eyes, beneath the chin, was a slashed
throat that mirrored Sky's wound. Erin shook his head
in disgust.

As far as he could see, he was the only living human
being for miles. Hundreds of bodies stretched out:
twisted, broken, limbs splayed in every direction. They
lay in heaps and stacks and small sad bundles. Bodies
crushed, bones splintered through the flesh, staring
eyes that could not, would not ever see again.

The wind whistling down from the great mountain
laughed at his musings, promised a gift of dark secrets
before the night ended.

Erin fought the surge of weakness. Fought the urge to just lie back down and let death take him. He froze his thoughts: he simply *had* to make it home. His people needed him.

When the pain and the fear began to dissipate, he realized that his stomach was utterly empty. Hunger, anesthetized by adrenaline and pain, roared awake. Feeling a bit ghoulish, he scavenged the pouches and belts of the men around him, managed to find some beef jerky. He hunched there, watching and chewing. There was nothing moving, nothing making a sound.

He tore a waterpouch from a dead man's grasp, sloshed it and found it half full. He drank deeply, splashed some on his face and then lashed the pouch to his belt. He ripped belts from two of the corpses and wrapped them around his left leg, below and above the knee. It was torn, but he thought that he could walk on it—he *had* to walk on it. He had to make it home, to the north, through miles of marshy ground.

He had a spear, a ten-inch knife and a pouch of water. It was enough or he wasn't a Crow.

He hobbled, walked through the battlefield through mounds of dead horses and dead men. He stumbled clumsily through them, sleepwalking through a crimson dream. The marsh stank of blood. Old blood, new blood, future blood.

Erin staggered on, the night flies buzzing around his mouth and nose.

"Help . . . help me . . ." The sound wafted from the west, over toward the bluff overlooking Killsister, and he hobbled over to it, hoping that it was one of his comrades.

Lying partially hidden beneath a bush lay a boy of the Horseclans. The lad was his own age, but thinner and taller. The boy's leg was shattered, his throat was slashed, but he was still alive. Blood pumped from the wound sluggishly, through a bandage made of a knotted scarf.

Erin hunkered down, uncertain what to do. He could not kill a wounded foe. In fact, he couldn't understand the slashed throats. The Crow performed no such mutilations of wounded foes. Would the Horseclansmen kill their own wounded? His head spun. Monsters!

The moonlight leeched the remaining blood from the boy's pale face. His mouth moved, lips trembled as he struggled to whisper. Fear lived in the pale eyes, but not fear of Erin, or the knife at Erin's side. These eyes had seen something that drove terror of the Crows from consciousness.

Erin hunkered close. He wet his hand and smeared it across the forehead of the dying boy. His body was burning up. The boy thrashed in fever. Finally a weak sound emerged from parched lips. "Kill . . . kill . . ." the clansman whispered.

What? A threat? A plea? Erin pulled back, alert for a trick.

The boy began to tremble. His eyes were fixed, staring out across that bloodsoaked marsh, toward the towering mountain to the west.

"Killsister," the boy said, and then the eyes were fixed and still, still directed at the mountains that stood wreathed in silence and mist, the peaks that had witnessed so much death and tragedy without judgment or mercy. Mountains that yielded no life and dealt no death. That had stood before Crow or clansmen had come a-hunting to this land, and would tower still when both had gone to dust.

Erin shuddered. He closed the boy's eyes with his fingertips. He had never touched a Horseclansman with gentleness before. The boy's skin had just been skin. Smooth and warm, like anyone's skin. He wiped his hand on his jerkin, wondering what it was that he had expected. Of course it was skin.

Just skin.

He continued on, suddenly weary to his very bones.

A few animal sounds broke the silence of the night. Erin heard the sound of night birds, a keening wind, fluttering the marsh reeds, the distant whisper of the river. Then he heard something else: a sound almost like laughter.

Erin stopped, listening. "I could have sworn . . ." he whispered. He had heard of animals, scavengers, that laughed while they ate. He had never seen one, nor had anyone he knew of. But they were supposed to be real.

On the other hand, there were his mother's stories. *There's things such as a madman never dreams.* . . .

Erin stood very still, peering out into the night.

Ahead, something moved, and he dove behind a bush, lungs frozen without breath.

He heard before he saw, heard a single guttural syllable.

"Meat," someone, or something, said in a voice like nothing he'd ever heard. There was another, more horrible laugh. A shadow detached itself from the surrounding terrain and humped toward one of the nearby bodies, hunkered over it.

Then a second shadow, hulking, brutelike, making that same horrendous giggling sound, joined the first. Something slender rose into the air, flashed like a sliver of sunlight, then fell with the horrible squashing sound of rending flesh.

Other shadows joined the first, giggling and tittering, and other axes sprouted against the clouds—

And rose and fell, and rose again, and then there was a long, long sound of tearing, *ripping* . . .

Erin shrank into the shadow as completely as he could, fighting to control the bile that rose in his throat.

They were *butchering* the bodies, tearing them into sections, like a man butchering a cow. There was no mistaking the actions, no mistaking the motion of those axes. Terror gripped him. This was something that he couldn't comprehend. Something beyond his own experience. Combat, death on the field of battle, he understood. But men eating other men!

An unknown wave of fear ran through him. More of the shadowy figures were coming now. From the darkness he watched the creatures come hulking in from east, from south and north, drawing a cordon around the entire battlefield.

Of course! Of course! The Maneaters had done this many, many times, lurking in the shadow of Killsister, rubbing their hands and licking their chops as the Crow and the men of the Horseclans fought. Waiting, knowing at the beginning of the day who the true victors would be at the end.

Only because his body had been hidden beneath a dead horse had he missed the initial kill, the hours when the advance guard prowled the field, slitting the throats of the wounded.

His limbs felt as if they had been immersed in freezing water. He had to move, and move quickly. To be found would be to die, and die more horribly than any clean death in battle. Hell would be a relief to one caught by these creatures.

For an insane moment he thought of lifting a corpse, hiding under it, playing dead again . . . but only for a moment. That idea would lead him to the stewpot.

The only answer was to sneak past, to make it through the line of ghouls.

Move lively.

The hooting, giggling laughter echoed around the battlefield—not just an expression of insane delight, but signals, greetings from one man-eater to another.

The river. The rushing waters would help to hide his own sound, might well be his best chance. On his belly, moving between breaths, Erin worked his way down to the river, the smell of the lush mud in his nose, the taste in his mouth. He paused when he reached a particularly wet patch and rolled slowly, smearing his body until he was completely covered, and then continued on.

Every ten feet he stopped and waited, listening to the thunder of his heart, fighting to keep from soiling himself.

Light flared suddenly to the east: a campfire. It was carefully shielded from wind and prying eyes; he could see it only dimly. But he didn't need to see to know that over it, on a wooden spit perhaps, turned a sizzling human haunch.

He froze as a heavy form walked flat-footed through the bushes. The cannibal stopped, sniffing the air. Erin gave thanks that the wind was with him. The man was a brute, squat and thick-bodied, like something prehuman, inhuman, more akin to ape than man. His muscles were thick and ropy, almost apelike, and there was little body fat between muscle and skin—too little. It was vile the way the man's cabled thews rolled under a layer of loose skin, like a writhing bag of pythons. His skin was unnaturally pale, his eyes almost glaringly white. He carried a heavy, two-headed axe, which he used to stir in the bushes, and he sniffed, the thick nose twitching slowly in the moonlight.

The ghoul smelled nothing. He grunted, and continued on through the brush.

Erin closed his eyes, fighting his urge to vomit, then slowly crawled away through the woods.

Distantly, he heard another giggle, and this time it was accompanied by a guttural voice: "Eat well. Long time till fresh meat again."

"Not so sure." Another tittering giggle. And those words were followed by hearty, giddy laughter. "They stupid stupid. Fight fight."

Erin crawled back on his knees and elbows, careful not to make a sound. He was one with the brush, one with the clouds above him, barely making furrows in the ground beneath him.

People that ate people. Not even the Horseclans had been accused of such things. Murder, yes. But cannibalism was something so . . . *wrong* that it was difficult for him to even hold the thought in his mind.

When he was so far away that he could no longer see their campfire or hear the guttural barks of their laughter, he oriented himself by the mountains and began to crawl more rapidly.

What kind of people would these be? Men who hunted men . . . how dangerous would they be? They would not trade with other men, so their skills in many ways would not be high. Their toolmaking would be unrefined. But be that as it may, there was no way to overestimate the danger of his position.

If he was very, very careful—

Pain. Sudden, bright agony flared in his leg, and he had to stop, sobbing for breath. He checked the belts around his knee, found that one of them had slipped. The leg was numb, and sore.

Erin had a brief urge to stop, to wait for the pain

to diminish. He was only human. He couldn't keep going . . .

He exhaled harshly. He was Erin the Warrior! The Slayer! He had a purpose, a reason to keep moving, and he would.

Although he crawled in the mud, his pride sustained him. He was a warrior of the greatest warrior people in the world. And he would survive.

As Tal and Steel Tooth had taught him, he tunneled his mind, focusing on the sounds of the songs that would be sung, the images of the dancing, the taste of the food, almost managing to mask the terrible whimpering sound which had begun in the back of his throat.

Erin forced a grim smile. He gripped his spear and crawled on, unmindful of the branches slapping against his face.

Erin, the survivor! The one who had outwitted the monsters, his thousand acts of battlefield valor already famous. Erin! Who would lead the Crow against a savage new enemy, new flesh to hone their lances against before renewing their feud with the Horseclans.

He stopped, curling himself against a tree as the ground shook with hoofbeats. Along a rocky path through the marshes there came a devil horse. A stallion as black and as terrible as an eclipse of the sun. Its hooves struck sparks as it galloped, and when it stopped, not ten yards from where Erin lay hidden, it pawed the ground into furrows, snorting like a wild animal.

The rider was gigantic, twice Erin's size. His arms and shoulders were animal knots of muscle. He was larger than Hezros, or even Steel Tooth. The ghoul carried an axe with a huge double-bladed head, darkly crusted with blood.

The moon was behind Erin's tree, and he rested in deep shadow. The cannibal could not see him.

The man's eyes were like open sores. His skin was very pale. His teeth were sharp, filed for eating raw meat. His eyes were large, and the whites too overpowering. The man searched through the underbrush, searching for something. What did those terrible, dead eyes search for?

With a thrill of nausea, Erin realized that he knew exactly what they were looking for.

They knew that somebody had survived. They'd found tracks. He crawled even farther back into the shadows, but as he watched that horse, tossing and pawing the ground, an idea began to blossom.

Silently, Erin felt around in the shadow until he found a chunk of rock as big as his fist, and then a second one that was even larger. He hefted the first carefully, took aim, and threw.

The horse reared violently as the rock hit it squarely between the eyes. As it shied, the man turned cat-quick, cursing gutturally. Erin hefted the second rock, the biggest and heaviest that he could throw accurately, and hurled it. The man groaned and sagged to his knees as it hit him in the back of the head.

Even hurt as he was, on his knees, he managed to turn, fought to bring the axe to guard. Erin steeled himself, shut the pain in his leg away, and leaped from the shadows. He barely managed to suck his gut in, to evade that first clumsy swing. His leg was aflame—he had no strength for a long fight, especially a long fight against a man as huge as this.

He had to hope that the man's head was as clouded as it seemed. Erin faked to the left, and the man tried to pivot on his knees to follow the feint. There was a moment of uncertainty, and Erin twisted to the right, gambled everything and drove the spear in. The momentum of the axe was too much for the man to redirect, and he didn't make it. The blade clanged against the spear, cleaving the haft as the head struck home. The man knelt there, staring unbelievingly at Erin, blood gushing blackly into the moonlight, and fell over onto his face.

Erin tumbled to the ground. His leg! The pain had doubled. He had torn something, or allowed splintered bone to tear through his flesh.

He forced himself to his knees and wrenched his broken spear out of the man's throat. He grabbed the horse's reins before the animal could get away from

him. Every breath more labored than the last, he
sucked wind and climbed onto the saddle, digging his
heels into its great flanks.

It sprinted forward as if released from a sling, plung-
ing wildly through the brush. At his strongest he would
have struggled to control such a beast. Now it was
more than he could do just to hang on. His eyesight
blurred in the darkness. Erin didn't see the branch
that smashed his face, didn't even know that he had
been hit until his back struck the ground. He lay
there, the world spinning around and around.

Distantly, he heard voices. He had to keep moving.
He forced himself to his knees, groping out in the
darkness. Where was his spear? Desperately he flailed,
until the nearness of the voices wrenched a sob of
despair from his lips. He staggered to his feet, hob-
bling in the direction of the river.

He barely saw the figure flickering to the left. He
threw himself to the ground, and a war axe buried
itself in the tree trunk behind him. A great hairy
figure launched after it, striking Erin before he could
get his knife from his belt. They rolled over and over
and around in the dirt, gasping and sweating. The
man's breath smelled like rotted human flesh.

Erin sank his fingers into the cannibal's throat, felt
the great corded muscles there in the same moment that
the man's hands found his own.

The man's throat was thicker than his own, his
hands stronger. Erin felt the awful pressure as the
fingers dug into his neck, crushed his throat closed.

Air! There was no air! His vision blackened, splashes
of red and silver flashing in the darkness. Desperately,
he rammed his head forward, smashing it into the face
of the man above him. There was a strangled snarl of
surprise and pain, and the tension on Erin's throat
eased.

He changed his grip so that his thumbs clawed at his
attacker's eyes. He squeezed with everything that he
had left. There was a long moment of resistance, and
then his thumbs plunged into warmth and wetness.

The beast-man atop him gave an awful, animal
scream, his hands clapping to ruined eyes. He flung

himself back, rolling on the ground making great whooping sounds.

Erin bashed the man's head against the ground once, twice, three times, striking his own fingers the last time, numbing and bruising them.

Staggering back to his feet, Erin could hear his pursuers crashing through the brush behind him, only a few seconds away.

He hobbled on. Just a little way to the river now. He could hear it. If he could just keep going! Every step stabbed him with pain, and his lungs were aflame now, even his good leg heavy as lead.

He couldn't run. Just couldn't.

Erin the Warrior! He couldn't quit. He had to live.

Keep your mind on the food, on the campfire. . . .

Don't think about your legs, your chest, the pounding of your heart. They were so close now—

He wrenched himself from his reverie in time to dig in his heels. Momentum slowed but not stopped, he smashed into a gnarled tree growing at the lip of the bluff above Killsister River.

He stared down at her twisting, rushing black depths. The lip of the cliff rose forty feet above the riverbank. Too steep to climb—with his bad leg.

The voices were right behind him now. There was time only for a desperate gambit.

Carefully, testing each step, he climbed down over the edge of the cliff. The tree roots had actually grown out the bottom, and he climbed down, finding the heaviest and sturdiest roots, clinging to them as he hung there over the lip of the abyss.

The sound of cursing and heavy steps. Finally, voices, "Must find him," one said, with a heavy, spitting sound. "If we don't"—another angry expulsion of air and viscous fluid—"trouble."

"Aye. They discover us, they come after us. Good eating gone."

The first grunted with disgust. "The easy eating over, for sure. Damn. So easy to goad them, so easy to make each think the other side broke the truce. What's left after the battle?" They all laughed heartily. "Heh heh. Is meat for us."

"Let's try around over to the west."

Erin hung beneath the tree, shocked, disbelieving.

The Horseclansmen were not their enemies? Had not been their enemies for decades?

And these horrible troll-people, these creatures who lurked like maggots in the shadow of Killsister, watching and waiting and prodding and goading—these things had been fueling the feuds all along?

Finding the bodies, and butchering them like cattle?

Erin lost control of his stomach, tasted acid, felt a sour fist squeeze him until he lost the water and jerky, vomiting over his own chest as he hung there in the tangle of roots. He thought of all the death, all the lives thrown away for nothing, and wanted to die. His brother Tal, dead these five years, whose death had fired him with hatred for the Horseclans. Tal had died to make meat for these monsters. If Erin could not somehow get back to his people the killing would go on, and on, and on, until there was nothing left of either tribe. Then perhaps the ghouls of Killsister would roam, like nomads, until they found more fools eager to kill each other to make meat for the cannibal table.

All thoughts of heroism were gone now. He had to reach his people with the awful truth. Their enemy was not the Horseclans. Their enemy was Death itself.

Erin pulled himself up from beneath the tree, shivering, shaking. He looked out at the distant peaks of the mountain. The mist surrounding them seemed to be countless thousands of souls, torn from their bodies by human teeth and denied rest until someone somewhere lived to tell the truth.

Erin began to move north. If he could reach a notch just ahead, he could get down to the river, and—

Something instinctive made him jerk his head aside. The axe grazed his ear and sailed out over the lip of the cliff and down to the water beyond. Before it disappeared the axeman hurled his own body after it, and Erin was caught around the knees. He brought his joined hands down on the neck, heard a groan, felt new pain as the cannibal *bit* him with those filed teeth. He screamed. A second man flew at him, hit him around the chest, knife flashing down.

Fighting a growing sensation of hopelessness, he caught the descending wrist and twisted, trying to get hold of the knife. He screamed again as a third man hit him from behind. The cannibals were laughing now.

"Thought you'd get away from us, boy! Ain't no way out—din't you know that? Gonna eat you *up*!"

Erin screamed again as teeth dug into his shoulder and his arm, and the three monsters dragged him down, eyes bright, mouths stained with his blood, giggling now, settling into the business of devouring him alive.

His head hung over the lip of the cliff. Below him, far below, hissed the waters of Killsister. Life to his people, life to the clans to the south, the last sight in his life . . .

Teeth tore at the tender flesh of his stomach, nuzzling for his vitals . . .

With strength born of rage and panic, born of some primal survival drive so deep that he had never suspected its existence, he convulsed his entire body, pushed with his good leg and with his one free arm, and suddenly all four of them were teetering on the brink of the cliff.

The ghouls howled with despair, and one of them wriggled like a worm on the hook, desperate to escape. Erin's gory fingers were twined in the monster's hair, and together the four of them teetered on the edge, tottered there, and they fell, tumbling down the rock face.

Erin felt flesh go, and bone—felt the injured leg shatter as he struck a boulder, bounced out away from the face of the cliff and down into the water, feeling his face go under, the gigantic splash drowning all consciousness and . . .

. . . at least . . .

. . . clean death . . .

A flash of sky, and the momentary, sliding grasp of desperate, drowning fingers, a moonlight glimpse of a white face, panicked eyes rolling and head sinking in the churning waters of Killsister . . .

And then nothing.

*   *   *

Dead. I must be . . .

His head throbbed terribly, his entire body seethed with pain. He couldn't move.

Somehow he managed to pry his eyes open. He tried to move: his hands were tied behind him, his body bound to the trunk of a tree. His leg was shattered, twisted at an ugly angle. Bone projected through the flesh. The pain was a dull throb, a pulse that beat more steadily every moment.

It was day, and from where he sat, he could see the waters of Killsister. Rippling calmly here, its rage spent. There was green to either side of it, a vast field, and beyond this a gentle rise of hills.

Behind him he heard horses, and the smell of stew and fresh-baked bread was in the air. Leather-shod feet slapped against hard earth.

A bearded figure leaned into his field of vision suddenly, grinned without humor. "Hezros! Rat is awake!" The bearded man squatted, picked at his brown teeth with a long fingernail. "You may wish you'd drowned, Rat."

Erin tried to remember something. Anything.

Tumbling, into the river. Something striking him—a log? A tree trunk? And he had clasped it.

And something else had, as well: one of the cannibals. He vaguely remembered a savage struggle, in a place beyond pain or exhaustion. Only the knowledge of the message that he carried, had to carry, kept him conscious and fighting.

And then the knife was gone, and his enemy was gone, swirling away, ruined face pumping black in the moonlight.

Erin had hitched himself up over the wood and passed out.

He had a faint memory of hands hauling him from the water, but nothing more until this moment.

He heard but could not see a general commotion. Four people approached from behind him, three tall men, and a clean-limbed dark-skinned woman who stood level with the tallest of them. She had a cold, brilliant smile, and her hair was cut close to her scalp.

The largest man caught his attention.

Erin would recognize Hezros anywhere, even without the leather armor. His jaw was immense, and carried a heavy dark beard. Half of his lower lip had been cut away, and three teeth were missing from the lower jaw. He was bare-chested, three varied wounds already dressed and swathed.

His chest was that of a giant, iron ribs and bands of stomach muscle as sharply defined as carved rock.

Hezros spoke first. "You may wonder why we pulled you from the river, Rat."

"My name . . . Erin."

"Shut up, Rat!" the man roared, in a voice that shook the earth. "I want the pleasure of killing you myself—"

"Because I killed your horse?"

Hezros shook his head as if dreaming. "You, Rat?" He peered closer, then a reluctant smile curled the mouth behind the dark beard. "So that was you. A pretty piece of nerve, Rat. I'm almost sorry it has to be you."

Erin gasped for breath. His bruised, constricted ribs made breathing cruelly painful. "What . . . has to be me?"

The woman spoke now, and her voice was even more vicious than Hezros'. "Someone has to pay. We sent peace envoys. You sent them back down the river in chunks. You." She prodded his throat with the tip of a knife. "you will be our return message."

"I . . . I didn't. We didn't . . ."

He couldn't find the breath, the words. Was just so damned tired.

"It wasn't us," he finally managed to gasp. "Killsister. Killsister."

Hezros stood, eyes hooded, as if trying to shield himself from the distasteful task ahead. "Kill him."

"Cannibals!" Erin screamed. "Cannibals on the battlefield. They killed your envoys. Our envoys. For years. I woke up, alive on the battlefield, under your horse. They hunted me. They caught me. I pulled three into the river with me. They were . . . eating me alive."

The flow of words emptied him, drained him. He had nothing left, and Hezros' face was unfathomable, unchanged.

They didn't believe, wouldn't believe. Then he had lost. Both the Crow and the Horseclans had lost.

Hezros opened his mouth to speak, but before he could, the woman bent and roughly grabbed one of Erin's arms, her eyes narrowing as she examined the wounds. Then she peered quizzically at a leg.

"Bite marks," she said.

Hezros knelt down and studied Erin's eyes. Erin didn't have the strength to meet that gaze. Finally, Hezros stood.

"Kill—"

There was a shout from downriver, and the ground thundered with hooves. Two men rode up, one of them dragging behind him a broken, bleeding figure.

They reined in just before they reached Erin and swung down lightly. "We pulled this from the river," the first man began, kicking the body over.

Hezros swore vilely. The squat, grayish figure was even paler by the light of day, a creature of shadow and darkness, a troglodyte, a creation of myth, of nightmare, of abnormal appetites.

A knife had been driven into its mouth, wedging the jaws open. The Horseclansman inspected the teeth: sharp, filed.

With a grunt, Hezros pulled the knife from between the dreadful teeth, then turned back to Erin.

Erin watched that blade grow huge, its razor tip prick the skin directly beneath his eye. This time, he found the will to meet Hezros' gaze.

"Is this your knife, Rat?" Hezros asked finally.

"Yes."

Hezros looked at his two lieutenants, and one of them shrugged. The woman touched Hezros' shoulder. "Perhaps. I have heard stories. A fairy tale. About a monster who ate children. Its name was Killsister."

"Just a tale," Hezros said slowly.

"Just a story," she agreed.

Hezros sat on the ground, heavily, as if nursing his wounded leg. "Damn," he said, disgusted with him-

self. "I may hate myself for this." Almost casually, his
hand blurred, and the knife buried itself in the tree
next to Erin's head. "All right. Let's hear your story.
Beginning to end." He grinned roughly. "One lie, and
you're dead. Erin."

Erin had never wanted to talk so badly in his entire
life, and he did, omitting nothing, not even his fear,
not even soiling himself.

And as he talked, they nodded, and their eyes grew
round. The pain grew more distant, and with a strange
sort of body knowledge Erin knew that his leg would
have to be severed to save his life.

Hezros swore vilely, looking north to Killsister, flex-
ing his great, gnarled fists. There was blood and slaughter in his eyes. Erin saw a crusade, Horseclans and
Crow together, sweeping through the mountains . . .

And he felt a kind of peace, was able to say goodbye to his shattered leg without sorrow.

Erin the Warrior was dead.

But there would certainly be room at the campfires
for Erin the Peacemaker.

The Enemy of My Enemy

by Mercedes R. Lackey

MERCEDES LACKEY says that of her published work to date (four novels and a host of short stories), her friends were most impressed by the fact that she got to write a Horseclans story. Her latest novel is *The Oathbound*.

The fierce heat radiating from the forge was enough to deaden the senses all by itself, never mind the creaking and moaning of the bellows and the steady tap-tapping of Kevin's youngest apprentice out in the yard working at his assigned horseshoe. The stoutly built stone shell was pure hell to work in from May to October; you could open windows and doors to the fullest, but heat soon built up to the point where thought ceased, mind went numb, and the world narrowed to the task at hand.

But Kevin Floyd was used to it, and he was alive enough to what was going on about him that he sensed that someone had entered his smithy, although he dared not interrupt his work to see who it was. This was a commissioned piece—and one that could cost him dearly if he did a less than perfect job on completing it.

Even under the best of circumstances the tempering of a swordblade was always a touchy bit of business. The threat of his overlord's wrath—and the implied loss of his shop—did not make it less so.

So he dismissed the feeling of eyes on the back of his neck and went on with the work stolidly. For the moment he would ignore the visitor as he ignored the heat, the noise, and the stink of scorched leather and many long summers' worth of sweat—horse sweat and man sweat—that permeated the forge.

Only when the blade was safely quenched and lying on the anvil for the next step did he turn to see who his visitor was.

He almost overlooked her entirely, she was so small, and was tucked up so invisibly in the shadowy corner where he kept oddments of harness and a pile of leather scraps. Dark, nearly black eyes peered up shyly at him from under a tangled mop of curling black hair as she perched atop his heap of leather bits, hugging her thin knees to her chest. Kevin didn't recognize her.

That, since he knew every man, woman, and child in Northfork by name, was cause for a certain alarm.

He made one step toward her. She shrank back into the darkness of the corner, eyes going wide with fright. He sighed.

"Kid, I ain't gonna hurt you—"

She looked terrified. Unfortunately, Kevin frequently had that effect on children, much as he liked them. He looked like a red-faced, hairy ogre, and his voice, rough and harsh from years of smoke and shouting over the forge noise, didn't improve the impression he made. He tried again.

"Where you from, huh? Who's your kin?"

She stared at him, mouth set. He couldn't tell if it was from fear or stubbornness, but was beginning to suspect the latter. So he persisted, and when she made an abortive attempt to flee, he shot out an arm to bar her way. He continued to question her, more harshly now, but she just shook her head at him, frantically, and plastered herself against the wall. She was either too scared now to answer, or wouldn't talk out of pure cussedness.

"Jack—" he finally shouted in exasperation, calling for his helper, who was around the corner outside the forge, manning the bellows. "Leave it for a minute and c'mere."

A brawny adolescent sauntered in the door from the back, scratching at his mouse-colored hair. "What—" he began.

"Where'd this come from?" Kevin demanded. "She ain't one of ours, an' I misdoubt she came with the king."

Jack snorted derision. "King, my left—"

Kevin shared his derision, but cautioned, "When he's here, you call him what he wants. No matter he's king of only about as far as he can see, he's paid for mercs enough to pound you inta the ground like a tent peg if you make him mad. Or there's worse he could do. What the hell good is my journeyman gonna be with only one hand?"

Jack twisted his face in a grimace of distaste. He looked about as intelligent as a brick wall, but his sleepy blue eyes hid the fact that he missed very little. HRH King Robert the Third of Trihtown had *not* impressed him. "Shit. Ah hell; king, then. Naw, she ain't with his bunch. I reckon that youngun came with them trader jippos this mornin'. She's got that look."

"What jippos?" Kevin demanded. "Nobody told me about no jippos—"

"Thass 'cause you was in here, poundin' away at His Highass' sword, when they rode in. It's them same bunch as was in Five Point last month. Ain't no wants posted on 'em, so I figgered they was safe to let be for a bit."

"Aw hell—" Kevin glanced at the waiting blade, then at the door, torn by duty and duty. There hadn't been any news about traders from Five Points, and bad news *usually* traveled faster than good—but, dammit, he had responsibility. As the duly appointed mayor, it was his job to cast his eye over any strangers to Northfork, apprise them of the town laws, see that they knew troublemakers got short shrift. And he knew damn well what Willum Innkeeper would have to say about his dealing with them so tardily as it was—pissant fool kept toadying up to King Robert, trying to get himself appointed mayor.

Dammit, he thought furiously. *I didn't* want *the damn job, but I'll be sheep-dipped if I'll let that suckass take it away from me with his rumor-mongering and back-stabbing. Hell, I have to go deal with these jippos, and quick, or he'll be on my case again.*

On the other hand, to leave King Robert's sword three-quarters finished—

Fortunately, before he could make up his mind, his dilemma was solved for him.

A thin, wiry man, as dark as the child, appeared almost magically, hardly more than a shadow in the doorway; a man so lean he barely blocked the strong sunlight. He could have been handsome but for the black eyepatch and the ugly keloid scar that marred the right half of his face. For the rest, he was obviously no native of any town in King Robert's territory; he wore soft riding boots, baggy pants of a wild scarlet, embroidered shirt and vest of blue and black, and a scarlet scarf around his neck that matched the pants. Kevin was surprised he hadn't scared every horse in town with an outfit like that.

"Your pardon," the man said, with so thick an accent that Kevin could hardly understand him, "but I believe something of ours has strayed here, and was too frightened to leave."

Before Kevin could reply, he had turned with the swift suddenness of a lizard and held out his hand to the girl, beckoning her to his side. She flitted to him with the same lithe grace he had displayed, and half hid behind him. Kevin saw now that she wasn't as young as he'd thought, but in late adolescence—it was her slight build and lack of height that had given him the impression that she was a child.

"I sent Chali aseeing where there be the smithy," the man continued, keeping his one eye on Kevin and his arm about the girl's shoulders. "For we were atold to seek the townman there. And dear she loves the forgework, so she stayed to be awatching. She meant no harm, God's truth."

"Well, neither did I," Kevin protested. "I was just trying to ask her some questions, an' she wouldn't answer me. I'm the mayor here, I gotta know about strangers—"

"Again, your pardon," the man interrupted, "but she *could not* give answers. Chali has been mute for long since. Show, mouse—"

At the man's urging the girl lifted the curls away

from her left temple to show the unmistakable scar of a hoofmark.

Aw, hellfire. Big man, Kevin, bullying a little cripple. Kevin felt about as high as a horseshoe nail. "Shit," he said awkwardly. "Look, I'm sorry—hell, how was *I* to know?"

Now the man smiled, a wide flash of pearly white teeth in his dark face. "You could not. Petro, I am. I lead the Rom."

"Kevin Floyd; I'm mayor here."

The men shook hands; Kevin noticed that this Petro's grip was as firm as his own. The girl had relaxed noticeably since her clansman's arrival, and now smiled brightly at Kevin, another flash of white against dusky skin. She was dressed much the same as her leader, but in colors far more muted; Kevin was grateful as he wasn't sure how much more of that screaming scarlet his eyes could take.

He gave the man a quick rundown of the rules; Petro nodded acceptance. "What of your faiths?" he asked, when Kevin had finished. "Are there things we must or must not be adoing? Is there Church about?"

Kevin caught the flash of a gold cross at the man's throat. Well, hey—no wonder he said "Church" like it was poison. A fellow Christer—not like those damn Ehleen priests. This was a simple one-barred cross, not the Ehleen two-barred. "Live and let be" was a Christer's motto, and "A godly man converts by example, not words nor force"—which might well be why there were so few of them. Kevin and his family were one of only three Christer families in town, and Christer traders weren't that common, either. "Nothing much," he replied. "King Robert, he didn't go in for religion last I heard. So, what's your business here?"

"We live, what else?" Petro answered matter-of-factly. "We have livestock for trading. Horses, mules, donkeys—also metalwork."

"Don't know as I care for that last," Kevin said dubiously, scratching his sweaty beard.

"Na, no, not ironwork," the trader protested. "Light metals. Copper, brass—ornament, mostly. A few kettles, pans."

"Now *that* sounds a bit more like! Tell you—you got conchos, harness studs, that kinda thing? You willin' to work a swap for shoein'?"

"The shoes, not the shoeing. Our beasts prefer the hands they know."

"Done." Kevin grinned. He was good enough at tools or weaponwork, but had no talent at ornament, and knew it. He could make good use of a stock of pretty bits for harnesses and the like. Only one frippery could he make, and that was more by accident than anything else. And since these people were fellow Christers and he was short a peace offering—

He usually had one in his apron pocket; he felt around among the horseshoe nails until his hand encountered a shape that wasn't a nail, and pulled it out.

"Here, missy," he said apologetically. "Little somethin' fer scarin' you."

The girl took the cross made of flawed horseshoe nails into strong, supple fingers, with a flash of delight in her expressive eyes.

"Hah! A generous apology!" Petro grinned. "And you cannot know how well comes the fit."

"How so?"

"It is said of my people, when the Christ was to be killed, His enemies meant to silence Him lest He rouse His followers against them. The evil ones made four nails—the fourth for His heart. But one of the Rom was there, and stole the fourth nail. So God blessed us in gratitude to awander wherever we would."

"Well, hey." Kevin returned the grin, and a thought occurred to him. Ehrik was getting about the right size to learn riding. "Say, you got any ponies, maybe a liddle horse gettin' on an' gentle? I'm lookin' for somethin' like that for m'boy."

The jippo regarded him thoughtfully. "I think, perhaps yes."

"Then you just may see me later on when I finish this."

Chali skipped to keep up with the wiry man as they headed down the dusty street toward the *tsera* of their *kumpania*. The town, of gray wood-and-stone buildings enclosed inside its shaggy log palisade, depressed her and made her feel trapped—she was glad to be heading out to where the *kumpania* had made their camp. Her eyes were flashing at Petro with the only laughter she could show. *You did not tell him the rest of the tale, Elder Brother,* she mindspoke. *The part that tells how the good God then granted us the right to steal whatever we needed to live.*

"There is such a thing as telling more truth than a man wishes to hear," Petro replied. "Especially to *Gaje.*"

Huh. But not all Gaje. *I have heard a different tale from you every time we come to a new holding. You tell us to always tell the whole of the truth to the Horseclans folk, no matter how bitter.*

"They are not *Gaje.* They are not *o phral,* either, but they are not *Gaje.* I do not know what they are, but one does not lie to them."

But why the rule? We have not seen Horseclans since before I can remember, she objected.

"They are like the Wind they call upon—they go where they will. But they have the *dook.* So it is wise to be prepared for meeting them at all times."

I would like to see them, one day.

He regarded her out of the corner of his eye. "If I am still *rom baro,* you will be hidden if we meet them. If I am not, I hope you will be wise and hide yourself. They have *dook,* I tell you—and I am not certain that I wish them to know that we also have it."

She nodded, thoughtfully. The Rom had not survived this long by giving away secrets. *Do you think my* dook *is greater than theirs? Or that they would seek me out if they knew of it?*

"It could be. I know they value such gifts greatly. I am not minded to have you stolen from us for the sake of the children you could bear to one of them."

She clasped her hands behind her, eyes looking downward at the dusty, trampled grass as they passed through the open town gate. This was the first time Petro had ever said anything indicating that he thought her a woman and not a child. Most of the *kumpania,* including Petro's wife, Sara, and their boy, Tibo, treated her as an odd mixture of child and *phuri dai*. Granted, she *was* tiny; perhaps the same injury that had taken her voice had kept her small. But she was nearly sixteen winters—and still they reacted to her body as to that of a child, and to her mind as to that of a *drabarni* of sixty. As she frowned a little, she pondered Petro's words, and concluded they were wise. Very wise. That the Rom possessed *draban* was not a thing to be bandied about. That her own *dook* was as strong as it was should rightly be kept secret as well.

Yes, rom baro, I will do as you advise, she replied.

Although he did not mindspeak her in return, she knew he had heard everything she had told him perfectly well. She had so much *draban* that any human and most beasts could hear her when she chose. Petro could hear and understand her perfectly, for though his mindspeech was not as strong as hers, he would have heard her even had he been mind-deaf.

That he had no strong *dook* was not unusual; among the Rom, since the Evil Days, it was the women that tended to have more *draban* than the men. That was one reason why females had come to enjoy all the freedoms of a man since that time—when his wife could make a man feel every blow, he tended to be less inclined to beat her, and when his own eyes burned with every tear his daughter shed he was less inclined to sell her into a marriage with someone she feared or hated.

And when she could blast you with her own pain, she tended to be safe from rape.

As she skipped along beside Petro on the worn ruts that led out of the palisade gate and away from town, she was vaguely aware of every mind about her. She and everyone else in the *kumpania* had known for a very long time that her *dook* was growing stronger every year, perhaps to compensate for her muteness. Even the herd-guard horses, those wise old mares, had been impressed, and it took a great deal to impress *them!*

Petro sighed, rubbing the back of his neck absently, and she could read his surface thoughts easily. *That was an evil day, when ill luck led us to the settlement of*

the Chosen. A day that ended with poor Chali sense-
less, her brother dead, and Chali's parents captured
and burned as witches. And every other able-bodied,
weapons-handy member of the kumpania *either wounded*
or too busy making sure the rest got away alive to
avenge the fallen. She winced as guilt flooded him—as
always.

You gave your eye to save me, Elder Brother. That
was more than enough.

"I could have done more. I could have sent others
with your mama and papa. I could have taken everyone away from that sty of pigs, that nest of—I will *not*
call them Chosen of God. Chosen of *o Beng* perhaps—"

And o Beng *claims his own, Elder Brother. Are we*
not o phral? *We have more patience than all the* Gaje
in the world. We will see the day when o Beng *takes*
them. Chali was as certain of that as she was of the sun
overhead and the grass beside the track.

Petro's only reply was another sigh. He had less
faith than she. He changed the subject, which was
making him increasingly uncomfortable. "So, when
you stopped being a frightened *tawnie juva,* did you
touch the *gajo,* the townsman's heart? Should we sell
him old Pika for his little son?"

I think yes. He is a good one, for Gaje. *Pika will like*
him; also, it is nearly fall, and another winter wander-
ing would be hard on his bones.

They had made their camp up against a stand of
tangled woodland, and a good long way off from the
palisaded town. The camp itself could only be seen
from the top of the walls, not from the ground. That
was the way the Rom liked things—they preferred to
be apart from the *Gaje.*

The *tsera* was within shouting distance by now, and
Petro sent her off with a pat to her backside. The
vurdon, those neatly built wooden wagons, were arranged in a precise circle under the wilderness of trees
at the edge of the grasslands, with the common fire
neatly laid in a pit in the center. Seven wagons, seven
families—Chali shared Petro's. Some thirty-seven Rom
in all—and for all they knew, the last Rom in the
world, the only Rom to have survived the Evil Days.

But then, not a great deal had survived the Evil Days. Those trees, for instance, showed signs of having once been a purposeful planting, but so many generations had passed since the Evil Days they were now as wild as any forest.

Chali headed, not for the camp, but for the unpicketed string of horses grazing beyond. She wanted to sound out Pika. If he was willing to stay here, this Mayor Kevin would have his gentle old pony for his son, and cheap at the price. Chali knew Pika would guard any child in his charge with all the care he would give one of his own foals. Pika was a stallion, but Chali would have trusted a tiny baby to his care.

Petro trusted her judgment in matters of finding their horses homes; a few months ago she had allowed him to sell one of their saddlebred stallions and a clutch of mares to mutual satisfaction on the part of the horses, Rom, and buyers. Then it had been a series of sales of mules and donkeys to folk who wound up treating them with good sense and more consideration than they gave to their own well-being. And in Five Points she had similarly placed an aging mare Petro had raised from a filly, and when Chali had helped the *rom baro* strain his meager *dook* to bid her farewell, Lisa had been nearly incoherent with gratitude for the fine stable, the good feeding, the easy work.

Horses were bred into Chali's blood, for like the rest of this *kumpania*, she was of the Lowara *natsiyi*—and the Lowara were the Horsedealers. Mostly, anyway, though there had been some Kalderash, or Coppersmiths, among them in the first years. By now the Kalderash blood was spread thinly through the whole *kumpania*. Once or twice in each generation there were artificers, but most of *rom baro* Petro's people danced to Lowara music.

She called to Pika without even thinking his name, and the middle-aged pony separated himself from a knot of his friends and ambled to her side. He rubbed his chestnut nose against her vest and tickled her cheek with his whiskers. His thoughts were full of the hope of apples.

No apples, greedy pig! Do you like this place? Would you want to stay?

He stopped teasing her and stood considering, breeze blowing wisps of mane and forelock into his eyes and sunlight picking out the white hairs on his nose. She scratched behind his ears, letting him take his own time about it.

The grass is good, he said, finally. *The* Gaje *horses are not ill treated. And my bones ache on cold winter mornings, lately. A warm stable would be pleasant.*

The blacksmith has a small son. . . . She let him see the picture she had stolen from the *gajo*'s mind, of a blond-haired, sturdily built bundle of energy. *The* gajo *seems kind.*

The horses here like him, came the surprising answer. *He fits the shoe to the hoof, not the hoof to the shoe. I think I will stay. Do not sell me cheaply.*

If Chali could have laughed aloud, she would have. Pika had been Romano's in the rearing—and he shared more than a little with that canny trader. *I will tell Romano—not that I need to. And don't forget,* prala, *if you are unhappy—*

Ha! the pony snorted with contempt. *If I am unhappy, I will not leave so much as a hair behind me!*

Chali fished a breadcrust out of her pocket and gave it to him, then strolled in the direction of Romano's *vurdon.* When this *kumpania* had found itself gifted with *dook,* with more *draban* than they ever dreamed existed, it had not surprised them that they could speak with their horses; Lowara Rom had practically been able to do that before. But *draban* had granted them advantages they had never *dared* hope for. . . .

Lowara had been good at horse stealing; now only the Horseclans could better them at it. All they needed to do was to sell one of their four-legged brothers into the hands of the one they wished to relieve of the burdens of wealth. All the Lowara horses knew how to lift latches, unbar gates, and find the weak spot in any fence. And Lowara horses were as glib at persuasion as any of their two-legged friends. Ninety-nine times out of a hundred, the Lowara would return to the *kumpania* trailing a string of converts.

And if the *kumpania* came across horses that were being mistreated—

Chali's jaw tightened. That was what had set the Chosen at their throats.

She remembered that day and night, remembered it far too well. Remembered the pain of the galled beasts that had nearly driven her insane; remembered how she and Toby had gone to act as decoys while her mother and father freed the animals from their stifling barn.

Remembered the anger and fear, the terror in the night, and the madness of the poor horse that had been literally goaded into running her and Toby down.

It was just as well that she had been comatose when the "Chosen of God" had burned her parents at the stake—*that* might well have driven her completely mad.

That anger made her sight mist with red, and she fought it down, lest she broadcast it to the herd. When she had it under control again, she scuffed her way slowly through the dusty, flattened grass, willing it out of her and into the ground. She was so intent on controlling herself that it was not until she had come within touching distance of Romano's brightly painted *vurdon* that she dared to look up from the earth.

Romano had an audience of children, all gathered about him where he sat on the tail of his wooden wagon. She tucked up against the worn side of it and waited in the shade without drawing attention to herself, for he was telling them the story of the Evil Days.

"So old Simza, the *drabarni*, she spoke to the *rom baro* of her fear, and a little of what she had seen. Giorgi was her son, and he had *dook* enough that he believed her."

"Why shouldn't he have believed her?" tiny Ami wanted to know.

"Because in those days *draban* was weak, and even the *o phral* did not always believe in it. We were different, even among Rom. We were one of the smallest and least of *kumpania* then; one of the last to leave the old ways—perhaps that is why Simza saw what she saw. Perhaps the steel carriages the Rom had taken to, and the stone buildings they lived in, would not let *draban* through."

"Steel carriages? *Rom chal*, how would such a thing move? What horse could pull it?" That was Tomy, skeptical as always.

"I do not know—I only know that the memories were passed from Simza to Yanni, to Tibo, to Melalo, and so on down to me. If you would see, look."

As he had to Chali when she was small, as he did to every child, Romano the Storyteller opened his mind to the children, and they saw, with their *dook*, the dim visions of what had been. And wondered.

"Well, though there were those who laughed at him, and others of his own *kumpania* that left to join those who would keep to the cities of the *Gaje*, there were enough of them convinced to hold to the *kumpania*. They gave over their *Gaje* ways and returned to the old—wooden *vurdon*, pulled by horses, practicing their old trades of horsebreeding and metalwork, staying strictly away from the cities. And the irony is that it was the *Gaje* who made this possible, for they had become mad with fascination for the ancient days and had begun creating festivals that the Yanfi *kumpania* followed about."

Again came the dim sights—half-remembered music, laughter, people in wilder garments than ever the Rom sported.

"Like now?" asked one of the girls. "Like markets and trade days?"

"No, not like now; these were special things, just for amusement, not really for trade. I am not certain I understand it; they were a little mad in those times. Well, then the Evil Days came—"

Fire, and red death; thunder and fear—more people than Chali had ever seen alive, fleeing mindlessly the wreckage of their cities and their lives.

"But the *kumpania* was safely traveling out in the countryside, with nothing needed that they could not make themselves. Some others of the Rom remembered us and lived to reach us; Kalderash, mostly."

"And we were safe from *Gaje* and their mad ways?"

"When have the Rom ever been safe?" he scoffed.

"No, if anything, we were in more danger yet. The *Gaje* wanted our horses, our *vurdon,* and *Gaje* law was not there to protect us. And there was disease, terrible disease that killed more folk than the Night of Fire had. One sickly *gajo* could have killed us all. No, we hid at first, traveling only by night and keeping off the roads, living where man had fled or died out."

These memories were clearer, perhaps because they were so much closer to the way the *kumpania* lived now. Hard years, though, and fear-filled—until the Rom learned again the weapons they had forgotten. The bow. The knife. And learned to use weapons they had never known—like the sharp hooves of their four-legged brothers.

"We lived that way until the old weapons were all exhausted. Then it was safe to travel openly, and to trade; we began traveling as we do now—and now life is easier. For true God made the *Gaje* to live so that we might borrow from them what we need. And that is the tale."

Chali watched with her *dook* as Romano reached out with his mind to all the children seated about him, and found what he had been looking for. Chali felt his exultation; of all the children to whom Romano had given his memories and his stories, there was one in whose mind the memories were still as clear as they were when they had come from Romano's. Tomy had the *draban* of the Storyteller; Romano had found his successor.

Chali decided that it was wiser not to disturb them for now, and slipped away so quietly that they never knew she had been there.

The scout for Clan Skaht slipped into the encampment with the evening breeze and went straight to the gathering about his chief's fire. His prairiecat had long since reported their impending arrival, so the raid leaders had had ample time to gather to hear him.

"Well, I have good news and bad news," Daiv Mahrtun of Skaht announced, sinking wearily to the bare earth across the fire from his chief. "The good news is that these Dirtmen look lazy and ripe for the picking—the bad news is that they've got traders with 'em, so the peace banners are up. And I mean to tell you, they're the weirdest damn traders I ever saw. Darker than any Ehleenee—dress like no clan I know—and—" He stopped, not certain of how much more he wanted to say, and if he'd be believed.

Tohnee Skaht snorted in disgust and spat into the fire. "Dammit anyway—if we break trade peace—"

"Word spreads fast," agreed his cousin Jahn. "We may have trouble getting other traders to deal with us if we mount a raid while this lot's got the peace banners up."

There were nearly a dozen clustered about the firepit; men and a pair of women, old and young—but all of them were seasoned raiders, regardless of age. And all of them were profoundly disappointed by the results of Daiv's scouting foray.

"Which traders?" Tohnee asked after a long moment of thought. "Anybody mention a name or a clan you recognized?"

Daiv shook his head emphatically. "I tell you, they're not like any lot I've ever seen *or* heard tell of. They got painted wagons, and they ain't the big trade wagons; more, they got whole families, not just the menfolk—and they're horsetraders."

Tohnee's head snapped up. "Horse—"

"Before you ask, I mindspoke their horses." This was a perfect opening for the most disturbing of Daiv's discoveries. *"This* oughta curl your hair. *The horses wouldn't talk to me.* It wasn't 'cause they couldn't, and it wasn't 'cause they was afraid to. It was like *I* was maybe an enemy—was surely an outsider, and maybe not to be trusted. Whoever, whatever these folks are, they got the same kind of alliance with their horses as we have with ours. And *that's* plainly strange."

"Wind and Sun—dammit, Daiv, if I didn't know you, I'd be tempted to call you a liar!" That was Dik Krooguh, whose jaw was hanging loose with total astonishment.

"Do the traders mindspeak?" Tohnee asked at nearly the same instant.

"I dunno," Daiv replied, shaking his head, "I didn't catch any of 'em at it, but that don't mean much. My guess would be they do, but I can't swear to it."

"I think maybe we need more facts," Alis Skaht broke in. "If they've got horse brothers, I'd be inclined to say they're not likely to be a danger to us—but we can't count on that. Tohnee?"

"Mm." He nodded. "Question is, how?"

"I took some thought to that," Daiv replied. "How about just mosey in open-like? Dahnah and I could come in like you'd sent us to trade with 'em." Dahnah was Daiv's twin sister—an archer with no peer in the clan, and a strong mindspeaker. "We could hang around for a couple of days without making 'em too suspicious. And a pair of Horseclans kids doin' a little dickerin' ain't gonna make the Dirtmen *too* nervous. Not while the peace banners are up."

Tohnee thought that over awhile, as the fire cast weird shadows on his stony face. "You've got the sense to call for help if you end up needing it—and you've got Brighttooth and Stubtail backing you."

The two young prairiecats lounging at Daiv's side purred agreement.

"All right—it sounds a good enough plan to me," Tohnee concluded, while the rest of the sobered clansfolk nodded slowly. "You two go in at first morning light and see what you can find. And I know I don't need to tell you to be careful, but I'm telling you anyway."

Howard Thomson, son of "King" Robert Thomson, was distinctly angered. His narrow face was flushed, always a bad sign, and he'd been drinking, which was worse. When Howard drank, he thought he owned the world. Trouble was, he was almost right, at least in this little corner of it. His two swarthy merc bodyguards were between Kevin and the doors.

Just what I didn't need, Kevin thought bleakly, taking care that nothing but respect showed on his face, *A damnfool touchy idiot with a brat's disposition tryin' to put me between a rock and a hard place.*

"I tell you, my father sent me expressly to fetch him that blade, *boy.*" Howard's face was getting redder by the minute, matching his long, fiery hair. "You'd better hand it over *now,* before you find yourself lacking a hand."

I'll just bet he sent you, Kevin growled to himself. *Sure he did. You just decided to help yourself, more like—and leave me to explain to your father where his piece went, while you deny you ever saw me before.*

But his outwardly cool expression didn't change as he replied stolidly, "Your pardon, but His Highness gave *me* orders that I was to put it into no one's hands but his. And he hasn't sent me written word telling me any different."

Howard's face enpurpled as Kevin obliquely reminded him that the Heir couldn't read or write. Kevin waited for the inevitable lightning to fall. Better he should get beaten to a pulp than that King Robert's wrath fall on Ehrik and Keegan, which it would if he gave in to Howard. What with Keegan being pregnant—better a beating. He tensed himself and waited for the order.

Except that just at the moment when Howard was actually beginning to splutter orders to his two merc bodyguards to take the blacksmith apart, salvation, in the form of Petro and a half-dozen strapping jippos, came strolling through the door to the smithy. They were technically unarmed, but the long knives at their waists were a reminder that this was only a technicality.

"*Sarishan, gajo,*" he said cheerfully. "We have brought you your pony."

Only then did he seem to notice the Heir and his two bodyguards.

"Why, what is this?" he asked with obviously feigned surprise. "Do we interrupt some business?"

Howard growled something obscene—if he started something *now* he would be breaking trade peace, and no trader would deal with him or his family again without an extortionate bond being posted. For one moment Kevin feared that Howard's temper might get the better of him anyway, but then the young man pushed past the jippos at the door and stalked into the street, leaving his bodyguards to follow as they would.

Kevin sagged against his cold forge, only now breaking into a sweat. "By all that's holy, man," he told Petro earnestly, "your timing couldn't have been better! You saved me from a beatin', and that's for damn sure!"

"Something more than a beating," the jippo replied slowly, "or I misread that one. I do not think we will sell any of our beasts *there*, no. But"—he grinned suddenly—"we lied, I fear. We did not bring the pony—we brought our other wares."

"You needed six men to carry a bit of copperwork?" Kevin asked incredulously, firmly telling himself that he would *not* begin laughing hysterically out of relief.

"Oh no—but I was not of a mind to carry back horseshoes for every beast in our herd by myself! I am *rom baro*, not packmule!"

Kevin began laughing after all, laughing until his sides hurt.

Out of gratitude for their timely appearance, he let them drive a harder bargain with him than he normally would have allowed, trading shoes and nails for their whole equipage for about three pounds of brass and copper trinkets and a set of copper pots he knew Keegan would lust after the moment she saw them. And a very pretty little set of copper jewelery to brighten her spirit; she was beginning to show, and subject to bouts of depression in which she was certain her pregnancy made her ugly in his eyes. This bit of frippery might help remind her that she was anything but. He agreed to come by and look at the pony as soon as he finished a delivery of his own. He was going to take no chances of Howard's return; he was going to deliver that sword himself, now, and straight into Robert's palsied hands!

"So if that one comes, see that he gets no beast nor thing of ours," Petro concluded. "Chali, you speak to the horses. Most like, he will want the king stallion, if any."

Chali nodded. *We could say Bakro is none of ours— that he's a wild one that follows our mares.*

Petro grinned approval. "Ha, a good idea! That way nothing of blame comes on us. For the rest—we wish to leave only Pika, is that not so?"

The others gathered about him in the shade of his *vurdon* murmured agreement. They had done well enough with their copper and brass jewelery, orna-

ments and pots—and with the odd hen or vegetable or
sack of grain that had found a mysterious way into a
Rom kettle or a *vurdon*.

"Well then, let us see what we can do to make them
unattractive."

Within the half hour the Rom horses, mules and
donkeys little resembled the sleek beasts that had come
to the call of their two-legged allies. Coats were dirty,
with patches that looked suspiciously like mange; hocks
were poulticed, and looked swollen; several of the
wise old mares were ostentatiously practicing their
limps, and there wasn't a hide of an attractive color
among them.

And anyone touching them would be kicked at, or
nearly bitten—the horses were not minded to have
their two-legged brothers punished for *their* actions.
Narrowed eyes and laid-back ears gave the lie to the
hilarity within. No one really knowledgeable about
horses would want to come near this lot.

And just in time, for Howard Thomson rode into
the camp on an oversized, dun-colored dullard of a
gelding only a few moments after the tools of their
deceptions had been cleaned up and put away. Chali
briefly touched the beast's mind to see if it was being
mistreated, only to find it nearly as stupid as one of
the mongrels that infested the village.

He surveyed the copper trinkets with scorn and the
sorry herd of horses with disdain. Then his eye lit
upon the king stallion.

"You there—trader—" He waved his hand at the
proud bay stallion, who looked back at this arrogant
two-legs with the same disdain. "How much for that
beast there?"

"The noble prince must forgive us," Petro fawned,
while Chali was glad, for once, of her muteness;
she did not have to choke on her giggles as some
of the others were doing. "But that one is none of
ours. He is a wild one; he follows our mares, which
we permit in hopes of foals like him."

"Out of nags like *those*? You hope for a miracle,
man!" Howard laughed, as close to being in good
humor as Petro had yet seen him. "Well, since he's

none of yours, you won't mind if my men take him."

Hours later, their beasts were ready to founder, the king stallion was still frisking like a colt, and none of them had come any closer to roping him than they had been when they started. The Rom were nearly bursting, trying to contain their laughter, and Howard was purple again.

Finally he called off the futile hunt, wrenched at the head of his foolish gelding, and spurred it back down the road to town—

And the suppressed laughter died, as little Ami's youngest brother toddled into the path of the lumbering monster, and Howard grinned and spurred the gelding at him—hard.

Kevin was nearly to the traders' camp when he saw the baby wander into the path of Howard's horse— and his heart nearly stopped when he saw the look on the Heir's face as he dug his spurs savagely into his gelding's flanks.

The smith didn't even think—he just *moved*. He frequently fooled folk into thinking he was slow and clumsy because of his size; now he threw himself at the child with every bit of speed and agility he possessed.

He snatched the toddler, curled protectively around it, and turned his dive into a frantic roll. As if everything had been slowed by a magic spell, he saw the horse charging at him and every move horse and rider made. Howard sawed savagely at the gelding's mouth, trying to keep it on the path. But the gelding shied despite the bite of the bit; foam flecks showered from its lips, and the foam was spotted with blood at the corners of its mouth. It half reared, and managed to avoid the smith and his precious burden by a hair— one hoof barely scraped Kevin's leg—then the beast was past, thundering wildly toward town.

Kevin didn't get back home until after dark—and he was not entirely steady on his feet. The stuff the Rom drank was a bit more potent than the beer and wine from the tavern, or even his own home brew. Pacing along beside him, lending a supporting shoulder and

triumphantly groomed to within an inch of his life and
adorned with red ribbons, was the pony, Pika.

Pika was a gift—Romano wouldn't accept a single
clipped coin for him. Kevin was on a first-name basis
with all of the Rom now, even had mastered a bit of
their tongue. Not surprising, that—seeing as they'd
sworn brotherhood with him.

He'd eaten and drunk with them, heard their tales,
listened to their wild, blood-stirring music—felt as if he'd
come home for the first time. Rom, that was what they
called themselves, not "jippos,"—and *o phral*, which
meant "the people," sort of. They danced for him—and
he didn't wonder that they wouldn't sing or dance
before outsiders. It would be far too easy for a dullard
gajo to get the wrong idea from some of those dances—
the women and girls danced with the freedom of the wind
and the wildness of the storm—and to too many men,
"wild" and "free" meant "loose." Kevin had just been
entranced by a way of life he'd never dreamed existed.

Pika rolled a not-unsympathetic eye at him as he
stumbled, and leaned in a little closer to him. Funny
about the Rom and their horses—you'd swear they
could read each other's minds. They had an affinity
that was bordering on witchcraft.

Like that poor little mute child, Chali. Kevin had
seen with his own eyes how wild the maverick stallion
had been—at least when Howard and his men had
been chasing it. But he'd also seen Chali walk up to
him, pull his forelock, and hop aboard his bare back
as if he were no more than a gentle, middle-aged pony
like Pika. And then watched the two of them pull
some trick-riding stunts that damn near pulled the
eyes out of his sockets. It was riding he'd remember
for a long time, and he was right glad he'd seen it.

But he devoutly hoped Howard hadn't.

Howard hadn't—but one of his men had.

Daiv and Dahnah rode up to the traders' camp in
the early morning, leaving Brighttooth and Stubtail
behind them as eyes to the rear. The camp appeared
little different from any other they'd seen—at first
glance. Then you noticed that the wagons were small,

shaped almost like little houses on wheels, and painted like rainbows. They were almost distracting enough to keep you from noticing that there wasn't a beast around the encampment, not donkey nor horse, that was hobbled or picketed.

I almost didn't believe you, Daivie, his sister said into his mind, wonderingly.

His mare snorted; so did he. *Huh. Thanks a lot, sis. You catch any broadbeaming?*

She shook her head, almost imperceptibly, as her mount shifted a little. *Not so much as a stray thought. . . .* Her own thought faded for a moment, and she bit her lip. *Now that I think of it, that's damned odd. These people are buttoned up as tight as a yurt in a windstorm.*

Which means what? He signaled Windstorm to move up beside Snowdancer.

Either they're naturally shielded as well as the best mindspeaker I ever met, or they do have the gift. And the first is about as likely as Brighttooth sitting down to dinner with an Ehleenee priest.

Only if the priest was my dinner, sister, came the mischievous reply from the grassland behind them. With the reply came the mock disgust and nausea from Stubtail that his littermate would even *contemplate* such a notion as eating vile-tasting Ehleenee flesh.

So where does that leave us? Daiv asked.

We go in, do a little dickering, and see if we can eavesdrop. And I'll see if I can get any more out of the horses than you did.

Fat chance! he replied scornfully, but followed in the wake of her mare as she urged her into the camp itself.

The fire on the hearth that was the only source of light in Howard's room crackled. Howard lounged in his thronelike chair in the room's center. His back was to the fire, which made him little more than a dark blot to a petitioner and cast all the available light on a petitioner's face.

Howard eyed the lanky tavernkeeper, who was now kneeling before him, with intense speculation. "You say the smith's been consorting with the heathen traders?"

"More than traders, m'lord," Willum replied humbly. "For the past two days there's been a brace of horse barbarians with the traders as well. I fear this means no good for the town."

"I knew about the barbarians," Howard replied, leaning back in his padded chair and staring at the flickering shadows on the wall behind Willum thoughtfully. Indeed he did know about the barbarians—twins they were, with hair like a summer sun; he'd spotted the girl riding her beast with careless grace, and his loins had ached ever since.

"I fear he grows far too friendly with them, m'lord. His wife and child spend much of the day at the trader's camp. I think that, unlike those of us who are loyal, he has forgotten where his duties lie."

"And you haven't, I take it?" Howard almost smiled.

"M'lord knows I am but an honest tavernkeeper—"

"And has the honest tavernkeeper informed my father of this possibly treacherous behavior?"

"I tried," Willum replied, his eyes not quite concealing his bitterness. "I have *been* trying for some time now. King Robert will not hear a word against the man."

"King Robert is a senile old fool!" Howard snapped viciously, jerking upright where he sat so that the chair rocked and Willum sat back on his heels in startlement. "King Robert is far too readily distracted by pretty toys and pliant wenches." His own mouth turned down with a bitterness to equal Willum's—for the talented flame-haired local lovely that had been gracing *his* bed had deserted it last night for his father's.

Willum's eyes narrowed, and he crept forward on his knees until he almost touched Howard's leg. "Perhaps," he whispered, so softly that Howard could barely hear him, "it is time for a change of rulers—"

Chali had been banished to the forest as soon as the bright golden heads of the Horseclans twins had been spotted in the grasslands beyond the camp. She was not altogether unhappy with her banishment—she had caught an unwary thought from one of them, and had shivered at the strength of it. Now she did not doubt the *rom baro*'s wisdom in hiding her. *Dook* that strong would surely ferret out her own, and she did not want to betray the secret gifts of her people until they knew more about the intent of these two. So into the forest she had gone, with cloak and firestarter and sack of food and necessaries.

Nor was she alone in her exile; Petro had deemed it wiser not to leave temptation within Howard's reach and sent Bakro, the king stallion, with her. They had decided to explore the woods—and had wandered far from the encampment. To their delight and surprise, they had discovered the remains of an apple orchard deep in the heart of the forest. The place had gone wild and reseeded itself several times over, and the apples themselves were far smaller than those from a cultivated orchard, hardly larger than crabapples. But they were still sweet—and most of them were ripe. They had both gorged themselves as much as they dared on the crisp, succulent fruits, until night had fallen. Now both were drowsing beneath a tree in Chali's camp, sharing the warmth of her fire, and thinking of nothing in particular—

—when the attack on the Rom *tsera* came.

Chali was awake on the instant, her head ringing with the mental anguish of the injured—and God, oh God, the dying! Bakro wasn't much behind her in picking up the waves of torment. He screamed, a trumpeting of defiance and rage. She grabbed a handful of mane and pulled herself up onto his back without being consciously aware she had done so, and they crashed off into the darkness to the source of that agony.

But the underbrush they had threaded by day was a series of maddening tangles by night; Bakro's headlong dash ended ignominiously in a tangle of vine, and when they extricated themselves from the clawing branches, they found their pace slowed to a fumbling crawl. They slower they went, the more frantic they felt, for it was obvious from what they were being bombarded with that the Rom were fighting a losing battle.

And one by one the voices in their heads—lost strength. Then faded.

Until finally there was nothing.

They stopped fighting their way through the brush,
then, and stood, lost in shock, in the blackness of the
midnight forest—utterly, completely alone.

Dawn found Chali on her knees, exhausted, face
tear-streaked, hands bruised from where she'd been
pounding them on the ground, over and over. Bakro
stood over her, trembling; trembling not from fear or
sorrow, but from raw, red hatred. *His* herd had survived, though most had been captured by the enemy
two-legs. But his two-leg herd—Chali was all he had
left. He wanted *vengeance*—and he wanted it now.

Slowly the hot rage of the stallion penetrated Chali's
grief.

I hear you, prala, *I do hear you,* she sent slowly,
fumbling her way out of the haze of loss that had
fogged her mind.

Kill! the stallion trumpeted with mind and voice.
Kill them all!

She clutched her hands at her throat, and encountered the thong that held the little iron cross. She
pulled it over her head, and stared at it, dully. What
good was a god of forgiveness in the light of this
slaughter? She cast the cross—and all it implied—
from her, violently.

She rose slowly to her feet, and put a restraining
hand on the stallion's neck. He ceased his fidgeting
and stood absolutely still, a great bay statue.

We will have revenge, prala, *I swear it,* she told him,
her own hatred burning as high as his, *but we will have
it wisely.*

Kevin was shoved and kicked down the darkened
corridor of the king's manor house with brutal indifference, smashing up against the hard stone of the
walls only to be shoved onward again. His head was
near to splitting, and he'd had at least one tooth
knocked out; the flat, sweet taste of blood in his
mouth seemed somehow unreal.

He was angry, frightened and bewildered. He'd awakened to distant shouts and screams, run outside to see

a red glow in the direction of the Rom camp—then he'd been set upon from behind. Whoever it was that had attacked him clubbed him into apparent submission. Then he had his hands bound behind him—and his control broke; he began fighting again, and was dragged, kicking and struggling, up to the manor house. He'd seen, when his vision had cleared, that his attackers were some of King Robert's own mercs. He'd stumbled and nearly fallen on his face from the shock— he'd figured that the town had been taken by Ehleenee or some marauding band.

The door to King Robert's quarters opened and Kevin was shoved through it, skidding on the flagstone floor to land sprawling on his face at someone's feet.

"And here is the last of the suspects, my lord," he heard Willum say unctuously.

He wrenched himself up onto his knees by brute force. Lounging at his ease in King Robert's favorite chair was Howard, sumptuously clad and playing with his father's new sword. Beside him, in the blue and red of Howard's livery, was Willum.

"What the hell is that shit supposed to mean, asshole?" Kevin was too angry to mind his tongue, and a blow from one of the mercs behind him threw him onto his face again, made his brains rattle in his head and jarred his teeth to their sockets. His vision swam and he saw double for a long moment.

He pulled himself back into a semi-kneeling posture with aching difficulty.

"Keep a civil tongue in your head in the presence of your king, boy," Willum told him, with a faint smile. "You're suspected of conspiring with those false traders—"

"To what? Invade the town? Don't make me laugh!" Kevin snorted. "Take over with a handful of men when— What the hell do you mean, *king?*"

"My father has met with an accident," Howard purred, polishing the blade of the sword he held with a soft cloth. The steel glinted redly in the firelight. "He went mad, it seems. I was forced to defend myself. I have witnesses."

Willum nodded, and it seemed to Kevin that there

was a glint of balefire in the back of the man's eyes.

"So *I* am king now—by right of arms. *I* have declared that those so-called traders were no such thing at all—and I have eliminated their threat."

Slowly Kevin began to understand what it was he was saying. "You—good God—that camp was mostly women, children—"

"The spawn of vipers will grow to be vipers."

"You broke the trade peace! You *murdered* innocent people, babies in their beds!"

"That hardly sounds like the words of a loyal subject—"

"Loyal my ass! *They* deserved my loyalty—all *you* should get is the contempt of every honest man in this town! We're the ones who're gonna suffer because of what you just did! *You broke your sworn word, you bastard!*" Bound hands or not, Kevin lunged for the two of them.

His arms were caught and blows rained down on his head and shoulders. Still he fought, screaming obscenities, and only being clubbed half unconscious kept him from getting to the oathbreakers and tearing their throats out with his teeth.

When he stopped fighting, he was thrown back at Howard's feet. He lay on the cold stone floor, and through a mist of dancing sparks he could see that Howard was purple again.

"Take him out and make an example of him," the patricide howled. "Burn him—hang him—tear his guts out!"

"No—" Willum laid a restraining hand on his ruler's arm. "Not a good idea—you *might* make him a martyr for those who would doubt you. No, I have a better idea. Did we get the horse barbarians as well? I seem to remember that you ordered them to be taken."

The new king regained his normal coloring. "Only the boy," Howard pouted, calming. "The girl managed to get herself killed. Damn! I *wanted* that little bitch! I thought about having the boy gelded and sold—"

"Good, do that. We'll put it out that it was the horse barbarians that killed the traders—and that the

smith conspired with them to raid both the traders and
the town. We'll have it that the boy confessed. I'll
have my men start passing the word. Then, by afternoon when the story is spreading, we'll put this fool
and his family out of the gates—banish them. The
barbarians aren't likely to let him live long, and they
certainly aren't likely to give an ear to any tales he
might tell."

Howard nodded, slowly. "Yes—yes, indeed! Willum,
you are going to go far in my service."

Willum smiled, his eyes cast humbly down. From his
vantage point on the floor, Kevin saw the balefire he
thought he'd glimpsed leap into a blaze before being
quenched. "I always intended to, my lord."

Chali crept in to the remains of the camp in the gray
light before dawn and collected what she could. The
wagons were charred ruins; there were no bodies. She
supposed, with a dull ache in her soul, that the mur-
derers had dragged the bodies off to be looted and
burned. She hoped that the *mule* would haunt their
killers to the end of their days.

There wasn't much left, a few bits of foodstuff, of
clothing, other oddments—certainly not enough to keep
her through the winter—but then, she would let the
winter take care of itself. She had something more to
concern her.

Scrabbling through the burned wood into the secret
compartments built into the floor of every *vurdon,* she
came up with less of use than she had hoped. She had
prayed for weapons—what she mostly found was coin,
useless to her.

After searching until the top of the sun was a finger's length above the horizon and dangerously near
to betraying her, she gave up the search. She *did*
manage to collect a bow and several quivers' worth of
arrows—which was what she wanted most. Chali had
been one of the best shots in the *kumpania.* Now the
Gaje would learn to dread her skill.

She began her one-person reign of terror when the
gates opened in late morning.

She stood hidden in the trees, obscured by the fo-

liage, but well within bowshot of the gates, an arrow
nocked, a second loose in her fingers, and two more in
her teeth. The stallion stood motionless at her side.
She had managed to convince the creatures of the
woods about her that she was nothing to fear—so a
blackbird sang within an arm's length of her head, and
rabbits and squirrels hopped about in the grass at the
verge of the forest, unafraid. Everything looked perfectly normal. The two men opening the gates died
with shafts in their throats before anyone realized that
there was something distinctly out of the ordinary this
morning.

When they *did* realize that there was something
wrong, the stupid *Gaje* did exactly the wrong thing;
instead of ducking into cover, they ran to the bodies.
Chali dropped two more who trotted out to look.

Then they realized that they were in danger, and
scrambled to close the gates again. She managed to
get a fifth before the gates closed fully and the bar on
the opposite side dropped with a *thud* that rang across
the plain, as they sealed themselves inside.

Now she mounted Bakro and arrowed out of cover.
Someone on the walls shouted, but she was out of
range before they even had time to realize that she
was the source of the attack. She clung to Bakro's
back with knees clenched tightly around his barrel,
pulling two more arrows from the quiver slung at her
belt. He ran like the wind itself, past the walls and
around to the back postern gate before anyone could
warn the sleepy townsman guarding it that something
was amiss.

She got him, too, before someone slammed the
postern shut, and picked off three more injudicious
enough to poke their heads over the walls.

Now they were sending arrows of their own after
her, but they were poor marksmen, and their shafts
fell short. She decided that they were bad enough
shots that she dared risk retrieving their arrows to
augment her own before sending Bakro back under
the cover of the forest. She snatched at least a dozen
sticking up out of the grass where they'd landed, leaning down as Bakro ran, and shook them defiantly at

her enemies on the walls as they vanished into the underbrush.

Chali's vengeance had begun.

Kevin was barely conscious; only the support of Pika on one side and Keegan on the other kept him upright. Ehrik was uncharacteristically silent, terribly frightened at the sight of his big, strong father reduced to such a state.

King Howard and his minions had been "generous," piling as much of the family's goods on the pony's back as he could stand before sending the little group out the gates. In cold fact that had been Willum's work, and it hadn't been done out of kindness; it had been done to make them a more tempting target for the horse barbarians or whatever strange menace it was that now had them hiding behind their stout wooden walls. That much Kevin could remember; and he waited in dull agony for arrows to come at them from out of the forest.

But no arrows came; and the pathetic little group, led by a little boy who was doing his best to be brave, slowly made their way up the road and into the grasslands.

Chali mindspoke Pika and ascertained that the smith had had nothing to do with last night's slaughter—that in fact, he was being cast out for objecting to it. So she let him be. Besides, she had other notions in mind.

She couldn't keep them besieged forever—but she could make their lives pure hell with a little work.

She found hornets' nests in the orchard; she smoked the insects into slumberous stupefaction, then took the nests down, carefully. With the help of a scrap of netting and two springy young saplings, she soon had an improvised catapult. It wasn't very accurate, but it didn't have to be. All it had to do was get those nests over the palisade.

Which it did.

The howls from within the walls made her smile for the first time that day.

Next she stampeded the village cattle by beaming

pure fear into their minds, sending them pounding against the fence of their corral until they broke it down, then continuing to build their fear until they ran headlong into the grasslands. They might come back; they might not. The villagers would have to send men out to get them.

They did—and she killed one and wounded five more before their fire drove her back deeper into the forest.

They brought the cattle inside with them—barely half of the herd she had sent thundering away. That made Chali smile again. With the cattle would come vermin, noise, muck—and perhaps disease.

And she might be able to add madness to that.

Bakro? she broadbeamed, unafraid now of being overheard. *Have you found the mind-sick weed yet?*

But to her shock, it was not Bakro who answered her.

Daiv struggled up out of a darkness shot across with lances of red agony. It hurt even to think—and it felt as if every bone in his body had been cracked in at least three places. For a very long time he lay without even attempting to move, trying to assess his real condition and whereabouts through a haze of pain. Opening his eyes did not lessen the darkness, but an exploratory hand to his face told him that although the flesh was puffed and tender, his eyes were probably not damaged. And his nose told him of damp earth. So he was probably being held in a pit of some kind, one with a cover that let in no light. Either that, or it was still dark.

Faint clanks as he moved and his exploring fingers told him that chains encircled his wrists and ankles. He tried to lever himself up into sitting position, and quickly gave up the idea; his head nearly split in two when he moved it, and the bones of his right arm grated a little.

He started then to mindcall to Dahnah—then he remembered.

Hot, helpless tears burned his eyes, scalded along the raw skin of his face. He didn't care. *Wind—oh Wind.*

For he remembered that Dahnah was dead, killed defending two of the traders' tiny children. And uselessly, for the children had been spitted seconds after she had gone down. She'd taken one of the bastards with her, though—and Stubtail had accounted for another before they'd gotten him as well.

But Daiv couldn't remember seeing Brighttooth's body—perhaps the other cat had gotten away!

He husbanded his strength for a wide-beam call, opened his mind—

And heard the stranger.

Bakro? came the voice within his mind, strong and clear as any of his kin could send. *Have you found the mind-sick weed yet?*

He was so startled that he didn't think—he just answered.

Who are you? he beamed. *Please—who are you?*

Chali stood, frozen, when the stranger's mind touched her own—then shut down the channel between them with a ruthless and somewhat frightened haste. She kept herself shut down, and worked her way deeper into the concealment of the forest, worming her way into thickets so thick that a rabbit might have had difficulty in getting through. There she sat, curled up in a ball, shivering with reaction.

Until Bakro roused her from her stupor with his own insistent thought.

I have found the mind-sick weed, drabarni, *and something else as well.*

She still felt dazed and confused.

What—she replied, raising her head from her knees.

And found herself looking into a pair of large, golden eyes.

Kevin had expected that the Horseclans folk would find them, eventually. What he had not expected was that they would be kind to him and his family.

He had a moment of dazed recognition of what and who it was that was approaching them across the waving grass. He pushed himself away from the pony, prepared to die defending his loved ones—

And fell over on his face in a dead faint.

When he woke again he was lying on something
soft, staring up at blue sky, and there were two atten-
tive striplings carefully binding up his head. When
they saw he was awake, one of them frowned in con-
centration, and a Horseclans warrior strolled up in the
next moment.

"You're damn lucky we found you," he said, speaking slowly so that Kevin could understand him. He
spoke Merikan, but with an odd accent, the words
slurring and blurring together. "Your mate about t'
fall on her nose, and your little one had heat-sick. Not
to mention the shape *you* were in."

Kevin started to open his mouth, but the man shook
his head. "Don't bother; what the pony didn't tell us,
your mate did." His face darkened with anger. "I
knew Dirtmen were rotten—but this! Only one thing
she didn't know—there were two of ours with the
traders."

The nightmare confrontation with Howard popped
into Kevin's mind, and he felt himself blanch, fearing
that this friendly barbarian would slit his throat the
moment he knew the truth.

But the moment the memory surfaced, the man
went absolutely rigid, then leaped to his feet, shouting. The camp boiled up like a nest of angry wasps. As
his two attendants sprang to *their* feet, Kevin tried to
rise.

Only to pass into oblivion again.

Chali stared into the eyes of the great cat, mesmerized.
My brother is within those walls, the cat said to her,
and I am hurt. You must help us. True, the cat was
hurt; a long cut along one shoulder, more on her flanks.

Chali felt anger stirring within her at the cat's impe-
rious tone. *Why should I help you?* she replied. *Your
quarrel is nothing to me!*

The cat licked her injured shoulder a moment, then
caught her gaze again. *We have the same enemy,* she
said shortly.

Chali pondered that for a moment. *And the enemy
of my enemy—is my friend?*

The cat looked at her with approval. *That,* she said, purring despite the pain of her wounds, *is wisdom.*

Daiv had just about decided that the mindcall he'd caught had been a hallucination born of pain when the stranger touched him again.

He snatched at the tentatively proffered thought-thread with near-desperation. *Who are you?* he gasped. *Please—*

Gently, brother, came a weaker mind-voice, joining the first. And that was one he knew!

Brighttooth!

The same. Her voice strengthened now, and carried an odd other-flavor with it, as if the first was somehow supporting her. *How is it with you?*

He steadied himself, willing his heart to stop pounding. *Not good. They've put chains on my arms and legs; my right arm's broken, I think. Where are you? Who's with you?*

A friend. Two friends. We are going to try to free you. No-Voice says that she is picking up the thoughts of those Dirteaters regarding you, and they are not pleasant.

He shuddered. He'd had a taste of those thoughts himself, and he rather thought he'd prefer being sent to the Wind.

We are going to free you, my brother, Brighttooth continued. *I cannot tell you how, for certain—but it will be soon; probably tonight. Be ready.*

It was well past dark. Chali, aided by Bakro, reached for the mind of Yula, the cleverest mare of the Rom herd. Within a few moments she had a good idea of the general lay of things inside the stockaded village, at least within the mare's line of sight—and she knew *exactly* where the Horseclans boy was being kept. They'd put him in an unused grain pit a few feet from the corral where the horses had been put. Yula told Chali that they had all been staying very docile, hoping to put their captors off their guard.

Well done! Chali applauded. *Now, are you ready for freedom?*

More than ready, came the reply. *Do we free the boy*

as well? There was a definite overtone to the mare's mind-voice that hinted at rebellion if Chali answered in the negative.

Soft heart for hurt colts, hm, elder sister? Yes, we free him. How is your gate fastened?

Contempt was plain. *One single loop of rawhide! Fools! It is not even a challenge!*

Then here is the plan—

About an hour after full dark, when the nervous guards had begun settling down, the mare ambled up to the villager who'd been set to guard the grain pit.

"Hey, old girl," he said, surprised at the pale shape looming up out of the darkness, like a ghost in the moonlight. "How in hell did *you* get—"

He did not see the other, darker shape coming in behind him. The hooves of a second mare lashing into the back of his head ended his sentence and his life.

At nearly the same moment, Brighttooth was going over the back wall of the stockade. She made a run at the stallion standing rock-steady beneath the wall, boosting herself off the scavenged saddle Bakro wore. There was a brief sound of a scuffle; then the cat's thoughts touched Chali's.

The guard is dead. He tasted awful.

Chali used Bakro's back as the cat had and clawed her own way over the pallisade. She let herself drop into the dust of the other side, landing as quietly as she could, and searched the immediate area with mindtouch.

Nothing and no one.

She slid the bar of the gate back and let Bakro in, and the two of them headed for the stockade and the grain pits. The cat was already there.

If it had not been for the cat's superior night sight, Chali would not have been able to find the latch holding it. The wooden cover of the pit was heavy; Chali barely managed to get it raised. Below her she could see the boy's white face peering up at her, just touched by the moonlight.

Can you climb? she asked.

Hell, no, he answered ruefully.

Then I must come down to you.

She had come prepared for this; there was a coil of scavenged rope on Bakro's saddle. She tied one end of it to the pommel and dropped the other down into the pit, sliding down to land beside the boy.

Once beside him, she made an abrupt reassessment. *Not* a boy. A young man; one who might be rather handsome under the dirt and dried blood and bruises. She tied the rope around his waist as he tried, awkwardly, to help.

From above came an urgent mindcall. *Hurry,* Brighttooth fidgeted. *The guards are due to report and have not. They sense something amiss.*

We're ready, she answered shortly. Bakro began backing, slowly. She had her left arm around the young man's waist, holding him steady and guiding him, and held to the rope with the other, while they "walked" up the side of the pit. It was hardly graceful—and Chali was grateful that the pit was not too deep—but at length they reached the top. Her shoulders were screaming in agony, but she let go of him and caught the edge with that hand, then let go of the rope and hung for a perilous moment on the verge before hauling herself up. She wanted to lie there and recover, but there was no time—

They have found the dead one!

Te xal o rako lengo gortiano! she spat. The young man was trying to get himself onto the rim; she grabbed his shoulders while he hissed softly in pain and pulled him up beside her.

What? he asked, having sensed something.

No time! she replied, grabbing his shoulder and shoving him at Bakro. She threw herself into the saddle, and wasted another precious moment while Bakro knelt and she pulled at the young man again, catching him off-balance and forcing him to fall facedown across her saddlebow like a sack of grain. *NOW, my wise ones! NOW!*

The last was broadbeamed to all the herd—and even as the perimeter guards began shouting their discovery, and torches began flaring all over the town, the Rom horses began their stampede to freedom.

The cat was already ahead of them, clearing the way

with teeth and flashing claws; her task was to hold the
gate against someone trying to close it. Chali clung to
Bakro's back with aching legs—she was having her
hands full trying to keep the young man from falling
off. He was in mortal agony, every step the stallion
took jarring his hurts without mercy, but he was fastened to her leg and stirrup iron like a leech.

The herd was in full gallop now, sweeping everything and everyone aside. There was only one thing to
stop them—the narrowness of the postern gate. Only
three horses could squeeze through at any one time. If
there was anyone with a bow and good sense, he
would have stationed himself there.

Chali heard the first arrow. She felt the second
hit her arm. She shuddered with pain, ducked, and
spread herself over the body in front of her, trying
to protect her passenger from further shots.

Bakro hesitated for a moment, then shouldered aside
two mules and a donkey to bully his own way through
the gate.

But not before Chali had taken a second wound,
and a third, and a fourth.

"I'll say this much for you, Dirtman, you're stubborn." The Horseclans warriors's voice held grudging
admiration as it filtered out of the darkness beside
Kevin. He had been detailed to ride at the smith's left
hand and keep him from falling out of his saddle. He
had obviously considered this duty something of an
embarrassing ordeal. Evidently he didn't think it was
anymore.

Kevin's face was white with pain, and he was nearly
blind to everything around him, but he kept his seat.
"Don't call me that. I told you—after what they did to
my blood brothers, *I'm not one of them.* I'm with
you—all the way. If that means fighting, I'll fight.
Those oathbreaking, child-murdering bastards don't
deserve anything but a grave. They ain't even human
anymore, not by my way of thinking."

That was a long speech for him, made longer still by
the fact that he had to gasp bits of it out between
flashes of pain. But he meant it, every word—and the

Horseclansman took it at face value, simply nodding, slowly.

"I just—" A shout from the forward scout stopped them all dead in their tracks. The full moon was nearly as bright as day—and what it revealed had Kevin's jaw dropping.

It was a mixed herd of horses, mules and donkeys—all bone-weary and covered with froth and sweat, heads hanging as they walked. And something slumped over the back of one in the center that gradually revealed itself to be two near-comatose people, seated one before the other and clinging to each other to keep from falling off the horse's saddle. The clan chief recognized the one in front, and slid from his horse's back with a shout. The herd approaching them stopped coming, the beasts moving only enough to part and let him through.

Then Kevin recognized the other, and tumbled off *his* horse's back, all injuries forgotten. While the clan chief and another took the semiconscious boy from the front of the saddle, cursing at the sight of the chains on his wrists and ankles, it was into Kevin's arms that Chali slumped, and *he* cursed to see the feathered shafts protruding from her leg and arm.

Chali wanted to stay down in the soft darkness, where she could forget—but They wouldn't let her stay there. Against her own will she swam slowly up to wakefulness, and to full and aching knowledge of how completely alone she was.

The *kumpania* was gone, and no amount of vengeance would bring it back. She was left with nowhere to go and nothing to do with her life—and no one who wanted her.

No-Voice is a fool, came the sharp voice in her head.

She opened her eyes, slowly. There was Brighttooth, lying beside her, carefully grooming her paw. The cat was stretched out along a beautifully tanned fur of dark brown; fabric walls stretched above her, and Chali recognized absently that they must be in a tent.

How a fool? asked a second mind-voice. Chali saw the tent wall move out of the corner of her eye—the

wall opened and became a door, and the young man
she had helped to rescue bent down to enter. He sat
himself down beside the cat and began scratching her
ears; she closed her eyes in delight and purred loudly
enough to shake the walls of the tent. Chali closed her
eyes in a spasm of pain and loss; their brotherhood
only reminded her of what she no longer had.

I asked you, lazy one, how a fool?

Chali longed to be able to turn her back on them,
but the wounds in her side made that impossible. She
could only turn her face away, while tears slid slowly
down her cheeks—as always, soundlessly.

A firm but gentle hand cupped her chin and turned
her head back toward her visitors. She squeezed her
eyes shut, not wanting these *Gaje* to see her loss and
her shame at showing it.

"It's no shame to mourn," said the young man
aloud, startling her into opening her eyes. She had
been right about him—with his hurts neatly bandaged and cleaned up, he *was* quite handsome. And his
gray eyes were very kind—and very sad.

I mourn, too, he reminded her.

Now she was even more ashamed, and bit her lip.
How could she have forgotten what the cat had told
her, that he had lost his twin—lost her in defending
her people.

For the third time, how a fool?

Brighttooth stretched, and moved over beside her,
and began cleaning the tears from her cheeks with a
raspy tongue. *Because No-Voice forgets what she herself told me.*

Which is?

The enemy of my enemy is my brother.

My friend. *I said, the enemy of my enemy is my
friend,* Chali corrected hesitantly, entering the conversation at last.

Friend, brother, all the same, the cat replied, finishing off her work with a last swipe of her tongue.
Friends are the family you choose, not so?

I—

"You're not gonna be alone, not unless you want
to," the young man said, aloud. "Brighttooth is right.

You can join us, join any family in the clan you want. There ain't one of them that wouldn't reckon themselves proud to have you as a daughter and a sister."

There was a certain hesitation in the way he said "sister." Something about that hesitation broke Chali's bleak mood.

What of you? she asked. *Would you welcome me as a sister?*

Something, he sent, shyly, *maybe—something closer than sister?*

She was so astonished that she could only stare at him. She saw that he was looking at her in a way that made her very conscious that she *was* sixteen winters old—in a way that no member of the *kumpania* had ever looked at her. She continued to stare as he gently took one of her hands in his good one. It took Brighttooth to break the spell.

Pah—two-legs! she sent in disgust. *Everything is complicated with you! You need clan; here is clan for the taking. What could be simpler?*

The young man dropped her hand as if it had burned him, then began to laugh. Chali smiled, shyly, not entirely certain she had truly seen that admiration in his eyes—

"Brighttooth has a pretty direct way of seein' things," he said, finally. "Look, let's just take this in easy steps, right? *One,* you get better. *Two,* we deal with when you're in shape t' think about."

Chali nodded.

Three—you'll never be alone again, he said in her mind, taking her hand in his again. *Not while I'm around to have a say in it. Friend, brother—whatever. I won't let you be lonely.*

Chali nodded again, feeling the aching void inside her filling. Yes, she would mourn her dead—

But she would rejoin the living to do so.

About the Editors

ROBERT ADAMS lives in Seminole County, Florida. Like the characters in his books, he is partial to fencing and fancy swordplay, hunting and riding, good food and drink. At one time Robert could be found slaving over a hot forge making a new sword or busily reconstructing a historically accurate military costume, but, unfortunately, he no longer has time for this as he's far too busy writing.

PAMELA CRIPPEN ADAMS is living proof of the dangers of being around science fiction writers. Originally a fan, she now spends her time as an editor and anthologist. When not working at these tasks, she is kept busy by their two dogs and ten cats.

For more information about Milo Morai, Horseclans, and forthcoming Robert Adams books contact the **NATIONAL HORSECLANS SOCIETY**, P.O. Box 1770, Apopka, FL 32704–1770.